FIREWALL

Henning Mankell has become a worldwide phenomenon with his crime writing, gripping thrillers and atmospheric novels set in Africa. His prizewinning and critically acclaimed Kurt Wallander thrillers are currently dominating best-seller lists all over the globe. His books have been translated into over forty languages and made into numerous international film and television adaptations: most recently the BAFTA-award-winning BBC television series *Wallander*, starring Kenneth Branagh. Mankell devotes much of his free time to working with Aids charities in Africa, where he is director of the Teatro Avenida in Maputo. In 2008 the University of St Andrews conferred on Henning Mankell an honorary degree of Doctor of Letters, in recognition of his major contribution to literature and to the practical exercise of conscience.

Ebba Segerberg teaches English at Washington University in St Louis, Missouri.

ALSO BY HENNING MANKELL

Kurt Wallander Series

Faceless Killers

The Dogs of Riga

The White Lioness

The Man Who Smiled

Sidetracked

The Fifth Woman

One Step Behind

Before the Frost

The Pyramid

The Troubled Man

Fiction

The Return of the Dancing Master

Chronicler of the Winds

Depths

Kennedy's Brain

The Eye of the Leopard

Italian Shoes

The Man from Beijing

Daniel

The Shadow Girls

Non-fiction

I Die, But the Memory Lives On

Young Adult Fiction

A Bridge to the Stars

Shadows in the Twilight

When the Snow Fell

The Journey to the End of the World

Children's Fiction

The Cat Who Liked Rain

HENNING MANKELL

Firewall

TRANSLATED FROM THE SWEDISH BY
Ebba Segerberg

VINTAGE BOOKS
London

Published by Vintage 2012

2 4 6 8 10 9 7 5 3 1

First published with the title *Brandvägg* by
Ordfronts Förlag, Stockholm 1998

First published in Great Britain in 2003 by
The Harvill Press

Vintage
Random House, 20 Vauxhall Bridge Road,
London SW1V 2SA

www.vintage-books.co.uk

Addresses for companies within The Random House Group Limited can be found at: www.randomhouse.co.uk/offices.htm

The Random House Group Limited Reg. No. 954009

A CIP catalogue record for this book
is available from the British Library

ISBN 9780099571766

The Random House Group Limited supports The Forest Stewardship Council (FSC®), the leading international forest certification organisation. Our books carrying the FSC label are printed on FSC® certified paper. FSC is the only forest certification scheme endorsed by the leading environmental organisations, including Greenpeace. Our paper procurement policy can be found at:
www.randomhouse.co.uk/environment

Printed and bound by CPI Group (UK) Ltd, Croydon, CR0 4YY

"A man who strays from the path of understanding comes to rest in the company of the dead"

PROVERBS 21:16

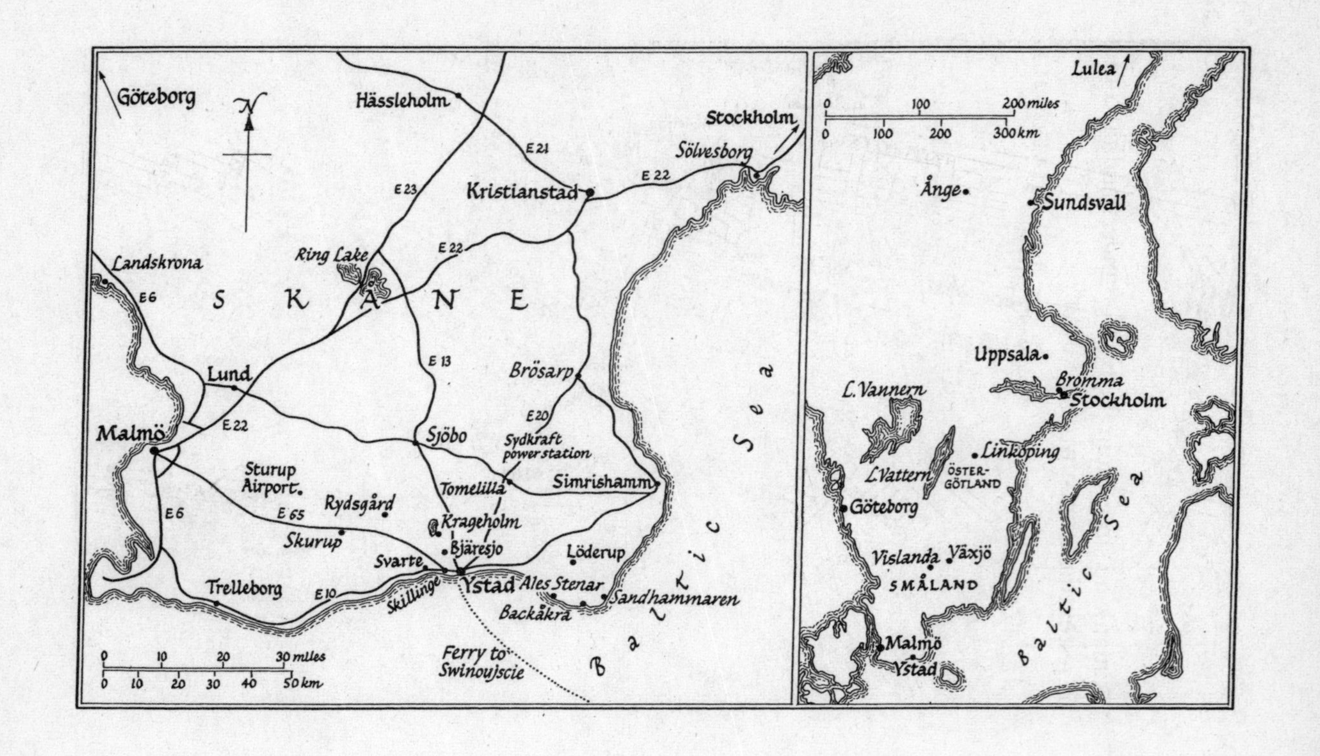
Göteborg
N
Hässleholm
Stockholm
E 21
Sölvesborg
E 22
E 23
Kristianstad
E 22
Landskrona
Ring Lake
E 6
S K Å N E
E 13
Brösarp
Lund
E 22
E 20
Malmö
Sjöbo
Sydkraft power station
Sturup Airport
Tomelilla
Simrishamn
Rydsgård
E 6
E 65
Krageholm
Skurup
Bjäresjo
Löderup
Svarte
Trelleborg
E 10
Skillinge
Ystad
Ales Stenar
Sandhammaren
Backåkra
Ferry to Swinoujscie
Baltic Sea
0 10 20 30 miles
0 10 20 30 40 50 km
Lulea
0 100 200 miles
0 100 200 300 km
Ånge
Sundsvall
Uppsala
L. Vannern
Bromma
Stockholm
Linköping
L. Vattern
ÖSTER-GÖTLAND
Göteborg
Vislanda
Växjö
SMÅLAND
Malmö
Ystad
Baltic Sea

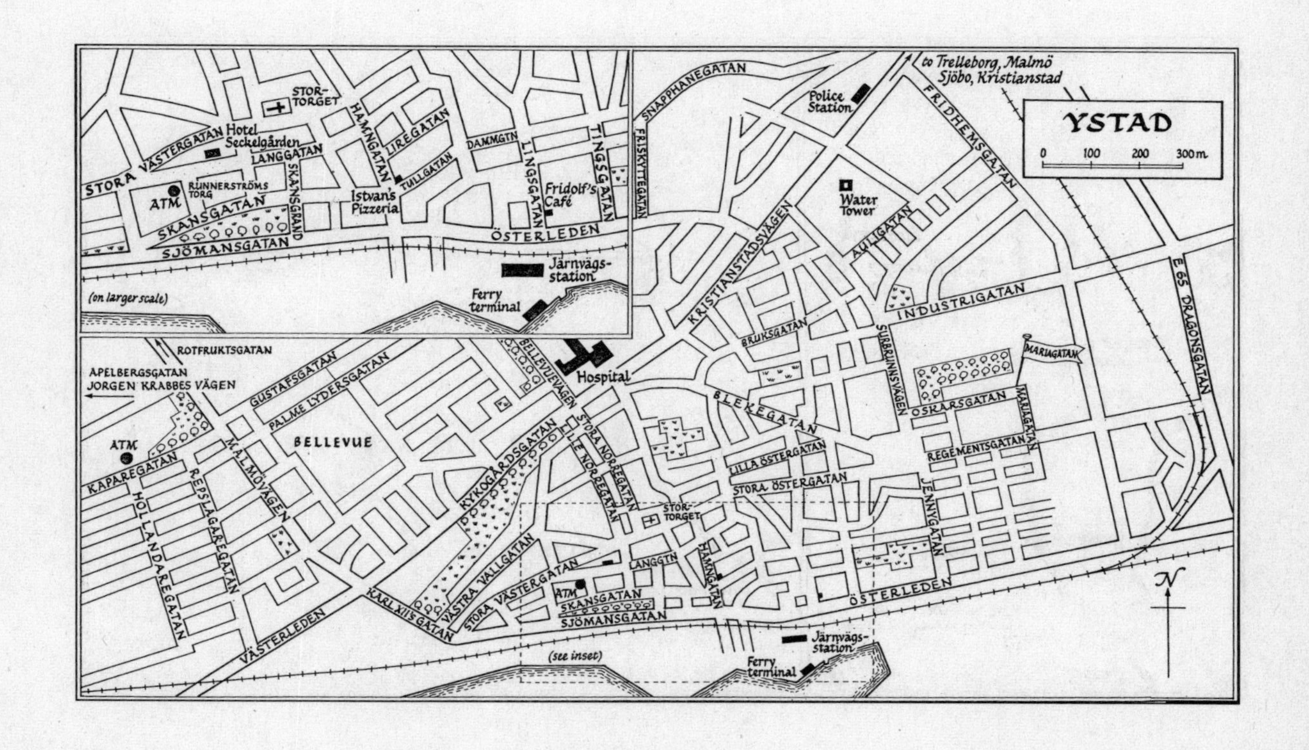
YSTAD
0
100
200
300 m
to Trelleborg, Malmö
Sjöbo, Kristianstad
N
Police Station
Water Tower
Hospital
BELLEVUE
ATM
Järnvägs-station
Ferry terminal
(see inset)
(on larger scale)
STOR-TORGET
Hotel Seckelgården
Istvan's Pizzeria
Fridolf's Café
RUNNERSTRÖMS TORG
SNAPPHANEGATAN
FRISKYTTEGATAN
FRIDHEMSGATAN
KRISTIANSTADSVÄGEN
AULIGATAN
INDUSTRIGATAN
E 65 DRAGONSGATAN
MARIAGATAN
SURBRUNNSVÄGEN
BRUKSGATAN
OSKARSGATAN
REGEMENTSGATAN
BLEKEGATAN
LILLA ÖSTERGATAN
STORA ÖSTERGATAN
JENNYGATAN
ÖSTERLEDEN
HAMNGATAN
LANGGTN
STORA NORREGATAN
LILLE NORREGATAN
BELLEVUEVÄGEN
KYKOGÅRDSGATAN
VÄSTRA VALLGATAN
STORA VÄSTERGATAN
SKANSGATAN
SJÖMANSGATAN
KARL XII'S GATAN
VÄSTERLEDEN
GUSTAFSGATAN
PALME LYDERSGATAN
MALMÖVÄGEN
REPSLAGAREGATAN
HOLLANDAREGATAN
KAPAREGATAN
ROTFRUKTSGATAN
APELBERGSGATAN
JORGEN KRABBES VÄGEN
TINGSGATAN
LINGSGATAN
DAMMGTN
LIREGATAN
TULLGATAN
LANGGATAN
SKANSGRAND

PART 1

The Catalyst

CHAPTER ONE

The wind died down towards evening, then stopped completely.

He was standing on the balcony. Some days he could see a sliver of ocean between the buildings across the way. Right now it was too dark. Sometimes he set up his telescope and looked into the lighted windows of the other flats. But he invariably began to feel as if someone were on to him and then he would stop.

The stars were very clear and bright.

It's already autumn, he thought. There may even be a touch of frost tonight, though it's early for Skåne.

A car drove past. He shivered and went back in. The door to the balcony was hard to close and needed some adjustment. He added it to the "to do" list he kept on a pad in the kitchen.

He walked into the living room, pausing in the doorway to look around. Since it was Sunday, the place was immaculately clean. It gave him a feeling of satisfaction.

He sat at his desk and pulled out the thick journal he kept in one of the drawers. As usual he began by reading his entry from the night before.

Saturday, October 4, 1997. Gusty winds, 8–10 metres per second according to the Meteorological Office. Broken cloud formations. Temperature at 6 a.m. 7ºC. Temperature at 2 p.m. 8ºC.

Below that he had added four sentences: *No activity in*

C-space today. No messages. C doesn't reply when prompted. All is calm.

He took off the top of the ink pot and carefully dipped the nib in the ink. It had been his father's pen, saved from his early days as an assistant clerk at a bank in Tomelilla. He himself would use no other pen for writing his journal.

The wind died away as he was writing. The thermometer outside the kitchen window read 3°C. The sky was clear. He recorded that cleaning the flat had taken three hours and 25 minutes, ten minutes faster than last Sunday.

He had also taken a walk down to the marina, after meditating in St Maria's Church for half an hour. He hesitated, then wrote: *Short walk in the evening.* He pressed the blotting paper over the lines he had written, wiped the pen and put the top back on the ink pot. Before closing the journal, he glanced at the old ship's clock on the desk. It was 11.20.

In the hall he put on his leather jacket and his old rubber boots. He checked that he had his wallet and his keys.

Once on the street, he stood for a while in the shadows and looked about him. There was no-one there, as he had expected. He walked down to the left, as he usually did, crossing the main road to Malmö, heading towards the department stores and the red-brick building that housed the Tax Authorities. He increased his pace until he found his normal, smooth late-night rhythm. He walked more quickly in the daytime to get his heart rate up, but the late-night walks had a different purpose. This was when he tried to empty his mind, preparing for sleep and the day to come.

Outside one of the department stores he passed a woman with an Alsatian. He almost always encountered her on his late-night walks. A car drove by at high speed, its radio blaring.

They have no inkling of what's in store for them, he thought. All these hooligans who drive around damaging for ever their hearing with their obnoxious music. They don't know. They know as little as that woman out walking her dog.

The thought cheered him up. He thought about the power he wielded, the sense of being one of the chosen. He had the power to do away with the ingrained, corrupt ways of this society and create a new order, something completely unexpected.

He stopped and looked up at the night sky.

Nothing is truly comprehensible, he thought. My own life is as incomprehensible as the fact that the light I see now from the stars has been travelling for aeons. The only source of meaning is my own course of action, like the deal I was offered 20 years ago and that I accepted without hesitation.

He continued on his way, going faster, because his thoughts were exciting him. He felt a growing impatience. They had waited so long for this. Now the moment was approaching when they would open the invisible dams and watch the tidal wave sweep over the world.

But not yet. The moment was not quite here, and impatience was a weakness he would not permit himself.

He turned round and started back. As he walked past the Tax Authority he decided to go to the cash machine in the square. He put his hand over the pocket where he kept his wallet. He wasn't going to make a withdrawal, just get an account balance and make sure all was as it should be.

He stopped in the light by the ATM and took out his

blue card. The woman with the Alsatian was long gone. A heavily loaded truck went by on the Malmö road, probably on its way to one of the Poland ferries. By the sound of it, the muffler was damaged.

He punched in his code and selected "account balance". The machine returned his card and he put it back in his wallet. He listened to the whirring and clicking and smiled. If they only knew, he thought. If people only knew what lay in store for them.

The paper slip showing his balance emerged from the slot. He felt around for his glasses before he realised he had left them in his other coat. He felt a twinge of irritation at this oversight.

He walked to where the light was brightest, under the street lamp, and studied the slip of paper. There was Friday's withdrawal, as well as the cash he had taken out on Saturday. His balance was 9,765 kronor. Everything was in order.

What happened next came without warning. It was as if he had been kicked in the chest by a horse. The pain was sudden and violent.

He fell forward, the piece of paper clutched in his hand. As his head hit the pavement he experienced an instant of clarity. His final thought was that he couldn't understand what was happening to him. A darkness enveloped him from all sides.

A second truck on its way to the night ferry drove past. Then calm returned to the streets.

It was just after midnight on Monday, October 6, 1997.

CHAPTER TWO

When Kurt Wallander got into his car on Mariagatan in Ystad, on the morning of October 6, 1997, it was with reluctance. It was just gone 8 a.m. As he drove out of the city, he wondered what had possessed him to say he would go. He had such a profound dislike of funerals. And yet that was his objective. Since he had plenty of time, he decided against taking the direct route to Malmö. Instead he took the coast road by way of Svarte and Trelleborg. He glimpsed the sea on his left-hand side. A ferry was approaching the harbour.

He thought about the fact that this was his fourth funeral in seven years. First there had been his colleague Rydberg, who died of cancer. It had been a protracted and painful end. Wallander had visited him often at home and finally at the hospital as slowly he wasted away. Rydberg's death had been a huge blow. It was Rydberg who had made a police officer of him, taught him to ask the right questions. Through watching him work, Wallander had learned how to read the information hidden at the scene of a crime. Before he started working with Rydberg, Wallander had been a very average policeman. It was only after Rydberg's death that Wallander realised he had become not only a stubborn and energetic detective, but a good one. He still held long conversations with Rydberg in his head when he tackled a new investigation and didn't know quite how to proceed. Almost every day he experienced a twinge of loss and sadness at Rydberg's absence. Those feelings would never leave him.

Then there was his father, who had died unexpectedly. He had collapsed from a stroke in his studio. That was three years ago. Even now, Wallander sometimes had trouble grasping the fact that his father wasn't there any more, surrounded by the smell of turpentine and oil paint. The house in Löderup had been sold. Wallander had driven past it a few times since then and seen that new people had moved in. He had never stopped and taken a closer look. From time to time he went to his father's grave, always with an inexplicable feeling of guilt. These visits were getting more infrequent. It was getting harder for him to conjure up his father's face.

A person who died eventually became a person who had never existed.

Then there was Svedberg, one of his own officers, who had died a terrible death only a year ago. That had made him realise how little he knew about the people he worked with. During the investigation he had uncovered a more complicated network of relationships in Svedberg's life than he would ever have dreamed of.

And now he was on his way to funeral number four, the only one he really didn't have to go to. She had called on Wednesday, just as Wallander was about to leave the office. It was late afternoon and he had a headache from concentrating on a depressing case involving smuggled cigarettes. The tracks seemed to lead to northern Greece, then went up in smoke. Wallander had exchanged information with both German and Greek police. But still they had not managed to arrest the smugglers. He realised now that the driver of the truck with the smuggled goods probably had no idea what had been in his load. All the same, he would go to jail for a couple of months at least. Nothing else would come of it. Wallander was sure contraband cigarettes landed by every ferry in Ystad. He doubted they would ever put a stop to it.

His day had also been poisoned by an argument with the prosecutor, the man filling in for Per Åkeson, who had taken charitable work in the Sudan two years ago and seemed to be in no hurry to come back. Wallander was filled with envy each time he received a letter from Åkeson. He had actually done what Wallander had only fantasised about: starting all over again.

Wallander was about to turn 50 and he knew, though he could scarcely admit it, that the decisive events of his life were behind him. He would never be anything but a police officer. The best he could do in the years leading up to retirement was to try to become better at solving crimes, and to pass on his knowledge to the younger generation. But there were no life-changing decisions in wait for him, no Sudan.

He was just about to put his jacket on when the telephone rang. At first he hadn't known who she was. Then he realised she was Stefan Fredman's mother. Memories and isolated images from three years ago rushed back in the space of a few seconds. It was the case of the boy who had painted himself to look like a Native American warrior and had revenged himself on the men who had driven his sister insane and filled his younger brother with terror. One of the victims had been the boy's own father. Wallander flinched at one of the last, most disturbing images: the boy kneeling by his sister's dead body, weeping. He didn't know what had happened afterwards, except that the boy had been sent to a secure psychiatric ward rather than prison.

Now Anette, his mother, had called to say the boy was

dead. He had thrown himself out of a window. Wallander had expressed his condolences and they had been genuine, though perhaps what he felt was a sense of hopelessness and despair rather than grief. He had not yet understood why she had called him. He stood with the receiver to his ear, trying to recall her face. He had only met her on two or three occasions, in her home in a suburb of Malmö, when he had been struggling with the idea that a 14-year-old boy had committed these heinous crimes. She had been shy and tense. There was something cringing about her, as if she always expected everything to turn out for the worst. In her case it often did. Wallander remembered and wondered if she were addicted to alcohol or prescription medication. But he didn't know. He could hardly bring her face to mind. Her voice he did not recognise at all.

She wanted Wallander to be at the funeral. There were so few people coming. She was the only one left now, apart from Stefan's younger brother Jens. Wallander had, after all, been someone who wished them well. He said he'd be there. He had changed his mind the moment he said it, but it was too late.

He rang one of Stefan's doctors, to try and find out what became of the boy, after his admittance to the psychiatric ward. He was told that Stefan had hardly said a word during the past few years, had shut himself off from the world outside. But the boy who came smashing down onto that slab of concrete on the hospital grounds had worn full-blown warrior warpaint. That disturbing mask of paint and blood held little clue as to who the young person locked inside had been, but it spoke volumes about the violent and largely indifferent society in which he had been formed.

Wallander drove slowly. He had been surprised when he put on his suit that morning and found that the trousers fitted him. He must have lost weight. Since being diagnosed with diabetes the previous year he had been forced to modify his eating habits, start exercising and lose weight. At the beginning he had put himself on the bathroom scales several times a day, until finally he threw them out in a rage.

But his doctor had not relented, and had insisted that Wallander do something about his unhealthy eating habits and his almost complete lack of exercise. His nagging had eventually borne fruit. Wallander had bought a tracksuit and trainers and was taking regular walks. When Martinsson suggested they run together, Wallander had drawn the line. He had established a regular circuit that took about an hour, from Mariagatan through the Sandskogen park, and back. He forced himself out on a walk at least four times a week, and had also forced himself to stay away from his favourite fast-food places. As a result his blood sugar levels had dropped and he had lost weight. One morning as he was shaving, he noticed in the mirror that his cheeks were hollow again. It was like getting his old face back after having worn an artificial padding of fat and bad skin. His daughter Linda had been delighted with the change when she last saw him. On the other hand, no-one at the station made any comments about his appearance. It's as if we never really see each other, Wallander thought. We work together, but we don't see each other.

Wallander drove by Mossbystrand, which was empty on this autumn morning. He thought of the time six years ago when a rubber dinghy had drifted ashore here with two bodies in it.

On a whim, he slammed on the brakes and turned round. He had plenty of time. He parked and got out. There was no wind and it was perhaps a couple of degrees above freezing. He buttoned his coat and followed the trail that snaked between the sand dunes to the sea. There was no-one there, but there were tracks of people and dogs in the sand. And horses. He looked out over the water. A flock of birds was flying south in formation.

He still remembered exactly where they had found them. It had been a difficult investigation and had led Wallander to Latvia. He had met Baiba in Riga. She was the widow of a Latvian police officer, a man Wallander had got to know and like.

They had started seeing each other. For a long time he had thought it was going to work, that she would move to Sweden. They had even looked at houses. But then she had begun to draw back. Wallander thought, jealously, that she had met someone else. He even flew to Riga once, without warning her, to surprise her. But there was no-one else, only Baiba's doubts about marrying another policeman and leaving her homeland where she had an underpaid but rewarding job as a translator. So it had ended.

Wallander walked along the shore and realised that a year had gone by since he had last talked to her. She sometimes appeared in his dreams still, but he never managed to take hold of her. Whenever he approached her or put out his hand to touch her she was gone. He asked himself if he really missed her. His jealousy was gone; he no longer flinched at the thought of her with another man.

I miss the companionship, he thought. With Baiba I managed to escape the loneliness I hadn't even been aware of.

He returned to the car. I should avoid deserted beaches in the autumn, he thought. They make me depressed. He had taken refuge once in a remote part of northern Jylland.

He had been on sick leave due to depression and thought he would never go back to his work as a police officer in Ystad again. It was many years ago, but he could recall in terrifying detail how he had felt then. He never wanted to experience it again. That bleak and blustery landscape had seemed to awaken his deepest anxieties.

He got back into the car and drove on to Malmö. He wondered what the coming winter was going to be like, if there would be much snow or if it would simply rain. He also wondered what he was going to do during the week of leave he was due in November. He had discussed with Linda taking a charter flight to somewhere warmer. It would be his treat. But she was still in Stockholm, studying something – he didn't know what – and said she really couldn't get away. He had tried to think of someone else he could go with, but he had practically no friends. There was Sten Widén, who raised horses on a stud farm outside Ystad, but Wallander was not sure he would be such a good travel companion. Widén drank like a fish, and Wallander was struggling to keep his own once considerable alcohol consumption to a minimum. He could ask Gertrud, his father's widow. But what would they talk about for a whole week? There was no-one else.

He would stay at home and use the money towards a new car. The Peugeot was getting old. It had started to sound pretty odd.

He was in the suburb of Rosengård soon after 10 a.m. The funeral was at 11.00. The church was a modern building. Nearby some boys were bouncing a football off a concrete wall. There were seven of them, three black. Another three also looked as though they might have immigrant parents. The last one had freckles and unruly blond hair. The boys were kicking the ball around with enthusiasm and a great deal of laughter. For a second Wallander felt an overwhelming urge to join them, but he stayed where he was. A man walked out of the church and lit a cigarette. Wallander got out of the car and approached him.

"Is this where Stefan Fredman's funeral is going to be held?" he said.

The man nodded. "Are you a relative?"

"No."

"I didn't think there would be very many people here," the man said. "I take it you know what he did."

"Yes, I know."

The man looked down at his cigarette. "Someone like him is better off dead."

Wallander felt himself get angry. "Stefan wasn't even 18 years old. Someone that young is never better off dead." He realised he was shouting.

The smoker looked at him with curiosity. Wallander shook his head angrily and turned away. At that moment the hearse drove up. The brown coffin was unloaded. There was only a single wreath on it. He should have brought flowers himself.

Wallander walked over to the boys who were still playing football. "Any of you know of a flower shop around here?" he said.

One of the boys pointed into the distance.

Wallander took out his wallet and held up a hundred-kronor note. "Run over and buy me some flowers," he said. "Roses. And hurry back. I'll give you ten kronor for your trouble."

The boy looked at him wide-eyed, but took the money.

"I'm a police officer," Wallander said. "A dangerous

police officer. If you make off with the money I'll find you."

The boy shook his head. "Then why aren't you wearing a uniform?" he asked in broken Swedish. "You don't look like a policeman. Not a dangerous one, anyway."

Wallander got out his police badge and showed it to him. The boy studied it for a while, then nodded and set off. The others resumed their game.

There's a good chance he won't be back, Wallander thought gloomily. It's been a long time since civilians had any respect for the police.

But the boy returned with the roses as promised. Wallander gave him 20 kronor, the ten he'd promised him and ten for actually coming back. He knew he was being overly generous, but it was too late now. A taxi drew up at the church steps and Stefan's mother got out. She had aged and was so thin she looked ill. A young boy of about seven stood by her side. He looked a lot like his brother. His eyes were wide and frightened. He still lived in fear from that time. Wallander walked over and greeted them.

"It's just going to be us and the minister," the woman said.

They walked into the church. The minister was a young man who was sitting on a chair next to the coffin, leafing through a newspaper. Wallander felt Anette Fredman suddenly grab hold of his arm. He understood.

The minister got up and put his newspaper away. They sat down to the right of the coffin. She was still clinging to Wallander's arm.

First she lost her husband, Wallander thought. Björn Fredman was an unpleasant and brutal man, who hit her and terrified his children, but he had been her husband and the father of her children. He was murdered by his own son. Then her oldest child, Louise, had died. And now here she is, about to bury her son. What's left for her? Half a life? As much as that?

Someone entered the church behind them. Fru Fredman did not seem to hear anything, or else she was trying so hard to stay in control of herself that she couldn't focus on anything else. A woman was walking up the aisle. She was about Wallander's age. Anette Fredman finally looked up and nodded to her. The woman sat down a few rows behind them.

"She's a doctor," she said. "Her name is Agneta Malmström. She helped Jens a while back when he wasn't doing so well."

Wallander recognised the name, but it took him a moment to remember that it was Agneta Malmström and her husband who had provided him with the most important clues in the Stefan Fredman case. He had spoken to her late one night with the help of Stockholm Radio. She had been on a yacht far out at sea, beyond Landsort.

Wallander heard organ music although he had not seen an organist. The minister had turned on a tape recorder. Wallander wondered why he had not heard any church bells. Didn't funerals always start with the ringing of church bells? This thought was pushed aside when Anette Fredman's grip on his arm tightened. He cast a glance at the boy by her side. Should a child his age be attending a funeral? Wallander didn't think so. But the boy looked fairly collected.

The music died away and the minister began to speak. He started by reminding them of Christ's words, "Let the little ones come unto me." Wallander concentrated on the wreath that lay on the coffin, counting the blossoms to keep the lump in his throat from growing.

The service was short. Afterwards, they approached the coffin. Fru Fredman was breathing hard, as if she were in the final few yards of a race. Dr Malmström stood right behind them. Wallander turned to the minister, who seemed impatient.

"Bells," Wallander said to him. "Why were there no bells? There should be bells ringing as we walk out, and not a recording either."

The minister nodded hesitantly. Wallander wondered what would have happened if he had pulled out his police badge. They started walking out. Jens and his mother went ahead. Wallander said hello to Agneta Malmström.

"I recognised you," she said. "We've never met, but I've seen your face in the papers."

"She asked me to come. Did she call you too?"

"No, I came of my own accord."

"What's going to happen now?"

Dr Malmström shook her head slowly. "I don't know. She's started drinking heavily. I have no idea how Jens is going to get on."

At this point they reached the vestibule where Fru Fredman and Jens were waiting for them. The church bells rang out. Wallander opened the doors, throwing one last look at the coffin. Some men were already carrying it through a side door.

Suddenly a flash went off in his face. There had been a press photographer waiting outside. Anette Fredman held up her hands to shield her face. The photographer turned from her and tried to get a picture of the boy. Wallander put out his arm to stop him, but the photographer was too quick. He got his picture.

"Why can't you leave us alone?" Fru Fredman cried.

The boy started to cry. Wallander grabbed the

photographer and pulled him aside. "What the hell do you think you're doing?" he hissed.

"None of your fucking business," the photographer said. He had bad breath. "I shoot whatever sells. Pictures of a serial killer's funeral sell. Too bad I didn't get here earlier."

Wallander reached for his police badge, then changed his mind and snatched the camera. The photographer tried to pull it out of his hands, but Wallander was stronger. He opened the camera and pulled out the film.

"There have to be limits," Wallander said, and handed the camera back to him.

The photographer stared at him, then took his mobile from his jacket pocket. "I'm calling the police," he said. "That was assault."

"Do it," Wallander said. "I'm a detective with the CID in Ystad. Inspector Kurt Wallander. Call my colleagues in Malmö and tell them whatever you want."

Wallander let the roll of film fall to the ground and broke open the casing under his shoe. The church bells stopped ringing. He was sweating and still enraged. Anette Fredman's shrill plea to be left alone echoed in his head. The photographer stared at the destroyed film. The group of boys were still playing football.

Fru Fredman had asked him to join them for coffee after the service when she called. He had not been able to say no.

"There won't be any pictures in the paper," Wallander said.

"Why can't they leave us alone?"

Wallander had nothing to say. He looked over at Agneta Malmström, but she had nothing to say either.

The flat in the shabby rental building was just as Wallander remembered. Dr Malmström came with them.

They sat in silence while they were waiting for the coffee to percolate. Wallander thought he heard a clink of glass from the kitchen.

Jens was on the floor playing quietly with a car. Wallander could see that Dr Malmström found it all as depressing as he did, but there was nothing to say.

They sat there with their coffee cups. Anette Fredman sat across from them with shiny eyes. Dr Malmström tried to discover how she was managing, now that she was unemployed. Fru Fredman answered in vague perfunctory phrases.

"We manage. Things will work out somehow. A day at a time."

The conversation died away. Wallander looked down at his watch. He got up and shook Anette Fredman's hand. She burst into tears. Wallander was taken aback. He didn't know what to do.

"You go," Dr Malmström said. "I'll stay with her a little while."

"I'll call to see how things are going," Wallander said. Then, awkwardly, he patted the boy's head and left.

He sat in the car for a while before starting the engine. He thought about the photographer who was so sure the pictures of a serial killer's funeral would sell.

I can't deny that this is how things are now, he thought. But that doesn't mean that I can understand a single bit of it.

He drove through the autumn landscape to Ystad. It had been a depressing morning.

An easterly wind had picked up. As he walked into the police station, he saw that a belt of cloud was moving in over the coast.

CHAPTER THREE

By the time Wallander reached his office, he had a headache. He looked in his desk drawers for some tablets. He heard Hansson walk past his door whistling. Finally, he found a crumpled packet of acetaminophen. He went to the canteen to get himself a glass of water and a cup of coffee. A group of young officers, who had been taken on during the last couple of years, was sitting at one table talking loudly. Wallander nodded in their direction and said hello. He heard them talking about their time at Police Training College. He walked back to his office and watched the two tablets dissolve in the glass of water.

He thought about Fru Fredman. He tried to imagine what the future might hold for the little boy in the impoverished suburb of Rosengård who had played so quietly on the living-room floor. He had seemed to be hiding from the world, carrying within him his memories of a dead father and two siblings, now both dead too.

Wallander drained the glass and immediately felt the headache lifting. He looked at a folder that Martinsson had put on his desk, *Urgent as all hell* on a red Post-it on the front. Wallander already knew the facts of the case. They had discussed it last week on the telephone while Wallander was at a national police conference on new directions for policing the violence associated with the growing motorcycle gang movement. Wallander had asked to be excused, but Chief Holgersson had insisted. She specifically wanted him on this. One of the gangs had just bought a farm outside Ystad and they had to be prepared to deal with them in the future.

Wallander opened the folder with a sigh. Martinsson had written a concise report of the events. Wallander leaned back in his chair and thought about what he had just read.

Two girls, one 19, the other not more than 14, had ordered a taxi from a restaurant at about 10 p.m. on Tuesday. They had asked to be driven to Rydsgård. One was in the passenger seat. As they reached the outskirts of Ystad she asked the driver to stop, saying she wanted to move to the back seat. When the taxi pulled over to the side of the road, the girl in the back hit the driver on the head with a hammer. The girl in the passenger seat stabbed him in the chest with a knife. They took the driver's wallet and his mobile and left. The driver was able to make an emergency call on the taxi radio despite his condition.

His name was Johan Lundberg and he was about 60 years old. He had been a taxi driver almost all his adult life. He had given good descriptions of both girls. Martinsson had been able to get their names by using these descriptions while interviewing other people who had been in the restaurant.

The girls had been arrested in their homes. Both were now in custody despite their age, because of the enormity of the crime and the violence involved. Lundberg had been conscious when admitted at the hospital, but his condition had deteriorated. He was now unconscious, and the doctors were unsure of the prognosis. As a motive for the crime, Martinsson reported, the girls had offered only the explanation that they "needed money".

Wallander made a face. He had never known anything like it – two girls responsible for an act of such pointless brutality. According to Martinsson's notes, the younger girl had excellent grades at school. The older one was a hotel receptionist and had earlier worked as a nanny in London. She had applied for a place on a foreign-language course at the university. Neither had been in trouble before.

I just don't get it, Wallander thought. This total lack of respect for human life. They could have killed that taxi driver, and it may even turn out that way. Two girls. If they had been boys I could maybe understand, if only because by now I'm used to it.

He was interrupted by a knock on the door. His colleague Ann-Britt Höglund was in the doorway. As usual she looked pale and tired. Wallander thought about the change in her life since she first came to Ystad. She had been one of the best in her class at Police Training College and had arrived with a great deal of energy and ambition. Today she still possessed a strong will, but she was changed. The paleness in her face came from within.

"Do you want me to come back later?" she said.

"No, not at all."

She sat down gingerly in the rickety chair opposite him. Wallander pointed to the papers in front of him. "Do you have anything to say about this?" he asked.

"Is it the taxi driver case?"

"Yes."

"I've talked to the older girl, Hökberg. She gave me clear and strong answers, answered everything. And seemed to have not a trace of remorse. The other girl has been in custody with the social welfare people because of her age."

"Can you understand it?"

Höglund paused before answering. "Yes and no. We know that crime has spread down to the ranks of the very young."

"Forgive me, but I don't recall a case of two teenage girls attacking anyone with a knife and a hammer. Were they drunk?"

"No. But I don't know if that should surprise us. Maybe the surprise is that something like this didn't happen sooner."

Wallander leaned over the desk. "You'll have to run that last part by me again."

"I don't know if I can explain it."

"Give it a try."

"Women aren't needed in the workforce any more. That era is over."

"But that doesn't explain why a young girl would assault a taxi driver."

"There has to be something more to it than we know. Neither you nor I believe that people are born evil."

Wallander shook his head. "I cling to that belief," he said, "though at times it's a challenge."

"Just look at the magazines young girls are reading. Now it's all about beauty again, nothing else. How to get a boyfriend and find meaning for life through his interests and dreams, that sort of thing."

"Wasn't that what they were always about?"

"No. Think of your own daughter. Didn't she have her own ideas about what to do with her life?"

Wallander knew that she was right. "Yes, but that doesn't get me to the point of knowing why they attacked Lundberg," he said.

"But you should know. Young girls are slowly starting to see through the messages society sends them. When they work out they aren't needed, that in fact they're superfluous, they react just as viciously as boys. And go on to commit crimes, among other things."

Wallander was quiet. He now understood the point Höglund had been trying to make.

"I don't think I can explain it any better," she said. "Shouldn't you talk to them yourself?"

"Martinsson has suggested it."

"Actually, I stopped by for another reason. Something I need your help on."

Wallander waited for her to continue.

"I said I'd give a talk to a women's club in Ystad. The meeting is on Thursday evening, but I don't feel up to it any more. There's too much going on in my life, and I can't seem to focus."

Wallander knew that she was in the throes of agonising divorce proceedings. Her husband was constantly away due to his work as an engineer. He was sent all over the world, and that meant that the process was dragging on. It was more than a year since she had first told Wallander about the marriage ending.

"Why don't you see if Martinsson would do it?" Wallander said. "You know I'm hopeless at lectures."

"You only have to tell them what it's like to be a police officer," she said. "And you'd only need to speak for half an hour to an audience of 30 or so women. Probably there will be questions too. They'll love you."

Wallander shook his head firmly. "Martinsson will be more than happy to do it," he said. "And he has experience in politics so he's used to this kind of thing."

"I already asked him. He can't."

"Holgersson?"

"The same. There's only you."

"What about Hansson?"

"He'd start talking about horse racing after a few minutes. He's hopeless."

Wallander saw that he would have to give in. He couldn't leave her in the lurch. "What kind of women's club?"

"It started as a book club, I think, which has grown into a society for intellectual and literary activity. They've been active for about ten years."

"Well, I don't want to do it but, since you're stuck, I will."

She was clearly relieved and gave him a piece of paper. "Here's the name and number of the contact person." The address was in the middle of town, not far from where he lived. Höglund got to her feet.

"They won't pay you anything," she said. "But you'll get plenty of coffee and cake."

"I don't eat cake."

"If it's any help, this kind of public service is exactly what the chief constable wants us to be doing. You know how we're always getting those memoranda about finding new ways of reaching out to the community."

Wallander thought of asking her how she was getting on in her personal life, but he let it pass. If she had a problem she wanted to discuss with him, she would be the one to bring it up.

"Weren't you going to go to Stefan Fredman's funeral?"

"I was just there, and it was exactly as depressing as you might imagine."

"How is the mother taking it? I can't remember her name."

"Anette. She's certainly been dealt a bum hand in life. But I think she's taking good care of the one child she has left. Or is trying to, at any rate."

"We'll have to wait and see."

"What do you mean by that?"

"What's the boy's name?"

"Jens."

"We'll have to wait and see if the name Jens Fredman starts popping up in our police reports in about ten years' time."

Wallander nodded. There was certainly that possibility.

Höglund left and Wallander went to fetch a fresh cup of coffee. The young officers were gone. Wallander walked to Martinsson's office. The door was wide open, but the room was empty. Wallander returned to his office. His headache was gone. He looked out of the window. Some blackbirds were screeching over by the water tower. He tried to count them, but there were too many.

The phone rang and he answered without sitting down at his desk. It was someone calling from the bookshop to let him know that the book he had ordered had come in. Wallander couldn't recall ordering a book, but said that he'd call in to pick it up the following day.

He remembered what the book was as soon as he put the receiver down. It was a present for Linda. A French book on restoring antique furniture. Wallander had read about it in a magazine at the doctor's surgery. He was still hoping that Linda would return to her idea of restoring furniture for a living, despite her subsequent experimentation with other careers. He had ordered the book and promptly forgotten about it. He pushed his coffee cup aside and decided to call her later that evening. It had been several weeks since they had talked.

Martinsson walked in. He was always in a hurry and seldom knocked. Over the years, Wallander had become steadily more convinced of Martinsson's abilities as a police officer. His chief weakness was that he would probably rather be doing something else. There had been times when he had seriously considered quitting, the worst one of which was set off by his daughter being attacked at school. The offenders maintained that it was for no other reason than that she was the daughter of a policeman. That had been enough to push him over the edge. But Wallander had eventually been able to talk him out of it. Martinsson's greatest strengths were that he was both stubborn and sharp. His stubbornness was sometimes overtaken by a certain impatience and then his sharp wits were not enough. Occasionally he turned in sloppy background work.

Martinsson leaned against the door frame. "I tried to ring you," he said, "but your mobile was turned off."

"I was in church," Wallander said. "I forgot to turn it on again."

"At Stefan's funeral?"

Wallander told Martinsson what he had told Höglund, that it was as grim as he could have imagined.

Martinsson gestured to the file on his table.

"I've read it," Wallander said. "And I still can't fathom what drove these girls to take a hammer and a knife and assault someone – anyone – like that."

"It says it right there," Martinsson said. "They needed the money."

"But why such violence? How is he, anyway?"

"Lundberg?"

"Who else?"

"He's still unconscious and on the critical list. They promised to call if there was any change. It doesn't look so good, though."

"Do you understand any of this?"

Martinsson sat down. "No," he said, "I certainly don't. And I'm not sure I want to."

"But we have to. If we're going to do our jobs, that is."

Martinsson looked at Wallander. "You know I've often thought about quitting. Last time you managed to talk me out of it. Next time it won't be as easy."

Wallander was worried. He didn't want to lose Martinsson as a colleague, any more than he wanted to see Höglund turn up in his office with her resignation. "Maybe we should go and talk to this Hökberg girl," he said.

"There's one more thing."

Wallander sat back in his chair. Martinsson had some papers in his hand.

"I want you to look at this. It happened last night. I was on duty and saw no reason to get you out of bed."

"Tell me."

Martinsson scratched his forehead. "A night patrolman called in at around 1 a.m., saying that there was a man lying dead in front of one of the cash machines outside a department store in the town."

"Which one?"

"The one next to the Inland Revenue."

Wallander nodded in recognition.

"We drove down to check it out. According to the doctor the man hadn't been dead long, a couple of hours at the outside. We'll have the autopsy report in a few days, of course."

"What had happened?"

"That's the question. He had an ugly wound on his head, but whether somebody hit him or whether he injured himself when falling to the ground, we couldn't tell."

"Had he been mugged?"

"His wallet was still there, with money in it."

Wallander thought for a moment. "No-one saw anything?"

"No."

"Who was he?"

Martinsson looked in his papers. "Name of Tynnes Falk. 47 years old and living nearby. He was renting the top-floor flat at 10 Apelbergsgatan."

Wallander raised his hand. "10 Apelbergsgatan?"

"That's right."

Wallander nodded slowly. A couple of years ago, soon after his divorce from Mona, he had met a woman during a night of dancing at the Hotel Saltsjöbaden. Wallander had been very drunk. He had gone home with her and woken up the next morning in a strange bed next to a woman he hardly recognised, whose name he couldn't remember. He had thrown his clothes on and left and never saw her again. For some reason, he was sure she had lived at 10 Apelbergsgatan.

"Do you recognise the address?" Martinsson said.

"I just didn't hear you."

Martinsson looked at him with surprise. "Was I mumbling?"

"Please go on."

"He was single, divorced actually. His ex-wife still lives here, but their children are all over the place. A boy of 19 is studying in Stockholm. The girl is 17 and works as a nanny at an embassy in Paris. The ex-wife has been notified."

"Where did he work?"

"He seems to have worked for himself. Some kind of computer consultant."

"And he wasn't robbed?"

"No, but he had just rung up his account balance at the cash machine before he died. He still had the slip in his hand when we found him."

"And he hadn't taken out any money?"

"The records say not."

"Strange. The most reasonable thing would be to assume that someone was waiting for him to withdraw money and then strike when he had the cash."

"That occurred to me as well, of course, but the last time he made a withdrawal was on Saturday, and that wasn't even a large sum of money."

Martinsson handed Wallander a plastic bag with a blood-spattered bank receipt. The time on it said 12.02 a.m. He handed it back to Martinsson.

"What does Nyberg say?"

"That nothing apart from the head wound points to a crime. He probably had a heart attack."

"Perhaps he had been expecting to see a higher figure than the one he found on the printout," Wallander said, thoughtfully.

"Why do you say that?"

Wallander wondered too. He stood up. "Let's wait for the autopsy report. Until then we'll assume no crime has been committed, so put it aside for now."

Martinsson gathered up his papers. "I'll contact the lawyer who was assigned to Hökberg. I'll let you know when he can be expected here so you can talk to her."

"Not that I want to," Wallander said. "But I suppose I should."

Martinsson left and Wallander walked to the toilets. He should be grateful at least that his days of constantly urinating due to elevated blood sugar were over.

For an hour he kept working on the contraband cigarettes case, while the thought of the favour he had agreed to do for Höglund nagged at the back of his mind.

At 4.02 p.m. Martinsson telephoned to say that Hökberg and her lawyer were ready.

"Who is he?" Wallander said.

"Herman Lötberg."

Wallander knew him. He was one of the older ones, and easy to work with. "I'll be there in five minutes," Wallander said, and hung up.

He walked back to the window. The wind had picked up and the blackbirds were gone. He thought about Mrs Fredman and the boy, playing quietly on the floor. He thought about his frightened eyes. He shook his head and thought instead of the questions he was going to ask the Hökberg girl. Martinsson's notes told him that she was the one in the back seat who had hit Lundberg on the head with a hammer. Many blows, not just one. As if she had been in a blind rage.

Wallander picked up a notebook and pen and left. Halfway there he realised that he had left his glasses behind. He went back.

There's really only one question, he thought as he returned to the conference room. Why did they do it? Their saying they needed money isn't enough. There's another answer somewhere, a deeper answer that I have to find.

CHAPTER FOUR

Sonja Hökberg did not look as Wallander had expected her to look. Afterwards he couldn't recall exactly what he had been expecting, but he knew it wasn't the person he had met in that room. Sonja Hökberg was sitting down when he came in. She was small and thin, almost to the point of transparency. She had shoulder-length blonde hair and blue eyes. She could have been a model on a poster for innocence and purity. Nothing indicated that she was a crazed hammer-wielding murderess.

Wallander had been met by her lawyer and Martinsson outside the room.

"She's very much in control of herself," Lötberg said to Wallander. "I'm not sure she understands the gravity of the charges she's facing."

"It's not a matter of accusation. She's guilty," Martinsson said, firmly.

"What about the hammer?" Wallander said. "Have we found it?"

"She put it under her bed. She hadn't even tried to wipe off the blood. The other girl got rid of her knife. We're still searching for it," Martinsson said, and left.

Wallander walked into the room with the lawyer. The girl looked at them expectantly. She didn't seem at all nervous. Wallander nodded in acknowledgement and sat down. There was a tape recorder on the table. Wallander looked at her for a long time. She looked back at him.

"Do you have any gum?" she said, at last.

Wallander shook his head and looked at Lötberg, who also shook his head.

"We'll see if we can't get you some later," Wallander said, and turned on the tape recorder. "First we're going to have a little chat."

"I've already said what happened. Why can't I have some gum? I can pay for it," she said, and held up a black handbag with an oak-leaf clasp. Wallander was surprised it hadn't been confiscated. "I won't talk until I get my gum."

Wallander reached over for the phone and called the reception desk. Ebba will take care of this, he thought. Only when an unfamiliar voice came on the line did he remember that Ebba was retired now. She had been gone for six months, but Wallander had still not grown used to the new receptionist. She was a woman in her thirties, named Irene. She had been an administrative assistant in a doctor's office, and was already well liked at the police station. But Wallander missed Ebba.

"I need some gum," Wallander said. "Do you know anyone who would have any?"

"Yes," Irene said. "Me."

Wallander hung up and walked out to the reception.

"Is it for the girl?" Irene said.

"Fast thinker."

He returned to the examination room, gave Sonja Hökberg the stick of gum and realised he had forgotten to turn off the tape recorder through all of this.

"Let's begin," he said. "It's 4.15 p.m. on October 6, 1997. Kurt Wallander is questioning Sonja Hökberg."

"So do I have to tell you everything all over again?" she said.

"Yes, try to speak clearly and direct your words at the microphone."

"What about the fact that I've said it all already?"

"I may have some more questions."

"I don't feel like going over it again."

For a moment Wallander was thrown by her total lack of anxiety.

"Unfortunately you'll just have to cooperate," he said. "You have been accused of a very serious crime, and what's more you have confessed. Right now you stand accused of assault in the third degree, but this serious charge may be upgraded if the taxi driver's condition deteriorates any further."

Lötberg gave Wallander a disapproving look but said nothing.

Wallander started at the beginning. "Your name is Sonja Hökberg, and you were born on February 2, 1978."

"That makes me an Aquarius. What's your sign?"

"That doesn't concern us at present. You're here to answer my questions and that is all. Understand?"

"Do I look stupid?"

"You live with your parents on 12 Trastvägen, here in Ystad."

"Yes."

"You have a younger brother Emil, born in 1982."

"He's the one who should be sitting in this chair, not me."

Wallander raised his eyebrows. "Why do you say that?"

"He never leaves my things alone. He's always looking through my stuff. We fight a lot."

"I'm sure it can be trying to have a younger brother, but let's leave it for now."

She's still so composed, Wallander thought. Her nonchalance was beginning to irritate him.

"Can you describe the events of last Tuesday evening?"

"It's such a drag to have to go over the same thing twice."

"That can't be helped. You and Eva Persson went out that evening?"

"There's nothing to do around here. I wish I lived in Moscow."

Wallander regarded her with surprise. Even Lötberg seemed startled.

"Why Moscow?"

"I just saw somewhere that exciting things often happen there. Have you ever been to Moscow?"

"No. Just answer my questions. So, you went out that night."

"You already know that."

"Were you and Eva good friends?"

"Why else would we have gone out together? Do I look like the kind of person who would go out with people I didn't like?"

For the first time Wallander thought he could detect a note of emotion in her voice. Impatience.

"How long have you known each other?"

"Not very long."

"How long?"

"A few years."

"She's five years younger than you."

"She looks up to me."

"What do you mean by that?"

"She's told me so herself. She looks up to me."

"Why is that?"

"You'll have to ask her yourself."

I will, Wallander thought. I have a lot of things to ask her. "Can you tell me what happened that night?"

"Jesus Christ!"

"You must, whether you want to or not. We can stay here all night if we have to."

"We had a beer."

"Even though Eva Persson is only 14?"

"She looks older."

"Then what happened?"

"We ordered another beer."

"And after that?"

"We called a taxi. But you know all this. Why do you keep asking?"

"Had you already decided to attack this taxi driver?"

"We needed the money."

"For what?"

"Nothing in particular."

"Let me see if I have this straight: you needed money, but not for anything in particular."

"Right."

No, that's not right, Wallander thought. He had detected a shade of insecurity in her answer. He grew more attentive.

"Normally, when you need money it is for something in particular."

"Not in our case."

Oh yes, it was, Wallander thought. But he decided to leave the matter for now.

"How did you come up with the idea of robbing a taxi driver?"

"We talked about it."

"At the restaurant?"

"Yes."

"So you hadn't talked about it earlier?"

"Why would we have done that?"

Lötberg was staring down at his hands.

"Would it be correct to say that you had no intention of assaulting the taxi driver before you went to the restaurant? Whose idea was it?"

"It was mine."

"Eva had no objections?"

"No."

This doesn't hang together, Wallander thought. She's lying, but she's remarkably calm.

"You ordered the taxi from the restaurant, then waited until it arrived. Is that correct?"

"Yes."

"But where did the hammer and knife come from? If you hadn't planned the attack in advance, I mean."

The girl looked steadily into Wallander's eyes. "I always carry a hammer with me," she said. "And Eva always has a knife."

"Why?"

"You never know what's going to happen."

"What do you mean by that?"

"The streets are full of crazy people. You have to be able to defend yourself."

"So you always go out with this hammer in your handbag?"

"Yes."

"Have you ever used it before?"

Lötberg looked up. "That question has no relevance to this case," he said.

"What does that mean?" Sonja Hökberg said.

"Relevance? That he has no business asking that question."

"I can answer anyway. I had never used the hammer before. But Eva cut someone once. Some creep who was trying to feel her up."

Wallander was struck by a thought and veered away from his earlier line of questioning. "Did you meet anyone at that restaurant? Had you made a date with anyone?"

"No."

"You don't have a boyfriend?"

"No."

That answer came a little too quickly, Wallander thought. He made a mental note of it.

"The taxi came and you left."

"Yes."

"What did you do then?"

"What do you think? We told him where we wanted to go."

"And you said you wanted to be driven to Rydsgård. Why?"

"I don't know. We had to say something and that was the first thing that came to mind."

"Eva sat up front with the driver, and you sat in the back. Did you decide on that beforehand?"

"That was the plan."

"What plan?"

"That we would get the driver to stop because Eva wanted to get in the back seat with me. And that's when we were going to get him."

"So you had already decided to use your weapons?"

"Not if he had been younger."

"What would you have done then?"

"Then we would have got him to stop by pulling up our skirts and being suggestive."

Wallander felt that he had started to sweat. Her insouciance was getting on his nerves.

"Suggesting what exactly?"

"What do you think?"

"You would entice him into thinking he could have sex with you?"

"You dirty old fuck."

Lötberg leaned forward. "You should watch your language."

Hökberg looked at him. "I'll use whatever language I please."

Lötberg sat back again. Wallander decided to move on.

"But, as it happened, the taxi driver was an older man. You got him to stop. Then what?"

"I hit him in the head. Eva stabbed him with the knife."

"How many times did you strike him?"

"I don't know. A couple of times. I wasn't counting."

"You weren't afraid of killing him?"

"We needed the money."

"That wasn't what I was asking. What I want to know is, were you aware that the wounds you were inflicting could have been mortal?"

Sonja Hökberg shrugged. Wallander waited, but she didn't say anything. He didn't feel he had the energy to repeat the last question.

"You say you needed money. For what?"

"Nothing special. I told you."

"Then what happened?"

"We took his wallet and the mobile phone and walked home."

"What happened to the wallet?"

"We divided up the cash, then Eva threw it away somewhere."

Wallander looked swiftly through Martinsson's notes. Lundberg had been carrying around 600 kronor. They had found the wallet in a waste-paper basket, after getting directions from Persson. Hökberg had taken the mobile phone. The police had found it in her bedroom.

Wallander gave the time and that he was concluding the interview and turned off the tape recorder. Hökberg followed his movements with her eyes.

"Can I go home now?"

"No, as a matter of fact, you can't," Wallander said. "You are 19 years old and that means you count as an adult in our courts. You have committed a felony, and you will be formally arraigned."

"And that means?"

"You'll have to stay here at the station."

"Why?"

Wallander looked at Lötberg, then stood up. "I think your lawyer can explain it to you."

Wallander left the room. He felt sick to his stomach. Hökberg had not been putting on an act in there. She had no sense of wrongdoing. Wallander walked into Martinsson's office and sat down. Martinsson was on the phone but gestured that he would be off soon. While Wallander waited he felt a strong urge to smoke. That almost never happened. But his meeting with Sonja Hökberg had been profoundly disturbing.

Martinsson put the phone down. "How did it go?"

"She confessed to everything. She's as cold as ice."

"Persson is the same way and she's only 14."

Wallander looked at Martinsson with something like pleading in his eyes. "What's happening to the world?"

"I don't know."

Wallander was visibly shaken.

"They're just little girls."

"I know, I know. And they have no remorse at all."

They were silent for a while and Wallander felt utterly empty inside. Martinsson was the one who finally spoke.

"Do you understand now why I think so often of quitting?"

Wallander roused himself. "And do you understand why it is so important you don't?" He got up and walked over to the window. "How is Lundberg?"

"Still critical."

"We have to get to the bottom of this, whether he dies or not. They didn't attack him like that just to get some cash. Either they needed the money for a particular purpose or the attack was about something else entirely."

"Such as?"

"I don't know. It's just a feeling that I have that there's a deeper layer to all this."

"Isn't the most probable scenario that they were a bit drunk and concocted this lunatic plan to get some money? Without thinking of the consequences?"

"Why do you think that?"

"I'm just sure it wasn't a random act, as you said."

Wallander nodded. "Well, we agree on that. But I want to know what their reasons were. Tomorrow I'll talk to Persson, as well as her parents. Do either of them have a boyfriend?"

"Persson said she had someone."

"Not Hökberg?"

"No."

"Then she's lying. She has someone and we'll find him."

Martinsson made a note. "Who will take that on? You or me?"

Wallander's response was immediate. "I'll do it. I want to know what's going on in this country."

"Suits me."

"You're not completely off the hook, though. Not you, not Hansson, not Höglund. We have to get to the bottom of this attack. I feel sure it was an attempted homicide and if Lundberg does die, then it's murder."

Wallander returned to his office. It was 5.30 p.m. and already it was dark outside. He thought about Sonja Hökberg and why the two girls had needed money so badly. Had there been another reason entirely? Then he thought of Anette Fredman.

He still had work to do, but he couldn't bear to stay in his office. He grabbed his coat and left. The sharp autumn wind burned his face. He heard the strange engine noise when he started the car. As he turned out of the parking area he decided to go shopping. His fridge was almost empty except for the bottle of champagne that he had won in a bet with Hansson. He could no longer remember what the bet had been. On an impulse he decided to drive past the cash machine, where the man had died the night before. He could do his shopping in one of the supermarkets near there.

After parking the car he walked up to the cash machine and waited while a woman with a pushchair withdrew some money. The concrete of the pavement was rough and uneven. Wallander looked around. There seemed to be no residential buildings nearby. In the middle of the night the square would be quite deserted. Even under the powerful street lamps, a man could cry out and collapse to the ground without anyone hearing or seeing him.

Wallander went into the nearest department store and found the food section. As usual he was plagued by boredom and indecision as he inspected the shelves. He quickly filled up his basket with an assortment of items, paid and left. Back in the car the mystery engine noise seemed to increase. He took off his dark suit as soon as he was back in his flat. He showered and noted that he was almost out of soap. He made some vegetable soup for dinner which tasted surprisingly good. He made some coffee and took a cup with him into the living room. He was tired. He flipped the channels without finding anything interesting, then reached for the phone and called Linda in Stockholm. She was sharing a flat in Kungsholmen with two women he only knew by name. To make ends meet she sometimes worked as a waitress in a nearby restaurant. Wallander had eaten dinner there last time he was in town and had enjoyed the food. But he was surprised she could stand the music, which was oppressively loud.

Linda was 26 years old now. They had a good relationship, but he missed being able to see her regularly.

An answering machine came on. Neither Linda nor her flatmates were at home. The message was repeated in English. Wallander said who he was and that it wasn't important. He put the phone down and stared at his coffee. It was cold. I can't keep living like this, he thought, irritatedly. I'm only 50 years old, but I feel ancient and weak.

He knew he should go for an evening walk and tried desperately to think of an excuse. Finally he put on his trainers and headed out.

It was 8.30 p.m. when he returned. The walk had cleared his mind and his spirits had lifted.

The phone rang and Wallander thought it must be Linda. But it was Martinsson.

"Lundberg has died. They just called from the hospital."

Wallander said nothing.

"That means Hökberg and Persson have committed murder."

"I know," Wallander said. "And we have one hell of a mess on our hands."

They agreed to meet at eight the next morning. There was nothing more to say.

Wallander stayed in front of the television and watched a news programme, his mind elsewhere. The dollar had gained more ground against the krona. The only story that managed to grab his attention was the story on the insurance company Trustor. It seemed bewilderingly simple these days to drain the resources of an entire corporation without anyone catching on until it was too late.

Linda didn't call. Wallander went to bed at 11 p.m. It took him a long time to fall asleep.

CHAPTER FIVE

Wallander woke up with a sore throat a little after 6 a.m. on Tuesday, October 7. He was sweating and he knew that he was coming down with flu. He stayed in bed for a while and debated whether or not he should remain at home, but the thought of Johan Lundberg's having died drove him up. He showered, made himself coffee and swallowed some pills to lower his fever. He tucked the bottle of pills into his pocket. Before leaving, he forced himself to eat a bowl of yoghurt. The street lamp outside the kitchen window was swaying in the gusty wind. It was overcast and only two degrees above freezing. Wallander rummaged on his shelves for a warm sweater. He wondered whether he should call Linda, but it was too early. When he reached the street he thought of the list of things he had to do, which he had left on the kitchen table. There was something he had been planning to buy today, but he couldn't remember what it was, and he didn't have the energy to go back and get it.

He took the usual route to the station. Each time he drove this way he felt guilty. He should be walking to work, to keep his blood sugar at a healthy level. Even today, he wasn't so weak from the flu that he couldn't have walked.

He parked and was on his way through reception as the clock was striking seven. As he sat down at his desk he remembered what he meant to buy. Soap. He wrote it down. Then he turned his concentration to the case.

Some of the unpleasant feelings from the day before

returned. He recalled Hökberg's lack of emotion. He tried to persuade himself that she had in fact manifested some inkling of human feeling, and that he had just not been able to pick up on it. But to no avail. His experience in these matters told him that he had not been wrong. He got up and went to get a cup of coffee from the canteen. He stopped at Martinsson's office since he, too, was an early riser. The door was open. Wallander couldn't imagine how Martinsson could work with an open door. For Wallander a closed door was a must if he was going to focus on something.

"I thought you'd be here," Martinsson said, when he saw Wallander in the doorway.

"I don't feel so good today," Wallander said.

"A cold?"

"I always get a sore throat in October."

Martinsson, who was forever worrying about getting ill, pulled his chair back a few inches.

"You could have stayed at home," he said. "This wretched Lundberg case is solved already."

"Only partially," Wallander said. "We don't have a motive yet. I don't believe the line that they needed extra money for nothing in particular. Have you found the knife?"

"Nyberg's dealing with it. I haven't talked to him yet."

"Call him."

Martinsson made a face. "He's not easy to talk to in the morning."

"Then I'll call him."

Wallander reached for Martinsson's phone and tried Nyberg's home number. After a few moments he was automatically transferred to his mobile number. Nyberg answered, but it was a poor connection.

"It's me, Kurt. I just wanted to know if you'd found the knife yet."

"How the hell are we supposed to find anything when it's still dark?" Nyberg said, angrily.

"I thought Persson said where she had left it?"

"We still have an area of several hundred cubic metres to comb. She threw it 'somewhere in the Old Cemetery', was what she said."

"Why don't you have someone bring her down?"

"If it's here we'll find it," Nyberg said.

They ended the conversation.

"I didn't sleep well myself last night," Martinsson said. "My daughter Terese knows Eva Persson. They're almost the same age. And Persson has parents too. What are they going through right now? As far as I know, she is their only child."

They both thought about what he had said. Then Wallander began to sneeze. He beat a hasty retreat. The conversation was left hanging.

They gathered in one of the conference rooms at 8 a.m. Wallander sat in his usual spot at the end of the table. Hansson and Höglund were there. Martinsson was standing by the window and talking to someone on the phone, probably his wife. Wallander had always wondered how they could have so much to say to one another after presumably having had breakfast together hardly an hour earlier. The main feeling in the room was despondency. Lisa Holgersson walked in and Martinsson finished his conversation.

Hansson got up and shut the door. "Isn't Nyberg supposed to be here?" he said.

"He's in the Old Cemetery, looking for the knife," Wallander said. "I think we can assume he'll find it."

He looked at Holgersson. She nodded to him to start

the meeting. He asked himself how many times he had found himself in exactly this situation. Up early in the morning, facing his colleagues across the conference table with a crime to solve.

They were waiting for him to begin.

"Johan Lundberg has died," he said. "In case anyone hasn't heard."

He pointed to a copy of the local newspaper, the *Ystad Allehanda*, on the table. The taxi driver's death was reported under a huge headline on the front page.

"This means that the two girls, Hökberg and Persson, have committed murder. We can't call it by any other name, since Hökberg in particular was so precise in her explanations. They planned this and they were carrying weapons. They were going to attack whichever taxi driver came their way. We have recovered the hammer, as well as Lundberg's empty wallet and his mobile phone. We have yet to find the knife. Neither girl has denied the charges, nor shifted the blame to the other. I'm assuming we can hand the matter over to the prosecutor tomorrow at the latest. Since Persson is so young, her case will be passed to the juvenile courts. The autopsy result isn't in yet, but I think we can say that our role in this unfortunate case is as good as concluded."

Wallander waited to see if anyone had anything to say.

"Why did they do it?" Holgersson finally asked. "It seems so pointless."

Wallander had hoped that someone would ask this question, so he wouldn't have to find a way to frame it himself.

"Hökberg was very firm on this point," he said. "In both her sessions, first with Martinsson and later with me. She said, 'We needed the money.' Nothing else."

"What for?" Hansson asked.

"We don't know what for. They won't tell us. If Hökberg is to be believed, they didn't even know themselves. They just wanted money." Wallander looked around the table before he continued. "I don't think they're telling the truth. I am certain Hökberg is lying. I haven't spoken with Persson yet, but still I'm convinced of it. They needed that money for some particular purpose. I also suspect that Persson was doing what Hökberg told her to do. That doesn't make her any less guilty, but it gives an appropriate picture of their relation to each other."

"Does it even matter?" Höglund said. "Whether they needed the money for clothes or something else?"

"I suppose not, at this point. The prosecutor certainly has enough evidence to convict Hökberg."

"They've never been in trouble with us before," Martinsson said. "I made a quick search of our database. And they were both doing well at school."

Wallander again sensed that they were taking the wrong approach to the case. Or at the least that they had been too hasty in writing off other explanations for the murder. But since he couldn't put this hunch into words, he said nothing. The motive for the murder could very well have been to do with money. They simply had to keep their eyes open for other possibilities.

The phone rang and Hansson answered. After a while he put the receiver down. "That was Nyberg," he said. "They found the knife."

Wallander nodded and shut the file in front of him. "Naturally, we still have to speak to the parents and make sure we conduct a thorough background investigation, but I think we can safely forward the preliminary information to the prosecutor."

Holgersson raised her hand to speak. "We need a press

conference. We've been barraged by calls from the media. It is still a far cry from normal that two young girls commit this kind of violent crime."

Wallander looked at Höglund, but she shook her head. Over the past few years she had often dealt with the media, a job he thoroughly despised. But not this time. Wallander understood.

"I'll do it," he said. "Do we have a time?"

"I'm going to suggest 1 p.m."

Wallander made a note.

They divided up the tasks and he brought the meeting to a close. Everyone wanted the matter disposed of as rapidly as possible. It was an exceptionally unpleasant case, and no-one wanted to spend more time on it than they had to. Wallander would visit the Hökberg family. Martinsson and Höglund would talk to Eva Persson and her parents.

Soon the room was empty. Wallander could feel the symptoms of his flu getting worse. At least maybe I'll infect a journalist, he thought and dug into his pockets for a tissue.

He bumped into Nyberg in the corridor. Nyberg was wearing boots and a warm coat, his hair splayed in all directions. He was clearly in a bad mood.

"I heard you found the knife," Wallander said.

"Looks like the county can no longer afford to pay for basic upkeep," Nyberg said. "We were ankle-deep in leaves, but we eventually found it."

"What kind of a knife?"

"Kitchen knife. Pretty big. The tip broke off, probably from hitting a rib, so she must have used a surprising amount of force. But then again it was a cheap knife."

Wallander shook his head.

"It's hard to believe," Nyberg said. "I don't know what happened to the basic respect for human life. How much money did they get?"

"We don't know yet, but probably about 600 kronor. It couldn't have been much more. Lundberg was at the beginning of his shift and he never carried a lot of cash at the start."

Nyberg muttered something under his breath and walked away. Wallander went back to his office. For a while he sat at his desk without knowing what to do next. His throat hurt. Finally, he opened the file with a sigh. The Hökbergs lived to the west of Ystad. He wrote down the address, got up and put on his coat. As he was leaving the phone rang. He picked it up. It was Linda. The noises and clatter in the background made him think she was calling from the restaurant.

"I got your message this morning," she said.

"This morning?"

"I wasn't at home last night."

Wallander knew better than to ask her where she spent the night. It would only make her cross and she'd slam down the phone.

"Well, I didn't call for anything special," he said. "I just wanted to know how you were."

"I'm fine. How about you?"

"I've got a slight cold. Otherwise things are the same. I was wondering if you had any plans to come down and visit soon?"

"I don't have time."

"I'm happy to pay your fare."

"I told you, I don't have time. It's not about the money."

Wallander realised he was not going to be able to change her mind. She was as stubborn as he was.

"How are you doing anyway?" she said, again. "Do you have any contact with Baiba these days?"

"That ended a long time ago. You know that."

"It's not good for you to go on like this."

"What do you mean?"

"You know what I mean. You're even starting to sound whiny. You never had that before."

"You think I sound whiny?"

"You're doing it right now. But I have a suggestion. I think you should contact a dating agency."

"A dating agency?"

"Where you can find someone. Otherwise you're going to turn into a whiny old man who worries about where I'm spending my nights."

She sees right through me, he thought. I'm an open book.

"You mean I should put an ad in the paper?"

"Yes, or use one of those companies."

"I'd never do that."

"Why not?"

"I don't believe in them."

"And why not?"

"I don't know."

"Well, it was just a suggestion. Think it over. I have to get back to work."

"Where are you?"

"At the restaurant."

They said goodbye and hung up. Wallander did wonder where she had spent the night. A couple of years ago Linda had been involved with a young man from Kenya who was at medical school in Lund. But that was over, and since then he had not known very much at all about who she was going out with, other than that every so often she started seeing someone new. He felt a pinch of irritation and jealousy. Though the idea of putting in a personal ad or of signing up with a dating agency had occurred to him before, he had always drawn back at the last minute. It was as if making that choice would mean sinking to an unacceptable level of desperation.

The strong wind chilled him as soon as he walked outside. He got into his car and started the engine, listening to the strange noises that were getting worse. Then he drove out to the townhouse where the Hökbergs lived. Martinsson's report had only given him the information that Hökberg's father was "self-employed". He didn't know what at. The small garden in the front was neat and tidy. He rang the doorbell. After a moment a man opened the door. Wallander knew at once that they had met before. He had a good memory for faces. But he didn't know when and where it had been. The man had also immediately recognised Wallander.

"It's you," he said. "I knew the police would be coming out, but I didn't expect it to be you."

He stepped to one side to let Wallander enter. He heard the sound of a television from somewhere. He could not remember where he had met this man before.

"I take it you remember me?" Hökberg said.

"Yes, I do," Wallander said. "But I'm having trouble placing you in the right context."

"Erik Hökberg doesn't ring a bell?"

Wallander searched his memory.

"And Sten Widén?"

Suddenly Wallander remembered. Widén, with his stud farm in Stjärnsund. And Erik. The three of them had shared a passion for the opera. Sten had been the most involved, but Erik was a childhood friend of his and had often sat around the record player with him as they listened to Verdi's operas.

"Yes, I remember now," Wallander said. "But your name wasn't Hökberg then, was it?"

"I took my wife's name. As a boy I was called Erik Eriksson."

Hökberg was a large man. The coat hanger he held out to Wallander looked small in his hand. Wallander had remembered him as thin, but now he was substantial. That must have been why it had been so hard to make the connection.

Wallander hung up his coat and followed Hökberg into the living room. There was a television in the middle of the room, but it was turned off. The sound was coming from another room. They sat down. Wallander tried to think of how to begin.

"It's horrible what's happened," Hökberg said. "Naturally I have no idea what got into her."

"Has she ever been violent before?"

"Never."

"What about your wife? Is she home?"

Hökberg seemed to have collapsed into a heap in his chair. Behind the rolls of fat in his face Wallander thought he could sense the outline of another face from a time that now seemed immeasurably distant.

"She took Emil and went to her sister in Höör. She couldn't stand to stay here. The reporters kept calling. They show no mercy. They called in the middle of the night, some of them."

"I'm afraid I have to speak to her."

"I know. I've told her the police would reach her there."

Wallander wasn't sure how to proceed. "You and your wife must have talked about what happened."

"She doesn't understand it any more than I do. It was a total shock."

"You have a good relationship with Sonja?"

"There were never any problems."

"And between her and her mother?"

"The same. They had fights from time to time but only stuff you would expect. There have never been any problems, at least as long as I've known her."

Wallander furrowed his brow.

"What do you mean by that?"

"You knew she was my stepdaughter?"

Wallander was sure that this had not been in the report. He would have remembered it.

"Ruth and I had Emil together," Hökberg said. "Sonja was about two when I came on the scene. That was 17 years ago. Ruth and I met at a Christmas party."

"Who was Sonja's father?"

"His name was Rolf. He never cared about her. He and Ruth were never married."

"Do you know where he is?"

"He died a few years ago. Drank himself to death."

Wallander looked for a pen in his coat pocket. He had already realised that he had forgotten both his glasses and notebook. There was a pile of old papers on the glass table.

"Do you mind if I tear off a piece?"

"Can't the police afford office supplies any more?"

"That's a good question. As it happens I've forgotten my notebook."

Wallander used a magazine as a pad. He saw that it was an English-language financial magazine.

"Do you mind if I ask you what you do for a living?"

The answer was a surprise.

"I play the stock market."

"I see. What does that entail?"

"I trade stocks, options, foreign currency. I also place some bets, mainly English cricket games. Sometimes American baseball."

"So you mean you gamble?"

"Not the usual kind. I never place bets on horses. But I suppose you can call trading stocks a form of gambling."

"And you do all this from home?"

Hökberg got up and gestured for Wallander to follow him. When he walked into the adjoining room Wallander paused in the doorway. There was not simply one television in this room, there were three. Various numbers flashed past in a dark ribbon on the bottom of the screens. On one wall there was a series of clocks showing the time in various parts of the world. It was like walking into an air-traffic control tower.

"People always say technology has made the world smaller," Hökberg said. "I think that's debatable. But the fact that it's made my world bigger is beyond dispute. From this flimsy townhouse at the edge of Ystad, I can reach all the markets in the whole world. I can connect to betting centres in London or Rome. I can buy options on the Hong Kong market and sell American dollars in Jakarta."

"Is it really so simple?"

"Not altogether. You need permits, good contacts and knowledge. But when I step into this room I'm in the middle of the world. Whenever I choose. Strength and vulnerability go hand in hand."

They returned to the living room.

"I would like to see Sonja's room," Wallander said.

Hökberg accompanied him up the stairs. They walked past a room that Wallander assumed belonged to their boy, Emil. Hökberg pointed to a door.

"I'll wait downstairs," he said. "If you don't need me, that is."

"No, I'll be fine."

Wallander heard Hökberg's heavy steps going down the stairs. He pushed open the door. There was a sloping ceiling in the room and one of the windows was ajar. A thin curtain wafted in the draught. Wallander knew from long experience that the first impression was often the most valuable. A closer examination could reveal dramatic details that were not immediately visible, but the first impression was something he always came back to.

A person lived here in this room. She was the one he was looking for. The bed was made, heaped with pink and flowery cushions. On one of the walls there was a shelf full of teddy bears. There was a mirror on the wardrobe door and a thick rug on the floor. There was a desk by the window, but there was nothing on its top. Wallander stood in the doorway for a long time and looked into the room. This was where Sonja Hökberg lived. He entered the room, kneeled by the bed and looked underneath it. There was a thin covering of dust everywhere except in one spot where an object had left an outline of itself. Wallander shivered. He suspected it was the spot where the hammer had been found. He got up and opened the drawers of the desk. None of them was locked. There weren't even any locks. He didn't know exactly what he was looking for. Maybe a diary or some photographs. But there was nothing in the desk that caught his attention. He sat down on the bed and thought about his meeting with the girl.

There was something that had struck him as soon as he saw her room from the doorway.

Something which didn't add up. Hökberg and her room didn't go together. He couldn't imagine her here among all the pink cushions and the teddy bears. But it was her room. He tried to work out what it could mean. Which was closer to the truth – the indifferent girl he had met at the police station, or the room where she had lived and hidden a hammer under her bed?

Many years ago Rydberg had taught him how to listen: each room has its own life and breath. You have to listen for it. A room can tell you many secrets about the person who lives there.

At first Wallander had been sceptical about Rydberg's advice, but in time he had come to realise that Rydberg had imparted a crucial piece of knowledge.

Wallander's head was starting to ache, especially in his temples. He got up and opened the wardrobe door. There were clothes on hangers and shoes on the floor. On the inside of the door was a poster from a film called *The Devil's Advocate*. The star was Al Pacino. Wallander remembered him from *The Godfather*. He shut the wardrobe door and sat on the chair by the desk. That gave him a new angle from which to view the room.

There's something missing, he thought. He remembered what Linda's room had looked like when she was a teenager. There had been some stuffed animals of course. But above all there were the pictures of her idols, who changed from time to time but were always there in some form or another.

There was nothing like that in Hökberg's room. She was 19 and all she had was a movie poster inside her wardrobe.

Wallander remained there for a few more minutes, then he left the room and walked back down the stairs. Hökberg looked at him carefully.

"Did you find anything?"

"I just wanted to have a look around."

"What's going to happen to her?"

Wallander shook his head. "She'll be tried as an adult. She's confessed to the crime. They're not going to be easy on her."

Hökberg didn't say anything. Wallander could see he was pained.

Wallander wrote down the number for Hökberg's sister-in-law in Höör. Then he left the townhouse and drove back to the station, feeling worse and worse. He was going to go home after the press conference and crawl into bed.

As he walked into reception, Irene waved him over. Wallander saw that she was pale.

"Something's happened?" he said.

"I don't know," she said. "They were looking for you, and as usual you didn't have your mobile with you."

"Who was looking for me?"

"Everyone."

Wallander lost his patience. "What do you mean 'everyone'? Give me some names, dammit!"

"Martinsson. And Lisa."

Wallander went straight to Martinsson's office. Hansson was there.

"What's happened?"

Martinsson said: "Hökberg has escaped."

Wallander stared at him in disbelief. "Escaped?"

"Gone. It happened about an hour ago. We've put all available personnel on the search, but she's disappeared into thin air."

Wallander looked at his colleagues. Then he took off his coat and sat down.

CHAPTER SIX

It didn't take Wallander long to grasp what must have happened. Someone had been careless, someone had disregarded the most basic security measures. But above all someone had forgotten the fact that Sonja Hökberg was not the innocent young girl she appeared to be, that she had committed a brutal murder only a couple of days before.

It was easy to reconstruct the chain of events. Hökberg was to be moved from one room to another. She had met her lawyer and was to be brought back to the holding cell. While she was waiting to be moved she had asked to go to the toilet. When she came back out she saw that the officer on guard had turned his back and was talking to someone in one of the offices. She had simply walked the other way. No-one had tried to stop her. She had walked straight out through the front hall. No-one had seen her. Not Irene, not anyone else. After about five minutes the officer in charge of her had gone into the toilet and discovered that she was gone. He had then looked into the room where she had talked to her lawyer, and once he had established she was not there either, alerted security. At which point Hökberg had had ten minutes to do her disappearing act.

Wallander groaned and felt his headache worsen.

"I've alerted all available personnel," Martinsson said. "And I called her father. You had just left the house. Did you discover anything that might tell us where she might be heading?"

"Her mother is staying with her sister in Höör." He gave Martinsson the number.

"She can hardly be planning to go there on foot," Hansson said.

"She has a driving licence," Martinsson said, with the telephone receiver pressed against his ear. "She could hitch a lift, steal a car."

"We have to talk to Persson," Wallander said. "And pronto. Juvenile or not, she's going to tell us everything she knows."

Hansson got up to leave and almost collided with Holgersson who had only just learned of the disappearance. While Martinsson was talking on the phone with Hökberg's mother, Wallander told Holgersson how the escape had happened.

"This is simply unacceptable," she said. She was furious.

Wallander liked that about her. The previous chief, Björk, would always worry about his own reputation at times like these.

"These things are not supposed to happen," Wallander said. "But they do. What matters is to track her down. Then we'll have to go over our security procedures and work out who's responsible for what went wrong in this case."

"Do you think there's a danger of more violence?"

Wallander thought for a moment. He saw an image of Hökberg's room, the stuffed animals sitting all in a row.

"We don't know enough about her at this point," he said. "But you couldn't rule it out."

Martinsson put the phone down.

"That was her mother," he said. "And I've talked to our colleagues in Höör. They know what to do."

"I'm not sure any of us knows that," Wallander said. "But I want that girl picked up as soon as possible."

"Was the escape planned?" Holgersson said.

"Not according to the officer in charge," Martinsson said. "I think she took advantage of the situation."

"Oh, it was planned," Wallander said. "She was waiting for the right moment, that's all. She wanted to get away from here. Has anyone spoken to her lawyer? Could he be of any help?"

"I doubt if anyone's thought of that yet," Martinsson said. "He left the station when he had finished talking to her."

Wallander got up. "I'll speak to him."

"What about the press conference?" Holgersson said. "What should we do about that?"

Wallander looked at his watch. It was 11.20 a.m.

"We'll do it as planned and we'll have to tell them what's happened, even if we would rather not."

"I suppose I should be there," Holgersson said.

Wallander didn't answer. He went back to his office, his head throbbing. Every time he had to swallow it hurt.

I should be in bed, he thought. Not running around after teenage girls who murder taxi drivers.

He found some tissues in a desk drawer and dabbed himself down as well as he could. He had a temperature and was sweating profusely. He called Hökberg's lawyer.

"This is unexpected," Lötberg said when Wallander had finished.

"What this is is a problem," Wallander said. "Do you have any information that might help us?"

"I don't think so. It was hard to make a connection with her. She seemed very calm on the surface, but as to what was going on underneath I have no idea."

"Did she mention a boyfriend? Anyone she wanted to see?"

"No."

"No-one?"

"She asked about Persson."

Wallander paused. "She didn't ask about her parents?"

"As a matter of fact, no."

This struck Wallander as odd, like the impression her room had given him. The feeling was growing that something didn't add up about Sonja Hökberg.

"I'll be in touch, of course, if she contacts me," Lötberg said.

Wallander was left with the image of her room in his head. It was a child's room, he thought. Not a 19-year-old's room. It was still the room of a 10-year-old, as if the room had stopped ageing even though the girl herself was still growing.

He couldn't develop this insight any further, but he knew it was important.

It took Martinsson less than half an hour to arrange the meeting with Eva Persson. Wallander was shocked when he saw her. She was short and looked no older than 12. He studied her hands and tried, without success, to picture her holding a knife and plunging it into the chest of her victim. But he soon recognised that there was something in her that reminded him of Hökberg. The look in her eyes, the same indifference.

Martinsson left them alone. Wallander would have liked Höglund there, but she was organising the search for Hökberg.

Persson's mother looked as if she had been crying. Wallander felt sorry for her. He shuddered to think what she was going through.

He came to the point at once. "Sonja has run away. I want you to tell me where you think she could have gone. Think carefully before you say anything, and make sure you tell me the whole truth. Do you understand?"

Persson nodded.

"Where do you think she's gone?"

"Home, probably. Where else would she have gone?"

His headache was making him impatient. "If she had gone home, we would already have found her," he said, raising his voice a little. The mother seemed to retreat into herself.

"I don't know where she is."

Wallander opened his notebook. "Who are her friends? Who does she normally go around with? Does she know anyone who has a car?"

"It's normally just her and me."

"What about her other friends?"

"There's Kalle, I suppose."

"What's his last name?"

"Ryss."

"His name is Kalle Ryss?"

"Yes."

"I don't want a single lie out of you, do you get that?"

"What the fuck are you screaming at me for, you old bastard?"

Wallander almost exploded, perhaps objecting most to being called "old".

"Just tell me who he is."

"He's a surfer. He goes to Australia a lot, but he's at home at the moment, working for his dad."

"What does his dad do?"

"He has a hardware store."

"And he's friends with Sonja?"

"They used to go out."

Persson was unable to think of anyone else that Hökberg might have contacted. She didn't know where she would be likely to go. In a last attempt to get some more information, Wallander turned to the mother, but she said she knew very little about Sonja.

"You must have known something about her; she was your daughter's best friend."

"I never liked her."

Persson swung round and hit her mother in the face. It happened so fast that Wallander had no time to catch her arm. The mother started screaming and the girl went on hitting her and yelling obscenities. She bit Wallander's hand, but he managed to drag them apart.

"Get rid of the old hag!" Persson yelled. "I don't want to see her any more!"

Wallander lost control. He slapped Persson. Hard. The girl was knocked to the ground. Wallander quickly left the room with his palm stinging. Holgersson came hurrying down the corridor and stared at him.

"What happened in there?"

Wallander didn't answer. He looked at his hand. It had turned red and was hurting. Neither one of them saw the journalist who had arrived early for the press conference. During the chaos of the last few moments he had reached the door unnoticed. He snapped two, three, four pictures. A headline was already taking shape in his mind.

The press conference started half an hour late. Holgersson had been clinging to the hope that a patrol would spot Hökberg. Wallander, who had been harbouring no illusions about the likelihood of this happening, had wanted to get started on time, in part also because his flu was now breaking out in full force.

He convinced her at last to go ahead. The reporters were only going to get irritated and make things more difficult for them.

"What do you want me to tell them?" she said.

"Nothing," Wallander said. "I'll handle it. I just want you to be there, that's all."

He excused himself and went to the toilet. He rinsed his face in cold water, then returned to the large conference room. He flinched when he saw how many reporters were there. He walked up to the podium with Holgersson. They sat down and Wallander looked out over the sea of faces. He recognised a good many. Some he knew by name, but some were complete strangers.

What should I tell them? he wondered. Even when you think you know what you are going to say it never comes out exactly the way you had imagined.

Holgersson welcomed the reporters and introduced Wallander.

I hate this, he thought bitterly. I don't just dislike it. All these meetings with the media. I know they are a fact of life, but I hate them.

He counted silently to three before he began.

"Last Tuesday evening in Ystad, a taxi driver was brutally assaulted and robbed. As you know, he died from the wounds that were inflicted. Two people have since been charged with the crime and they have both confessed. One of the assailants is a juvenile and consequently we will not be releasing any names at this press conference."

One of the reporters raised his hand.

"Isn't it true that the assailants were both women?"

"I'll get there, don't worry," Wallander said.

The reporter was young and pushy. "This press conference was supposed to start at 1 p.m. and it's already past 1.30. Don't you realise that we have deadlines to meet?"

Wallander ignored this question.

"This case is therefore a homicide," he said. "There's no reason not to disclose that this was an unusually savage killing. It is therefore comforting to know that we were able to resolve the investigation as rapidly as we did."

Then he took a deep breath. He felt as if he were diving into a pool without knowing how deep it was.

"Regrettably there has been a complication. One of the assailants has escaped. We have, I should add, every expectation of catching her shortly."

At first there was complete silence in the room. Then the questions burst from all sides.

"What's her name?"

Wallander looked over at Holgersson, who nodded.

"Sonja Hökberg."

"Where was she being detained?"

"Here at the police station."

"How could that happen?"

"We're conducting an inquiry into the matter."

"What does that mean?"

"Exactly what you think it means. That we're looking into how Hökberg was able to escape from custody."

"Would it be correct to describe her as dangerous?"

Wallander hesitated. "We don't know yet if she poses a threat to the public."

"She either poses a threat or she doesn't, surely? Which is it?"

Wallander was on the verge of losing his temper, for the umpteenth time in this one day. He wanted very much to bring proceedings to a close and go home and go to bed.

"Next question."

The reporter was not going to give up. "I want a definite answer. Is she dangerous or not?"

"I've given you my answer. Next question."

"Is she armed?"

"We don't know."

"Lundberg, the taxi driver: how was he attacked?"

"With a knife and with a hammer."

"Have you recovered the murder weapons?"

"Yes."

"Can we see them?"

"No."

"Why not?"

"For reasons linked to the progress of the investigation. Next question."

"Have the police nationwide been alerted?"

"At this point there is only regional involvement. And that's all we have to tell you for the time being."

Wallander's closing words were met with a storm of protest. He knew there were many more or less important questions left, but he got up and pulled Chief Holgersson up with him.

"That will have to do for now," he said.

"Shouldn't we stay longer?"

"Then you'll have to take over. They've got the information they need. They'll fill in the rest better than we could have done."

Reporters from television and radio stations wanted interviews. Wallander had to wade through a throng of microphones and camera lenses.

"You'll have to deal with this yourself," he said to Holgersson. "Or Martinsson. I need to go home."

They had reached the corridor. She looked at him with surprise.

"You're going home?"

"I give you permission to lay your hand on my brow, should you so wish. I'm sick. I am running a temperature. There are officers here more than capable of finding Hökberg, and of answering all these damned questions from the media."

He left without waiting for a response. What I'm doing is wrong, he thought. I should stay and try to sort out this chaotic situation. But I just don't have the energy.

He reached his office and put on his coat. A note left on the desk caught his attention. It was Martinsson's handwriting. *According to pathologist's report, Tynnes Falk died from natural causes. No crime. Shelve it for now.*

It took Wallander a couple of seconds to remember that this was in reference to the man found dead by the cash machine. One less thing to worry about, he thought.

He slipped out through the garage to avoid reporters. The wind was very strong now. He had to hunch over and run directly into it to get to his car. When he turned the key nothing happened. He tried again, several times, but the engine was completely dead.

He undid his seat belt and left the car without bothering to lock the door. On his way back to Mariagatan he remembered the book he was supposed to pick up. But it would have to wait. Everything would have to wait. Right now all he wanted to do was to sleep.

When he woke, it was as if he had come running out of a dream at full tilt. He had been in the middle of a press conference, but this one had been held at Hökberg's house. Wallander had not been able to answer a single question.

Then he had suddenly spotted his father at the very back of the room. He seemed undisturbed by the television cameras and was calmly painting his favourite autumn landscape.

That was the point at which Wallander woke up. He lay in bed, listening for sounds. The wind blew against the window. He turned his head. The clock on his bedside table read 9.30 p.m. He had been sleeping for almost seven hours. He tried to swallow. His throat was still swollen and sore. But his temperature had gone down. He felt sure that Hökberg was still on the run. Someone would have called him. He got up and went into the kitchen. There was the reminder to buy soap. He added to the list the book he had to pick up. Then he made some tea. He looked in vain for a lemon. There were some old tomatoes and a half-rotten cucumber in the vegetable bin, which he threw out. When the tea was ready, he carried the cup into the living room.

He reached for the phone and called the station. The only person he managed to reach was Hansson.

"How is it going?"

Hansson sounded tired when he answered.

"She's disappeared without a trace."

"Not a single sighting?"

"No-one, nothing. The national chief of police has called and expressed his displeasure."

"I don't doubt it. But I suggest we ignore him for the moment."

"I heard you're sick."

"I'll be fine tomorrow."

Hansson told him how the investigation was proceeding. Wallander had no objections to the way things were being handled. They had declared a regional search for

Hökberg and had alerted the rest of the force in case they had to operate nationally. Hansson said he would call if there were significant developments.

Wallander put on a CD of Verdi's *La Traviata*. He lay on the sofa and closed his eyes. He thought about Persson and about her mother, the girl's violent outburst and her puzzlingly indifferent gaze. Then the phone rang. Wallander sat up and turned the music down.

"Kurt?"

He recognised the voice immediately. It was Sten Widén, one of Wallander's few close friends and probably the oldest.

"It's been a while."

"It's always been a while when we talk to each other. How are you doing? When I tried to reach you at the station someone said you were sick."

"I have a sore throat. It's nothing."

"It would be nice to see you."

"Now is not the best time. Have you seen the news?"

"I never watch the news or read a paper. Apart from the racing sections."

"Someone managed to escape from custody. I have to find her. Then we can meet."

"I wanted to say goodbye."

Wallander felt something go tight in his stomach. Was Sten sick? Had his alcohol abuse finally got to his liver?

"Why? Why do you need to say goodbye?"

"I'm selling my place and taking off."

The last few years Widén had talked about leaving. The stud he had inherited from his father had stopped being profitable many years ago. Wallander had listened, on countless occasions, to his dreams of starting a new life but he had never taken Widén's ideas seriously, just as he never took his own dreams seriously. That had apparently been a mistake. When Sten was drunk, as he often was, he tended to exaggerate. But now he seemed sober and full of energy. The normal slowness of his speech was gone.

"Is this for real?"

"Yes. I'm going."

"Where to?"

"I haven't decided yet."

Wallander was no longer tensing up his stomach, but he felt envy instead. Sten Widén's dreams had turned out to have more life in them than his own.

"I'll come as soon as I can. Maybe in a few days."

"I'll be here."

Wallander sat deep in thought for a long time. He couldn't hide from his envy. His dreams of leaving behind his work as a police officer felt extremely remote. What Widén was doing now, Wallander could never do.

He drank his tea and then carried the cup into the kitchen. The thermometer outside the window read one degree above freezing. It was cold for the beginning of October.

He walked back to the sofa. The music was still playing softly. He reached for the remote control. The power went out.

At first he thought a fuse had blown, but after feeling his way over to the window he saw that even the street lamps had gone out. He went back to the sofa and waited.

A large part of Skåne lay in darkness.

CHAPTER SEVEN

Olle Andersson was asleep when the phone rang.

He tried the bedside lamp, but it wouldn't go on. That told him what the call was about. He turned on the strong flashlight he always kept beside his bed and lifted the receiver. As he had guessed, the call was from the Sydkraft main office, staffed round the clock. It was Rune Ågren. Andersson had already known that Ågren was the one on duty that night, October 8. He was from Malmö and had worked for various utility companies for more than 30 years. He was due to retire next year. He got straight to the point.

"Twenty-five per cent of Skåne is without power."

Andersson was surprised. There had been gusting winds these past few days, but there had been nothing close to a storm.

"The devil only knows what happened," Ågren said. "But it's the Ystad power substation that's been affected. You'd better get dressed and go down there to take a look."

Andersson knew it was urgent. In the complicated network that conveyed electricity to cities and houses across the countryside, the Ystad power substation was one of the central points of connection. If anything happened to it, most of Skåne would be affected one way or another. Someone was always responsible for making sure that didn't happen. This week Andersson was on call for the Ystad area.

It took him 19 minutes to reach the substation. The area was completely dark. Every time the power went out and he was out looking for the problem, he was struck by the same thought: that as little as a hundred years ago this impenetrable darkness had been the norm. The advent of electricity had changed everything. No-one now living could remember what life had been like before electricity. But he would also think about how vulnerable society had become. In the worst-case scenario, one single snag in the power grid could plunge a third of the country into darkness.

"I'm here," he told Ågren on his radio transmitter.

"Hurry up, then."

The power substation stood in a field. It was surrounded by barbed-wire fencing. At regular intervals there were "No Trespassing" and "Danger! High Voltage" signs. He hunched over against the wind, a set of keys in his hand and wearing a pair of protective glasses he had constructed himself with two small powerful flashlights attached to the frames. He found the right keys and stopped in front of the gates. They were open. He looked around. There was no car, no sign of anyone else. He took up his radio again and called Ågren.

"The gates have been busted open," he said.

Ågren had difficulty hearing him because of the wind. Andersson had to repeat himself.

"It doesn't look as though anyone's here. I'm going in."

The gates had been broken open before, and it was always reported to the police. Sometimes the police managed to catch the guilty party, usually drunken teenagers on a vandalism kick. But they had also considered the possibility of someone bent on sabotaging the grid. In fact, Andersson had been in a meeting only this last September where one of the Sydkraft safety engineers had proposed the installation of a whole new set of security measures.

He turned his head. Since he had his hand-held torch too, three spots of light travelled across the metal frame of the substation. A little grey building set deep among the steel towers was the heart of the structure. It housed the transformers. It had a thick steel door that could be opened only with two different keys, or by the use of powerful explosives. Andersson had marked the various keys on his chain with coloured tape. The red key opened the gates, the yellow and blue were for the steel door of the transformer building. He looked around. There was no-one there. The only thing he heard was the wind. He started walking but stopped after only a few steps. Something had caught his attention. He looked around again. Was there anyone behind him? He could hear Ågren's raspy voice coming from the radio dangling from his jacket. He didn't bother to answer. What was it that had made him stop? There was nothing there in the darkness, at least nothing that he could see. There was, however, a bad smell, but that probably came from the fields, he thought. The farmer must have fertilised them recently. He continued towards the transformer building. The bad smell lingered. Then he stopped short. The steel door was ajar. He took a few steps back and clutched the radio.

"The door's open," he said. "Can you hear me?"

"I hear you. What do you mean the door is open?"

"Just what I said."

"Is anyone there?"

"I don't know. It doesn't look as if it's been forced."

"But then how could it be open?"

"I don't know."

The radio was quiet. Andersson felt very alone.

Ågren spoke up. "Do you mean the door is unlocked?"

"That's what it looks like to me. And there's a strange smell."

"You'll have to go in and see what it is. There's a lot of pressure from above right now to get this thing cleared up. The bosses keep calling and asking what the hell happened."

Andersson took a deep breath and walked all the way up to the door, opened it further and directed his flashlight inside. At first he didn't know what he was looking at. The stench was overwhelming. Slowly it dawned on him what had happened. The power had gone out in Skåne this October evening because a burned corpse lay among the power lines. A person had caused this power cut.

He stumbled back out of the building and called for Ågren to come in.

"There's a corpse in the transformer building."

A few seconds went by before Ågren replied. "Can you repeat that?"

"There's a burned body in there. A person has short-circuited the entire region."

"Are you serious?"

"You heard me. Something must have gone wrong with the relay safety."

"We'll call the police. You stay where you are. We'll try to reconnect the power grid to bypass you."

The radio went dead. Andersson realised he was shaking. He couldn't believe what had happened. What could drive a person to go down to a power substation and kill themselves with high-voltage electrical current? It was like choosing execution by the electric chair. He felt sick to his stomach and tried to keep himself from throwing up by walking back to the car.

The wind was still gusting and it had started to rain.

The police in Ystad were alerted shortly after midnight. The officer who took the call from Sydkraft wrote down the information and made a quick decision. Since a death was involved he called Hansson, the senior officer on duty. He said he'd drive out right away. He had a candle by the phone. He knew Martinsson's number by heart. It took Martinsson a while to answer. He was sound asleep and had no idea that the power was off. He listened to what Hansson had to say and knew it was a serious matter. When the conversation was over he called Wallander.

Wallander had fallen asleep on the sofa while he had been waiting for the power to come back on. When the phone rang and woke him up it was still dark. He knocked the phone down on the floor as he was reaching for the receiver.

"It's Martinsson. Hansson just called me."

Wallander sensed that something serious had happened. He held his breath.

"A body has been found on one of Sydkraft's stations outside Ystad."

"Is that why there's no power?"

"I don't know. But I thought you should be notified, even if you are sick."

Wallander swallowed. His throat was still sore, but his temperature was normal.

"My car has broken down," he said. "You'll have to pick me up."

"I'll be there in ten minutes."

"Make that five," Wallander said. "If it's true, the whole region is without power."

He got dressed in the dark and went down to wait on the street. It was raining. Martinsson was there in seven minutes. They drove through the dark city. Hansson was waiting by one of the roundabouts on the outskirts of town.

"It's one of the substations north of the waste-management plant," Martinsson said.

Wallander knew where it was. He had been on a walk once in a forest close by, when Baiba had been visiting.

"What happened exactly?"

"I don't know any details. Sydkraft made an emergency call claiming to have found a dead body out there when they were investigating the power cut."

"Is it affecting a large area?"

"According to Hansson a quarter of Skåne is without power."

Wallander looked at him in disbelief. Blackouts were rarely so extensive. It happened occasionally after a big winter storm. It had happened after the hurricane in the autumn of 1996. But not when the weather was like this.

They turned off the main road. It was raining more heavily now. Martinsson's windscreen wipers were on full. Wallander regretted not having brought his raincoat or the boots that he kept in the back of the car now stuck down at the station.

Hansson stopped his car. Flashlights were on in the dark. Wallander saw a man in overalls who was gesturing for them to follow him.

"This is a high-voltage station," Martinsson said. "It won't be a pretty sight."

They stepped out into the rain. The wind was stronger here in the open fields. The man who came towards them was clearly shaken. Wallander no longer had any doubts that something serious had occurred.

"In there," the man said and pointed behind him.

Wallander went ahead. The rain whipped him in the face and made it hard to see. Martinsson and Hansson were somewhere behind him. Their shaken guide was walking to one side.

"In there," he repeated, when they stopped in front of the transformer building.

"Is anything still live in there?" Wallander asked. "I mean the power lines."

"Nothing. Not any more."

Wallander took Martinsson's torch and went in. He could smell it now, the stench of scorched human flesh. It was a smell he had never been able to get used to, although he had been exposed to it on frequent occasions when houses burned down and people were trapped inside. Hansson will probably be sick, Wallander thought, vaguely. He can't take the smell of burned bodies.

The corpse was completely blackened and sooty. The face was gone. It was trapped in a mess of lines, switches and circuit breakers.

Wallander moved aside so that Martinsson could take a look.

"Oh Christ," Martinsson groaned.

Wallander called out to Hansson to get Nyberg on the line and organise the back-up they needed.

"And tell them to bring a generator," he said. "We'll need it to get some light in here."

He turned back to Martinsson.

"What's the guy's name, the one who discovered the body?"

"Olle Andersson."

"What was he doing here?"

"Sydkraft had sent him down to take a look. They always have trained men on call in case of emergencies."

"Have a chat with him. See if you can get some specifics on the sequence of events from him. And don't walk around too much in here or Nyberg will be on your case."

Martinsson took Andersson with him to one of the cars. Wallander was left alone. He crouched down and shone his torch on the body. Nothing remained of the clothes. It was like looking at a mummy, or a body that had been discovered in a bog after a thousand years. But this was a twentieth-century substation. He tried to think back to when the power had been cut off. That had been some time around 11 p.m. Now it was almost 1 a.m. If the body had caused the power cut then this happened about two hours ago.

Wallander got up and let his torch rest on the floor. What had happened here? A person goes to a remote power substation and causes a major blackout by killing him or herself. Wallander made a face. That made no sense. The questions were starting to pile up. He bent down to pick up the torch. The only thing to do was to wait for Nyberg.

At the same time something was bothering him. He let the beam of light from the torch travel over the blackened remains. He didn't know what was causing this feeling, but it was as if he were sensing something that was no longer there. But that *had* been there.

He walked out of the building and examined the reinforced steel door. He could see no signs of a forced entry. There were two impressive locks. Wallander started walking back the way he had come. He tried to retrace his steps so that he wouldn't interfere with any tracks that might also be there. At the gates he examined the lock. It had been forced open. What did that mean? The gates had been clumsily cut open, but a reinforced steel door had posed no problem?

Martinsson was in Andersson's car. Hansson was making phone calls from his own car. Wallander tried to shake the rain off his coat and got into Martinsson's car. The engine was running and the windscreen wipers were still on high. He turned up the heat. His throat ached. He turned the radio on to get the latest news. He listened and began to realise the enormity of what was happening.

A quarter of Skåne was without power. It was dark from Trelleborg to Kristianstad. The hospitals were using their emergency generators, but otherwise the power cut was total. A Sydkraft executive had been reached and had said that the problem had been located. He was expecting the power in most areas to be restored in half an hour.

There won't be any power coming from here in half an hour, that's for sure, Wallander thought. He wondered if the executive really knew what had happened.

I have to let Lisa Holgersson know about this, he thought. He reached for Martinsson's mobile phone and dialled her number. It took a while for her to answer.

"Wallander here. Have you noticed the power's off?"

"A blackout? I was sleeping."

Wallander explained the situation. She became fully alert.

"Do you want me to come down?"

"I think you should get in touch with Sydkraft and tell them that their power problem now also involves a police investigation."

"What do you think has happened? Is it a suicide?"

"I can't tell. I don't know."

"What about sabotage? A terrorist act?"

"I don't think we can answer that question yet either. In fact, we can't rule out any of these things."

"I'll call Sydkraft. Keep me posted."

Wallander hung up. Hansson came running through the rain over to the car. Wallander opened the door.

"Nyberg is on his way. How did things look in there?"

"Pretty bad. There was nothing left, not even a face."

Hansson didn't answer. He ran through the rain, back to his own car.

Twenty minutes later Wallander saw the lights of Nyberg's car appear in the rear-view mirror. Wallander stepped out of the car and greeted him. Nyberg looked tired.

"What is it that's happened exactly? I couldn't get one coherent sentence out of Hansson."

"We have a dead body in there. Burned to a crisp. Nothing left."

Nyberg looked around. "That's what usually happens when high-voltage transformers are involved. Is that why the power's out?"

"Seems so."

"Does that mean half of Skåne will be waiting for me to finish?"

"We're not going to take that into consideration. I think they're working on restoring the power anyway, working their way around this substation."

"We live in a vulnerable society," Nyberg said, and immediately started instructing his crew of technicians.

Erik Hökberg said the same thing, Wallander thought. We live in a vulnerable society. His computers will have been shut off by this, if he sits up with them at night trying to make more money.

Nyberg worked quickly and efficiently. Soon all the

spotlights were up and running, connected to a noisy generator. Martinsson and Wallander went back to the car. Martinsson flipped through his notes.

"Andersson was called by a central command employee called Ågren. They had pinpointed the blackout to this substation. Andersson lives in Svarte. It took him 20 minutes to get here. He found that the outside gates had been tampered with, but that the inner steel door was simply unlocked. When he looked in he saw what had happened."

"Did he see anything else?"

"There was no-one here when he arrived and he didn't see anyone walking around."

Wallander thought for a moment. "We have to get to the bottom of this business of the keys," he said.

Andersson was talking with Ågren on the radio when Wallander got into his car. He immediately finished the conversation.

"I understand that you're pretty shaken up by this," Wallander said.

"I've never seen anything so terrible. What happened exactly?"

"We don't know that yet. Now, when you arrived on the scene the gates had been forced open, but the steel door had been opened without any visible sign of its being forced. How do you explain that?"

"I can't."

"Who else has a copy of these keys?"

"Only another repairman called Moberg. He lives in Ystad. And the main office, of course. There the security is always very tight."

"But someone did unlock the steel door?"

"That's what it looks like."

"I take it that these keys can't be copied."

"The locks are made in the United States. They're supposed to be impossible to force."

"What's Moberg's first name?"

"Lars."

"Is it possible that someone forgot to lock the door?"

Andersson shook his head. "That would be grounds for instant dismissal. The security is very thorough. If anything, it has got tighter in the past few years."

Wallander had no other questions for the moment. "I'd like you to remain here for now," he said, "in case any other puzzles come up. I'd also like you to call Moberg and ask him if he still has his keys for the steel door."

Wallander got out of the car. The rain was tailing off. The conversation with Andersson had increased his anxiety. It was just possible that someone wanting to commit suicide had come out here to this substation, but the facts were starting to line up against this hypothesis. Among other things was the fact that the steel door had been opened with keys. Wallander knew where this thought was leading: murder. The victim had then been disposed of in the power lines to destroy the clues.

Wallander walked into the beam of the spotlights. The photographer had just finished taking his pictures and video clips. Nyberg was kneeling by the body. He muttered irritably when Wallander walked into his light.

"What's your take on this?"

"That it's taking the pathologist an awfully long time to get out here. I want to move the body to see if there's anything behind it."

"I mean your take on what could have happened."

Nyberg thought for a while. "It's a macabre way to commit suicide. If it's murder, it's exceptionally brutal. It would be the equivalent of executing your victim in the electric chair."

That's right, Wallander thought. That leads us to the possibility that it's an act of revenge. Taking revenge through executing someone in a very special kind of electric chair.

Nyberg went on with his work. One of his technicians had started to scout the area between the building and the gates. The pathologist arrived, a woman Wallander had met before. Her name was Susann Bexell and she was a woman of few words. She got down to business at once. Nyberg got his thermos from his bag and had a cup of coffee. He offered Wallander some. Wallander decided to accept. They would get no more sleep that night anyway. Martinsson turned up at their side, wet and stiff. Wallander passed him his cup of coffee.

"They're beginning to restore power," Martinsson said. "Parts of Ystad already have some light. I have no idea how they managed to do that."

"Has Andersson spoken to his colleague Moberg about the keys?"

Martinsson walked off to find out. Wallander saw that Hansson was sitting rigidly behind his steering wheel. He walked over and told Hansson to return to the station. Most of Ystad was still dark, after all, and he would be of more use there than here. Hansson nodded gratefully and drove away. Wallander walked over to the pathologist.

"Have you learned anything about him?"

Susann Bexell looked up.

"Just enough to tell you that this is a woman."

"Are you sure?"

"Yes, but I'm not going to answer any other questions for now."

"Just one more. Was she dead when she got here, or was it the power that killed her?"

"I don't know that yet."

Wallander turned round, lost in thought. He had been assuming the victim was a man.

At that moment the technician, searching between the gates, came to Nyberg with something in his hand. Wallander joined them. It was a woman's handbag. Wallander stared at it. At first he thought he was making a mistake. Then he knew he had seen it before. More specifically, yesterday.

"I found it to the north by the fence," said the technician, whose name was Ek.

"Is the body in there a woman?" Nyberg asked, in surprise.

"Not only that," Wallander said. "Now we know who she is."

The handbag had been on a desk inside the interrogation room. It had a clasp that looked like an oak leaf. There was no mistaking it.

"This bag belongs to Sonja Hökberg," he said. "She's the one in there."

It was 2.10 a.m. The rain came on more heavily.

CHAPTER EIGHT

The power in Ystad was restored shortly after 3 a.m. At that time Wallander was still working with the technicians at the substation. Hansson called from the police station and told him the news. Wallander could see lights come on in the distance on the outside of a barn.

The pathologist had finished her work, the body had been removed and Nyberg had been able to continue his forensic investigation. He had asked Andersson to explain the complicated network of lines and switches inside the transformer building. Outside, his technicians worked to find any traces that might have been left behind. The rain was making for difficult working conditions. Martinsson slipped in the mud and bruised his elbow. Wallander was shivering with cold and longed for his wellingtons.

Soon after the power was restored in Ystad, Wallander took Martinsson with him to one of the police cars. There they mapped out the information they had gathered so far. Hökberg had escaped from the police station about 13 hours earlier. She could have made it to the substation on foot, but neither Wallander nor Martinsson thought it plausible. It was, after all, 3 kilometres to Ystad.

"Someone would have seen her," Martinsson said. "Our cars were out looking for her."

"Double-check to see if a patrol car came this way."

"What's the alternative?"

"That someone gave her a lift. Someone who left her and drove off."

They both knew what that implied. The question of how Hökberg had died was still the most pressing. Did she commit suicide or was she murdered?

"The keys," Wallander said. "The gates were forced, but not the door. Why?"

They searched for a rational explanation.

"We need a list of anyone who could possibly have had access to the keys," Wallander said. "I want every key holder accounted for, and what they were doing last night."

"I have trouble getting this to hang together," Martinsson said. "Hökberg commits murder. Then she gets murdered herself? Suicide makes more sense."

Wallander didn't answer. There were a number of thoughts in his head, but they weren't connecting with each other. He went over and over the one and only conversation he had had with Hökberg.

"You talked to her first," Wallander said. "What was your impression of her?"

"Same as yours. That she felt no remorse, and might just as well have killed an insect as an old taxi driver."

"That doesn't suggest suicide to me. Why would she kill herself if she felt no remorse?"

Martinsson turned off the windscreen wipers. They could see Andersson waiting in his car and beyond him Nyberg was helping to move a spotlight. His movements were brusque. Wallander could tell that he was both angry and impatient.

"Well, is there anything that suggests it was murder?"

"No," Wallander said. "There's nothing to indicate either possibility, therefore we have to keep them both open. But I think we can rule out accidental death."

After a while Wallander asked Martinsson to make sure the investigative team was ready to meet at 8 a.m. Then he got out of the car. The rain had stopped. He felt how tired he was, and how cold. His throat ached. He walked over to Nyberg, who was wrapping up work in the transformer building.

"Have you found anything?"

"No."

"Does Andersson have anything to say?"

"About what? Forensic investigations?"

Wallander silently counted to ten before going on. Nyberg was in a very bad mood. Saying the wrong thing would make him impossible to talk to.

"He can't determine what happened," Nyberg said after a while. "The body caused the power break, but whether it was a dead body or a living person who was thrown down there only the pathologist can say. And she may not be able to tell either."

Wallander nodded. He looked down at his watch. It was 3.30 a.m. There was no point in staying any longer.

"I'm going to take off now. But we have a meeting at 8 a.m."

Nyberg muttered something unintelligible. Wallander took that to mean he would be there. Then he returned to the car where Martinsson was making notes.

"We're going," he said. "You'll have to take me home."

They returned to Ystad in silence. When Wallander got back to his flat he ran a bath. While the bath was filling up he swallowed the last of his painkillers and added them to the list on the kitchen table. He wondered, helplessly, when he would next be able to stop at the chemist's.

His body thawed out in the warm water. He dozed off for a while, his mind a blank, but then the images returned.

Sonja Hökberg and Eva Persson. Slowly he rehearsed the events. He proceeded steadily so as not to forget anything. Nothing made any sense. Why had Lundberg been killed? What had motivated Hökberg and made Persson go along with it? He was sure it wasn't a random impulse. They needed the money for something very particular, or else it was all about something entirely different.

There had only been about 30 kronor in the handbag that they had found at the substation. The money from the robbery had been confiscated by the police.

She ran away, he thought. Suddenly she sees a chance to get away. It's 10 a.m. Nothing could have been planned in advance. She leaves the police station and disappears for 13 hours until her body is found 8 kilometres from Ystad.

How did she get there? he thought. She could have hitch-hiked. But she could also have called someone to come and pick her up. And then what? Does she ask to be driven to a spot where she commits suicide? Or is she murdered? And who has access to the keys that open the door, but not the ones for the gates?

Wallander got out of the bath. There are two central questions, he thought. If she had decided to commit suicide, why pick the substation, and how did she get the keys? And if she was murdered, then why? And by whom?

Wallander crawled into bed and pulled up the sheets. It was 4.30 a.m. His head was spinning and he was too tired to think. He had to sleep. Before turning out the light he set his alarm clock. He then pushed the clock as far away from his bed as possible, so he would be forced to get out of bed to turn it off.

When he woke up he felt as if he had only been sleeping for a couple of minutes. He tried to swallow. His throat was still sore, but it seemed better than the day before. He felt his forehead. The fever was gone, but he was congested. He walked to the bathroom and blew his nose, avoiding his reflection in the mirror. His whole body ached with fatigue. While he was waiting for the water for his coffee, he looked out of the window. It was still windy, but the rain clouds were gone. It was 5°C. He wondered, vaguely, when he would ever have time to do anything about his car.

They met in one of the conference rooms at the station a little after 8 a.m. Wallander looked at Martinsson and Hansson's tired faces and wondered what his own face must be like. Holgersson, however, who also could not have slept many hours, seemed undimmed. She called the meeting to order.

"We need to be perfectly clear about the fact that last night's power cut was one of the most serious ever to have hit Skåne. That displays the extent of our vulnerability. What happened should have been impossible, but happened anyway. Now the authorities, power companies and law enforcement will have to discuss how security can be stepped up. This is just by way of introduction."

She nodded to Wallander to carry on. He gave a brief summary of the events.

"In other words, we don't know what happened," he said finally. "We don't know if it was an accident, suicide or murder, although we can reasonably rule out an accident. Either she was alone or she had someone with her who had broken through the outside gates. After that they apparently had access to keys. The whole thing is bizarre to say the least."

He looked round at the others gathered around the table.

Martinsson reported that several police cars had on different occasions driven along the road to the power substation while they were looking for Hökberg.

"Then we know this much," Wallander said. "Someone drove her there. Were there any car tracks found?"

He directed that question to Nyberg who sat at the other end of the table with bloodshot eyes and wild hair. Wallander knew how much he was looking forward to his retirement.

"Apart from our own cars and that of Andersson, we found tracks belonging to two other vehicles. But there was a hell of a rainstorm last night and the impressions weren't too clear."

"But two other cars had been there?"

"Andersson seemed to think one of them could have belonged to his colleague, Moberg. We're still checking that."

"That leaves one set of tracks unaccounted for?"

"Yes."

Ann-Britt Höglund, who hadn't said anything up to this point, now raised her hand.

"Could it really be anything other than murder?" she said. "Like all of you, I don't see Hökberg committing suicide. And even if she had decided to end her life, I can't imagine she would have chosen to *burn* herself to death."

Wallander was reminded of an incident that occurred a few years earlier. A young woman from somewhere in Central America had burned to death by pouring petrol all over herself in the middle of a linseed field. It was one of his most horrific memories. He had been there, he had seen the girl set light to herself, and he had not been able to do anything about it.

"Women take pills," Höglund was saying. "Women rarely

shoot themselves. And I don't think they would throw themselves on a power line."

"I think you're right," Wallander said. "But we have to wait for the pathologist's report. None of us who were out there last night was able to determine what happened."

There were no other questions.

"The keys," Wallander said. "We need to make sure none of the keys were stolen. That's the first thing we need to establish."

Martinsson volunteered to check on the keys. They ended the meeting and Wallander went to his office, collecting a cup of coffee on his way there. The telephone was ringing. It was Irene from reception.

"There's someone here to see you," she said.

"Who is it?"

"His name is Enander and he's a doctor."

Wallander searched his mind without being able to come up with a face. "Send him to someone else."

"I've tried that, but he insists on speaking to you. And he says it's urgent."

Wallander sighed. "I'll be right out," he said and put the phone down.

The man in reception was middle-aged, he had cropped hair and was dressed in a tracksuit. Wallander noted his firm handshake. He said his name was David Enander.

"I'm very busy," Wallander said. "The power cut last night has created a good deal of chaos. I can only spare a few minutes. What is it you wanted to see me about?"

"I'd like to clear up a misunderstanding."

Wallander waited for him to continue, but he didn't. They walked to his office. The armrest came off the chair that Enander sat down in.

"Don't worry about it," Wallander said. "It was broken already."

Enander got right to the point. "I'm here about Tynnes Falk."

"That case is closed as far as we're concerned. He died of natural causes."

"That's the misunderstanding I wanted to raise with you," Enander said, stroking his cropped hair with one hand.

Wallander saw he was anxious about something. "I'm listening."

Enander took his time. He chose his words carefully. "I've been Falk's physician for many years. He became my patient in 1981, that is, 15-plus years ago. He came to me first because of a rash on his hands. I was working at that time in the skin clinic at the hospital, but I opened a private practice in 1986 and Falk followed me there. He was rarely sick, but I looked after his regular check-ups. He was a man who wanted to know the state of his health. He took great care of himself. He ate well, exercised and had very regular habits."

Wallander wondered what Enander was driving at and was growing impatient.

"I was away when he died," Enander said. "I only found out last night."

"How did you hear?"

"His ex-wife called me."

Wallander nodded for him to continue.

"She said the cause of death was a massive coronary."

"That's what we were told."

"The thing is, that can't possibly be true."

Wallander raised his eyebrows. "And why not?"

"It's very simple. As little as ten days ago I did a complete physical check-up on Falk. His heart was in excellent condition. He had the stamina of a 20-year-old."

Wallander thought this through. "So what is it you're saying? That the pathologist made a mistake?"

"I'm aware that a heart attack can, in rare cases, strike down a perfectly healthy person. But I can't accept that this was what happened in Falk's case."

"What else could he have died of?"

"That I don't know. But I wanted it clear that whatever killed him it wasn't his heart."

"I'll pass on what you've told me," Wallander said. "Was there anything else?"

"Something must have happened," Enander said. "I don't know if I'm right about this, but I gather he had a head wound. I think he was probably attacked. Killed."

"Nothing points to that conclusion. His wallet wasn't taken."

"I'm neither a pathologist nor a forensic specialist, so I can't tell you what killed him," Enander said. "But it wasn't his heart. I'm sure of it."

Wallander made a note of Enander's phone number and address. Then he got up. The conversation was over. He didn't have any more time.

Wallander saw Enander back to reception, then returned to his office. He put the notes about Falk in a drawer and used the following hour to write up the events of the night before.

As he typed, he thought about the fact that he had once thought of his computer with distaste. But then one day he realised that it actually made his work easier. His desk was no longer drowning in random notes jotted on odd pieces of paper. He still typed with two fingers and often made mistakes, but nowadays when he wrote up his reports he no longer had to use Tipp-Ex to remove all his mistakes. That in itself was a huge blessing.

Martinsson came in with the list of people who had keys to the power substation. There were five altogether. Wallander glanced at the names.

"Everyone can account for their keys," Martinsson said. "Not one of them has let them out of their possession. Apart from Moberg, no-one has been to the substation in the past few days. Should I look into what they were doing during the time that Hökberg was missing?"

"Let's hold on that," Wallander said. "Until the forensic reports come back we can't do much except wait."

"What should we do with Persson?"

"She should be questioned again, more thoroughly."

"Are you going to do that?"

"No thanks. I thought we would leave that to Höglund. I'll put it to her."

By noon, Wallander had brought her up to date on the Lundberg case. His throat was feeling better, but he still felt tired. He had tried, without success, to start his car and, in despair, he called a garage and asked them to collect it. He left the keys with Irene and walked into town to have lunch. At the next table, people were talking about the power cut. Afterwards he went to the chemist's and bought soap and painkillers. When he returned to the station his car was gone. He called the mechanic, but they hadn't had time to identify the problem. When he asked how much the repair was going to cost the answer was vague. He hung up and decided that enough was enough. He was going to get a new car.

Then he let himself sink down into his thoughts. The more he thought about it the more he was convinced that

Hökberg had not ended up at that substation by accident. And it was no coincidence that it was one of the most vulnerable points in Skåne's power distribution system.

He reached for Martinsson's list. Five people, five sets of keys: Andersson, line repairman; Lars Moberg, line repairman; Hilding Olofsson, power manager; Artur Wahlund, safety manager; Stefan Molin, technical director.

The names still told him as little as when he had first looked at them. He called Martinsson, who answered immediately.

"These key people," he said. "You haven't by any chance looked them up in the police register, have you?"

"Should I have?"

"Not necessarily, but I know you're very thorough."

"I can do it now, if you like."

"Perhaps it's not a priority. There's nothing from the pathologist?"

"I don't think they'll be able to give us anything until tomorrow at the earliest."

"Then plug in the names. If you have time."

In contrast to Wallander, Martinsson loved his computer. If anyone at the station was having a problem they always turned to him for help.

Wallander turned back to the Lundberg murder case. At 3 p.m. he went for some coffee. He was starting to feel better; his throat was almost back to normal. Hansson told him that Höglund was talking to Persson. Everything is flowing nicely, he thought. For once we have time for everything we need to do.

He had just sat down with his paperwork when Holgersson appeared at his door. She had one of the evening papers in her hand. Wallander could see from her face that something had happened.

"Have you seen this?" she asked and handed him the newspaper.

Wallander stared at the photograph. It was a picture of Eva Persson sprawled on the floor of the interrogation room. It looked as if she had fallen.

He felt a knot form in his stomach as he read the caption: WELL-KNOWN POLICEMAN ASSAULTS TEENAGE GIRL. WE HAVE THE PICTURES.

"Who took this picture?" Wallander said, in disbelief. "There were no journalists there, were there?"

"There must have been."

Wallander had a vague recollection of the door being slightly open to the corridor and there might have been a shadow of a person there.

"It was before the press conference," Holgersson said. "Maybe one of the reporters came early and was hanging around the hallway."

Wallander was paralysed. He had often been involved in scuffles and fist fights in his 30-year career, but that had always been during a difficult arrest. He had never jumped anyone in the middle of an interrogation, however irritated he had become.

It had only happened once, and that once there had been a photographer present.

"There's going to be trouble here," Holgersson said. "Why didn't you say anything?"

"She was attacking her mother. I slapped her to keep her from hurting her mother."

"That's not the story the picture tells."

"That's how it was."

"Why didn't you tell me?"

Wallander had no answer.

"I hope you understand I'm forced to order an investigation into this."

Wallander heard the disappointment in her voice. It angered him. She doesn't believe me, he thought.

"Am I suspended?"

"No, but I want to hear exactly what happened."

"I've told you already."

"Persson gave a different version to Ann-Britt. She said your assault came out of the blue."

"Then she's lying. Ask her mother."

Holgersson hesitated before answering. "We did," she said. "She says her daughter never hit her."

Wallander was quiet. I'm going to resign, he thought. I'm going to resign from the force and leave this place. And I'm never coming back. Holgersson waited for an answer, but Wallander said nothing. Finally she left the room.

CHAPTER NINE

Wallander left the station immediately. He wasn't sure if he was running away or just going out for air. He knew he was right about what happened, but Holgersson didn't believe him and that upset him. It was only when he was outside that he remembered he didn't have a car. He swore. When he was upset he liked to drive around until he had calmed down again.

He went down to the off-licence and bought a bottle of whisky. Then he went straight home, unplugged the phone and sat at the kitchen table. He opened the bottle and took a couple of deep draughts. It tasted awful. But he felt he needed it. If there was one thing that made him feel helpless it was being accused of something he hadn't done. Holgersson hadn't spelled it out for him, but he wasn't wrong about her doubts. Maybe Hansson had been right all along, he thought angrily. Never have a woman for a boss. He took another swig. He was beginning to feel better, and was even starting to regret the fact that he had come straight home. That could be interpreted as a sign that he was guilty. He plugged in the phone. He felt a sense of childish impatience over the fact that no-one called him. He dialled the station and Irene answered.

"I just wanted to let you know I've gone home for the day," he said. "I have a cold."

"Hansson has been asking for you, and Nyberg. Also people from several newspapers."

"What did they want?"

"The papers?"

"No, Hansson and Nyberg."

"They didn't say."

She probably has the paper in front of her right now, Wallander thought. She and all the rest of them. Probably no-one's talking about anything else. Some of them are probably even gleeful about the fact that that bastard Wallander has finally got what's been coming to him.

He asked Irene to put him through to Hansson's office. It was a while before he answered. Wallander suspected that Hansson had been pouring over some complicated betting sheets that were supposed to get him that big jackpot, but never helped him do much more than break even.

"How are the horses doing?" Wallander asked when Hansson answered.

He said that to let him know that the story in the evening papers hadn't affected him.

"What horses?"

"You're not betting on horses these days?"

"No, not right now. Why do you ask?"

"It was just a joke. What was it you wanted to ask me?"

"Are you in your office?"

"I'm at home with a cold."

"I wanted to tell you that I've worked out the times that our cars went up and down that road. I've talked to the drivers and no-one saw Hökberg. All in all that stretch of road was covered four times."

"Then she didn't walk. She must have had a lift. The first thing she did when she left the station was call someone. Or else she walked to someone's house first. I hope Ann-Britt knew enough to ask Persson about that, about who could have given Hökberg a lift. Have you talked to Ann-Britt?"

"I haven't had time."

There was a pause. Wallander decided to be the first to bring it up.

"That picture in the paper wasn't too flattering, I suppose."

"No."

"The question is what was a photographer doing floating around the corridor of the station. They're always brought in as a group for the press conferences."

"It's odd that you didn't notice someone taking pictures."

"With today's cameras it's not so easy."

"What exactly happened?"

Wallander told him what had happened. He used the same words that he had used when he described it to Holgersson.

"There were no witnesses?" Hansson said.

"No-one apart from the photographer and he's going to lie. Otherwise his picture wouldn't be worth anything."

"You'll have to make a public rebuttal and tell your side."

"And how well would that work? An ageing police officer's word against a mother and her daughter? It'll never work."

"You forget that this particular girl committed murder."

Wallander wondered if that was really going to help. A policeman using excessive force was always a serious matter. That was his own opinion. It didn't help that the details of the situation had been quite unusual.

"I'll think about it," he said and asked Hansson to put him through to Nyberg.

By the time Nyberg came on the line Wallander had

taken a few more swigs from his whisky bottle and was beginning to feel tipsy, but the pressure was lifting from his chest.

"Have you seen the papers?" Wallander said.

"Which papers?"

"The picture? The picture of the Persson girl?"

"I don't read the evening papers, but I heard about it. I understand she had been attacking her mother."

"That's not what the picture caption says."

"So what does that matter?"

"It means I'm in big trouble. Lisa is going to set up a formal investigation."

"So then the truth comes out. Isn't that what you want?"

"I just wonder if the media will buy it. Who cares about an old policeman when there's a young, fresh-faced murderess involved?"

Nyberg sounded surprised. "Since when have you cared what they write in the paper?"

"Maybe I still don't. But it's different when they publish a picture saying I've punched out a young girl."

"But she's committed murder."

"It still makes me uncomfortable."

"It'll blow over. Look, I just wanted to confirm that one of the car prints was from Moberg's car. That means that all the sets of tracks have been accounted for except one, but that unknown one is using common tyres."

"So we know someone drove her out there. And left her."

"There's one other thing," Nyberg said. "Her handbag."

"What about it?"

"I've been trying to work out why it was so far away, over by the fence."

"Don't you think he just threw it there?"

"But why? He couldn't have expected us not to find it."

Nyberg was right. This was important.

"You mean: why didn't he just take it with him? Especially if he was hoping the body wouldn't be identified."

"Something like that."

"What would the answer be?"

"That's your job. I'm just giving you the facts. The handbag was lying 15 metres from the transformer building."

"Anything else?"

"No."

The conversation was over. Wallander lifted up the bottle of whisky but then quickly put it down. He had had enough. If he kept on drinking he would cross a threshold he didn't even want to think about. He walked into the living room. It felt strange to be home in the middle of the day. Was this what retirement would be like? The thought made him shiver. He walked to the window and looked into the street. It was already getting dark. He thought about the doctor who had paid him a visit and about the man who had been found dead next to the cash machine. Wallander decided to call the pathologist the next day and tell him what Enander had said. It wouldn't change anything, but at least he would have passed on the information.

He switched to thinking about what Nyberg had said about Hökberg's handbag. There was really only one conclusion, and it was one that brought out his keenest investigative instincts. The bag was where it was because someone wanted it to be found.

Wallander sat on his sofa and thought it through. A body can be burned beyond recognition, he thought. Especially if it is burned with a high-voltage charge that can't be controlled. A person who is executed in the electric chair is boiled from the inside out. Hökberg's murderer knew it would be hard to identify her body. That's why the handbag was left behind.

That still didn't explain what it was doing by the fence, however. Wallander thought it through again, but still could not come up with a sensible explanation. He abandoned the question of the bag. In any case, he was proceeding too quickly. First they had to confirm that Hökberg had in fact been murdered.

He returned to the kitchen and made some coffee. Still no telephone call and it was 4 p.m. He sat at the kitchen table with his coffee and called in again. Irene told him that the papers and television had been on the line all afternoon. She had not given out his number: it had been unlisted for a couple of years now. Wallander thought again that his absence was going to be interpreted as an admission of guilt, or at least as a sign of deep embarrassment about the matter. I should have stood my ground and stayed put, he thought. I should have talked to every damned reporter who called and told them the truth: that both Persson and her mother were lying.

The moment of weakness was over. He was starting to get angry. He asked Irene to put him through to Höglund. He should have started with Holgersson and told her once and for all that her attitude was unacceptable. But he put the phone down before there was an answer. He didn't want to talk to either one of them. Instead he dialled Sten Widén's number. By the time he picked up, Wallander had almost had time to regret it. But he was fairly sure Widén would not yet have seen the picture in the papers.

"I was thinking of coming over," Wallander said. "The only problem is that my car is in the garage."

"I'll pick you up if you like."

They decided on 7 p.m. Wallander glanced in the direction of the whisky bottle, but didn't touch it.

The doorbell rang. Wallander jumped. No-one ever came to his flat unannounced. It was probably a reporter who had somehow got hold of his address. He put the whisky in a cabinet and opened the front door. But it wasn't a reporter, it was Höglund.

"Is this a bad time?"

He stood aside to let her in and turned his face away so she wouldn't smell the alcohol on his breath. They sat down in the living room.

"I have a cold," Wallander said. "I didn't have the energy to keep working."

She nodded, but he didn't for a second suppose that she believed him. She had no reason to. Everyone knew Wallander always kept working through whatever fevers or ailments he was suffering from.

"How are you holding up?" she said.

The moment of weakness is over, Wallander thought. Even if it has just retreated for now and I know it's still in there. But I'm not going to show it.

"If you are referring to the picture in the papers, I know it looks bad. On the other hand, how can a photographer find his way unseen all the way to our interrogation rooms?"

"Lisa is very concerned."

"She should listen to what I have to say," Wallander said. "She should support me, not immediately believe everything they say in the paper."

"She can't just ignore what's in the picture."

"I'm not saying she should. I hit the girl, but only because she was laying into her mother."

"You know that they have a different story."

"They're lying. But maybe you believe them?"

She shook her head. "The question is only how to prove that they're lying."

"Who's behind it?"

Her answer came quickly and firmly. "The mother. I think she's smart. She sees an opportunity to turn the attention away from what her daughter has done. And now that Hökberg is dead they can try to pin everything on her."

"Not the bloody knife."

"Oh, but they can. Even though it was recovered with Persson's help she can claim that Hökberg was the one who used it on Lundberg."

She was right. The dead can't speak. And there was a large colour photograph of a policeman who had knocked a girl to the ground. The picture was somewhat fuzzy, but no-one could have any doubts as to what it depicted.

"The prosecutor's office has demanded a quick investigation."

"Who in particular?"

"Viktorsson."

Wallander didn't like him. He had only been in Ystad since August, but Wallander had already had a couple of run-ins with him.

"It's going to be my word against theirs."

"And there's two of them, of course."

"The strange thing is that Persson doesn't even like her mother," Wallander said. "It was very clear to me when I spoke to her."

"She's probably realised that she's in deep trouble, even though she's a juvenile and won't go to jail. Therefore she's declared a temporary truce with her mother."

Wallander suddenly felt he couldn't keep talking about the subject any longer. Not right now.

"Why did you come round?"

"I heard you were sick."

"But not at death's door. I'll be back tomorrow. Tell me instead what you learned from your conversation with Persson."

"She's changed her story."

"But she can't know that Hökberg is dead?"

"That's what's so strange."

It took a while for Wallander to understand what Höglund had just said. Then it dawned on him. He looked at her.

"You're thinking something?"

"Why does one change one's story? Persson couldn't have known that Hökberg was dead when I started questioning her. But that's when she wholly changed her story. Now Hökberg is the one who did everything. Persson is innocent. They were never going to rob a taxi driver. They weren't going out to Rydsgård. Hökberg had suggested they visit her uncle who lived in Bjäresjö."

"Does he exist?"

"I've called him. He says he hasn't seen his niece in five or six years."

Wallander thought this over. "In that case there's only one explanation," he said. "Persson would never have been able to rescind her confession and fabricate another story if she wasn't sure that Hökberg would never be able to contradict it."

"I can't find another explanation either. Naturally I asked her why she hadn't said all this earlier."

"What was her answer?"

"That she hadn't wanted all the blame to fall on Sonja."

"Since they were friends?"

"Yes."

They both knew what it meant. There was only one explanation: that Persson knew that Hökberg was dead.

"What are you thinking?" Wallander said.

"That there are two possibilities. One is that Hökberg could have called Persson after she left the station. She could have told her she was planning to commit suicide."

"That doesn't sound likely."

"I don't think so either. I don't think she called Persson. I think she called someone else."

"Who later called Persson and told her Hökberg was dead?"

"It's possible."

"That would mean that Persson knows who killed Hökberg. Assuming it was a murder."

"Could it have been anything else?"

"I doubt it, but we have to wait for the result of the autopsy."

"I tried to get a preliminary report, but I suppose it takes time to work with badly burned bodies."

"I hope they realise it's urgent."

"Isn't it always?"

She looked down at her watch and got up.

"I have to get home to the kids."

Wallander thought he should say something to her. He knew what a hellish experience it was to end a marriage.

"How are things going with the divorce proceedings?"

"You've been through it yourself. You know what it's like."

Wallander walked her to the door.

"You should have a whisky," she said, "you need it."

"I already have," Wallander said.

* * *

At 7 p.m., Wallander heard a car horn below. From his kitchen window he could see Widén's rusty old van. Wallander tucked the whisky bottle in a plastic bag and went down.

They drove out to the farm. As usual Wallander asked to see the stables first. Many of the stalls were empty. A girl of about 17 was hanging up a saddle when they came in. When she had mucked out they were left alone. Wallander sat on a bale of hay. Widén leaned against a wall.

"I'm leaving," he said. "The stud has been put up for sale."

"Who do you think will buy it?"

"Someone crazy enough to think he'll make money on it."

"Can you get a decent price?"

"No, but it will probably be enough. If I live cheaply I can probably survive on the interest."

Wallander was curious to know how much money was involved, but couldn't think of the right way to ask.

"Have you decided where to go?" he said, instead.

"First I have to sell. Then I'll decide where to go."

Wallander got out the whisky.

"You'll never be able to live without your horses," he said. "What will you do?"

"I don't know."

"You'll drink yourself to death."

"Or else it'll be just the opposite. Maybe that's when I'll be able to kick the habit for good."

They left the stables and walked across the yard to the house. It was a chilly evening. Wallander felt his usual pang of envy. Widén was on his way to an unknown but surely very different future. He, on the other hand, was splashed across the front pages of the paper for assaulting a 14-year-old girl.

Sweden has become a place people try to escape from, he thought. The ones who can afford to. And those who can't afford it join the hordes who scavenge for enough money to leave. How had that happened? What had changed?

They settled down in the untidy living room that also served as an office. Widén poured himself a glass of cognac.

"I've been thinking about becoming a stage technician."

"What do you mean?"

"Exactly what I say. I could go to La Scala in Milan and operate the curtain."

"You don't really think that that's done by hand any more, do you?"

"Well, I'm sure the occasional prop is still moved by hand. Just think about being able to be backstage every night and hear that singing without paying a single cent for it. I would even work for free."

"Is that what you're going to do?"

"No. I have a lot of ideas. Sometimes I even think about heading up to northern Sweden and burying myself in some cold and unpleasant snowdrift. I just don't know. The only thing I know is that the stud is going to be sold and I'll have to go somewhere. What about you?"

Wallander shrugged without answering. He'd had too much to drink. His head was starting to feel heavy.

"Are you still chasing booze smugglers?"

Widén had a teasing tone in his voice. Wallander felt himself get angry.

"Murderers," Wallander said, "people who kill other people by smashing their heads with a hammer. I take it you heard about that taxi driver?"

"No."

"Two girls hit and stabbed a taxi driver to death the other day. They are the kind of people I chase. Not smugglers."

"I don't understand how you can keep at it."

"Neither do I. But someone has to do it, and I probably do it as well as anybody else."

Widén looked smilingly at him. "You don't have to get so defensive. Of course I think you're an excellent policeman. I've always thought so. I just wonder if you're going to make time for anything else in your life."

"I'm not a quitter."

"Like me?"

Wallander didn't answer. He was suddenly aware of the distance between them and wondered how long it had been so without their knowing it. Once upon a time they had been very close. Then they had grown up and gone their separate ways. When they met up years later, they thought they could build on the friendship they had once had. They had never grasped that the continuation of that friendship was utterly different. Only now could Wallander see clearly. Widén had probably come to the same conclusion.

"One of the girls who killed this taxi driver had a stepfather," Wallander said. "Erik Hökberg. Or Eriksson, as we know him."

Widén looked at him with surprise. "Seriously?"

"Seriously. It looks as if the girl has now been murdered herself. I don't have the time to take off, even if I wanted to."

He put the whisky back in the plastic bag.

"Could you call a taxi for me?"

"Are you going already?"

"I think I am."

A wave of disappointment ran over Widén's face. Wallander felt the same. Their friendship had come to an end. Or rather: they had finally discovered that it had ended a long time ago.

"I'll take you home."

"No," Wallander said. "You've been drinking yourself."

Widén didn't argue. He went over to the phone and called the taxi company.

"It'll be here in ten minutes."

They went out. It was a clear autumn evening with no wind.

"What did we expect?" Widén said suddenly. "When we were young, I mean."

"I've forgotten. But I'm not the kind to look back very often. I have enough on my plate with the present, and my worries for the future."

In time the taxi arrived.

"Make sure you write and tell me what happens," Wallander said.

"Will do."

Wallander climbed into the back seat. The car drove through the darkness of Ystad.

Wallander had just stepped into his flat when the phone rang. It was Höglund.

"Are you home now? I've tried to call you a million times. Why isn't your mobile turned on?"

"What's happened?"

"I tried the coroner's office in Lund again. I spoke to the pathologist. He didn't want to be held to this, but he's found something. Hökberg had a skull fracture in the back of the head."

"Was she dead when she hit the power lines?"

"Maybe not, but probably unconscious."

"Could she have somehow hurt herself?"

"He was pretty sure it could not have been self-inflicted."

"That settles it," Wallander said. "She was murdered."

"Haven't we known that all along?"

"No," Wallander said. "We suspected it, but we haven't known it until now."

Somewhere in the background a child started crying. Höglund was in a hurry to get off the phone. They arranged to meet at 8 a.m. the next day.

Wallander sat at the kitchen table. He thought about Widén and Hökberg, but above all about Persson.

She must know, he thought. She does know who killed Sonja Hökberg.

CHAPTER TEN

Wallander was catapulted from sleep at around 5 a.m. on Thursday. As soon as he opened his eyes in the dark he knew what had awakened him. It was something that had slipped his mind: his promise to Höglund. Today was the day he was supposed to give a talk at the Ystad women's literary society about life as a police officer.

He lay paralysed in the darkness. How could he have forgotten about it so completely? He had nothing prepared, not even scribbled notes. He felt the anxiety settle in his stomach. The women he was going to address would almost certainly have seen the pictures of Eva Persson. And Höglund must have called them by now to tell them he was speaking in her place.

I can't do it, he thought. All they are going to see is a brutal man who assaulted a little girl. Not the person I actually am. Whoever that is.

As he lay in bed he tried to plot a way out of his dilemma, but he soon realised there was no escaping this time. He got up at 5.30 a.m. and sat down at the kitchen table with a pad of paper in front of him. He wrote the word *Lecture* at the top of the page. He asked himself what Rydberg would have told a group of women about his work. But in the back of his mind he suspected that Rydberg would never have allowed himself to be roped into something like this in the first place.

By 6 a.m., he had still only written this one word. He

was about to give up when he had a sudden thought. He could tell them about what they were involved in right now: the investigation of the taxi driver's death. He could even start by telling them about Stefan Fredman's funeral. A few days in a policeman's life – the way it really was, without any editing. He made a few notes. He wouldn't be able to avoid the incident with the photographer and so his speech could seem like a defence. But in a way of course it was. It was a chance for him to tell it the way it had happened.

He put down his pen at 6.15 a.m. He was still anxious about the evening, but no longer felt quite so helpless. He called the garage and asked about his car. The conversation was depressing. Apparently they were considering taking the engine apart. The clerk promised to call him with a quote later in the day.

The thermometer outside read 7°C. There was a soft wind and some clouds, but no rain. Wallander watched an old man walking slowly down the street. He stopped by a rubbish bin and leafed through its contents with one hand but, apparently, found nothing. Wallander thought back to his visit to Widén. All trace of envy was gone. It had been replaced by a vague melancholy. Widén was going to disappear from his life. Who was left who connected him to his earlier life? Soon there would be no-one.

Wallander forced himself to halt this train of thought and left the flat. On his way to the station he thought about what he should say in his speech. A patrol car pulled up alongside him and the officer asked him if he wanted a lift. Wallander thanked him but declined the offer. He wanted to walk.

A man was waiting for him in reception. When

Wallander walked past the man turned to face him. Wallander recognised the face but could not place it.

"Kurt Wallander," the man said, "do you have a minute?"

"That depends. Who are you?"

"Harald Törngren." Wallander shook his head. "I was the one who took the picture."

Wallander remembered the man's face from the press conference.

"You mean, you were the one skulking around the corridor."

Törngren smiled. He was in his thirties, had a long face and short hair.

"I was looking for the toilet and no-one stopped me."

"What do you want?"

"I thought you might like to comment on the picture. I'd like to interview you."

"You'd never write what I say."

"How do you know that?"

Wallander thought about asking Törngren to leave. But he saw an opportunity and decided to take it. "I want a third party present," he said.

Törngren kept smiling. "A witness to the interview?"

"I've had bad experiences with reporters."

"As far as I'm concerned, you're welcome to ten witnesses."

Wallander looked at his watch. It was 7.25 a.m.

"I'll give you half an hour."

"When?"

"Right now."

Irene said that Martinsson was in already. Wallander told Törngren to wait. Martinsson was doing something on his computer. Wallander explained the situation.

Martinsson seemed to hesitate. "As long as you don't flare up."

"Do I usually say things I don't mean?" Wallander said.

"It happens." Martinsson was right.

"I'll keep it in mind. Come on."

They sat down in one of the smaller conference rooms. Törngren put his tape recorder on the table. Martinsson kept himself in the background.

"I spoke to Eva Persson's mother last night," Törngren said. "They have decided to press charges against you."

"For what?"

"For assault. Do you have a reaction to that?"

"There was never any question of assault."

"That's not what they say. And I have a picture of what happened."

"Do you want to know what happened?"

"I'd be glad to hear your version."

"It's not a version. It's the truth."

"It's their word against yours, you know."

Wallander was starting to realise the impossibility of what he was trying to do and regretted agreeing to the interview, but it was too late now. He told him what happened: Persson had attacked her mother and Wallander had tried to separate them. The girl had been wild. He had slapped her.

"Both the mother and the girl deny this."

"Nonetheless, it's what happened."

"Do you really expect me to believe that she started hitting her mother?"

"The girl had just confessed to murder. It was a tense moment. At such times unexpected things can happen."

"Eva Persson told me last night that she had been forced to confess."

Wallander and Martinsson looked at each other. "Forced?"

"That's what I said."

"And who forced her to do this?"

"The officers who interrogated her."

Martinsson was upset. "That's the damnedest thing I ever heard," he said. "We most certainly do not coerce anyone during our interrogations."

"I'm just repeating what she said. She now denies everything. She says she's innocent."

Wallander looked hard at Martinsson who didn't say anything else. Wallander felt completely calm.

"The pre-investigation is far from complete," he said. "Persson is tied to the crime and if she has decided to retract her confession that doesn't change anything at this point."

"You're saying she's lying."

"I am not going to answer that."

"Why not?"

"Because to do so I would need to give you information about an ongoing investigation. Information that is still classified."

"But are you saying that she's lying?"

"Those are your words. I can only tell you what happened."

Wallander could see the headlines, but he knew what he was doing was right. Persson and her mother were cunning, but it wasn't going to help them in the long run, nor would exaggerated and emotional newspaper coverage.

"The girl is very young," Törngren said. "She claims she was drawn into these tragic events by her much older friend. Doesn't that sound plausible? Couldn't Eva be telling the truth?"

Wallander considered telling him the truth about

Hökberg. The most recent events had yet to be made public, but he decided against it. Anyway, it still gave him an advantage.

"You and your newspaper are not the ones in charge of this investigation. We are. If you wish to draw your own conclusions and arrive at your own judgement, we can't stop you. But the truth is going to turn out quite different. Not that your editor will give it much space."

Wallander let his hands fall palms down on the table to signal the end of the interview.

"Thank you for your time," Törngren said and started putting his tape recorder away.

"Inspector Martinsson will show you out," Wallander said.

He left the room without shaking hands. While he was collecting his post he tried to judge how the interview had gone. Was there something he should have added? Was there something he should have expressed differently? He carried a cup of coffee back to his office with his letters tucked under his arm. He decided that the conversation with Törngren had gone rather well, even if he couldn't influence what eventually appeared in the published report. He sat down and went through the post. There was nothing that couldn't wait. He reminded himself of Enander's visit, rifled through his notes in the top desk drawer and called the coroner's office in Lund. He was in luck and was put through at once to the pathologist in question. Wallander told him what Enander had said. The pathologist listened and evidently took notes. He promised to let Wallander know if any of this new information was likely to lead to a revision of the conclusions of the autopsy.

At 8 a.m., Wallander got up and went to the large conference room. Holgersson was already there, as well as the lawyer Lennart Viktorsson. Wallander felt a surge of adrenalin when he caught sight of him. Most people would probably keep a low profile after turning up in such circumstances on the front page of a newspaper. Wallander had gone through his moment of weakness the day before when he left the station early. Now he was ready for battle. He sat in his chair and started speaking.

"As you all know, the evening papers ran a photograph last night of Eva Persson, with a caption, saying that she had fallen down because I slapped her. The girl and her mother may deny this, but what happened was that the girl was hitting her mother in the face and I was trying to intervene. She was in a fury. To snap her out of it, I slapped her. Not hard, but it was enough to knock her off balance and she fell over. This is also what I told the reporter who was creeping around the station. I met him this morning, as Martinsson can report."

He paused before continuing and looked round at those who were gathered around the table. Chief Holgersson seemed put out. Probably she had wanted to be the one to bring it up.

"I have been told that there will be an internal investigation of the matter, which is fine with me. But for now I think we should turn our attention to the most important matter at hand, Lundberg's murder and sorting out what actually happened to Hökberg."

Holgersson started speaking as soon as he had finished. Wallander didn't like the expression on her face. He still felt as though she were letting him down.

"I think it goes without saying that you will not be allowed to question Eva Persson," she said.

Wallander nodded. "Even I understand that."

I should have said more, he thought. That a police

officer's first duty is to stand by his colleagues – not uncritically, not at any price. But for as long as it is a question of one person's word against another's. Persson's lie is easier for her to swallow than standing up for the uncomfortable truth.

Viktorsson lifted his hand and interrupted Wallander's train of thought. "I will be following this internal investigation closely and I suggest that we seriously consider Eva Persson's new version of what happened. It's quite possible that it was as she says, that Sonja Hökberg was solely responsible for the planning and execution of the assault."

Wallander couldn't believe his ears. He looked around the room trying to elicit support from his closest colleagues. Hansson in his checked flannel shirt looked lost in thought. Martinsson was rubbing his chin and Höglund was slumped in her chair. No-one met his gaze, but he decided to interpret from what he saw that they were still with him.

"Persson is lying," he said. "Her first story is the true one. That's the version we will also be able to prove, if we get down to business and do our jobs."

Viktorsson wanted to go on, but Wallander didn't let him. He didn't think that most of them had been told what Höglund had called to tell him about last night.

"Hökberg was murdered," he said. "The pathologist has advised us that fractures have been found consistent with a heavy blow to the back of the head. It may have been the cause of death; at the very least it made her unconscious. Thereafter she was thrown among the power lines. At any rate, we need have no more doubts about whether or not she was murdered."

He had been correct. Everyone in the room was surprised.

"I should emphasise that this is the pathologist's

preliminary report," he said. "There may be more information forthcoming."

No-one said anything and he felt he had control of the proceedings now. The photograph in the papers nagged at him and gave him renewed energy, but he couldn't get over Holgersson's open distrust of him.

He went on to give a thorough report of the investigation to date.

"Johan Lundberg is murdered in what appears to be a hastily planned and quickly executed robbery. The girls say they needed money, but not for anything in particular. They make no attempts to hide from the police after the attack. When we bring them in, both confess almost immediately. Their stories are consistent and neither shows any remorse. We also find the murder weapons. Then Hökberg escapes from the police station in what looks to have been a spur-of-the-moment decision. Twelve hours later she is found murdered in one of the Sydkraft power substations. Establishing how she got there will be of crucial importance for us. Also we don't know *why* she was murdered. Parallel to these developments, something else happens that is also crucial: Persson retracts her earlier confession. She lays the whole blame for what happened on Hökberg. She gives new information that cannot be checked because Hökberg is dead. The question is: how did Persson know this – she must have known it. News of the murder has not been released. The people who know about it are very few in number; yesterday that number was even smaller. Yet that was when Persson suddenly changed her story."

Wallander leaned back in his chair. The level of attentiveness in the room had risen sharply. Wallander had isolated the decisive issues.

"What did Hökberg do when she left the station?" Hansson said. "That's what we need to find out."

"She didn't walk to the substation," Wallander said. "Even if it will be hard to prove 100 per cent. We have to assume that she was driven."

"Aren't we going a little too fast?" Viktorsson said. "She could have been dead when she got there."

"I haven't finished yet," Wallander said. "That is, of course, a possibility."

"Is there indeed anything that speaks against this assumption?"

"No."

"Isn't it in fact the most logical conclusion? What reason could we have for supposing that she went there of her own volition?"

"Only that she knew the person who drove her there."

Viktorsson shook his head. "Why would anyone seek out a power substation, one located in the middle of a field? Wasn't it raining all this time? Doesn't this tell us that she was in fact killed somewhere else?"

"Hold on," Wallander said. "We're just trying to lay all the alternatives on the table. We shouldn't be homing in on any one of them yet."

"Who drove her?" Martinsson said. "If we know that, we'll know who killed her, even if we won't know why."

"That will have to come later," Wallander said. "My thought is that Persson could not have found out about Hökberg's death other than through the person who killed her. Or at the very least from a witness." He looked at Holgersson. "That means Persson is our key to working out what happened. She's a juvenile and she's lying, and now we have to turn up the heat. I want to know how she learned of Hökberg's death." He stood up. "Since I won't be involved in her interrogation, I'll get on with attending to other matters."

He walked from the room, pleased with his exit. It was a childish display, he knew, but he thought it would hit its mark. He assumed that Höglund would be given the responsibility of talking to Persson. She knew what to ask; he didn't have to prepare her.

Wallander collected his coat and left. He would be using his time to check something else. Before leaving the station he put two photographs from the case file into his pocket. He walked down towards the centre of town. One aspect of the case had continued to bother him. Why had Hökberg been killed, and why in such a way as to cut power to large parts of Skåne? Had that been intended or mere chance?

He crossed the main square and ended up on Hamngatan. The restaurant where Hökberg and Persson had had their beers wasn't yet open. He peered in through a window. Someone was there, and it was a man he recognised. He knocked on the pane. The man went on with his work behind the counter. Wallander knocked harder and the man looked up. When he recognised Wallander, he smiled and came to open the door.

"It's not even nine yet," he said. "Do you want pizza already?"

"Sort of," Wallander said. "A cup of coffee would be nice. I need to talk to you."

István Kecskeméti had come to Sweden from Hungary in 1956. He had run a number of restaurants in Ystad and Wallander had made it a habit to eat at one or other of them when he didn't have the energy to cook for himself. He talked a lot at times, but Wallander liked him. He was also one of the few people who knew of Wallander's diabetes.

"You don't stop by very often," István said. "When you come, we're closed. That means you want something other than food." He raised his arms and sighed. "Everyone comes to István for help. Sports clubs and charities, someone who wants to start a cemetery for animals – all want money. They promise some advertising in return. But how is advertising in a pet cemetery to help a pizzeria? Perhaps you also want something? Is it a donation to the Swedish Police Force?"

"Answers to a couple of questions will do fine," Wallander said. "Last Wednesday – were you here?"

"I'm here always. But last Wednesday is a while ago."

Wallander put the two photographs on the table. The lighting was poor.

"See if you recognise either of these faces."

István took the photographs to the bar. He looked at them for a long time before he said, "I think so."

"Did you hear about the taxi murder?"

"A terrible thing – how can it happen? And such young people." Then István understood the connection. "These two?"

"Yes. And they were here that evening. I badly need you to tell me everything you remember. Where they sat, who they were with, that kind of thing."

István strained to remember the evening, while Wallander waited. He picked up the photographs and walked around the restaurant. He walked slowly and seemed to be searching. He's looking for his guests, Wallander thought. He's doing what I would have done. The question is: will he find them?

István stopped at a table by the window. Wallander walked over to it.

"I think here," István said.

"Who sat in which seat?"

István looked troubled. Wallander waited again while István walked around the table a couple of times. Then, as if he were handing out menus, he put the photographs of Hökberg and Persson in front of their seats.

"Are you sure?"

"Yes."

But Wallander saw him wrinkle his brow. He was still trying to remember something.

"There was something that happened that evening," he said. "I remember them because I had doubts about one of them being 18."

"She wasn't," Wallander said. "But forget it."

Wallander waited. He saw how István was struggling to remember.

"Something happened that evening," he said, again. Then he remembered what it was. "They changed places," he said. "At some point that evening they switched seats."

Wallander sat in the chair where Hökberg had spent the first part of the evening. From that seat, he could see a wall and the window over the street. Most of the restaurant was behind him. When he changed seats he saw the front door. Since a pillar and a booth hid much of the rest of the room, he had a clear view of only one table, a table for two.

"Did anyone sit there?" he said, pointing to the table. "Did anyone sit there when the girls changed places?"

"Actually, yes," István said. "Someone did come in and sit there, but I'm not sure if it was when they changed seats or not."

Wallander realised he was holding his breath. "Can you describe him? Did you know him?"

"I had never seen him before, but he's easy to describe."

"What do you mean?"

"Well, he was Chinese. Or at least he looked Asian."

Wallander was close to something important.

"Did he stay on after the girls left in the taxi?"

"Yes, an hour at least."

"Did they seem to make contact?"

István shook his head. "I don't know. I didn't notice anything, but it's possible."

"Do you remember how the man paid his bill?"

"I think it was by credit card, but I'm not sure."

"Good," Wallander said. "I want you to find that charge slip."

"I will have sent it in. American Express, if I remember rightly."

"Then we'll find your copy," Wallander said.

He felt a sense of urgency. Sonja Hökberg saw someone walking down the street, he thought. She changed places in order to see him. He was Asian.

"What is it you're looking for?" István said.

"I'm just trying to understand what must have happened," Wallander said. "I haven't got any further than that."

He said goodbye to István and left the restaurant. A man of Asian descent, he thought. A powerful wave of anxiety overtook him. He began to walk faster.

CHAPTER ELEVEN

Wallander was out of breath by the time he arrived at the station. He had walked rapidly because he knew that Höglund was interrogating Persson. He had to tell her what he had learned at István's restaurant so she could ask questions that now needed answers. Irene handed him a little pile of messages that he stuffed unread into a pocket. He called Höglund in the room where the interrogation was taking place.

"I'm almost finished here," she said.

"Hold on," Wallander said. "I have a few more questions for you. Take a break. I'll be outside."

Wallander was waiting impatiently for her in the corridor when she emerged. He told her at once about the seat changes and the man who had been sitting at the only table of which Hökberg had a clear view. He could see that she was not convinced.

"An Asian man?"

"Yes."

"Do you really think this is important?"

"Hökberg changed seats because she wanted to have eye contact with someone. That has to mean something."

She shrugged. "I'll ask Persson. But what is it exactly that you want an answer to?"

"Why they changed places, and when. Watch to see if she's lying. And did she notice the man who sat behind her?"

"It's hard to tell anything about what's going on inside her."

"Is she sticking to her new story?"

"Hökberg both hit and stabbed Lundberg. Persson knew nothing in advance."

"How did she react when you told her that Hökberg was dead?"

"She acted sad, but she didn't do a very good job. I think she was in fact quite shocked."

"So you don't think she already knew?"

"No. The mother has hired a lawyer, Klas Harrysson. He's filed charges against you."

Wallander didn't recognise the name.

"He's a young, ambitious lawyer from Malmö. Seems very sure of himself."

Wallander was smitten by a wave of tiredness. Then the anger came back, as well as the sense of being unfairly treated.

"Did you get anything new?"

"Honestly, I think Persson is a little stupid but she's sticking to her story – the later version. She sounds like a recording."

"There's something more than meets the eye with Lundberg's murder," Wallander said. "I'm convinced of it."

Höglund went back to questioning Persson, and Wallander went back to his room. He tried, without success, to find Martinsson. Hansson wasn't in either. Then he leafed through the messages Irene had handed him. Most of the callers were reporters, but there was also a message from Tynnes Falk's ex-wife. Wallander put the message aside, called Irene and told her to hold all incoming calls for a while. He called information and was given the phone number for the American Express office. He started to explain what he wanted and was transferred to someone called Anita. She asked to return his call as a security check. Wallander put down the phone and waited. After a few minutes he remembered that he had asked Irene to hold his calls. He swore and dialled the American Express number. This time they managed to arrange the security callback and Wallander was able to ask for the information he needed.

"It will take us some time," the girl said.

"So long as you understand how important it is."

"We'll do what we can."

Wallander called the garage. Eventually, the man he had spoken to earlier came on the line and quoted him a price that took his breath away. The car would be ready the following day. It was the parts that were expensive, not the labour. Wallander said he would come and collect the car at noon.

After he put the receiver down his thoughts wandered. He was in the interrogation room with Höglund. It irritated him that he couldn't be there. She could be a bit soft, wasn't good at applying real pressure. Moreover, Holgersson had not given him the benefit of the doubt, and he wasn't going to forgive her for that.

To fill the time, he dialled the number of Falk's ex-wife. She answered almost at once.

"This is Inspector Wallander. Is that Marianne Falk?"

"I'm so glad you called. I've been waiting for you."

She had a high, pleasant-sounding voice. She sounded like Mona. Wallander felt a distant, brief pull of emotion. Was it sadness?

"Has Dr Enander been in touch with you?" she asked.

"I've talked to him."

"Then you know that Tynnes did not die of a heart attack."

"I'm not sure that we can rule out the possibility."

"Why not? He was attacked."

Wallander's curiosity was piqued. "You don't sound surprised."

"I'm not. Tynnes had many enemies."

Wallander pulled a pen and some paper towards him. He was already wearing his glasses.

"What kind of enemies?"

"I don't know. But he was constantly on his guard."

Wallander searched his memory for the information that had been in Martinsson's report.

"He was some kind of computer consultant, isn't that right?"

"Yes."

"That doesn't sound so dangerous."

"I think it depends on what you do."

"And what exactly did he do?"

"I don't know."

"But you are convinced that he was attacked?"

"I knew him well, even if we didn't live together. This past year he was particularly anxious."

"He never told you why?"

She hesitated before answering. "I know it sounds strange that I can't be more specific," she said. "Though we were together for a long time and had two children."

"'Enemy' is a strong word."

"Tynnes travelled extensively. He always did. I have no idea what sort of people he must have met, but sometimes he came home very excited. At other times when I met him at Sturup airport he would be visibly worried."

"But he must have said something, like why he had enemies, or who they were?"

"He was a quiet man, but I could read the anxiety in his face."

Wallander wondered if the woman wasn't a little highly strung.

"Was there anything else?"

"It wasn't a heart attack. I want the police to find out what really happened."

Wallander thought for a moment before answering.

"I've made a note of what you've said. We'll be in touch if we need to ask you anything else."

"I'm counting on you to find out what happened. We were divorced, Tynnes and I, but I still loved him."

Wallander wondered if Mona would say that she loved him still, though they were divorced and she was married to another man. He doubted it. Then he asked himself if she had ever really loved him. He brushed these thoughts angrily aside and went over what Marianne Falk had told him. Her unease seemed genuine. On the other hand, she had not really said anything concrete. He still didn't have a clear sense of what sort of man Tynnes Falk had been. He looked for Martinsson's report, then called the coroner's office in Lund. All the time he was listening for Höglund's footsteps at his door. The outcome of Persson's interrogation was his primary interest. Falk had died of a heart attack, and that fact wasn't going to be changed by an ex-wife just because she was convinced he had been surrounded by enemies. Wallander telephoned the pathologist who had conducted the autopsy on Falk. He told him about his conversation with Falk's wife.

"Heart attacks can come, seemingly, out of the blue," the pathologist said. "The autopsy revealed this incontrovertibly as the cause of death. Neither Falk's wife nor what his doctor said change my view in any way."

"And the head wound?"

"That was caused by his head hitting the pavement."

Wallander thanked him and hung up. As he closed Martinsson's report, he had the nagging feeling that he had overlooked something, but he couldn't spend precious time worrying about the products of other people's imagination.

He poured himself another cup of coffee in the canteen. It was almost 11.30 a.m. Martinsson and Hansson were still out, and no-one knew where they were. Wallander returned to his office. He was impatient and cross. Widén's decision to get away was needling him. It was as if he had ended up in a race he never expected to win, but one in which he didn't want to end up last. It was not a clear thought, but he knew what was bothering him. Time was rushing away from him, that was what he felt.

"I can't live like this," he said out loud. "Something has to change."

"Who are you talking to?"

Wallander looked up. Martinsson was in the doorway. Wallander hadn't heard him come in. No-one at the station moved as quietly as Martinsson.

"I was talking to myself," Wallander said firmly. "Don't you ever do that?"

"I talk in my sleep, according to my wife. Maybe that's the same thing."

"What do you want?"

"I've checked everyone who had access to the sub-station keys. Not one of them has a previous record."

"We didn't really expect them to," Wallander said.

"I've been trying to puzzle out why the gates were forced," Martinsson said. "I can only think of two possibilities: one, that the key to the gates was missing. Two, someone's trying to throw us off the track."

"For what reason?"

"Vandalism, destruction for its own sake, I don't know."

Wallander shook his head. "The steel door was opened with a key. Maybe the person who forced the gates was not the same person who unlocked the door."

Martinsson wrinkled his brow. "And how would you explain that?"

"I can't explain it. I'm only offering you another alternative."

When Martinsson left, it was noon. Wallander went on waiting. Höglund appeared at 12.12 p.m.

"One thing you can't accuse that girl of is talking too fast," she said. "I've never met a young person who talked so slowly."

"Perhaps she's afraid of saying the wrong thing," Wallander said.

Höglund sat down in his visitor's chair.

"I asked her what you told me," she said. "But she never saw any Chinese person."

"I didn't say Chinese, I said Asian."

"Well, she says she never saw anyone like that. They changed seats because Hökberg complained about a draught from the window."

"How did she react when you asked her that question?"

Höglund looked worried. "Just as you would expect. The question took her by surprise and her answer was a pure lie."

Wallander slammed the desktop. "Then we know," he said. "There's a connection here to the man who came into the restaurant."

"What connection?"

"That we don't know. But the killing certainly wasn't a spur-of-the-moment business."

"I don't know how we're going to get any evidence to prove that."

Wallander told her about his call to American Express.

"That will give us a name," he said. "And if we have a name, we will have made progress. While we're waiting for that, I'd like you to visit Persson's home. I want you to look at her bedroom. Where's her father, by the way?"

Höglund checked her notes. "His name is Hugo Lövström. According to his daughter, he's a homeless drunk. She's filled with hate, that girl. I don't know who she hates the most, her mother or her father."

"Have they no regular contact?"

"It doesn't sound like it."

"We don't see clearly yet," Wallander said. "We have to find the real reasons behind it all. It may be that I'm simply too naive, that young people nowadays – even girls – see nothing wrong with murdering people. In that case I give up. But not just yet. Something must have driven them to do this."

"Maybe we should come at it from another direction," Höglund said.

"What do you mean?"

"Shouldn't we be looking more closely at Lundberg?"

"Why? They couldn't have known who their driver was going to be?"

"That's true."

But Wallander saw that she was on to something. He waited.

"There's just this possibility," she said thoughtfully, "that maybe it was an impulsive act after all. They order a taxi, and then one or both of them recognise Lundberg."

Wallander saw what she was getting at.

"You're right," he said. "That is possible."

"We know the girls are armed," she said. "They have a hammer and a knife. Apparently all young people carry some kind of weapon these days. The girls realise that Lundberg is their driver. Then they kill him. It could have happened like that, even if it seems unlikely."

"No more unlikely than anything else," Wallander said. "So let's try to establish whether they had had any earlier contact with Lundberg."

Höglund got up and left. Wallander reached for his pad and tried to jot down the outline of what Höglund had said. By 1 p.m., he felt as if he were no further forward. He was hungry and walked out to the canteen to see if there were any sandwiches left. They were all gone. He picked up his coat from his office and left the station. This time he remembered to take his mobile and to instruct Irene to refer calls from American Express to that number. He went to the café closest to the station. He could tell that some of the customers there recognised him. He felt sure that the picture in the papers had been a topic of discussion in most Ystad homes. He felt self-conscious and ate in a hurry. When he was back on the street his phone rang. It was Anita.

"We've found the information," she said. "That card number belongs to someone called Fu Cheng."

Wallander stopped, took a scrap of paper from his pocket and wrote it down.

"It's a Hong Kong-based account," she said. "There's only one problem. It's a false account."

"He stole it?"

"Worse than that. The account is fictitious. American Express has never opened an account with a Fu Cheng."

"What does that mean?"

"Well, it's good that we discovered it so quickly. The

restaurant will not, unfortunately, get paid. Hopefully the owner is insured against fraud."

"Does that mean Fu Cheng doesn't exist?"

"Oh, I'm sure he exists, but he has a fake credit card, as well as a fake address."

Wallander thanked her and hung up. A man who possibly came from Hong Kong had turned up at István's restaurant in Ystad and paid with a fake credit card. At some point he had made eye contact with Sonja Hökberg.

He hurried back to the station. He could no longer put off the next task: preparing the lecture he had undertaken to give. Even though he had decided to speak plainly about the murder investigation he was involved in, he still needed to write down the points he wanted to make. Otherwise his nervousness would get the better of him.

He started writing but had trouble concentrating. The image of Hökberg's charred body kept returning. He reached for the phone and called Martinsson.

"See if you can find anything on Persson's father," he said. "Name of Hugo Lövström. He's supposed to be in Växjö. An alcoholic and a vagrant, apparently."

"I'll do that through our colleagues in Växjö," Martinsson said. "I'm also checking out Lundberg."

"Did you think of that on your own?" Wallander was surprised.

"Höglund asked me. She's just gone to check out Persson's home. I don't know what she expects to find."

"One more name for your computers," Wallander said. "Fu Cheng."

"What was that?"

Wallander spelled it.

"Who is this?"

"I'll explain later. Can we have a meeting this afternoon? I suggest 4.30 p.m. It'll be short."

"His name is Fu Cheng? Is that all?" Martinsson said.

Wallander didn't bother to reply. He set about the plan of his lecture. After only a short while, he already hated what he had written. The year before, he had given a lecture about his experiences as a crime fighter at Police Training College. In his opinion it had been a complete disaster, but many students had come up to him afterwards to thank him. He never knew what they were thanking him for.

At 4.30 p.m. he gave up. Now it was in the lap of the gods. He picked up his notes and headed for the conference room. No-one was there yet. He tried to gather his thoughts and come up with a clear summary of the events of the case so far, but he was distracted.

It doesn't hang together, he thought. Lundberg's murder doesn't fit with these two girls. Nor does Hökberg's murder. This investigation lacks a common foundation, even though we know what happened. What we don't have is the crucial "why".

Hansson arrived with Martinsson in tow, Höglund behind them. Wallander was glad that Holgersson didn't come. It was a short meeting.

Höglund told them about her visit to Persson's home. "Everything seemed very normal," she said. "It's a flat on Stödgatan. Her mother works as a cook at the hospital. The girl's room was what you'd expect."

"Did she have any posters on the wall?" Wallander said.

"Only pop stars I didn't recognise," Höglund said. "But nothing out of the ordinary. Why do you ask?"

Wallander didn't elaborate.

The transcript of Höglund's conversation with Persson was ready and Höglund distributed copies. Wallander told them of his visit to István's restaurant and the subsequent revelation of the fake credit card.

"We need to find this man," he said. "If for no other reason than to be able to rule out any involvement on his part with this case."

They continued to sift through the day's work. Martinsson told them what he had done, then Hansson. Hansson had talked to Kalle Ryss, whom Persson had called Hökberg's boyfriend. He had only said that he knew very little about her.

"He said she was very secretive," Hansson said. "Whatever that means."

After 20 minutes, Wallander tried to sum up. He stressed the fact that they had more work ahead of them than they had at this stage expected.

The meeting was over shortly before 5 p.m. Höglund wished him good luck.

"They're going to accuse me of being a violent misogynist," Wallander said.

"I don't think so. You have a good reputation."

"I thought it was destroyed a long time ago."

Wallander went home. There was a letter from Per Åkeson in the Sudan. He put it on the kitchen table to be opened later. Then he showered and put on a clean shirt and a suit. He left the flat at 6.30 p.m. and walked to the place where he was supposed to meet all these unknown women. He stood for a moment staring up at the lighted house before he found the courage to go in.

It was past nine when he re-emerged from the house. He was running with sweat. He had talked longer than he had planned, and there had been more questions than he could have expected. But the women there had inspired him.

Most of them were his own age and their attention had flattered him. When he left, part of him had even wanted to stay longer.

He walked slowly home. He could hardly remember what he had talked about, but they had listened. That had been the most important thing.

There was one woman in particular who stood out in his mind. He had exchanged a few words with her before he left. She had said her name was Solveig Gabrielsson. She had made a real impression on him. When he got home he wrote down her name. He didn't know why.

The phone rang. He answered it before even taking his coat off.

It was Martinsson. "How did the lecture go?" he said.

"Good, I think. But that can't be why you're calling."

"I'm just here working," Martinsson said slowly. "There's been a phone call from the coroner's office in Lund that I don't quite know what to do with."

Wallander caught his breath.

"Do you remember Tynnes Falk?" Martinsson said.

"The man by the cash machine. Yes, of course."

"Well, it seems his body has disappeared."

Wallander frowned. "I thought bodies disappeared only into coffins."

"One would think so, but in this case it appears that someone has actually made off with the corpse."

Wallander didn't know what to ask next. He tried to think.

"And one other thing," Martinsson said. "It's not just that the body has gone missing. Something was left in its place on the stretcher in the morgue."

"What was that?"

"A broken relay."

Wallander wasn't exactly sure what a relay was, other than that it had something to do with electricity.

"It's not just an ordinary relay," Martinsson said. "This one is large."

Wallander's heart was beating faster. He sensed what was coming. "And where does one normally find large relays?" he asked.

"In power substations, like where Hökberg's body was found."

Wallander was silent. They had a connection. But not the kind he had been expecting.

CHAPTER TWELVE

Martinsson was waiting in the canteen.

It was 10 p.m. on Thursday. The faint sound of a radio came from the control room that handled incoming emergency calls. Otherwise all was quiet. Martinsson was drinking tea and eating rusks. Wallander sat across from him without taking off his coat.

"How did your lecture go?"

"You've already asked me that."

"I used to enjoy public speaking, but I don't know if I'd be any good at it any more."

"I'm sure you'd still be better at it than me. But since you ask, I had 19 middle-aged women listening to bloodthirsty stories about our socially responsible profession with baited breath. They were very nice and asked me polite and friendly questions that I answered in a manner which even the national chief of police would not have been able to fault. Does that give you the picture?"

Martinsson nodded and brushed the crumbs from his mouth before pulling out his notes.

"I'll take it from the top. At 8.51 p.m. the officer in charge in the control room puts a call through to me since he knows it doesn't involve sending out patrol cars. If I hadn't been here the caller would probably have been told to call back tomorrow morning. The caller's name was Pålsson. Sture Pålsson. I don't know what his position is, but he's in the coroner's office in Lund. Anyway, at around

8 p.m. he checked the morgue and noticed that one of the lockers – do they call them lockers? – wasn't shut properly, and when he pulled the gurney out, the body was gone and an electrical relay was lying in its place. He called home to the janitor who had been working there that day. Name of Lyth. He was able to confirm that the body had been there at 6 p.m. when he left for the day. The body disappeared sometime between 6 and 8 p.m. On one side of the morgue, there's a back entrance that opens onto the yard. Pålsson checked the door and discovered that the lock had been broken. He called the Malmö police. The whole thing went very fast. A patrol car was there within 15 minutes. When they heard that the body in question was from Ystad and had been the subject of an investigation they told Pålsson to contact us, which he did." Martinsson put his notes down. "The task of finding the body falls to our colleagues in Malmö," he said. "But I suppose it's also something that we have to concern ourselves with."

Wallander turned the matter over in his mind. It was a strange and unpleasant incident. His anxiety grew.

"We'll have to assume that our colleagues will think of searching for fingerprints," he said. "I don't know exactly what category this kind of crime falls into. Desecration of the dead? But there is a good chance they won't take it as seriously as we would like. Did Nyberg manage to secure any fingerprints from the substation?"

Martinsson thought about that. "I think so. Would you like me to call him?"

"Not right now. But I'd like Malmö to look for fingerprints on the relay and around the morgue."

"Right now?"

"I think that would be best."

Martinsson left to make the call. Wallander poured himself a cup of coffee and tried to understand what this could mean. A connection had emerged, but it might turn out to be an unlikely coincidence. He had experienced such things before. Yet something told him that it wouldn't be the case here. Someone had broken into a morgue and stolen a body, leaving an electrical relay in its place. It made Wallander think of something Rydberg had said many years ago, when they first started working together: "Criminals often leave a greeting at the scene of the crime. Sometimes it's deliberate, sometimes by accident."

This is no mistake, he thought. No-one just happens to have a big electrical relay on them. We were obviously going to find it and it was hardly a message for the pathologists. It was meant for us.

This led to the other question: why was the body stolen? He had heard of cases where the bodies of people who had been members of strange sects were removed. That hardly applied in the case of Falk, although it couldn't be entirely ruled out. But there was only one plausible explanation: the body had been removed so as to conceal something.

Martinsson returned. "We're in luck," he said. "They've put the relay in a plastic bag."

"Any prints?"

"They're working on it now."

"No sign of the body?"

"No."

"No witnesses?"

"Not as far as we know."

Wallander told him what he had been thinking. Martinsson agreed. The relay had to be a message, and the body removed to conceal something from them. Wallander also told him about Enander's visit and the phone call from Falk's ex-wife.

"I didn't put too much stock in what they told me," he said. "You have to be able to trust the coroner's report."

"Just because the body's been stolen doesn't mean Falk was murdered."

Martinsson was right.

"But if you remove the body, can it be other than to hide the manner of death?"

"What do we do now?"

"We need to determine who Falk was," Wallander said. "Since we closed the case so quickly, we had no need to look at his life closely. When I talked to the wife, she said that Falk was nervous and that he claimed to have enemies. In fact, she said a number of things that suggested he had a complicated life."

Martinsson made a face. "A computer consultant with enemies?"

"That is what she said, but none of us have spoken to her in any detail."

Martinsson was carrying the file with all the information they had on the Falk case.

"We never talked to his children," he said, checking the report. "We never talked to anyone since we concluded that he had died of natural causes."

"That's what we're still assuming," Wallander said. "It's as likely at this stage as anything else. What we have to acknowledge, however, is that there is some kind of connection between him and Hökberg. Perhaps even to Persson."

"Why not also with Lundberg?"

"You're right. Maybe also with the taxi driver."

"At least we know that Falk was already dead when Hökberg was killed," Martinsson said.

"And if we assume Falk was murdered, it may be by the same man who killed Hökberg."

Wallander saw that they were delving into something they didn't understand. We have to find the part where it comes together, he thought. We have to go deeper.

Martinsson yawned. He was usually asleep by this time, Wallander knew.

"The question is whether we can really get much further," he said. "We're not in a position to send out people to look for a missing body. Anyway, that's for Malmö to do."

"We should take a look at his flat," Martinsson said, stifling a new yawn. "He lived alone. We can start there and then talk to the wife."

"Ex-wife. He was divorced."

Martinsson got up. "I have to get some sleep. How's the car?"

"It'll be ready tomorrow."

"Do you want a lift?"

"No, I'm going to stay for a while."

Martinsson hesitated. "I know it must have upset you," he said. "The business with the picture in the paper."

Wallander looked at him closely. "What's your take on it?"

"On what?"

"Whether or not I'm guilty?"

"Clearly you slapped her. But I believe you. She was attacking her mother and you were trying to restrain her."

"Well, my mind's made up," Wallander said. "If they try to pin it on me, I'm resigning."

He was surprised by his own words. It had never before

occurred to him to resign if the internal investigation came back with a guilty verdict.

"In that case we will have swapped roles," Martinsson said.

"How do you mean?"

"Then I'll be the one trying to convince you to stay."

"You'll never do it."

Martinsson didn't answer. He took the file and left. Wallander stayed at the table. A while later, two patrol officers on the night shift walked through the room. They nodded at him. Wallander listened absently to their conversation. One of them was thinking of buying a motorcycle in the spring. Once they had poured themselves coffee and left, Wallander was alone again. Without being entirely conscious of it, he had already arrived at a decision. He looked at his watch. It was almost 11.30 p.m. He ought to wait until the morning, but the sense of urgency was too great. He left the station shortly before midnight. He had a set of pass keys in his pocket.

It took him ten minutes to walk to Apelbergsgatan. It was overcast. There was a soft breeze and it was a few degrees above freezing. The town felt deserted. Some heavily laden trucks barrelled past him on their way to the Poland ferries. It occurred to Wallander that it was at about this time of night that Falk had died.

Wallander stopped in a shadow and looked at the apartment building at 10 Apelbergsgatan. The top floor was dark. That was Falk's floor. The flat below was also dark, but in the first-floor flat the lights were on. Wallander shivered. That was where he had once fallen asleep in the arms of a total stranger. He had been so drunk that when he woke up he hadn't known where he was.

He fingered the pass keys in his pocket and hesitated. What he was about to do was unnecessary as well as unlawful. There was no overwhelming reason not to wait until the morning. He could then arrange to get the keys to the flat, but his sense of urgency wouldn't let up. It was something he had learned to trust over the years.

The front door to the building was unlocked. The stairway was dark. He turned on the flashlight he had with him and listened for any sounds before starting up the stairs. There were two doors on the top floor. The one to the right was Falk's. He listened again, putting his ear to both doors. No sound. Then he gripped the little flashlight between his teeth and got out the pass keys. If Falk had fitted his door with special locks he might have been forced to give up at the outset, but he had only ordinary locks. That doesn't fit with what Mrs Falk said, he thought. That her ex-husband was worried and had enemies. She must have exaggerated.

It took him longer than expected to open the door. The pass keys felt strange in his hands and he had started to sweat. When the door finally opened he thought he heard breathing coming at him from out of the darkness. But then it was gone. He stepped into the hall and shut the door noiselessly behind him.

The first thing he always noticed about a flat was the smell. But here there wasn't one, as if the flat were new and no-one had moved in yet. He made a mental note of it and started to walk through the flat with the torch in his hand, expecting at any moment to find someone there. Only when he had assured himself that he was alone did he take off his shoes, shut the curtains, put on a pair of rubber gloves, and turn on a lamp.

Wallander was in the hall when the phone rang. He

flinched and held his breath. The answering machine in the living room cut in and he hurried over to it. But the caller didn't leave a message. Who would have called a dead person's number in the middle of the night?

Wallander walked to one of the windows overlooking the street. He peered through a tiny slit in the curtains. The street was empty. He tried to penetrate the shadows with his gaze, but he saw no-one.

He started his search in the living room after turning on the desk lamp. Then he stood in the middle of the room and looked around. This is where Tynnes Falk lived, he thought. His story starts with a clean and well-ordered living room that is the very opposite of everyday chaos. There is leather furniture, a collection of maritime art on the walls. There's a big bookcase along one wall.

He walked to the desk. There was an old brass compass beside a green writing pad. Pens lay neatly in line next to an antique oil lamp made of clay.

Wallander continued out into the kitchen. There was a coffee cup on the counter, and a notepad on the kitchen table. Wallander turned on the light and looked at it. "Door to balcony," he read. Maybe Tynnes Falk and I have a lot in common, he thought. We both keep notepads in our kitchens. He walked back into the living room and tried the balcony door. It was too stiff to open. He walked into the bedroom. The double bed was made. Wallander kneeled and looked under it. He saw a pair of slippers.

He opened the wardrobe and pulled out all the drawers. Everything was neatly arranged. He went back to the living room. The instructions for the answering machine had been tucked in underneath it. When he was sure he could listen to the messages without erasing anything, he pressed the button.

First there was a message from someone called Jan who asked him how he was doing. He didn't say when he was calling. Then there were two calls from someone who only breathed at the other end. Wallander had the feeling it was the same person. The fourth call was from a tailor in Malmö, to let him know that his trousers were ready. Wallander made a note of the name. Then the most recent call, from the person who only breathed. Wallander listened to the sequence again and wondered if Nyberg could determine whether the mystery calls were from the same person.

He put the instruction manual back in its place. There were three framed, postcard-sized photographs on the desk, two of them probably of Falk's children. There was a boy and a girl. The boy was sitting on a rock in a tropical setting, smiling at the camera. He was around 18 years old. Wallander turned it over. "Jan, 1996, Amazonas". That must have been the boy who left the message on the answering machine. The girl was younger. She sat on a bench surrounded by pigeons. Wallander turned that picture over and read "Ina, Venice, 1995". The third photograph was of a group of men in front of a white stone wall. It was slightly out of focus. Wallander turned it over, but there was no legend. He studied the men's faces. They were of varying ages. To the far left there was a man who looked Asian. Wallander put the frame down and tried to think. Then he slipped the photograph into his pocket.

He lifted the green writing pad and found a newspaper clipping. "To make fish fondue". He went through the drawers, which were in the same meticulous order. In the third drawer he found a thick diary. Wallander opened it at the last entry. Sunday, October 5, Falk had noted that the wind had died down and that it was 3°C. The sky was clear and he had cleaned the flat. It had taken him 3 hours and 25 minutes, 10 minutes longer than last time.

Wallander frowned. The notes about the house cleaning perplexed him. Then he read the last line: "A short walk in the evening?" Did that mean he had already been for a walk, or was he about to go?

Wallander glanced at the entry for the previous day: *Saturday, October 4, 1997. Gusty winds, 8–10 metres per second according to the Meteorological Office. Broken cloud formations. Temperature at 6 a.m. 7°C. Temperature at 2 p.m. 8°C. No activity in C-space today. No messages. C doesn't reply when prompted. All is calm.*

Wallander read the last lines without being able to make sense of them. He flipped through the diary and saw that all the entries were similar, giving information about the weather as well as "C-space". Sometimes all was quiet, sometimes there were messages, but what kind of messages they were Wallander could not guess. Finally he closed the book and put it back.

It was strange that Falk had not written a single name anywhere, not even those of his children. He wondered if Falk was crazy. The diary entries could easily have been those of a manic or confused person.

Wallander walked to the window again. The street was still empty. It was already past 1 a.m.

He made one last search of the desk and found some business material. It seemed that Falk was a consultant who helped corporate clients choose and install the right computer system for their business. Wallander couldn't tell exactly what that involved, but he noted that a number of prominent companies, including several banks and Sydkraft Power, had been his clients. There was nothing really surprising anywhere. Wallander closed the last drawer.

Tynnes Falk is a person who doesn't leave any traces, he thought. Everything is impersonal, well ordered and impenetrable. I can't find him.

Somehow Hökberg's murder was connected to Falk's death, and also to the fact that his body had now disappeared. And there was perhaps a link to Johan Lundberg.

Wallander took the photograph frame from his pocket. He put it back. He wanted to make sure no-one found out about his visit. In case Mrs Falk let them in, he didn't want anything to be missing.

Wallander walked around the flat and turned out all the lights, then he opened all the curtains. He listened for sounds before opening the door. He checked the outside of the door, but the pass keys had left no mark.

Once he was back out on the street he paused and looked around. No-one was in sight, the town was quiet. He began walking home. It was 1.25 a.m. He never saw the shadow following him at a distance.

CHAPTER THIRTEEN

Wallander woke to the phone ringing. He sprang out of bed as if he had been lying in wait for the call rather than deeply asleep. As he put the receiver to his ear he glanced at the time. It was 5.15 a.m.

"Kurt Wallander?"

He did not recognise the voice on the line.

"Speaking."

"Excuse me for calling so early. I wanted to ask you one or two questions regarding the alleged assault."

Wallander was instantly alert. The man gave his name and the name of his newspaper. Wallander thought that he should have foreseen this. Any of his colleagues would have rung his mobile. At least that number was still totally private.

But it was too late now. He had to say something. "As I've already explained, it wasn't assault."

"So the photograph is a lie?"

"It doesn't tell the whole truth."

"Would you care to tell it now?"

"Not so long as I'm involved in the investigation."

"But you must be able to say something?"

"I already have. It wasn't assault."

Wallander hung up and unplugged the phone. He could already see the headlines: DEFENSIVE SILENCE FROM POLICE. OFFICER HANGS UP ON REPORTER. He sank back on to his pillows. The street light outside his window was swaying in the wind. The light flickered across the wall.

He had been dreaming something when the phone had rung. The images slowly re-emerged from his subconscious. They were images from last autumn, when he had taken a trip to the Östergötland archipelago. He had been invited by the postman who delivered post on the islands. He had accepted the invitation somewhat hesitantly. They had met during one of the worst cases Wallander had ever been involved in. One early morning the postman had taken him to explore one of the remote islands on the edge of the archipelago, where craggy rocks poked out of the sea like fossilised creatures from the ice age. As he had wandered around the small island on his own he had experienced a remarkable feeling of clarity. He had often returned to this moment in his thoughts, and longed to experience this feeling again. The dream is trying to tell me something, he thought. I just don't know what.

He stayed in bed until 5.45 a.m. when he got up and plugged the phone back in. He drank a cup of coffee as he tried to go through everything that had happened in his head, trying to make sense of the new connection drawn between Hökberg's death and the man whose flat he had searched last night.

By 7 a.m., he gave up trying to make sense of it and went in to the station. It was colder than he had anticipated. He wasn't yet accustomed to the fact that it was autumn. He wished he had put on a warmer sweater. As he walked he felt his left foot getting damp. He stopped and discovered a hole in the sole. It made him unaccountably furious. It was as much as he could do not to tear off both his shoes and continue in his stockinged feet.

As he passed through reception, he asked Irene who was in already. She told him that Martinsson and Hansson had arrived. Wallander asked her to send them in to see him. Then he changed his mind and decided to meet in one of the conference rooms. He asked her to send Höglund to join them when she arrived.

Martinsson and Hansson came in together.

"How did the lecture go?" Hansson asked.

"Let's not waste our time on that," Wallander said irritably, then felt bad that he should have taken his mood out on Hansson.

"I'm tired," he said.

"Who isn't?" Hansson said.

Höglund opened the door and came in.

"That's some wind," she said, taking off her jacket.

"Autumn is here," Wallander said. "All right, let's start. Something happened last night that dramatically alters the investigation."

He nodded to Martinsson, who told the others about the disappearance of Falk's body.

"At least this is something new," Hansson said when Martinsson had finished. "I don't think we've ever had a stolen body before. I know there was that rubber raft. But not a dead body."

Wallander made a face. He remembered the rubber raft that had floated ashore on Mossbystrand, and how afterwards the raft had mysteriously and by means still unclear disappeared from the station.

Höglund looked at him. "So are we to accept a connection between the man who died at the cash machine and Lundberg's murder? That seems ludicrous."

"Yes," Wallander said. "But I don't think we can avoid working with this assumption for now. I think we should also be prepared for the fact that this will be a difficult case. We thought we were dealing with an unusually brutal but clear-cut case of murder. We saw this scenario dissolve when Hökberg escaped and was later found dead at the power substation. We knew that a man had been found dead close to a cash machine, but we had already declared that case closed for lack of evidence that any crime had been committed. This conclusion still cannot be ruled out. Then the body disappears, and someone puts an electrical relay in its place."

Wallander paused and thought back to the questions he had regarding Hökberg and Persson's visit to the restaurant and the identity of the Asian man. He saw that they would have to start from a quite different angle.

"Someone breaks into a morgue and steals a body. We can't be sure of the motive, but it seems that someone wants to conceal something. At the same time the relay is left, as a kind of message, for us to find. Obviously it wasn't left by accident."

"Which can only mean one thing," Höglund said. "That someone wants us to see a connection between Hökberg and Falk."

"Couldn't it be a red herring?" Hansson said. "Put there by someone who's read about the girl being burned to death?"

"Malmö have assured me the relay is large and heavy," Martinsson said. "It's hardly the kind of thing you would carry around with you."

"We'll take it step by step," Wallander said. "Nyberg will examine the relay and determine whether it originates from our substation. If it does, then we're home and dry."

"Not necessarily," Höglund said. "It could still be partly symbolic."

Wallander shook his head. "I don't get that feeling in this case."

Martinsson telephoned Nyberg while the others went

to get coffee. Wallander told them about the reporter who had woken him up that morning.

"It'll soon blow over," Höglund said.

"I hope you're right."

They returned to the conference room.

"Listen," Wallander said. "We have to get serious with Persson. It doesn't matter any more that she's a juvenile. We've got to throw away the kid gloves and start getting some real answers. That will be up to you, Ann-Britt. You know what questions to ask and I don't want you to give up until she starts telling the truth."

They planned the next stages of the investigation. Wallander realised that his cold had gone and that his strength was returning. They finished around 9.30. a.m. Hansson and Höglund disappeared down the corridor to their appointed tasks. Wallander and Martinsson were going to examine Falk's flat together. Wallander was tempted to tell him about his visit the night before, but decided against it. It was one of his faults, this tendency not to advise his colleagues of all the avenues he was exploring in a case, but he had long ago given up hope that he would be able to mend this trait.

While Martinsson arranged to get keys to the flat, Wallander went to his office with a newspaper that Hansson had earlier thrown on the table. He flipped through it. There was a small item about a police officer suspected of the use of excessive force against a juvenile offender. He was not named, but his sense of outrage revived.

He was about to put the paper aside when his gaze fell on the personal ads. He started reading. There was an ad from a divorced 50-year-old woman who said she felt lonely now that her children were grown up. She listed her interests as travel and classical music. Wallander tried to imagine what she looked like, but he kept seeing the face of a woman called Erika whom he had met at a roadside café in Västervik a year ago. He had thought about her from time to time. He threw the paper into the waste-paper basket, but just before Martinsson appeared he fished it out, tore off the page with the ad and slipped it into a drawer.

"His wife will meet us there with the keys," Martinsson said. "Do you want to walk or take the car?"

"The car," Wallander said. "I have a hole in my shoe."

Martinsson gave him an amused look. "What would the national chief of police say about that?"

"We've already put in train his community policing ideas," Wallander said. "Why not expand them to include barefoot policing?"

They left the station in Martinsson's car.

"How are things with you?" Martinsson said.

"I'm fed up," Wallander said. "You'd think you get used to all this, but you don't. During my years in the force I've been accused of almost everything, with the possible exception of being lazy. You'd think you'd develop a thick skin, but you don't. At least not in the way you'd hope."

"Did you mean what you said yesterday?"

"What did I say?"

"That you'd leave if they found you guilty."

"I don't know. I don't think I have the energy to think about it right now."

Wallander didn't want to talk more about it and Martinsson knew to leave him alone. They parked outside 10 Apelbergsgatan. A woman was waiting for them.

"That must be Marianne Falk," Martinsson said. "She obviously kept her name after the divorce."

Martinsson was about to open the car door when Wallander stopped him.

"Does she know what's happened? About the body being missing?"

"Someone rang her."

They got out. The woman standing there in the wind was very well dressed. She was tall and slender and reminded Wallander vaguely of Mona. They said hello. Wallander could tell that she was angry and upset. He was immediately alert.

"Have they found the body? How can things like this happen?"

Wallander let Martinsson answer. "It's very unfortunate, of course."

"Unfortunate? It's unacceptable. What do we have a police force for anyway?"

"There's a question," Wallander said. "But I think we should deal with that another time."

They went into the building and went upstairs. Wallander was uneasy. Had he left anything behind last night?

Marianne Falk walked ahead of them. When she came to the top landing she stopped, pointing to the door. Martinsson was right behind her. Wallander pushed him aside. Then he saw. The door to the flat was wide open. The locks he had taken so much trouble with, trying to leave no trace of his visit, had been broken with something like a crowbar. Wallander listened for sounds. Martinsson was beside him. Neither of them was carrying a weapon. Wallander hesitated. He signalled them to go down to the floor below.

"There could be someone in there," he whispered. "We had better get some back-up."

Martinsson got out his phone.

"I want you to wait in your car," Wallander told Mrs Falk.

"What's happened?"

"Please just do as I say. Wait in your car."

She disappeared down the stairs. Martinsson was talking to someone at the station.

"They're on their way."

They waited motionless on the stairs. There were no sounds coming from the flat.

"I told them not to turn on the sirens," Martinsson whispered.

Wallander nodded.

Eight minutes later Hansson appeared on the stairs with three other officers. Hansson had a gun. Wallander took a gun from one of the other policemen.

"Let's go in," he said.

The hand holding the gun was very slightly shaking. Wallander was afraid. He was always afraid when he was about to tackle a situation where anything was possible. He established eye contact with Hansson, then called out into the flat. There was no answer. He shouted again. Then the door behind them opened and he jumped. An old woman appeared, peering into the hall. Martinsson forced her back inside. Wallander called out a third time. Still no answer.

Then they went in.

The flat was empty. But it was not the flat he had left the night before with an impression of meticulous order. All the drawers had been pulled out and emptied onto the floor. Paintings hung askew and a record collection lay shattered on the floor.

"There's no-one here," he said. "Let's get Nyberg and

his people here as soon as possible. I don't want us disturbing the area more than we have to."

Hansson and the others left. Martinsson set off to interview the neighbours. Wallander stood in the doorway to the living room and looked about him. How many times had he stood in a flat like this where a crime had been committed? Without being able to put his finger on it, he knew there was something changed. Something was missing. He let his gaze travel slowly through the room. When he was looking at the desk for the second time he realised what it was. He took off his shoes and approached the table.

The photograph of the group of men against the white stone wall was gone. He bent over and looked under the desk. One by one he lifted the pieces of paper that had fallen on the ground. But it was nowhere to be seen. And something else was gone too. The diary. He took a step back and held his breath. Someone knew I was here, he thought. Someone saw me come and go. Was it an instinctive sense of this that had made him walk to the windows twice and look out at the street? There had been someone out there he hadn't been able to see. Someone hidden deep within the shadows.

His thoughts were interrupted by Martinsson. "The woman opposite is a widow by the name of Håkansson. She hasn't seen or heard anything unusual."

Wallander thought about the time he was drunk and had ended up spending the night in the flat below.

"Talk to everyone who lives here. Find out if anyone has seen anything."

"Can't we get someone else to do it? I have more than enough to do as it is."

"It's important it be done right," Wallander said. "Not so many people live here anyway."

Martinsson departed again and Wallander waited. One of Nyberg's team turned up after 20 minutes.

"Nyberg is on his way," he said. "But he was doing something out at the substation that was apparently important."

Wallander nodded. "Take a look at the answering machine," he said. "I want everything you can find on it."

The officer made a note.

"The whole flat should be videotaped," Wallander said. "I want it examined down to the last detail."

"Are the people who live here away?"

"The person who lived here was the man who was found dead by the cash machine," Wallander said. "It's very important that the forensic investigation is thorough."

He left the flat and walked out on to the street. There were no clouds in the sky. Mrs Falk was smoking in her car. When she saw Wallander she got out.

"What happened?"

"There's been a break-in."

"I wouldn't have believed anyone could have such utter disrespect for the dead."

"I know you were divorced, but were you familiar with his flat?"

"We were on good terms. I visited him here many times."

"I'm going to ask you to return later today," Wallander said. "When the forensic team has finished, I want you to go through the flat with me. You may be able to notice something that's gone."

"Oh, I doubt that," she said, without hesitation.

"Why do you say that?"

"I was married to him for many years. I knew him fairly well then, but not later on."

"What happened?"

"He just changed."

"In what way?"
"I didn't know what he was thinking any more."
Wallander looked at her thoughtfully.
"But even so, you may be able to see if something's been taken. You said yourself that you visited him here many times."
"I could probably tell you if a lamp or a painting was missing, but nothing else. Tynnes had many secrets."
"What do you mean by that?"
"Just what it says. I didn't know what he was thinking or what he did. I tried to explain this to you during our first telephone conversation."
Wallander was reminded of what he had read in Falk's diary the night before.
"Do you know if your husband kept a diary?"
"I'm sure he didn't."
"Did he ever keep one?"
"Never."
She's right on one score, he thought.
"Was your ex-husband interested in outer space?"
Her surprise seemed genuine.
"Why do you ask?"
"Just wondering."
"We used to look up at the stars, when we were young, but I can't think of any sign of interest after that."
Wallander switched to a new topic. "You said that your husband had many enemies, and that he appeared worried."
"Yes, he actually said that to me."
"What else did he say?"
"That people like him always had enemies."
"Was that all?"
"Yes."
"People like me always have enemies?" he repeated.

"Yes."

"What did you think he meant?"

"I've already told you, I no longer understood him."

A car drew up where they were standing and Nyberg got out. Wallander decided to end the conversation for now and wrote down her phone number. He said he would be in touch later in the day.

"One last question: can you think of any reason why someone would steal his body?"

"Of course not."

Wallander had no more questions. When she had climbed into her car and backed out of her parking space, Nyberg came over.

"What's happened?" he said.

"A break-in."

"Do we really have time for this right now?"

"It's connected to the other events. I don't know exactly how yet, but I'd like to see if you find anything in there."

Nyberg blew his nose. "You were right," he said. "Once our colleagues in Malmö brought in that relay it was obvious. The substation workers were able to show us exactly where it belonged."

Wallander suppressed his excitement. "No room for doubt?"

"None at all."

Nyberg went into the building. Wallander looked down the street in the direction of the department stores and the cash machine. The connection between Hökberg and Falk was confirmed. But what it meant he didn't yet know. He started back to the police station. After only a few yards he picked up his pace. Anxiety drove him on.

CHAPTER FOURTEEN

When he got back to the station, Wallander set about constructing a reliable outline of the now chaotic mix of details, but the key events remained sharply separated in his mind. They collided only to continue on their separate ways.

Shortly before 11 a.m. he went to the gents' and rinsed his face in cold water. That too was something he had picked up from Rydberg. Nothing is better for you when your impatience is threatening to take over your mind. Nothing is ever better than cold water.

Then he went on to the canteen to get more coffee, but the machine was broken, as it often was. Martinsson had at some point suggested that they all pitch in to buy a new one. His argument was that no-one could reasonably expect good work from police officers without dependable access to coffee. Wallander looked unhappily at the machine and remembered that he had a tin of instant coffee somewhere in his desk. He returned to his room and started looking for it. He found it in the bottom drawer with some shoe-cleaning equipment and a pair of frayed gloves.

Then he compiled a list of the events of the case. He made a time line in the margin. He was trying to break through the surface of the case to the layer in which all the events were connected. He knew it had to be there.

When he had finished he felt as if he were looking at a nasty and incomprehensible fairy tale. Two girls went out and had some beers. One of the girls was so young she had no business being served in the first place. Some time during that evening they changed places. This happened at the same time as an Asian man came into the restaurant and sat down at a nearby table. This man paid with a fake credit card in the name of Fu Cheng, with a Hong Kong address.

After a couple of hours the girls ordered a taxi, asked to be driven to Rydsgård and in due course attacked the driver. They took his money and left, each going to their separate homes. When they were taken in by the police they at once owned up, sharing the blame and saying that their motive was money. The older of the two girls took advantage of a momentary lapse in security and escaped from the police station. Later her charred corpse was found at the power substation outside Ystad. In all likelihood she was murdered. The substation in turn is an important link in the power distribution grid for southern Sweden. When Hökberg died, much of the region of Skåne was plunged into darkness. After this event Persson retracted her earlier confession and changed her story.

At the same time, a parallel story was unfolding. There is a possibility that this parenthesis, this minor story, is in fact connected to the very heart of the other occurrence somehow. A divorced computer consultant by the name of Tynnes Falk cleaned his flat one Sunday, and then went for an evening walk. He was later found dead in front of a cash machine. After a preliminary investigation that included a conclusive autopsy report, the police eliminated any suspicion of a crime and considered the case closed. Later the man's body was removed from the morgue and an electrical relay from the Ystad substation was left in its place. Falk's flat was also broken into and – at the least – a diary and a framed photograph were taken. At the periphery of all these events, appearing in a group photograph and as a customer in a restaurant, was an Asian man.

Wallander read through all that he had written. It was still early in the investigation, but while he had been laying out his summary he had seen a new connection. If Hökberg had been murdered it had to be because someone wanted to be sure she didn't talk. Falk's body had been removed to conceal something. This was the common denominator. The question is what needs to be covered up, Wallander thought, and by whom?

Wallander was about to push his notes aside when something popped into his head. It was something Erik Hökberg had said, something about the vulnerability of modern society. Wallander looked again at his notes.

What happened if he placed the power substation at the centre? With the grisly aid of a human body, someone had managed to disrupt the power in large areas of southern Sweden. It could therefore be viewed as sabotage. And why had the electrical relay been placed on the gurney when Falk's body was stolen? The only reasonable explanation was that someone had wanted the connection between Hökberg's fate and Falk to be made perfectly clear. But what did this connection mean?

Wallander pushed his notes aside in irritation. It was too early to think of reaching a conclusion. They had to keep searching for more clues, without preconceived ideas.

He drank his coffee absent-mindedly, rocking back and forth in his chair. Then he reached for the page he had torn from the newspaper and kept looking through the personal ads. What would I say in an ad? he wondered. Who would be interested in a 50-year-old policeman with diabetes and increasing doubts about his career choice? Someone who isn't particularly interested in walks in the forest, evenings in front of the fire or sailing? He put the page down and started writing.

His first attempt was somewhat disingenuous: *50-year-old police officer, divorced, grown-up daughter, tired of being lonely. Appearance and age not important, but you should enjoy the comforts of home and opera. Send your answer to "Police '97".*

Lies, he thought. Appearance does matter. I'm not looking to end my loneliness. I want companionship. That's something completely different. I want someone to sleep with, someone who will be there when I want her. And someone who will leave me alone when I feel like it. He tore up the page and started again. This time the text was more truthful: *50-year-old police officer, diabetic, divorced, grown-up daughter, wishes to meet someone to spend time with. The woman I'm looking for is attractive, has a good figure and is interested in sex. Send your answer to "Old Dog".*

Who would respond to something like that? he wondered. Hardly anyone stable.

He turned the page over to start afresh, but was almost immediately interrupted by a knock on the door. It was already midday. It was Höglund. He realised too late that the personal section of the newspaper was still lying face up on his desk. He crumpled it and threw it in the waste-paper basket, but he thought she had seen what he was doing, and it irritated him.

I'm never going to write a personal ad, he thought angrily. The chances are too great that someone like Höglund would answer.

She looked tired.

"I've just finished questioning Persson," she said and sat down heavily.

Wallander pushed all thoughts of personal ads aside.

"How was she?"

"She didn't change her story. She insists that Hökberg used both the knife and the hammer."

"I asked how she was."

Höglund thought about it before answering. "She was different. She seemed more prepared for the questions."

"What made you think that?"

"She spoke faster. Many of her answers seemed prepared in advance. It was only when we got to the questions she wasn't expecting that she started speaking in that slow, apathetic way. That's how she protects herself, giving herself time to think. I don't know how intelligent she is, but she's not confused. She keeps track of her lies. I didn't catch a single instance of her contradicting herself in the two hours that we were at it. That's pretty impressive."

Wallander reached for his notepad. "We'll take the most important stuff now, your impressions. The rest I'll read about in your report."

"I am convinced that she's lying. Quite honestly I don't understand how a 14-year-old girl can be so hard-boiled."

"Because she's a girl?"

"I think it would be unusual even for a boy her age."

"You didn't manage to budge her at all?"

"No, not really. She sticks to her new story that she is innocent and only said what she said because she was afraid of Hökberg. I tried to get her to tell me why she was afraid, but she wouldn't. All she said was that Hökberg could be very tough on her."

"She's probably right about that."

Höglund looked at her notes. "She denied taking any calls from Hökberg, or anyone else, after Hökberg's escape from the station."

"When did she find out Hökberg was dead?"

"Erik Hökberg called her mother."

"Did Hökberg's death come as a shock to her?"

"She claims it did, but I certainly couldn't tell. Maybe she was surprised. She had no explanation as to why Hökberg would have gone out to the substation, nor any idea who could have taken her there."

Wallander got up and walked over to the window. "Did she really have no reaction? No regret, no pain?"

"In my opinion she was in control and utterly cold. Many of her answers were prepared in advance, some pure lies. But I got the impression that she wasn't surprised by what had happened, though she claims she was."

Wallander was struck by a thought that seemed important. "Did she seem afraid of anything happening to her?"

"No, I thought about that. I don't think what happened to Hökberg made her worried for her own life."

Wallander returned to the desk. "Let's assume that's the case. What does that mean?"

"It means Persson is at least partly telling the truth. Not about Lundberg's murder, since I'm convinced she had a hand in it. But I don't think she had much idea what else Hökberg was involved in."

"And what would that be?"

"I don't know."

"Why did they switch seats in the restaurant?"

"Because Hökberg complained of a draught. She won't change her line on that."

"And the man sitting behind them?"

"She claims not to have seen him or anyone else. She also says she didn't notice Hökberg having contact with anyone other than her."

"She didn't notice anyone as they were leaving the restaurant?"

"No. That may even be true. I don't think she would qualify for the title of the World's Most Observant Person."

"Did you ask her if she had ever heard of Tynnes Falk?"

"She said she had never heard the name."

"Was that true?"

Höglund paused. "There might have been a very slight hesitation on her part, but I can't be sure."

I should have talked to her myself, Wallander thought helplessly. If Eva Persson had been holding something back, I would have seen it.

Höglund seemed to be reading his thoughts.

"I don't have your certainty about these things. I wish I could have given you a better answer."

"We'll get to the bottom of this sooner or later. If the main entrance is closed, you try the back door."

"I've been trying to make sense of it," Höglund said. "But nothing hangs together."

"It will take time," Wallander said. "I wonder if we shouldn't get reinforcements. We don't have the manpower we need, even if we shelve our other duties and concentrate on this case."

Höglund looked at him with surprise. "I never thought I'd hear you say that. Usually you insist on us carrying out the investigation alone."

"Maybe I've changed my mind. I just want to make sure we're able to carry out the footwork necessary in this investigation. I'll talk to Lisa about it. If she hasn't already suspended me, that is."

"Persson is sticking to that story as well – that you hit her without provocation."

"Of course she is. If she's lying about everything else she might as well lie about that too."

Wallander got up. He told her in a nutshell about the break-in at Falk's flat.

"Has the body been found?"

"Not as far as I know."

Höglund was still in her chair. "Do you understand any of this?"

"No," Wallander said. "It worries me. Don't forget that a large area of Skåne was left without power."

They walked into the corridor together. Hansson put his head out of his door to say that the police in Växjö had found Persson's father.

"They say he lives in a run-down shack somewhere between Växjö and Vislanda. They're wondering what it is we want to know."

"Nothing for now," Wallander said. "We have more important questions to cover."

They decided to meet again at 1.30 p.m., when Martinsson was back. Wallander went to his office to call the garage. His car was ready. He walked down Frihemsgatan towards Surbrunn's Torg. A gusting wind came and went.

The mechanic's name was Holmlund and he had worked on several of Wallander's cars over the years. He was especially fond of motorcycles. He had a number of teeth missing and spoke with such a strong Skåne accent that Wallander had trouble understanding him. His appearance hadn't changed a bit since he first met him. Wallander still couldn't have said if he was 50 or 60.

"It's going to cost you," Holmlund said and smiled his

gap-toothed smile. "But you'll recoup some of the cost if you sell the car pretty soon."

When Wallander drove away, the erratic noise from the engine was gone. The thought of a new car excited him. The only question was would he stick with a Peugeot or try a new make. He decided to ask Hansson, who knew as much about cars as horse racing.

Wallander drove to a fast-food place by Österleden and had a meal. He tried to read a newspaper, but he couldn't concentrate on it. His thoughts kept returning to the case. He had been trying to find a new focal point and had considered the blackout as a candidate. Then they wouldn't be looking only at a murder but at a highly calculated form of sabotage. But what if he tried to focus his inquiries around something else, such as the man who had appeared at the restaurant? He had made Hökberg switch places. He had a forged identity. And he was in a photograph in Falk's living room – a photograph that had since been stolen. Wallander cursed himself for not taking it himself, as he had been intending. Then he could have asked István to identify him.

Wallander put down his fork and called Nyberg's mobile number. He was about to hang up when Nyberg answered.

"Have you by any chance come across a group photo?" he asked. "Something with a large group of men?"

"I'll ask."

Wallander waited and picked at the tasteless piece of fried fish in front of him.

Nyberg came back. "We have a photo of three men holding up a salmon for the camera. A fishing trip in Norway from 1983."

"Is that it?"

"Yes. How would you know that he would have a photograph like that anyway?"

He's not stupid, Wallander thought. Luckily he had prepared an answer ahead of time.

"I don't know. But I'm trying to find as many pictures as I can of Falk's acquaintances."

"We're almost done here," Nyberg said.

"Found anything interesting?"

"It seems to be a standard breaking-and-entering. Possibly a drug addict."

"No clues?"

"We have fingerprints, but they could all belong to Falk. I'm not sure how we're going to verify that now that the body is gone."

"We'll find it sooner or later."

"I doubt it. If someone steals a body it's surely to bury it."

Nyberg was right. He had an idea, but Nyberg got there first.

"I asked Martinsson to look up Falk in the police files. We couldn't rule out the possibility that we already had something on him."

"And what did he find?"

"He was there in fact. But not his fingerprints."

"What had he done?"

"According to Martinsson, Falk had been sued and fined for damaging property."

"In connection with what?"

"You'll have to get the details from Martinsson," Nyberg said irritably.

It was 1.10 p.m. Wallander filled up the car and returned to the station. Martinsson walked in at the same time.

"None of the neighbours heard or saw anything," Martinsson said as they crossed the car park together. "I managed to talk to all of them. Some are retired and home most of the day. One of them was a physiotherapist, about your age."

Wallander had no comments to make. Instead he said, "What was all that business about Falk damaging property?"

"I have the paperwork in my office. Something about a mink farm."

Wallander read the report in Martinsson's office. Falk had been arrested in 1991, north of Sölvesborg. One night, a mink farmer had discovered that someone was opening the cages. He had called the police and two patrol cars had been dispatched. Falk had not been alone, but he was the only one caught. He had confessed and told the officer that he was vehemently opposed to animals being killed for fur. He had, however, denied acting on behalf of any organisation and had never given the names of his accomplices.

Wallander put down the report. "I thought only young people did things like this," he said. "Falk was 40-plus in 1991."

"I suppose we could be more sympathetic to their cause," Martinsson said. "My daughter is a Greenpeace supporter."

"There's a difference between wanting to protect the environment and taking away a mink farmer's livelihood."

"These organisations teach you an enormous respect for animal life."

Wallander didn't want to be dragged into a debate he felt he would eventually lose, but he was perplexed by Falk's involvement in animal rights activism.

Wallander called Mrs Falk. An answering machine cut in, but as he started leaving his message her voice came on the line. They agreed to meet in the flat on Apelbergsgatan around 3 p.m. Wallander arrived in good time. Nyberg and his forensic team had left. A patrol car was parked outside. As Wallander was walking up the stairs to the flat the door to the flat below, the one he would rather have forgotten about, opened. The door was opened by a woman who looked familiar, but he wasn't sure.

"I saw you from the window," she said, smiling. "I just wanted to say hello. If you remember me, that is."

"Of course I do," Wallander said.

"You know, you never got in touch as you promised."

Wallander couldn't remember making any promises, but he knew it was possible. When he was drunk and strongly attracted to a woman, he was capable of promising almost anything.

"Things came up," he said. "You know how it is."

"I do?"

Wallander mumbled something.

"Would you like to come in for a cup of coffee?"

"As you may have heard, there's been a break-in upstairs. I don't have time right now."

She pointed to her door. "I had a security door put in several years ago. Almost all of us did. Everyone except Falk."

"Did you know him?"

"He kept to himself. We said hello if we met on the stairs, but that was it."

Wallander suspected she wasn't telling the truth, but he decided not to prove it. The only thing he wanted was to get away.

"I'll have to take a rain check on that coffee," he said.

"We'll see," she said.

The door closed. Wallander was sweating. He ran up the last flight. At least she had produced a significant fact.

People in the building had put in security doors, but not Falk, the man whom his wife described as anxious and surrounded by enemies.

The door had not yet been repaired. He walked into the flat and saw that Nyberg and his team had left the chaos intact. He walked into the kitchen and sat at the table. It was very quiet in the flat. He looked at his watch. It was 2.50 p.m. He thought he could hear footsteps on the stairs. Falk was probably too mean to have it put in, he thought. Security doors cost somewhere between 10,000 and 15,000 kronor. Or maybe Marianne Falk is wrong. There were no enemies. But Wallander was doubtful. He thought about the mysterious notations in the diary. There was also the fact that Falk's body had been stolen, and that someone had broken into his flat and made off with the diary and a photograph. That could mean only one thing: someone didn't want the picture or the diary to be studied by the police. Wallander cursed himself once again for not taking the photograph when he had had the chance.

He heard footsteps on the stairs outside. Mrs Falk. The door to the flat softly opened. Wallander got up to greet her. He stepped into the hall.

He sensed danger instinctively and pulled back. But it was too late. A violent explosion ricocheted through the flat.

CHAPTER FIFTEEN

Wallander's instincts saved his life. Nyberg extracted the bullet from the wall next to the living-room door jamb. In the reconstruction of events and from examining the entry hole in Wallander's jacket, they were able to determine what had happened. Wallander had walked into the hall to greet Marianne Falk. As he reached for the front door he sensed a threat behind it. Whoever it was behind the door was not Mrs Falk. He had jerked back and tripped on the rug. The bullet aimed at his chest passed between his body and his left arm. It had torn through his jacket, leaving only a small hole.

That evening he measured the distance from his shirt-sleeve to where he thought his heart was. Nine centimetres. He reflected, as he was pouring himself a glass of whisky, that the rug had saved him. It reminded him of the time, long ago, when he had been a young officer in Malmö. He had been stabbed and the blade had come within 10 centimetres of his heart. He had created a kind of mantra for himself – "There is a time for living, a time for dying." He was struck by the worrying fact that his margin of survival during the past 30 years had decreased by exactly 1 centimetre.

Wallander did not know who had fired the shot. He had not been able to glimpse more than a rapidly moving shadow beyond the door, a figure that seemed to dissolve the moment the echo of the gunshot had bounced across the flat and he had found himself on the floor of the hall cupboard under Falk's coats.

He thought he had been hit. He thought the cry he heard as the deafening roar of the shot echoed in his ears must be his own. But it came from Mrs Falk, who had been knocked down on the stairs by the fleeing shadow. She had not got a good look at him either. She heard the shot, but she had thought it came from below her. She had stopped and turned to look down. Then, when she heard someone running from above her, she turned but, as she did so, she was hit in the face and tumbled backwards, clutching the banister.

Most extraordinary perhaps was that neither of the officers in the patrol car outside saw anything. Wallander's assailant can only have left the building by the front entrance, since the door to the cellar was locked, but the officers noticed no-one leave the building. They had seen Mrs Falk go in, then they had heard the shot without realising immediately what it was, but they had not seen anyone come out of the building.

Martinsson reluctantly accepted this, after having the building searched from top to bottom. He obliged all the nervous senior citizens and the somewhat more controlled therapist to have their flats scoured by policemen. They peered into every cupboard and under every bed, but there was no trace of the assailant. But for the bullet buried in the wall, Wallander would have started to wonder if it had been a figment of his imagination. But he knew it was real enough, and he knew something else that he didn't yet want to admit to himself. He knew that the rug had been more of a blessing than he first thought. Not only because tripping on it saved his life, but because his fall had persuaded the assailant that he had hit his mark. The bullet that Nyberg extracted from the wall behind him was the kind that made a crater-like wound in its victim. When Nyberg showed him the bullet, Wallander understood why the marksman had fired only one shot. One hit would have been fatal.

A regional alert had gone out, but no-one thought it would bear fruit, because they didn't know who they were looking for. Neither Mrs Falk nor Wallander could give a description. Wallander and Martinsson sat in the kitchen, while Nyberg's team worked on the bullet. Wallander had handed them his jacket as well. His ears still hurt from the explosion. Holgersson arrived with Höglund, and Wallander had to explain what had happened all over again.

"The question is why did he fire?" Martinsson said. "There's already been a break-in here. Now an armed assailant."

"We can speculate that it was the same person," Wallander said. "But why did he come back? I can't see any other explanation than that he's looking for something – something he didn't manage to get the first time."

"Aren't we forgetting something else?" Höglund said. "Who was he trying to kill?"

Wallander had asked himself the same question from the outset. Did this have anything to do with the night he had come here to search the flat? Had it been a mistake to look out of the window? Had someone been watching him? He should tell his colleagues about it, but something kept him from doing so.

"Why would anyone want to shoot me?" Wallander said. "I think it was just plain bad luck that I was here when he returned. What we should ask ourselves is what was he here for, which in turn means that Mrs Falk should be brought back as soon as possible."

She had gone home to change.

Martinsson left the flat with Holgersson. The forensic team was tidying up. Höglund stayed with Wallander in the kitchen. Mrs Falk called to say she was on her way.

"How does it feel?" Höglund said.

"Not too good. You know what it's like."

A year or so ago, Höglund had been shot and wounded in a field outside Ystad. It had been partly Wallander's fault, since he had ordered her to advance without realising that the suspect had the gun that Hansson had dropped earlier. She had been badly hurt and it had taken her a long time to mend. When she returned to her post she was a changed person. She had told Wallander about the fear that surfaced in her dreams.

"At least I wasn't hit," Wallander said. "I was stabbed once, but so far I have never stopped a bullet."

"You should talk to someone. There are support groups."

Wallander shook his head impatiently. "No need," he said. "And I don't want to go on talking about it now."

"Why do you always have to be so pig-headed about these things? You're a fine police officer, but you are no less human than the rest of us, whatever you like to think."

Wallander was surprised by the anger boiling over in her. And she was right. When he put on his role as a policeman he tended to forget about the person inside.

"I think you should go home."

"What good would that do?"

At the same moment Mrs Falk walked into the flat. Wallander saw an opportunity to be rid of Höglund and her annoying questions.

"I'd prefer to talk to her alone," he said. "Thanks for your help."

"What help?" Höglund said, and left.

Wallander felt dizzy when he stood up.

"What on earth happened?" Mrs Falk said.

Wallander could see a big bruise starting on the left side of her jaw.

"I was here, waiting for you. I heard someone at the door. I thought it was you."

"Who was it?"

"I don't know, and apparently you don't either."

"I didn't have a chance to look at him."

"But it was a man?"

She was surprised by the question and took a moment to answer.

"Yes," she said finally. "It was a man."

Wallander had no way of proving it, but he was sure she was right. "Let's start in the living room," he said. "I want you to look everywhere, take stock of everything. Let me know if you think anything's missing. Then check the bedroom, and so on. Take your time, open drawers and look behind curtains."

"Tynnes would never have allowed such a thing. He was so secretive."

"We'll talk later," Wallander interrupted her. "Start with the living room."

He stood in the doorway and watched her as she went around the room. She was trying her best to do as he said. The longer he looked the more beautiful she seemed to him. He wondered what kind of an ad he would have to compose to get her to answer. She continued into the bedroom. He was alert for signs of hesitation. When she had finished with the kitchen, half an hour had passed.

"Did anything seem to be gone?"

"Nothing that I could see."

"How well did you know the flat?"

"We never lived here together. This was where he moved after the divorce. He called from time to time and we had dinner together. But even the children probably saw more of him than I did."

Wallander tried to remember the facts that Martinsson had laid out for him when they first discussed Falk's case.

"Does your daughter live in Paris?"

"Yes. Ina is only 17. She's working as a nanny at the Danish Embassy. She's learning French."

"And your son?"

"Jan? He's a student in Stockholm. He's 19."

Wallander turned the conversation back to the flat.

"Do you think you would have noticed if anything had been stolen?"

"Only if it was something I'd been aware of before."

Wallander excused himself, he went into the living room and took away one of three china cockerels from the window ledge. When he came back to the kitchen he asked her to go through the living room one more time. She spotted the missing rooster almost at once. They weren't going to get any further, Wallander realised. She had a good eye, even if she didn't know what Falk kept in his cupboards.

They sat in the kitchen. It was almost 5 p.m. and the autumn darkness was blanketing the city.

"Tell me what you know about his work," Wallander said. "He was self-employed, I know, and worked with computer systems."

"He was a consultant."

"What does that actually mean?"

She looked at him with surprise. "The whole country is run by consultants nowadays. Soon even party leaders will be replaced by consultants. Consultants are highly paid outsiders who fly around to various companies and come up with solutions for their problems. If things go badly, they get the blame, but they're well rewarded for their suffering."

"And your husband was a consultant who specialised in computer systems?"

"I would appreciate it if you wouldn't refer to Tynnes as my husband."

Her comment made Wallander impatient.

"What more can you tell me of what he did?"

"He was expert at designing systems for companies."

"What does that mean?"

She smiled for the first time. "I don't think I can explain it to you if you don't have even a basic grasp of how computers work."

She was right. He didn't.

"Who were his clients?"

"As far as I know, he worked a lot for banks."

"Which banks?"

"I wouldn't know."

"Who would know?"

"He had an accountant."

Wallander felt in his pockets for something to write the name on. All he found was the receipt for the work on the car.

"His name is Rolf Stenius and his office is in Malmö. I don't have an address or phone number."

Wallander put his pen down. He thought that he had overlooked something and he tried to catch hold of it. Mrs Falk took a packet of cigarettes from her bag.

"Do you mind if I smoke?"

"Not at all."

She got a saucer from under the sideboard and lit up.

"Tynnes would be spinning in his grave if he could see this. He hated cigarettes. All the time we were married he chased me out to the street to smoke. I guess this is my chance for revenge."

Wallander took the opportunity to shift the conversation.

"When we talked the first time, you said he had enemies and that he was anxious."

"Yes, he gave that impression."

"It's possible to see if a person is anxious or not. But you can't tell from observing them that a person has enemies. He must have said something that gave you that idea."

She paused before answering. She smoked and looked out of the window. It was dark now.

"It started a couple of years ago," she said. "I could see that he was anxious, but also that he was excited. As if he were in a kind of manic state. He started making strange comments. For example, if I were here having coffee with him he could say something like, 'If people knew what I was doing, they would do away with me' or 'You can never know how close your pursuers are.'"

"He actually said those things?"

"Yes."

"But he never gave you an explanation?"

"No."

"Did you ask him?"

"He would get upset and tell me to be quiet."

Wallander thought carefully before continuing.

"Do you think either of your children experienced these things that you describe? The anxiety or the talk about enemies?"

"I doubt it. They didn't have that much contact with

him. They lived with me, and Tynnes wasn't always that eager to have them over. I don't say these things to be mean. I think Jan and Ina would agree with me."

"He must have had some friends."

"Very few. I realised soon after our wedding that I had married a hermit."

"Who knew him well besides you?"

"He used to have regular contact with a woman who was also a computer consultant. Her name is Siv Eriksson. I don't have her number, but she has an office in Skansgränd, next to Sjömansgatan. They worked on some assignments together."

Wallander made a note of the name. Mrs Falk put out her cigarette.

"One last question," Wallander said. "At least for now. A couple of years ago Tynnes was caught on a mink farm by the police. He was letting minks out of their cages. He was charged and fined for this."

She looked at him, genuinely startled. "I never heard a word about that."

"Does it fit any sort of pattern?"

"To be letting minks out of their cages? Why on earth would it?"

"So you don't know of his being in contact with organisations who get into this kind of thing?"

"What organisations would those be?"

"Militant environmental groups. Animal rights activists."

"I'm not sure I can get my head round all this," she said.

Wallander knew she was telling the truth. She got up.

"I will need to speak to you again," Wallander said.

As he was showing her out, she stopped by the hole left in the wall.

"Do you carry a weapon in self-defence?"

"No."

She shook her head, stretched out her hand and said goodbye.

"One more thing," Wallander said. "Did Tynnes have any interest in outer space?"

"What sort of thing?"

"Spaceships, astronomy . . ."

"You asked me that already, and I'll give you the same answer. As far as I know, not. If he ever did look at the stars, it would have been to make sure they were still there. He was pragmatic rather than romantic by nature."

She went down the stairs and Wallander went back into the flat and sat again in the kitchen. That was where he first had the feeling he was missing something. It was Rydberg who had taught him to listen to his inner alarm system. Even in the high-tech and necessarily rational world of police work, intuition remained crucially important.

He sat without moving for a few minutes. Then he caught hold of it. Marianne Falk had not been able to find anything that was missing. Could it be that the man who broke in and later fired the shot at Wallander was coming to put something back? Wallander shook his head at the idea. He was about to get up when he jumped. There was a knock at the door. Wallander's heart was racing. It was only when the knocking stopped that he realised it could hardly be someone announcing their intention to take another shot at him. He went into the hall and opened the door. There was an old man on the landing, holding a cane.

"I want to talk to Mr Falk," he said in a stern voice. "I have a complaint."

"May I ask who you are?" Wallander said.

"My name is Carl-Anders Setterkvist and I own this building. There have been a number of complaints from other residents lately about excessive noise and loud visits by military men. I would prefer to speak to Mr Falk about it personally, if possible."

"Mr Falk is dead," Wallander said brusquely.

Setterkvist stared at him. "Dead? Whatever do you mean?"

"I'm a police officer," Wallander said, "CID. There's been a burglary here. But Mr Falk died last Monday. There are no military personnel running up and down these stairs, they're police."

Setterkvist seemed to be trying to gauge whether Wallander was telling the truth.

"I would like to see your identification badge, please," he said.

"Badges disappeared a long time ago," Wallander said, "but you can see my identification card." Setterkvist studied it carefully.

Wallander told him briefly what had happened.

"How unfortunate," Setterkvist said. "What will happen to the flats?"

Wallander frowned. "The flats?"

"I simply mean that it's difficult when new people move in. One wants to know what kind of people they are before renting the place, especially in this sort of building with a number of elderly tenants."

"Do you live here yourself?"

Setterkvist was clearly insulted. "I live in a house outside town."

"You said 'flats'."

"What else would I have called them?"

"Did you mean that Falk rented more than one flat?"

Setterkvist gestured that he wanted to be let in. Wallander stepped aside for him.

"I should warn you that it's so messy in here because there's been a burglary."

"I've been the victim of a burglary myself," Setterkvist said calmly. "I know how it is."

Wallander ushered him into the kitchen.

"Mr Falk was an excellent tenant," Setterkvist said. "Never late with the rent. At my age one is surprised by nothing, but I must admit to being a little shaken by the complaints that have come in these past few days. That is why I am here in person."

"He rents more than one flat, did you say?"

"I have a wonderful old building by Runnerströms Torg," Setterkvist said. "Falk had a small flat there, in the attic. He needed it for his work."

That would explain the absence of computers, Wallander thought. There certainly isn't anything in this flat to suggest that he worked here.

"I need to see that office," Wallander said.

Setterkvist thought for a moment, then drew out the largest set of keys Wallander had ever seen. Setterkvist knew at once which keys he needed. He removed them from the key chain.

"I'll write out a receipt," Wallander said.

Setterkvist shook his head.

"One has to be able to trust people," he said. "Or rather, one has to be able to rely on one's own judgement."

Setterkvist marched off, while Wallander called the station and arranged for someone to come and help him seal the flat. Then he walked straight down to Runnerströms Torg. It was close to 7 p.m. The wind buffeted him. Wallander was cold. Martinsson had lent him a coat, but it was thin. He thought about the bullet. It still seemed unreal. He wondered what his reaction would be in a couple of days, when the realisation of how close to death he had been sank in.

The house on Runnerströms Torg was a three-storey, turn-of-the-century building. Wallander walked to the other side of the street and stared up at the attic windows. No lights. Before he walked to the front door he looked about him. A man cycled past, then he was alone. Wallander let himself in. He heard music coming from one flat. He turned on the light in the hall. When he had climbed all the way to the attic floor there was only one door on the landing. It was a security door, no name or letter box. Wallander listened, but heard nothing. He unlocked the door. Pausing in the doorway, he listened again. For a split second he thought he heard someone breathing in the darkness and he almost jumped out before he realised it was his imagination. He turned on the light and let the door close behind him.

It was a large room, almost empty. The only furniture was a desk and a chair. There was a large computer on the desk. Wallander approached it and saw that on the desk next to the computer there was something like a blueprint. He turned on the desk lamp. It took him a moment to see what it was. He was looking at a blueprint of the power substation where Hökberg had been killed.

CHAPTER SIXTEEN

Wallander held his breath. At first he thought he was mistaken. It had to be a blueprint of something else. Then all doubt disappeared. He knew he was right. Carefully, he laid the paper back on the desk, next to the computer with its large dark screen. He could see his face reflected in it. There was a phone on the desk. He thought he should call someone, either Martinsson or Höglund. And Nyberg. But he didn't lift the receiver. Instead he started slowly walking around the room. This is where Falk worked, he thought. Behind a reinforced steel door that would have been very hard for someone to open without a key. This is where he worked. A computer consultant. One evening his body is found next to an ATM. His body disappears from the morgue, and now I find a blueprint for the power substation next to his computer.

For one breathtaking moment he thought he could see the connection. But the kaleidoscope of facts was too confusing. Wallander kept walking around. What is here, he thought, and what is missing? There is a computer, a chair, a desk, a lamp. There is a telephone and a blueprint, but no shelves, no binders, no books. Not one pen.

He turned the lampshade so that the beam of light was directed at the wall. He turned it so that each wall in turn was illuminated. The light was strong, but he could detect no hidden places. He sat in the chair. The silence was overwhelming. If Martinsson had been here,

Wallander would have asked him to turn on the computer. Martinsson would have loved that job. Wallander didn't dare touch it himself. Again he thought that he should call him, but hesitated. I have to understand how this hangs together, he thought. That's the most important thing right now. Many new connections have been revealed in a much shorter span of time than I would have thought. The problem is just that I can't see the pattern yet.

He decided to call Nyberg. It didn't help that it was almost 8 p.m. and Nyberg had been working for the last few days with hardly any sleep. Someone else would probably have decided that the search of the flat could wait until the following day. But Wallander was plagued by a sense of urgency that was only growing stronger. Nyberg listened without saying anything. He made a note of the address, and once they ended the conversation, Wallander made his way to street level to wait for him.

Nyberg arrived alone. Wallander helped him carry up his bags.

"What am I looking for here?" Nyberg asked once they were in the attic flat.

"Prints. Secret compartments."

"Then I won't need anyone else for now. Can we wait on the photography and videotape?"

"Do it in the morning."

Nyberg took off his shoes. He found a pair of plastic shoes in one of his bags. Nyberg had always been frustrated with the protective shoe covers that were commercially available. He had finally designed his own and found someone to make them. Wallander assumed he had paid for them out of his own pocket.

"Are you good at computers?" he said.

"I know as little as the next man about how they actually work," Nyberg said. "But I can probably get it started for you."

"Martinsson would never forgive me if I let anyone else deal with it," Wallander said.

Then he showed Nyberg the paper on the table. Nyberg saw at once what it was. He looked questioningly at Wallander.

"What does this mean? Did Falk kill the girl?"

"He died before she was murdered."

Nyberg got a magnifying glass out of his bags and sat down. He studied the blueprint while Wallander waited in silence.

"This is an original," Nyberg said.

"Are you sure?"

"Not 100 per cent, but almost."

"You'd think someone should be missing it."

"I talked to that man Andersson about the security procedures at the power company," Nyberg said. "It should have been virtually impossible for anyone to make a copy of this blueprint, much less steal it."

This was important. If the blueprint had been stolen from inside the power company a whole new avenue of clues would open up.

Nyberg positioned his spotlights. Wallander decided to leave him alone.

"I'm going to the station. Call if you need me."

Nyberg was already lost in his work.

Once on the street, Wallander realised that his mind was taking a slightly different direction. He wasn't going to go straight to the station. Mrs Falk had referred to a Siv Eriksson. She should be able to tell him more about Falk's work as a consultant. Her flat was nearby, or at least her office was. Wallander left his car. He walked down Långgatan towards the town centre and turned right on Skansgränd. The streets were deserted. He spun round twice, but there was no-one following him. The wind was strong still, and he was cold. He started thinking about the bullet. He wondered when he was going to take a hit, and he wondered how he would react.

When he arrived at the building that Mrs Falk had described, he at once saw the sign. *Serkon. Siv Eriksson, consultant.*

The office should be on the second floor. He pushed the buzzer and crossed his fingers. If this was only her office he would somehow have to discover her home address.

But someone answered. Wallander announced himself and said what he wanted. The door was unlocked and Wallander went in.

She was waiting for him in the doorway. Although the light in the hall was strong for his eyes, he recognised her at once. She had been at his lecture. He had been introduced to her, but had of course forgotten her name. It was odd that she hadn't explained who she was. She surely knew that Falk was dead. It threw him for a moment. Did she still not know? Was he going to be the bearer of this dreadful news?

"I'm sorry to bother you," he said.

She let him into the flat. There was the smell of an open fire coming from somewhere. Now he saw her clearly. She was in her forties, with medium-length dark hair and sharp features. He had been too nervous when he met her yesterday to notice her appearance, but the woman he now saw made him self-conscious, the way he always felt when he saw someone he found attractive.

"I should explain why . . . I know that Tynnes is dead. Marianne phoned me."

He was relieved. He would never get used to telling a relative, or a friend even, of a death. He noticed that she seemed sad. "As colleagues you must have been close," he said.

"Yes and no," she said. "We were close, very close. But only when it came to work."

Wallander wondered if their close working relationship had ever grown to be more than that. He felt an unreasonable pang of jealousy.

"You must have something important to discuss with me since you are here so late," she said, and handed Wallander a coat hanger.

He followed her into a stylish living room with a log fire burning in the grate. It seemed to Wallander that both the furniture and the paintings were probably as expensive as they looked.

"Can I offer you anything?"

I really could do with a whisky, Wallander thought. "Thank you, but that won't be necessary," he said.

He sat on a dark blue sofa, and she sat in an armchair. He silently admired her shapely legs and noticed that she had guessed his thoughts.

"I came straight from Falk's office," he said. "Where there appears to be only a computer."

"Tynnes was an ascetic. He wanted everything around him as pared back, as minimalist as possible. It helped him work."

"That's my real reason for being here, to ask you what his work consisted of. What your work consisted of, I should say."

"We worked together on some things, but not all the time."

"May we begin by your telling me what he did when he worked alone?" Wallander regretted not having called

Martinsson. There was a good chance he was going to get answers he wouldn't be able to understand. It wasn't too late to call him, even now, but for the third time this evening Wallander decided to let it go.

"I should warn you I don't know a great deal about computers," he said. "You'll have to be very clear, or I won't be able to follow you."

She smiled. "That surprises me," she said. "From your lecture last night I gathered that computers are a police officer's best friend."

"That doesn't go for me personally. Some of us still have to engage in the old-fashioned process of talking to people, not just running names through the computer registers. Or batting e-mails back and forth."

She got up and walked over to the hearth, bending down to rearrange the logs. Wallander watched her, but swiftly lowered his gaze as she turned around.

"What exactly do you want me to tell you? And why?"

Wallander began with the second question. "We're not 100 per cent sure that Falk died of natural causes, although the autopsy report pointed pretty conclusively to his having suffered a heart attack."

"A heart attack?" She was astonished, and Wallander thought immediately of the doctor who had come to see him. "There was nothing wrong with his heart. Tynnes was in terrific shape."

"That's what I've been told. That's one of the reasons we wanted to have one more look at the case. The question then is: what else could it have been? An attack, or perhaps an accident."

She shook her head. "Not an attack. Tynnes would never have let anyone get that close."

"How do you mean?"

"He was forever on his guard. He often talked about how he felt vulnerable in public. So he was prepared, and I know that he was quick on his feet. He was quite advanced in some martial art that I forget the name of."

"He could split bricks with his bare hands?"

"That sort of thing."

"So you believe it was an accident?"

"Yes. It had to be."

Wallander paused. "I had other reasons for coming at this hour, but I think we'll put those aside for the moment."

"You must realise that that makes me curious." She poured herself a glass of wine, and carefully balanced it on the armrest.

"I can't, unfortunately, share much information with you at this stage." That's nonsense, Wallander thought. I could tell her a lot more if I wanted to. For some reason I'm enjoying having some momentary hold over her.

She interrupted his thoughts. "What else was it you asked me?"

"About his work."

"Right. He was a highly accomplished creator of computer systems."

Wallander waited for more.

"He designed computer programs for businesses. Sometimes he just customised and improved existing systems. When I say he was highly accomplished, I mean it. He had offers from heavyweight companies in Asia and in North America. But he always declined them for all that they would have earned him a great deal of money."

"Why do you think he did that?"

"I honestly don't know," she said, and an anxious frown crossed her brow.

"Did you ever talk about the offers he received?"

"He told me what they were and how much money they were offering. Personally, I would have accepted them on the spot."

"And he never told you why he turned them down."

"He just didn't want the work. He didn't need it."

"He must have been very well off."

"I don't think it was that. Sometimes he had to borrow from me."

Wallander sensed that they were nearing a watershed.

"He never went into any detail, for example, about the companies themselves?"

"No, nothing. He just didn't need the extra work, he said. If I tried to keep asking, he cut me off. He could be quite aggressive. He set the limits, not me."

What was the real motivation for saying no? Wallander wondered. It doesn't make sense.

"What determined the kind of project you would work on together rather than separately?"

Her answer surprised him. "The degree of tedium involved."

"I don't understand."

"Some parts of our work will always be rather tedious. Tynnes could be impatient and he often siphoned off the more mundane tasks to me so that he could give his full attention to the more challenging aspects of a project. Especially if it involved something on the cutting edge, something that hadn't been cracked before."

"And you accepted this arrangement?"

"You have to accept your limitations. It was never as boring for me as it would have been for him. I didn't have his extraordinary talents."

"How did you first meet?"

"Until the age of 30 I was a housewife. Then I got

divorced and got myself an education. Tynnes gave a lecture in one of my classes. I was fascinated by him, and I asked him if he had any work for me. He said no, but a year later he called me. Our first project working together was designing a security system for a bank."

"What did that involve?"

"Today money is transferred between accounts at an astonishing speed, between private accounts and companies, between the banks of various countries, and so on. There are always people out there who want to disrupt these transfers for their own ends. The way to thwart them is to stay a step ahead. It's a constant battle."

"That sounds difficult."

"It is."

"It also sounds like a task that would be too big for a lone computer consultant in Ystad, however gifted."

"One of the advantages of the new technology is that you can be in the middle of things no matter where you are based. Tynnes was in constant contact with companies, computer manufacturers and other programmers all around the world."

"From his office here?"

"Yes."

Wallander was unsure how to proceed. He didn't feel that he had any sort of grasp of Falk's work, and he also saw the futility in continuing this conversation without Martinsson being there. They should also get in touch with the IT division at the national crime investigation centre.

Wallander changed tack and watched her face carefully while he asked the next question. "Did he have any enemies that you knew of?"

"Not as far as I know," she said, showing no emotion, but surprise at his question.

"Did you notice a change in him recently, in the last year, say?"

She thought for a while before answering. "He was the same as always."

"And how was that?"

"Moody. He worked very long hours."

"Where did you meet to discuss the work you did together?"

"Always here. Never in his office."

"Why not?"

"I think Tynnes was something of a germophobe, to be honest. I think he didn't want anyone leaving dirt on his carpets. He was manic about cleanliness."

"He seems to have been a very complicated man."

"Not when you got to know him. He wasn't so different from other men."

Wallander looked at her with interest. "And what is it that men are like?"

She smiled. "Is that your personal question or are we still discussing Tynnes?"

"I'm not here to ask personal questions."

She sees right through me, Wallander thought. It can't be helped.

"Men are often childish and vain, although they deny it."

"That's a rather broad characterisation."

"I mean it."

"Falk was like that?"

"Yes. But not always. He could be generous. For example, he always paid me more than he had to. But you could never predict his moods."

"He had been married and had children."

"We never talked about his family. It was only after about a year of working with him that I learned he had one."

"Did he have any interests outside his work?"

"None that I knew of."

"Any friends?"

"He had some friends that he corresponded with via e-mail. I never saw him get so much as a postcard through the post."

"How can you know that if you were never at his office?"

She made a little gesture of applause. "Good question. He used my address for his post, as it happens. But nothing was ever addressed to him."

Wallander frowned.

"This is a bit confusing. He used your address, but no post, no bills, no letters ever actually came for him?"

"He got junk mail, but that's all."

"He must have had another postal address as well, then."

"Probably, but in that case I don't know what it was."

Wallander thought about Falk's two flats. There had been nothing in the office at Runnerströms Torg, but he also could not remember seeing any post at Apelbergsgatan.

"We'll have to look into this," he said. "Falk comes across as strangely secretive."

"Some people don't like getting mail, while others love the sound of another letter coming through the letter box."

I'm going too fast, Wallander thought. First we have to see what's in his computer. If he had a life, that's surely where we'll find it.

She poured herself more wine and asked him if he had changed his mind. Wallander shook his head.

"You said you were close. Did you ever visit him at home?"

"No."

That answer came a little too quickly, Wallander thought.

The question was whether there hadn't been something between Falk and his female assistant after all.

It was 9 p.m. The fire had burned down to glowing embers.

"I take it there's been no post for him in the past few days?"

"No, nothing."

"And how would you sum up everything that's happened?"

"I always thought that Tynnes would become an old man. It can only have been an accident."

"You don't think he could have had some illness you didn't know about?"

"Yes, of course that's possible. But I don't think so."

Wallander wondered if he should tell her about the disappearance of Falk's body. But he decided to wait. He switched tack again.

"There was a blueprint of a power substation on his desk. Do you know anything about that?"

"I don't think I would know what one is."

"It's a structure just outside Ystad belonging to Sydkraft Power."

She thought hard. "He did work for Sydkraft some years ago," she said. "But I wasn't involved."

Wallander had a thought. "I'd like you to make a list of all the jobs he had over the past two years," he said. "Those he worked on alone and those you worked on together."

"Tynnes may have had projects I didn't know about."

"I'll talk to his accountant," Wallander said. "He must have given him the information. But I'd be grateful if I could see your list."

"Straight away?"

"Tomorrow is fine."

She got up and stirred the embers. Wallander tried to

compose a personal ad in his head that would tempt Siv Eriksson to reply. She returned to her chair.

"Are you hungry?"

"No. I should get going."

"It doesn't seem as if my answers have helped you."

"I know more about Tynnes Falk than I did before I came. Police work requires patience."

He had no more questions and knew he should leave. Finally, he got to his feet.

"I'll get in touch tomorrow," he said. "Do you think you could fax me the list of clients to the police station?"

"How about an e-mail attachment?"

"That would be fine as well, though I have no idea how to download those or even what address I have."

"Let me find out."

Wallander put on his coat. "Did Falk ever discuss mink farming?" he said.

"Why on earth would he?" she said.

"Just wondering."

She opened the front door. Wallander felt a strong urge to stay.

"It was a great lecture," she said. "But you were very nervous."

"That's par for the course when you're on your own talking to so many women."

They said goodbye. Wallander walked down the stairs. Just before he opened the door to the street his phone rang. It was Nyberg.

"How fast can you get here?"

"Pretty fast," Wallander said. "Why do you ask?"

"You'd better come now."

Nyberg hung up. Wallander's heart was beating faster. Nyberg would only call if it really mattered.

CHAPTER SEVENTEEN

It took Wallander less than five minutes to return to the building at Runnerströms Torg. At the top of the stairs, he saw Nyberg smoking on the landing outside the flat. He realised how extremely tired Nyberg was. He never smoked unless he was almost at the point of collapse. The last time that had happened was during the difficult homicide investigation that led to the capture of Stefan Fredman.

Nyberg stubbed the cigarette out in his matchbox and nodded to Wallander to follow him in.

"I started looking at the walls," Nyberg said. "There was a discrepancy. It happens sometimes in old buildings; renovations end up changing the original floor plan. But I started measuring the room anyway, and found this –" Nyberg led Wallander to the far end of the room. A part of the wall jutted into the room at a sharp angle.

"I started tapping on the walls. Here it sounded hollow. Then I saw this." He pointed to the floor.

Wallander crouched down. If you looked closely you could see that the skirtingboard had been sawn loose from the floor. There was also a thin crack in the wall from which Nyberg had removed part of a tape which had been painted over.

"Have you looked to see what's behind?"

"I wanted to wait for you."

Wallander nodded. Nyberg carefully pulled away the rest of the tape, revealing a low door, about 1.5 metres high.

Then he stepped aside. Wallander pushed the door open, which gave way without a sound. Nyberg shone his flashlight into the opening.

The hidden space was bigger than Wallander had imagined. He wondered if Setterkvist knew about this. He took Nyberg's flashlight and looked around for the light switch.

The room was perhaps 8 metres square with no window but one small air vent. The room was empty save for a table that looked like an altar. There were two candles on it. There was a photograph of Falk on the wall. Wallander had the feeling that the picture had been taken in this very room. He asked Nyberg to hold the flashlight while he went closer to study the photograph. Falk was staring straight into the camera. His expression was serious.

"What's that in his hand?" Nyberg said.

Wallander took out his glasses and then peered at the photograph again.

"I don't know what you think," he said, finally straightening up, "but it looks to me as if he has a remote control in his hand."

Nyberg came to the same conclusion.

"Tell me what I'm looking at," said Wallander. "I'm at a loss."

"Did he worship himself?" Nyberg said in a confounded tone of voice. "Was the man a lunatic?"

"I don't know yet," Wallander said.

They turned their attention to the rest of the room, but there was nothing else to look at. Wallander put on a pair of rubber gloves and carefully removed the picture. He looked on the back, but there was no writing. He handed the picture to Nyberg.

"You'll have to look it over."

"Maybe this room is part of a series of rooms," Nyberg

said, doubtfully. "Like a series of Chinese boxes. Maybe there's another secret space further along."

Together they searched the room but found nothing. The walls were all solid.

They returned to the living room.

"You haven't found anything else?" Wallander said.

"No. It seems as if the room was cleaned recently."

"Falk was a clean freak," Wallander said. He recalled both the diary entries and what Eriksson had told him.

"I don't think I can do much more tonight," Nyberg said. "But I'll come back tomorrow to finish up."

"We'll also bring in Martinsson," Wallander said. "I want to know what's in that computer."

Wallander helped Nyberg collect his things.

"How the hell can someone worship himself?" Nyberg asked when they had finished and were ready to leave.

"I can show you countless examples," Wallander said.

"I won't have to deal with any more of this in a couple of years," Nyberg said. "Lunatics praying before their own image."

They loaded the bags into Nyberg's car. Wallander saluted him and watched him drive off. The wind had picked up. It was close to 10.30 p.m. He was hungry, but the thought of going home and cooking something was not appealing. He got into the car and drove to a fast-food place that was open. When his meal came some boys had started playing a noisy video game. He decided to take his hot dogs and mashed potatoes out to the car. With the very first bite he managed to spill something on Martinsson's coat. His first reaction was to open the door and throw everything on the ground, but he managed to calm himself down.

Once he had finished eating he wasn't sure if he should

go home or go back to the station. He needed to sleep, but his anxiety wasn't letting up. He drove to the station. There was no-one in the canteen, but the coffee machine had been fixed. Someone had written an angry note about not pulling too hard on the levers.

What levers? Wallander thought helplessly. I put my cup down and push a button. I've never seen a lever. He took his coffee back to his office. The corridor was deserted. He didn't know how many late nights he had spent there alone.

Once, when he was still married to Mona and Linda was a young child, Mona had turned up at his office, seriously cross, and told him he had to make a choice between his family and his work. That time he had immediately gone home with her. But there had been many times when he had chosen to stay on and work.

He took Martinsson's coat with him to the gents' and tried to clean it, but without success. Then he returned to his office and spent half an hour making notes about his conversation with Eriksson. When he had finished he yawned and stretched. It was 11.30 p.m. and he knew he should go home and try to sleep, but he forced himself to read through what he had written. He kept thinking about Falk's strange personality and his secret room with an altar to his own image. And the fact that no-one knew where he had his post sent. Then he thought about the thing Eriksson had said that had stuck in his mind: Falk turned down a number of lucrative job offers because he felt he had enough as it was.

Wallander checked the time. It was 11.40 p.m. He wanted to talk to Mrs Falk, to ask about Falk's will. It was too late to call, even though something told him that she wouldn't be asleep. Wallander yawned again. He put on his coat and turned off the light. As he was walking through reception one of the officers on the night shift stuck his head out of the control room.

"I think I have something for you," he said.

Wallander shut his eyes tight and hoped it wasn't something that would keep him up all night. He walked over and took the receiver the officer held out to him.

"Someone has discovered a body," he said.

Not another one, Wallander thought. We can't take that. Not right now. He held the receiver to his ear. "Kurt Wallander. What seems to be the matter?"

The man speaking on the other end was clearly agitated. He was screaming into the phone. Wallander held the receiver further away.

"Please speak more slowly," Wallander said. "Clearly and slowly. Otherwise we're not going to be able to get anywhere."

"My name is Nils Jönsson. There's a dead man on the street."

"Where is that?"

"In Ystad. I tripped over him. He's naked and he's dead. It's horrible. I shouldn't have to see things like this. I have a weak heart."

"Calm down," Wallander said. "Nice and easy, now. You say there's a naked dead man on the street?"

"Isn't that what I said?"

"Yes, you did. Now tell me what street you're on."

"I don't know. It's a fucking car park."

Wallander shook his head.

"Is it a street or a car park?"

"It's something in between."

"And where is it?"

"I'm on my way from Trelleborg to Kristianstad. I was going to fill up the car and then he was just lying there."

"So you're calling from a petrol station?"

"I'm in my car."

Wallander had begun to hope the man was simply intoxicated and imagining things. But his agitation seemed real.

"What can you see from your car?"

"I think it's a department store."

"Is there a name?"

"I can't see any. I took the exit."

"What exit?"

"The one for Ystad, of course."

"From Trelleborg?"

"From Malmö. I was on the main road."

A thought had come crawling out of Wallander's subconscious, though he had trouble believing it could be true.

"Can you see a cash machine from your car?" he said.

"That's where he is. On the pavement."

Wallander held his breath. The man kept talking and Wallander handed the phone to the officer who had been listening in the background.

"It's where Falk was found," Wallander said. "Maybe we've found him again."

"Who do you want me to send down there?"

"Call Martinsson and Nyberg. How many patrol cars are out right now?"

"Two. One is in Hedeskoga sorting out a domestic dispute. Birthday party that got out of hand."

"The other?"

"In town."

"Tell them to make for the car park on Missunnavägen, right away. I'll get there on my own."

Wallander left the station. He was freezing in the thin coat. During the short journey he wondered what he was about to find, but he was pretty sure it would be Tynnes Falk, returned to the place of his death.

Wallander and the patrol car arrived almost simultaneously. A man jumped out of a red Volvo when they arrived. He was waving his arms. Wallander got out of his car and the man approached him, shouting and pointing. He had bad breath.

"Wait here," Wallander told him.

Then he walked over to the cash machine. It was Falk. He was lying on his stomach with his hands tucked underneath his chest. His head was turned to the left. Wallander told the officers to seal off the area and to take down Nils Jönsson's statement, something he didn't have the energy to do himself. He didn't expect the man to have anything important to tell them. The person or persons who had returned Falk's body would most likely have chosen a time when no-one could see them.

Wallander had never encountered anything like this before. The reconstruction of a death, a body returned to the scene of the crime. He couldn't make head nor tail of it. He walked slowly around the body as if he were expecting Falk to get to his feet. One could say I'm looking at a divine figure, he thought. You worshipped yourself, Mr Falk. According to Eriksson you were planning to become a very old man. But you didn't even live as long as me.

Nyberg arrived in his car. He stared at the body for a full minute, then turned to Wallander.

"Wasn't he already dead? Then how did he end up back here? Was this where he wanted to be buried?"

Wallander saw Martinsson park behind the patrol cars. He walked over to meet him.

Martinsson got out of his car. He was dressed in a

tracksuit. He eyed the stain on the coat Wallander was wearing with disapproval, but he didn't say anything.

"What's happened?"

"Falk has come back."

"Is this your idea of a joke?"

"I'm just telling you what's happened. Tynnes Falk is lying in the spot where he died."

They walked over to the cash machine. Nyberg was talking on the phone to one of his forensic team. Wallander wondered gloomily if he was going to have to see Nyberg faint again.

"There's one important thing I want you to check out," Wallander told him. "See if you think he's lying in the same position as when he was first found."

Martinsson nodded and slowly circled the body. Wallander knew he had an excellent memory. Martinsson shook his head.

"He was lying further away from the machine before. And one leg was bent."

"Are you sure?"

"Yes."

Wallander thought for a moment.

"We really don't need to wait for a doctor this time," he said after a while. "Falk was pronounced dead more than a week ago. I think we can turn him over without breaking any rules."

Martinsson hesitated, but Wallander insisted. He could see no reason to wait. Once Nyberg had taken photographs of the body, they turned it over. Martinsson flinched and drew back. A few seconds went by before Wallander realised why. Two fingers were missing. The index finger on the right hand and the ring finger on the left. He got up.

"What kind of animals are we dealing with?" Martinsson groaned. "Body snatchers? Corpse mutilators? Necrophiliacs?"

"Heaven knows what, but clearly this means something. Someone went to a lot of trouble to steal the body and now to return it here."

Martinsson was pale and Wallander pulled him aside.

"We need to get a hold of the nightwatchman, the one who discovered the body the first time," he said. "We also need the security guards' schedule to establish the time they patrol this area. Then we'll be in a better position to zero in on the time that he was dropped back here."

"Who found him this time?"

"A man from Trelleborg, called Nils Jönsson."

"Was he getting cash?"

"He says he stopped to fill up with petrol."

Wallander went to talk to the officer who had taken down Jönsson's statement. He had indeed said nothing of interest.

Martinsson came over with information from the night guard. "Someone drove by here around 11 p.m.," he said.

It was now 12.30 a.m. Wallander recalled that the first time Falk was found the call came into the station around midnight. Jönsson said he had discovered the body this time at around 11.45 p.m.

"The body can only have been here for about an hour," Wallander said. "And I am certain that whoever brought him back knew exactly what time the guards would do their rounds."

"What do you think our chances are of finding a witness?"

"Negligible. There aren't many residential buildings here, from which someone might have looked out of a window. And who comes here late at night?"

"People out walking their dogs."

"Maybe."

"They may at least have noticed a car or some unusual activity. People with dogs tend to have habitual natures and they would notice something out of the ordinary."

Wallander agreed. It was worth a try.

"We'll put an officer down here tomorrow night," he said. "He can talk to every dog walker and jogger that goes by."

"Hansson loves dogs," Martinsson said.

So do I, Wallander thought. But I'll be thankful if I don't have to stand out here tomorrow night.

A car slowed down and stopped by the police tape. A young man in a tracksuit that looked like the one Martinsson was wearing stepped out. Wallander felt like he was slowly being surrounded by the members of a football team.

"That's our security guard," Martinsson said. "The one from last Sunday. He was off tonight."

He walked over to talk to him. Wallander went back to the body.

"Someone has cut off two of his fingers," Nyberg said. "It gets worse and worse."

"I know you aren't a doctor," Wallander said. "But you used the word 'cut'?"

"Both of them look like clean cuts. There is a small possibility it could have been another kind of instrument if it was powerful enough. That's up to the doctor to determine. She's on her way."

"Susann Bexell?"

"I don't know for sure if it's her."

Half an hour later, Bexell arrived. Wallander explained the situation. The dog unit that Nyberg had requested arrived soon after. They were to search for the missing fingers.

"I really don't know what I'm supposed to be doing out here," Bexell said when Wallander had finished telling her everything. "If he's dead there's not a great deal I can do."

"I need you to look at his hands. Two of his fingers are missing."

Nyberg was smoking again. Wallander was surprised he wasn't feeling more exhausted himself. The dog officer had started his work. Wallander remembered a time when a dog had found a blackened finger. How long ago was that? He couldn't say. Five, maybe ten years ago.

Bexell worked quickly. "I think these fingers were cut off with pliers," she said. "But where that happened I can't say."

"It definitely wasn't here," Nyberg said.

No-one disputed this declaration, nor did anyone bother to ask him how he arrived at this conviction.

Bexell finished up and directed the loading of the body into the morgue van.

"Let's hope the body won't disappear again," Wallander said. "It would be nice if they could actually bury it this time."

Bexell and the morgue van drove away. The dog had given up the search.

"He would have found a couple of fingers if they had been anywhere here," his trainer said. "That's an easy job for him."

"I want the area searched again tomorrow," Wallander said, thinking of Hökberg's handbag. "Whoever removed them may have dropped them a little further away. Just to make our job harder."

It was 1.45 a.m. and the security guard had gone home.

"He agreed with me," Martinsson said. "The body was in a different place."

"That could mean one of two things," Wallander said. "Either they simply couldn't be bothered putting it in the original position. Or else they didn't know where that was."

"But how could that be? And why bring it back at all?"

"I don't know, but I don't think there's any use in staying here. We need to sleep."

Nyberg was packing up his bags for the second time this evening. The area would remain cordoned off until the next day.

"I'll see you tomorrow at 8 a.m.," Wallander said.

Then they went their separate ways. Wallander went home and made himself a cup of tea. He drank about half a cup and then went to bed. His back and legs ached. The street lamp swayed outside the window. Just as he was about to fall asleep, he was jerked back into consciousness. At first he didn't know what it was. He listened for noise, but then he realised the disturbance had come from within. It was something to do with the fingers.

He sat up in bed. It was 2.20 a.m. I have to know now, he thought. It can't wait until tomorrow.

He got out of bed and walked out into the kitchen. The phone book lay on the table. It took him less than a minute to find the phone number he was looking for.

CHAPTER EIGHTEEN

Eriksson was asleep. Wallander hoped he wasn't tearing her from a dream she didn't want to leave. She answered the phone after the eleventh ring.

"This is Kurt Wallander."

"Who?"

"I came to your place last night."

She seemed to be waking up slowly. "Oh, the policeman. What time is it?"

"It's 2.30 a.m. I wouldn't have called if it wasn't urgent."

"What's happened?"

"We found the body."

There was a scratchy sound at the other end. He thought she was probably sitting up in bed.

"Come again?"

"We have found Falk's body."

Wallander realised as he was saying this that he had never told her about it being missing in the first place. He was so tired that it had slipped his mind. So he told her. She listened without interrupting him.

"Do you really expect me to believe all this?" she said.

"It sounds strange, I know, but every word is true."

"Who would do something like that? And why?"

"That's what we're trying to find out."

"And you found the body where it was found the first time?"

"Yes."

"Oh my God!"

He heard her breathing hard.

"But how could it have ended up there?"

"We don't know that yet, but I'm calling because I'm hoping you'll be able to help me with something else."

"Are you planning to come over?"

"The phone is fine."

"Don't you ever sleep, by the way?"

"Things get a little hectic at times. Now, the question I have to ask you will seem a little odd."

"That's no surprise. I think everything about you is a little odd, if you don't mind my being completely honest while we're talking like this in the middle of the night."

Her comment threw him. "I don't understand."

She laughed. "Don't take it to heart. I didn't mean it so seriously. It's just that I find it funny when people who are obviously thirsty decline a drink, and people who are dying of hunger won't accept any food. That's all."

"I wasn't thirsty or hungry. If you're referring to me, that is."

"Who do you think?"

Wallander wondered why he couldn't tell her the truth. What was he afraid of? He didn't think she believed him.

"Have I offended you?"

"Not at all," he said. "Can I ask you my question?"

"Of course."

"Could you tell me how Falk used a computer keyboard?"

"That was your question?"

"Yes."

"He used a keyboard the way anyone would."

"But people often type in different ways. The stereotype of a policeman, for example, is someone pecking away at an old typewriter with two index fingers."

"I see what you're getting at."

"Did he use all his fingers when he was typing?"

"I don't think many people do."

"So he used a couple of fingers?"

"Yes."

Wallander held his breath. He was about to find out if his hunch had been correct.

"Which fingers did he use?"

"I have to think about it. To make sure I'm right."

Wallander waited with excitement. She was fully awake now and he knew she was trying her best to help him.

"I'd like to call you back," she said. "There's something I'm not sure about. It'll be easier if I sit down at the computer. That will jog my memory."

Wallander gave her his home phone number. Then he waited at the kitchen table. His head ached. Tomorrow I have to try to get an early night, he thought. Whatever happens. He wondered how Nyberg was doing. If he was sleeping or tossing restlessly.

Ten minutes later the phone rang. He wondered nervously if it could be another journalist but decided it was too early for that. He picked up the receiver. She launched directly into what she had to say.

"It was the second finger on the right hand and the fourth finger on the left hand."

Wallander felt a stir of excitement. "Are you positive?"

"Yes. It's a pretty unusual way of typing, but that's what he did."

"Good," Wallander said. "That confirms something for us."

"You will understand that you've made me very curious."

Wallander considered telling her about the missing fingers, but decided to hold off.

"Unfortunately I can't tell you more at this point. Perhaps at a later date. Don't forget to fax me the list of clients tomorrow. Good night, and thank you."

"Good night."

Wallander got up and walked to the window. The temperature had risen to about 7°C. The wind was still strong and there was a light rain. It was 2.56 a.m. Wallander went back to bed, but the missing fingers danced in front of his eyes for a long time before he managed to sleep.

The man in the shadows in Runnerströms Torg was counting his breaths. He had learned to do this as a child. Breathing and patience were connected. A person had to know when it was best to wait. Listening to his own breathing was also a way to keep his anxiety in check. There had been too many unanticipated happenings. It wasn't possible to have total control over a situation, he knew, but Tynnes Falk's death had been a huge blow. They were busy reorganising and control would soon be established, which was just as well since time was running out. If there was no more interference, they would be able to stay on track with their original schedule.

He thought about the man who lived far away in tropical darkness. He held everything in his hand. A man he had never met, yet one he both feared and respected. There could be no mistakes. Mistakes would not be tolerated. But there were no grounds for his anxiety. Who would be able to break into the computer that functioned at the heart of the operation? It was simply a failure of confidence. If there was any mistake so far it was that he had not managed to kill the policeman in Falk's flat. But even so they were safe. The policeman probably didn't know anything.

Falk himself had often said: nothing and no-one is ever

completely safe. And he had been right. Now he was dead. No-one could ever be totally safe.

They had to take care. The man who now stood alone at the helm had told him to hold off and see what happened next. If the policeman was attacked a second time it would only attract unnecessary attention.

He had kept watch outside the building on Apelbergsgatan, and when the policeman made his way to Runnerströms Torg he had followed him. He had been expecting this, that they would find the secret office. A little later another policeman had arrived, carrying bags. The first policeman had then left the flat only to return about an hour later. Then they had both left Falk's office before midnight.

He had continued to wait, all the while counting his breaths. Now it was 3 a.m. and the square was deserted. He was cold. He decided it was very unlikely that anyone would come at this time. Finally, he slid out of the shadows and walked across the street. He unlocked the front door and ran soundlessly up the stairs. He had his gloves on when he unlocked the door to the flat. He walked in, turned on his flashlight and looked around. They had found the door to the inner room, but he had expected that. Without really knowing why, he had developed a kind of respect for the policeman he had tried to kill. His reflexes had been very quick, despite the fact that he was no longer a young man. He must have learned this early in life. It was always a mistake to underestimate an opponent.

He trained the flashlight on the computer and started it up. The monitor came on and after a while he was able to search out the file that showed him when the computer was last booted up. Six days ago. The policemen had not touched it.

It was too soon to feel safe, however. It might simply be a question of time. They could be planning to use a specialist and that caused him a twinge of anxiety, but the bottom line was that no matter who they used they would not be able to break the codes. Not in a thousand years. Someone with an extreme and heightened intuition might have some luck, but how likely was it when they didn't know what they were looking for? They couldn't imagine what this computer was set up to do, not in their wildest dreams.

He left the flat as silently as he had come and melted back into the night.

When Wallander woke the next morning, he felt as if he had overslept. But when he looked at the clock it was only 6.05 a.m. He had slept for 3 hours. He fell back against the pillows. His head was pounding from lack of sleep. I need 10 more minutes, he thought. Make that 7. I can't get up right now. But he forced himself up and walked unsteadily to the bathroom. His eyes were bloodshot. He stepped into the warm spray of the shower and leaned against the wall like a horse. Slowly he came back to life.

At 6.55 a.m., he was in the station car park. It was still raining. Hansson was unusually early. He was in the reception area flipping through a newspaper. He was also wearing a suit and tie. His normal outfit consisted of wrinkled corduroy trousers and shirts that hadn't been ironed.

"Is it your birthday?" Wallander said.

Hansson shook his head. "I happened to see myself in the mirror the other day. Not a pretty picture. I thought I should try to make more of an effort. Anyway, it's Saturday. We'll see how long it lasts."

They walked to the canteen together and had the obligatory cup of coffee. Wallander told him what had happened during the night.

"That's crazy," Hansson said. "What kind of a sicko dumps a corpse on the street?"

"That's what we're paid to find out," Wallander said. "By the way, you're in charge of looking out for dogs tonight."

"What does that mean?"

"It's Martinsson's idea. He says someone walking a dog might have noticed something unusual along Missunnavägen last night. We thought you could be posted there to stop them as they walk by."

"Why me?"

"You like dogs, don't you?"

"I have plans tonight. It's Saturday, remember?"

"You'll be able to do both. It's fine if you get there shortly before 11 p.m."

Hansson nodded. Wallander had never liked him much, but he had to commend him for his willingness to put in the time when needed.

"I'll see you at 8 a.m. in the conference room," Wallander said. "We need to review and discuss the developments."

"It doesn't seem as if we do anything else. And where does it get us?"

Wallander sat at his desk, looked over his notes and let himself sink deeply into thought. Nothing in all of this makes any sense, he thought. I can't find a beginning or an end. I have no idea why these people have died. But there has to be a motive in here somewhere.

He got up and walked to the window, coffee cup in hand.

What would Rydberg do? he thought. Would he have had

any advice in this situation? Or would he feel as lost as I do?

Rydberg remained silent.

It was 7.30 a.m. Wallander sat down again. He had to prepare for their meeting. After all, he was the one who had to lead the work. He backtracked to try to gain a new perspective. Which events lay at the core of all this? What were the connections? It was charting a solar system where the planets circled not a sun, but a black hole.

There's a main figure in all this, he thought. There's always a protagonist. Not everyone is of equal importance. Not all the people who have died are major players. But who is who, and how am I supposed to tell them apart? What story is being enacted?

He was back where he started. The only thing he felt sure of was that the taxi driver's murder was neither a likely centre nor a catalyst for the events that followed.

That left Falk. There had to be a connection between him and Hökberg, indicated by the relay and the power substation blueprint. That's what they had to concentrate on. The connection was so far inexplicable, but it was there. He pushed away his notes, and sat there for a few more minutes. I can't see anything in what I've written, he thought. He heard Höglund laugh in the corridor. That didn't happen every day. He gathered up his papers and headed to the conference room.

They made a thorough review of the case material. It took almost 3 hours. The tired and despondent mood in the room slowly lifted.

Nyberg had appeared at 8.30 a.m. He sat at the far end of the table without saying a word. Wallander looked at him, but Nyberg shook his head. He had nothing crucial to tell them.

"Could someone be laying out false tracks deliberately?" Höglund wondered while they were taking a break to stretch their legs. "Maybe this is all very simple when it comes down to it. Maybe all we need is a motive."

"And what would that be?" Martinsson said. "A person who steals from a taxi driver has a very different motive from someone who burns a young woman to death, and causes blackouts in much of Skåne. And bear in mind that we don't know for sure whether Falk was murdered. My inclination is still to chalk it up to a natural death, or just possibly to an accident."

"It would be easier if he was murdered," Wallander said. "Then we could be sure that we were dealing with a related series of crimes."

They closed the windows and sat back down at the table.

"It seems to me that the most serious event so far is that someone tried to shoot you," Höglund said. "It's very rare that a burglar is ready to shoot dead someone who happens to cross his path."

"I don't know that I would call it more serious than anything else here," Wallander said. "But it does say something about the degree of ruthlessness in the people behind all this. Whatever it is they're trying to do."

They continued analysing the various crimes, turning each in as many directions as possible. Wallander didn't say much, but he listened attentively to all the others. During difficult investigations it had sometimes happened that a casual phrase or even a rephrasing of something had caused the case to break open. They were looking for openings now, and a centre.

During the final hour each person went through the tasks they had completed and read out what was still to be done. Shortly before 11 a.m. Wallander decided that they could go no further.

"This will take time," he said. "It is also possible that we're going to need help. I'll talk to Holgersson. I don't think there's any use staying here any longer, though that doesn't mean we can take the weekend off. We need to keep going."

Hansson left to speak to a prosecutor who had demanded to be kept up to date. Martinsson went to his office to call home. Wallander had asked him earlier to accompany him to the office on Runnerströms Torg when the meeting was over. Nyberg sat at the table for a while longer pulling at his thin wisps of hair. Then he got up and left without saying a word. Höglund was the only one left. Wallander realised she wanted to talk to him about something, so he closed the door.

"I've been thinking," she said. "That man who shot at you."

"Yes?"

"He saw you. And he didn't hesitate to shoot, not for a second."

"I'd rather not think too much about that."

"But maybe you should."

Wallander looked at her closely. "What are you getting at?"

"I just think that you should be extra careful. He may have been taken by surprise, but I don't believe we can rule out that he thinks you know something. And for that reason he may try again."

It frightened him that he hadn't considered this himself.

"I don't want to scare you," she said. "But I had to say it."

"I'll think about it. The question is: what could he think I know?"

"Maybe he's right and you do know something that's dangerous to him. But you're just not aware of what you know."

Another thought came to Wallander. "Maybe we should post some officers at Apelsbergsgatan and Runnerströms Torg. No patrol cars, nothing too noticeable. Just in case."

She agreed and left to arrange it. Wallander was left with his fear. He thought about Linda. Then he shook out his arms and shoulders and walked out to the reception area to wait for Martinsson.

They arrived at the flat at Runnerströms Torg shortly before noon. Although Martinsson was mainly interested in the computer, Wallander wanted to show him Falk's secret room and altar first.

"Too much time in cyberspace makes people a little strange," Martinsson said. "This whole flat gives me the creeps."

Wallander was thinking about Martinsson's choice of words. Cyberspace. C-space. The same word Falk had written in his diary.

"C-space is quiet." No messages from his friends.

What message was he waiting for? Wallander thought. I'd give an awful lot to know that right now.

Martinsson took off his coat and sat at the computer. Wallander stood behind him, looking over his shoulder.

"There are some pretty advanced programs here," Martinsson said once the computer had been switched on. "And it has an extremely fast processor. Some of this may be more than I can handle."

"I'd still like you to do what you can. If you get stuck, we'll call in the National Police Technology Division and get some of their computer whizzes on it."

Martinsson didn't answer. He was absorbed in his task, staring straight ahead at the screen. Then he got up and walked around to look at the computer from the back. As Wallander watched him he returned to the chair. The screen had come alive, with a number of symbols flitting by. Then the screen settled into an image of the night sky.

Cyberspace. At least Falk is consistent, Wallander thought.

"The computer seems automatically to connect with a server when you turn it on," Martinsson said. "Do you want me to talk you through what I'm doing?"

"I don't think I'd be able to follow you."

Wallander put on his glasses and leaned closer to the screen as Martinsson tried to open one of the files on the hard drive. After clicking on the file, Martinsson frowned.

"What happened?" Wallander asked.

Martinsson pointed to a corner of the screen where a cursor was blinking.

"I'm not 100 per cent sure about this," he said slowly. "But I think someone was just notified that we tried to open this file."

"How could that happen?"

"Well, this computer is connected to others."

"And someone at the other end of one of those could now have seen what we're trying to do?"

"Yes, something like that."

"Where is this person?"

"He could be anywhere," Martinsson said. "A ranch off the beaten track in California. An island off the coast of Australia. Or in another flat in this building."

Wallander shook his head in bafflement.

"When you're hooked up to the Internet you're in the middle of the world wherever you are," he quoted.

Martinsson had started working on the file again. After about 10 minutes he pushed back his chair.

"Everything's locked," he said. "There are complicated codes and barriers to everything. There's no way in."

"Is it time to give up?"

Martinsson smiled. "Not just yet," he said. He resumed his tapping on the keyboard, but stopped almost at once.

"What is it?"

Martinsson looked at the screen with surprise. "I'm not sure, but I think someone else used this computer only a few hours ago."

"Can you find out for sure?"

"I think so."

After about 10 minutes he got up. "I was right," he said. "Someone was using this computer yesterday. Or rather, last night."

"That means someone other than Falk has access to this material."

"And that someone didn't have to break into the flat to get to it," Martinsson said. "How does that change the picture?"

"We don't know yet," Wallander said. "It's too early."

Martinsson sat back down at the computer and kept working.

•

They took a break at 4.30 p.m. Martinsson invited Wallander to come home with him and have supper. They were back at the flat at 6.30. Wallander realised his presence was superfluous, but he didn't want to abandon Martinsson.

Martinsson kept working until 10 p.m. and then he finally gave up.

CHAPTER NINETEEN

Hansson had parked outside the Tax Authority building. Wallander saw him from a distance, leaning against a street light reading the newspaper. You can tell from here he's a policeman, Wallander thought. No-one can fail to see he's on the job, though it's not clear what he's up to. But he's not warmly enough dressed. Apart from the golden rule of making it through the day alive, there's nothing more important in the policeman's rule book than dressing warmly when working outside.

Hansson was absorbed in his newspaper. He didn't notice Wallander until he was right beside him. He was reading the racing section.

"I didn't hear you," Hansson said. "I wonder if my hearing is going."

"How are the horses today?"

"I suppose I'm living in cloud cuckoo land, like most people. I think that one day I'll sit there with all the right numbers. But it's funny, the horses don't run the way they're supposed to. They never do."

"And the dogs?"

"I only just got here. I haven't seen anyone yet."

Wallander looked around. "When I first came to Ystad, this part of town was an empty field," he said. "None of this was here."

They started along the street. Wallander told him about Martinsson's valiant efforts to break the code of

Falk's computer. They got to the cash machine and stopped.

"It's funny how quickly you get used to things," Hansson said. "I can hardly remember life before these machines. Not that I have a clue how they actually work. Sometimes I imagine a little man sitting inside, someone who counts out all the notes and sends it through to you."

Wallander thought again about what Erik Hökberg had said, about how vulnerable society had become. The black-out a few days ago had proved him right.

They walked back to Hansson's car. Still they saw no-one out walking their dogs.

"I'm off now. How was the dinner?"

"I never went. What's the point of eating if you can't have a glass or two?"

Wallander was about to leave when Hansson mentioned having had a conversation earlier in the day with the prosecutor.

"Did Viktorsson have anything to say?"

"Not really."

"He must have said *something*."

"He said he couldn't see any reason to narrow the investigation at this point. The case should still be attacked on all fronts. Without fixed ideas."

"Policemen never work without fixed ideas," Wallander said. "He should know that by now."

"Well, that was what he said."

"Nothing else?"

"Not really."

Wallander had the feeling that he was holding something back. He waited, but Hansson didn't add anything.

"I think 12.30 a.m. should do it," Wallander told him. "I'll see you in the morning."

"I should have worn warmer clothes. It's a chilly night."

"Soon enough it'll be winter," Wallander said.

He walked back into town. He was convinced that Hansson hadn't told him everything. By the time he got to Runnerströms Torg he realised it had to mean that Viktorsson had made some comment about him, about the Persson girl and the internal investigation. He was irritated that Hansson hadn't told him what he had said, but it didn't surprise him. Hansson made a career of trying to be everyone's friend. Wallander suddenly felt how tired he was. Or perhaps he was simply demoralised.

He looked around. The undercover police car was still parked in its spot. Apart from that the street was deserted. He unlocked his car and got in. Just as he was about to start the engine his mobile phone rang. He fished it out of his pocket. It was Martinsson.

"Where are you?" Wallander said.

"I went home."

"Why? Couldn't you get hold of Molin?"

"Modin. Robert Modin. No, I began to wonder if it was such a good idea after all."

"Why?"

"You know how it is, regulations. We can't simply bring in whoever we want on a case from outside the force. And remember, Modin has been convicted of a crime – even if his sentence was only for a month or so."

Martinsson was getting cold feet. That had happened before. At times it had even led to conflict between them. Sometimes Wallander thought Martinsson was too careful. He never used the word "pusillanimous", but that was what he meant.

"Strictly speaking we should first get approval from the

prosecutor," Martinsson said. "At the very least we should talk to Lisa."

"I'll take full responsibility," Wallander said.

"Even so."

Martinsson had clearly made up his mind.

"Give me Modin's address," Wallander said. "That way you'll be absolved of all responsibility."

"You don't think we should wait?"

"No. Time is running out and I want to know what's in that computer."

"What you really need to do is sleep, you know. Have you looked in the mirror recently?"

"Yes, I know," Wallander said. "Now give me the address."

He found a pen in the glove compartment which was stuffed full of papers and folded-up paper plates from burger bars. Wallander wrote down what Martinsson said on the back of a petrol receipt.

"It's almost midnight," Martinsson said.

"I know," Wallander said. "See you tomorrow."

He hung up and put his phone on the passenger seat. But before he started the engine he thought about what Martinsson had said. He was right about one thing. They needed to sleep. What was the point of going out to Löderup in the middle of the night? Modin was probably sleeping. I'll let it go until tomorrow, he thought.

He started the engine and drove in the direction of Löderup. He drove fast to try to wake himself up. He wasn't even acting on his own decisions any more.

He didn't need to consult the scrap of paper with the address. He knew exactly where it was even as he had been writing it down. It was in an area only a few kilometres from where his father's house had been. Wallander had the feeling, too, that he had met Modin's father. He wound down the window and let the cold air wash over his face. He was annoyed with both Hansson and Martinsson. They're bending to pressure, he thought. Kowtowing to Chief Holgersson.

He turned off the main road at 12.15 a.m. There was a good chance that he was going to arrive at a house where everyone was sleeping. But his anger had chased the tiredness away. He wanted to see Robert Modin, and he wanted to take him to Runnerströms Torg.

He drove up to the house, which was in deep country. There was a large garden and a paddock to one side with a lone horse. The house was whitewashed. There was a jeep and a smaller car parked in front. There were still lights on in several of the downstairs windows.

Wallander turned off his engine and got out. The porch light came on and a man walked out of the house. Wallander had been right. They had met before somewhere. He walked over and greeted the man. He was around sixty, thin and slightly bowed. His hands didn't feel like a farmer's.

"I recognise you," Modin said. "Your father lived not too far from here."

"I know we've met before," Wallander said. "But I can't remember the context."

"Your father was out walking in one of the fields around here," Modin said. "He was carrying a suitcase."

Wallander remembered that time. His father had had one of his episodes of confusion and had decided to go to Italy. He packed his suitcase and started walking. Modin had seen him tramping through the mud and had called the police.

"I haven't seen you since he passed away," Modin said. "The house is sold of course."

"Gertrud moved to be close to her sister in Svarte. I don't even know who ended up buying the place."

"It's someone from up north who claims to be a businessman," Modin said. "I suspect he's actually a booze smuggler."

Wallander had an image of his father's studio converted into a still.

"I suppose you've come on account of Robert," Modin said. "I thought he had paid for his sins?"

"I'm sure he has," Wallander said. "Though you're right that I'm here to see him."

"What's he done now?"

Wallander heard the dread in the father's voice.

"Nothing, nothing. In fact, it seems he may be able to help us with something."

Modin looked surprised, but also relieved. He nodded at the door and Wallander followed him inside.

"The wife's sleeping," Modin said. "She wears earplugs."

Wallander remembered that Modin was a surveyor. He didn't know how he knew this.

"Is Robert here?"

"He's at a party with some friends. But he has his phone with him."

Modin showed him into the living room.

Wallander was startled to see one of his father's paintings hanging above the sofa. It was the landscape motif without the woodgrouse.

"He gave it to me," Modin said. "Whenever it snowed heavily I would go over and shovel his driveway for him. Sometimes I stayed and we talked. He was an unusual man, in his own way."

"That's an understatement," Wallander said.

"I liked him. There aren't too many of his kind any more."

"He wasn't always easy to deal with," Wallander said. "But I miss him. And it's true, old men like him are getting more rare. One day there won't be any left."

"Who is easy to deal with anyway?" Modin said. "Are you? I don't think I could say that about myself. Just ask my wife."

Wallander sat down on the sofa. Modin was cleaning out his pipe.

"Robert is a good boy," he said. "I thought he was treated harshly, even if it was only a month. It was all just a game to him."

"I don't know the whole story," Wallander said, "other than that he broke into the Pentagon's computer network."

"He's very good with computers," Modin said. "He bought his first one when he was 9 years old, with money he had saved up picking strawberries. Then he was engulfed by it. But as long as he continued to do all right in school, it was fine with me. Of course my wife was against it from the start, and now she feels justified by what happened."

Wallander had the feeling that Modin was a somewhat lonely person, but however much he would have liked to sit and chat with him, Wallander had to move on. There was no time to waste.

"I need to get hold of Robert as soon as possible," he said. "His computer expertise could be of help to us with a case."

Modin puffed on his pipe. "Can I ask in what way?"

"I can only tell you that it involves a complicated computer system."

Modin nodded and got up. "I won't ask any more questions."

He walked out into the hall. Wallander heard him speaking on the phone. He twisted around on the sofa to look at his father's painting.

Modin came back. "He's on his way," he said. "They were in Skillinge, so it'll be a little while."

"What did you tell him?"

"That he wasn't to worry, but that the police needed his help."

Modin sat down again. His pipe had gone out.

"It must be important since you're here in the middle of the night."

"Some things can't wait."

Modin understood that Wallander didn't want to say anything more about it.

"Can I get you anything?"

"Some coffee would be nice."

"In the middle of the night?"

"I'm planning to put in a couple more hours of work. But I'm fine without it."

"Of course you should have some coffee," Modin said.

They were sitting in the kitchen when a car drew up outside the house. The front door opened and Robert Modin came in. Wallander thought he looked 13 years old. He had short hair, round glasses and a slight build. He was probably going to look more and more like his father as he got older. He was wearing jeans, a dress shirt and a leather jacket. Wallander got up and shook his hand.

"I'm sorry I bothered you in the middle of a party."

"We were about to leave anyway and a friend dropped me home."

"I'll leave you two to talk," his father said, and left.

"Are you tired?" Wallander asked.

"Not particularly."

"Good. There's something I want you to take a look at. I'll explain as we go."

The boy was on his guard. Wallander attempted a smile.

"Don't worry."

"I'll have to change my glasses."

He went upstairs to his room. Wallander walked into the living room and thanked Modin for the coffee.

"I'll make sure he gets home safely. But I have to take him with me to Ystad right now."

Modin looked worried again. "Are you sure he's not involved with anything?"

"I promise. It's exactly as I told you – there's something I want him to look at."

The boy came back and they left the house. It was 1.20 a.m. The boy got in on the passenger side and moved Wallander's phone.

"Someone called you," Robert said.

Wallander checked his voice mail. It was Hansson. I should have brought the phone in with me, Wallander thought.

He dialled Hansson's number. It took a while before anyone answered.

"Were you sleeping?"

"Of course I was sleeping. What do you think? It's 1.30 a.m. I was there until 12.30. At that point I was so tired I thought I was going to pass out."

"You tried to call."

"I think actually we got something."

Wallander sat up, alert.

"Someone saw something?"

"There was a woman with an Alsatian. She says she saw Falk the night he died."

"Good. Did she see anything else?"

"Very observant woman. Her name is Alma Högström, she's a retired dentist. She said she often used to see Falk in the evenings. He took regular walks, too, apparently."

"What about the night the body was put back?"

"She said she thought she saw a van that night. Around 11.30 p.m. It was in front of the cash machine. She noticed because it wasn't in the car park."

"Did she see the driver?"

"She said she thought she saw a man."

"Thought?"

"She wasn't sure."

"Could she identify the van?"

"I've asked her to come to the station tomorrow."

"Good," Wallander said. "This may give us something."

"Where are you? At home?"

"Not exactly," Wallander said. "I'll see you tomorrow."

It was 2 a.m. by the time Wallander pulled up outside the building in Runnerströms Torg. Wallander looked around. If anything dangerous were to happen, Modin would also be at risk. But there was no-one around. The rain had stopped.

Wallander had tried to explain the situation on the way from Löderup. He simply wanted Modin to access the information on Falk's computer.

"I know you're very good at this sort of thing," Wallander said. "I don't care about your business with the Pentagon. What I care about is what you know about computers."

"I should never have been caught," Robert said suddenly in the dark. "It was my own fault."

"What do you mean?"

"I was sloppy about cleaning up after myself."

"Cleaning up?"

"If you break into a secured area you always leave a trace. It's like cutting a fence. When you leave you have to try to fix it so that no-one can see you were there. But I didn't do that well enough. That's why I was caught."

"So there were people in the Pentagon who could see that someone in Löderup had paid them a visit?"

"They couldn't see who I was or know my name. But they knew it was my computer."

They went into the building and up the stairs. Wallander realised he was tense in anticipation. Before unlocking the door to the flat he listened for noise. Modin watched him closely, but said nothing.

Once inside, Wallander closed the curtains, turned on the light and pointed to the computer. He offered Modin the chair. He sat down and turned on the machine without hesitation. The usual succession of numbers and symbols started flickering across the screen. Wallander hung back. Modin's fingers were hovering above the keyboard as if he were about to launch into a recital. He kept his face very close to the screen, as if he were searching for something Wallander couldn't see. Then he started tapping on the keyboard.

He kept at it for about a minute, then he switched the computer off without warning and turned to face Wallander.

"I've never seen anything like this," he said simply. "I'm not going to be able to get through it."

Wallander sensed the disappointment, both in himself and in the boy. "Are you absolutely sure?"

The boy shook his head. "At the very least I need to sleep first," he said. "And I'll need time. Lots of it, and without being rushed."

Wallander realised the futility of bringing him out here in the middle of the night. Martinsson had been right. He grudgingly conceded that it had been Martinsson's hesitation that had spurred him on.

"Do you have anything else planned for tomorrow?"

"I can be here all day."

Wallander turned off the light and locked the door behind him. Then he followed the boy out to the patrol car and asked the officer to drive him home. Someone would be by to pick him up around noon, when he had had a chance to sleep.

Wallander drove back to Mariagatan. It was almost 3 a.m. by the time he crawled into bed. He fell asleep quickly, after deciding he would not go into the office before 11 a.m. the next day.

The woman had been to the police station on Friday, shortly before 1 p.m. She had asked for a map of Ystad and the receptionist had told her to try either the local tourist information office or the bookshop. The woman had thanked her politely, then asked to use the toilet. The receptionist showed her the way. The woman had locked the door and opened the window. Then she closed it again, but only after covering the catches with tape. The cleaner on Friday evening noticed nothing.

Early on Monday, around 4 a.m., the shadow of a man ascended the wall of the station and disappeared through the toilet window. The corridors were deserted. Only the faint sound of a radio came from the control room. The man had a plan of the building obtained by breaking into a computer at an architectural firm. He knew exactly where to go.

He gently opened the door to Wallander's office. A coat with a large yellow spot on the right lapel was hanging on the back of the door.

The man walked over to the desk. He looked at the computer for a moment before flicking it on. What he was about to do would take around 20 minutes, but he wasn't worried that anyone would come in during that time. It was child's play to go into Wallander's files and examine what was there. When he had finished, he switched off the computer and then the light and opened the door. The corridor was empty. He left the same way he had come.

CHAPTER TWENTY

Sunday morning, October 12, Wallander woke at 9 a.m. Even though he had only slept six hours he felt fully rested. Before going into the station he decided to take a walk. The rain from the night before was gone. It was a fine and clear autumn day. It was almost 9°C.

He walked through the front doors of the police station at 10.15 a.m. Before going to his office he walked past the control room and asked which of his colleagues had come in.

"Martinsson is here. Hansson had to go and pick someone up. Höglund hasn't been in yet."

"I'm here." Wallander heard her voice behind his back. "Did I miss anything?"

"No," Wallander said. "But why don't you come with me."

"I'll just take my coat off."

Wallander told the officer on duty he needed a patrol car to be sent out around noon to pick up Robert Modin. He gave the directions.

"Make sure it's an unmarked car," he added. "That's very important."

A few minutes later Höglund came into his office. She looked a little less tired today. He thought about asking her how things were going at home. But then as usual he wondered if it was the right moment. Instead he told her about the potential eyewitness that Hansson had found and was bringing in as they spoke. He also told her about

Robert Modin, who would perhaps be able to help them access the information in Falk's computer.

"I remember him," she said, when Wallander had finished. "Do you think he'll find something important in that computer?"

"I don't think anything. But we have to know what Falk was hatching. It seems to me that more and more people nowadays are really just electronic personalities."

He went on to talk about the woman Hansson was bringing down to the station.

"She will be the first person we have who has actually seen anything," Höglund said. She was leaning against the door frame. It was a newly acquired habit. She used to come right in and sit in his visitor's chair. "I did some thinking last night. I was watching TV, but I couldn't concentrate. The children had gone to bed."

"Your husband?"

"My ex-husband. He's in Yemen right now, I think. Anyway, I turned off the TV and sat in the kitchen with a glass of water. I tried to picture everything that had happened, as simply as possible, stripped of unnecessary details."

"That's an impossible task," Wallander said. "I mean the part about the details. You can't know what's unnecessary at this point."

"You're the one who's taught me to weigh facts against each other and discard what is less important."

"What was your conclusion?"

"Certain things seem firmly established, for example that there is a connection between Falk and Hökberg. The electrical relay gives us no choice in that department. But there's something about the timing of events that points to a possibility we haven't yet explored."

"And what would that be?"

"That Falk and Hökberg may not have had anything directly to do with each other."

Wallander saw where she was going. It might be important. "You mean that they are only indirectly connected? By way of someone else?"

"The reason Hökberg died may lie somewhere entirely removed from them both, since Falk was dead himself when Hökberg was burned to death. But the person who killed her could later have moved Falk's body."

"That still doesn't tell us what we're looking for," Wallander said. "There's no common denominator."

"Maybe we have to start again at the beginning," Höglund said thoughtfully. "With Lundberg, the taxi driver."

"Do we have anything on him?"

"His name doesn't appear in any register we have. I've spoken to a few of his colleagues and his widow and no-one had anything bad to say about him. He drove his taxi all day and spent his time off with his family. A normal, peaceful Swedish existence that came to an unexpectedly brutal end. What struck me last night while I was sitting in the kitchen was that his reputation seemed a bit *too* flawless. There isn't a smear anywhere. If you have nothing against it, I'd like to keep digging in his life for a bit."

"That sounds good. Did he have any children?"

"Two boys. One lives in Malmö, the other lives here in town. I was going to try to get hold of them today."

"Go ahead. It's crucial to determine once and for all whether there was anything to Lundberg's murder other than a simple robbery."

"Are we meeting today?"

"I'll let you know if we do."

Wallander thought about what she had said, then went out to the canteen and helped himself to coffee. He picked up a copy of the paper lying on a table. Once he got back to his office he started leafing through it, but stopped when something caught his eye. An ad for a dating agency, with the unoriginal name of "Computerdate". Wallander read the ad thoroughly. He switched on his computer and quickly sketched an application. He knew that if he didn't do it now he never would. No-one would have to know. He could be anonymous. He tried to write something as simple and direct as possible: *Policeman, divorced, one child, seeking companionship. Not marriage, but love.* He chose the name "Labrador" rather than "Old Dog". He printed it out and saved a copy on his hard drive. He put it in an envelope, wrote the address and stamped it. Then he put it in his pocket. He realised that he actually felt excited. Probably he would not get any replies, or if he did they would be ones he would immediately discard. But the excitement was there. He could not deny it.

Then Hansson appeared in the doorway.

"She's here," she said. "Alma Högström, our witness."

Wallander got up and followed him to one of the small conference rooms. An Alsatian was lying on the floor next to the woman. It regarded them suspiciously. Wallander greeted her, sensing that she had dressed up for her visit to the station.

"Your willingness to help the police in this matter is very much appreciated," he said. "Especially on a Sunday."

He marvelled at the stilted phrases. How could he sound so dry and impersonal after all these years?

"If the police need any information one may have, surely it is one's duty to try to be of assistance."

She's worse than I am, he thought. It's like watching a bad film from the 1930s.

Slowly they went through what she thought she had seen. Wallander let Hansson do the questioning while he wrote down her answers.

She had observed a dark van at 11.30 p.m. She was sure of the time because she had just consulted her watch, she said.

"It's an old habit. It's ingrained in me by now. I always had one client in the chair and a whole waiting room full of others. Time always went too fast."

Hansson tried to get her to pinpoint the kind of van it had been. He had brought with him a folder he had assembled a few years ago. It had pictures of different models of cars, as well as a colour chart. Naturally there were all kinds of computer programs for this now, but Hansson, like Wallander, had trouble adjusting his work habits.

They concluded it had possibly been a Mercedes. Either navy blue or black. She hadn't noticed the number plate, nor had she seen whether there was anyone in the van or not. But she had seen a shadowy figure behind the van.

"Well, I wasn't the one who saw him," she explained. "It was Steadfast, my dog. He pricked up his ears and strained in that direction."

"I know it may be hard to describe what you saw," Hansson said. "But I'd like you to try. Was it a man or a woman?"

She thought for a long time before answering. "I think it was a man," she said finally.

"What happened after that?"

"I took my usual walk."

Hansson spread a map on the table. She told him her route.

"That means you passed by the cash machine on your way back. Was the van gone then?"

"Yes."

"What time would that have been?"

"About 12.10 a.m."

"And how do you know that?"

"I came home at 12.25 a.m. It takes me 15 minutes to walk home from that spot."

She showed him on the map where she lived. Wallander and Hansson agreed with her. It would take about that long.

"But you didn't see anything in that area when you walked home?" Hansson said. "And your dog didn't react in any way?"

"No."

"Isn't that surprising?" Hansson said to Wallander.

"The body must have been stored at a low temperature," Wallander said. "It wouldn't have had a smell. We can ask Nyberg, or one of the dog units."

"I'm very glad I didn't see anything," Alma Högström said firmly. "It's terrible even to imagine it. People delivering dead bodies in the middle of the night."

"Did you know that this man you normally saw during your evening walks was called Falk?" Wallander said.

Her answer came as a surprise. "He was my patient once upon a time. He had good teeth. I only saw him a couple of times, but I have a good memory for faces and names."

"He often took walks at night?" Hansson said.

"I used to meet him several times a week. He was always alone. I said hello sometimes, but he didn't seem to want to be disturbed."

Hansson looked over at Wallander who nodded.

"We may be in touch if we need anything else," he said.

"If you think of anything else in the meantime we would of course like to hear from you."

Hansson followed her out. Wallander remained where he was. He thought about what she had told them. Nothing had emerged that helped them make more sense out of this case.

Hansson came back and picked up his folders. "A black or navy blue Mercedes van," he said. "We should look into cars that have been stolen recently."

Wallander nodded. "And talk to one of the dog units about the question of smell. At least we have a fixed time. That counts for a lot at this stage."

Wallander returned to his office. It was 11.45 a.m. He called Martinsson and told him what had happened during the night. Martinsson listened without saying a word. It irritated Wallander but he managed to control himself. He told Martinsson that a patrol car was going to collect Modin. Wallander said he would see him in reception and give him the keys to the flat.

"Maybe I'll learn something," Martinsson said when he saw him. "Watching a real master climb the firewalls."

"I assure you the responsibility is still all mine," Wallander said. "But I don't want him left alone."

Martinsson noticed Wallander's gentle irony, and immediately became defensive.

"We can't all be like you," he said. "Some of us actually take police regulations seriously."

"I know," Wallander said patiently. "And you're right of course. But I'm still not going to the prosecutor or Lisa for permission on this."

Martinsson disappeared out through the front doors.

Wallander felt hungry. He walked into town and had lunch at István's pizzeria. István was very busy. They never had a chance to talk about Fu Cheng and his fake credit card. On the way back to the station Wallander posted his letter to the dating agency. He remained convinced that he would not get a single reply.

The phone was ringing as he reached his office. It was Nyberg. Wallander went back into the corridor. Nyberg's office was on the floor below. When Wallander got there, he saw lying, in plastic bags, on Nyberg's desk, the hammer and the knife that had been used in Lundberg's murder.

"As of today I've been a policeman for 40 years," Nyberg said grumpily when he came in. "I started on a Monday but of course my meaningless anniversary has to fall on a Sunday."

"If you're so sick of your job, you should just quit," Wallander said.

He was surprised that he lost his temper. He had never done such a thing with Nyberg. In fact, he always tried to be as tactful as possible around his irascible colleague. But Nyberg didn't seem to take offence. He looked at Wallander, curious.

"Well, well," he said. "I thought I was the only one around here with a temper."

"Forget it. I didn't mean it," Wallander mumbled.

That made Nyberg angry. "Of course you meant it. That's the whole point. I don't know why people have to be so afraid of showing a little temperament. And anyway, you're right. I'm just bitching."

"Maybe that's what we're all reduced to in the end," Wallander said.

Nyberg pulled the plastic bag with the knife impatiently towards him.

"The results of the fingerprinting have come back," he said. "There are two different sets on this knife."

Wallander leaned in attentively.

"Persson and Hökberg?"

"Exactly."

"So Persson may not be lying in this particular case?"

"It seems it's at least a possibility."

"That Hökberg is responsible for the murder, you mean?"

"I'm not implying anything. That's not my job. I'm just telling you the facts. It's a legitimate possibility, that's all."

"What about the hammer?"

"Only Hökberg's prints. No-one else's."

Wallander nodded. "That's good to know."

"We know more than that," Nyberg said, leafing through the papers strewn across his desk. "Sometimes the pathologists exceed even their own expectations. They have determined that the blows were inflicted in stages. First he was hit with the hammer, then with the knife."

"Definitely not the other way around?"

"No. And not at the same time."

"How on earth can they know that?"

"I can only tell you the approximate answer to that, and it's hard to explain."

"Does this mean Hökberg switched weapons in the course of her attack?"

"I believe so. Persson had the knife in her bag, but she gave it to Hökberg when asked."

"Like an operation," Wallander said with a shudder. "The surgeon asking for tools."

They thought about this for a moment. Nyberg broke the silence.

"There was one more thing. I've been thinking about that bag out at the power substation. It was lying in the wrong place."

Wallander waited for him to continue. Nyberg was an excellent and thorough forensic technician, but he could also sometimes demonstrate unexpected investigative skills.

"I went out there," he said, "and I took the bag with me. I tried throwing it to the spot by the fence where it was found, but I couldn't throw it that far."

"How so?"

"You remember what the place looks like. There are towers, poles, high-voltage lines and barbed wire everywhere. The bag always got stuck on something."

"That means someone must have carried it over there?"

"Maybe. But the question then is why?"

"Do you have an idea?"

"The obvious explanation would be that the bag was put there deliberately because someone wanted it to be found – but maybe they didn't want it to be found right away."

"Someone wanted the body to be identified, but not immediately?"

"Yes, that's what I was thinking. But then I discovered something else. The place where the bag was found is in the direct beam of one of the spotlights."

Wallander sensed where Nyberg was going, but said nothing.

"I'm simply wondering now if the bag was there because someone had been rifling through it, looking for something."

"And maybe found something?"

"That's what I think, but it's your job to work these things out."

Wallander got up. "Good work," he said. "You may have hit on something."

Wallander went back up the stairs and stopped at Höglund's office. She was bent over a stack of papers.

"I want you to contact Hökberg's mother," he said. "Find out what the girl usually had in her bag."

He told her about Nyberg's idea. He didn't bother to wait while she made the call. He felt restless and started back to his office. He wondered how many miles he had covered walking to and fro in these corridors all these years. He heard the phone in his office and hurried over. It was Martinsson.

"I think it's time for you to come down here," he said.

"Why?"

"Robert Modin is a proficient young man."

"What's happened?"

"Exactly what we were hoping for. We're in. The computer has opened its doors."

Wallander hung up. It's finally happened, he thought. It's taken some time, but we finally did it.

He took his coat and left the station.

It was 1.45 p.m. on Sunday, October 12.

PART 2

The Firewall

PART 2

The Firewall

[illegible]

... [illegible] was a white man [illegible] ...
[illegible] in modern countries [illegible] ...
given. If [illegible] been one of the poor, [illegible] would have
robbed people [illegible] self.

As sudden[illegible] it had stopped, the air-conditioning
started up [illegible]. That meant it wasn't the work of
bandits, it was [illegible]mply a technical glitch. The power
lines were [illegible] over from the Portug[illegible]ese colonial

CHAPTER TWENTY-ONE

Carter woke up at dawn because the air-conditioning unit suddenly stopped. He lay listening to the darkness, frozen between the sheets. There was the steady drone of cicadas and a dog barked in the distance. The power had gone out again. That happened every other night in Luanda. Savimbi's bandits were always looking for ways to cut the power to the city. In a few minutes the room would be stifling hot, but he didn't know if he had the energy to go down to the room past the kitchen and start up the generator. He didn't know what was worse: the insufferable heat or the throbbing of the generator.

He turned and looked at the time. It was 5.15 a.m. He heard one of the guards outside, snoring. That was probably José. As long as Roberto kept himself awake it didn't matter. He shifted his head and felt for the muzzle of his gun under the pillow. When it came down to it, beyond the guards and the fences, this was his real protection against the burglars hiding in the dark. He understood them, of course. He was a white man, he was wealthy. In a poor and downtrodden country like Angola, crime was a given. If he had been one of the poor, he would have robbed people himself.

As suddenly as it had stopped, the air conditioning started up again. That meant it wasn't the work of bandits, it was simply a technical glitch. The power lines were old, left over from the Portuguese colonial times. How many years ago that was, he could no longer remember.

Carter had trouble getting back to sleep. He thought about the fact that he was about to turn 60. In many ways it was a miracle that he had reached this age, given his unpredictable and dangerous way of life.

He pushed away the sheet and let the cool air touch his skin. He didn't like to wake up at dawn. He was most vulnerable during the hours before sunrise, left to the dark and his memories. He could get worked up over old wrongs that had been done to him. It was only when he focused on the revenge he was planning that he could calm himself. By then several hours might have passed. The sun would be up, the guards would have started talking and Celine would be unlocking the door to the kitchen to come in and make his breakfast.

He pulled the sheet back over his body. His nose started to itch and he knew he was about to sneeze. He hated to sneeze. He hated his allergies. They were a weakness he despised. The sneezing could come at any time. Sometimes they interrupted him in the middle of a lecture and made it impossible for him to continue. Other times he broke out in hives. Or else his eyes kept filling with tears. He pulled the sheet all the way up and over his mouth. This time he won. The need to sneeze died away. He thought about all the years that had gone by and all that had occurred which had led to his lying in a bed in Luanda, capital of Angola.

Thirty years ago he had been a young man working at the World Bank in Washington, DC. He had been convinced that the bank had the potential to do good in the world, or at the very least shift the balance of justice in the Third World's favour. The World Bank had been founded to provide the huge loans needed in the poverty-stricken parts of the world and which exceeded the capacity of individual nations and banks to provide. Many of his friends at the University of California had told him that he was wrong, that no reasonable solutions to the economic inequality of the world were addressed at the World Bank, but he had maintained his beliefs. At heart he was no less radical than they. He too marched in the anti-war demonstrations. But he had never believed in the potential of civil disobedience to reshape the world. Nor did he believe in the small and squabbling socialist organisations. He had come to the conclusion that the world had to be changed from within existing social structures. If you were going to try to shift the balance of power, you had to stay close to its source.

He had, however, a secret. It was what had made him leave Columbia and go to university in California. He had been in Vietnam for one year, and he had liked it. He had been stationed close to An Khe most of the time, along the important route west from Qui Nhon. He knew he killed many soldiers during that year and that he had never felt remorse over this. While his buddies had turned to drugs for solace, he had maintained a disciplined approach to his work. He knew he was going to survive the war, that he would not be one of the bodies sent home in a plastic bag. And it was then, during the stifling nights patrolling the jungle, that he had arrived at his conviction that you had to stay close to the source of power in order to affect it. Now, as he lay in the damp heat of the Angolan nights, he sometimes experienced the feeling that he was back in the jungle. He knew he had been right.

He had understood that there was going to be an opening at the executive level in Angola and he had immediately learned Portuguese. His career climb had been meteoric. His bosses had seen his potential, although there were others with more experience who applied for the same post. He had been appointed to a desirable post with little or no discussion.

That was his first contact with Africa, with a poor and shattered country. His time in Vietnam didn't count, he had been an unwelcome intruder. Here he was welcome. At first he spent his time listening, seeing and learning. He had marvelled at the joy and dignity that flourished amid the hardship.

It had taken him almost two years to see that what the bank was doing was wrong. Instead of helping the country to gain true independence and enable the rebuilding of the war-torn land, the bank merely served to protect the very rich. He noted that the people around him treated him with deference to his high rank. Behind the radical rhetoric there was only corruption, weakness and greed. There were others – independent intellectuals and the occasional politician – who saw what he saw, but they were not in positions of power. No-one listened to them.

At last he could stand it no longer. He tried to explain to his superiors that the strategies of the bank were misdirected, but he received no response, despite time and time again making transatlantic flights to persuade the staff at the top in the head office. He wrote countless memos, but he never had an answer that conveyed more than well-meaning indifference. At one of these meetings he finally understood that he had been labelled as difficult, as someone who was beginning to fall outside the pale. One evening he spoke with his oldest mentor, a finance analyst called Whitfield who had followed his career since his undergraduate days and who had helped recruit him. They met for dinner at a restaurant in Georgetown and Carter had asked him straight out: was he alienating everyone? Was there really no-one who could see that he was right and that the bank was wrong? Whitfield had answered just as candidly and told him he was asking the wrong question. It didn't matter that Carter was right or wrong. What mattered was bank policy.

Carter flew back to Luanda. As he leaned back into his first-class seat, a dramatic decision was taking shape.

It took several sleepless nights for him to see what it was he wanted. It was also at this time that he met the man who would play a decisive role in convincing him that he was doing the right thing. With hindsight Carter had often marvelled at the mixture of conscious decision and random coincidence that shaped a person's life.

It had been an evening in March in the middle of the 1970s. He had suffered a long period of sleeplessness as he searched for a way out of his dilemma. One evening, feeling restless, he decided to go to one of the restaurants in Luanda's harbour, Metropol. He liked going there because there was little chance he would run into anyone from the bank. Or any of Angola's élite, for that matter. He was usually left in peace at the Metropol. At the next table that night there had been a man who spoke very poor Portuguese and, since the waiter couldn't speak English, Carter had stepped in to translate.

Then the two of them had started talking. It turned out that the man was Swedish and was in Luanda on a consulting project commissioned by the state-owned telecom sector, which was grossly neglected and underdeveloped. Carter could never afterwards say exactly what it was that sparked his interest in the man. He was usually someone who maintained a stern reserve. But there had been something about this man that lowered his guard, even though Carter was a suspicious person by nature. His usual attitude was that most of the people he met were his enemies.

It had not taken Carter long to understand that the man at the next table – who soon joined him at his own – was highly intelligent. He was not only an able engineer and technician, but someone who seemed to have read up on and understood much of Angola's colonial history and present political situation.

The man's name was Tynnes Falk. He had only learned this when it was late and they had said goodbye. They had been the last to leave the establishment. A lone waiter was slumped half asleep at the bar. Their chauffeurs were waiting outside. Falk was staying at the Hotel Luanda. They decided to meet the following evening.

Falk had only meant to stay in Luanda for the three months that the project was expected to take. When the work was over, Carter had offered him a new consulting project. It was mainly an excuse to hold on to him, so that they could continue their conversations.

Falk had therefore come back to Luanda two months later. That was when he told Carter he was unmarried. Carter had likewise remained unmarried, though he had lived with a succession of women and fathered three girls and one boy, whom he almost never saw. In Luanda he now had two black lovers. One was a professor at the local university, the other the ex-wife of a cabinet minister. He kept these liaisons secret, except from his staff. He had avoided forming relationships within the bank. Since Falk seemed very lonely, Carter guided him into a suitable relationship with a woman named Rosa, the daughter of a Portuguese businessman and his Angolan housekeeper.

Falk had started to feel at home in Africa. Carter got him a pleasant house with a garden and a view of Luanda's beautiful harbour. He also wrote a contract that rewarded Falk excessively for the modest work he was expected to carry out.

They continued their conversations. Whatever subject they discussed on those long tropical nights, they always found that their political and moral opinions coincided. It was the first time Carter had met anyone in whom he could fully confide. Falk felt the same way.

It was during these long African nights that the plan began to take shape. Carter listened with fascination to the surprising things Falk told him about the electronic world in which he lived and worked. Through Falk he had come to understand that he who controlled electronic communication controlled everything. It was above all what Falk told him about how wars would be fought in the future that excited him. Bombs would be nothing more than computer viruses smuggled into the enemy's storehouse of weapons. Electronic signals could eliminate the enemy's stock markets and telecom networks. The days of nuclear submarines were over. Future threats would come barrelling down the miles of fibre-optic cables that were now entangling the world like a spider's web.

They were in agreement from the beginning about the need for patience. Never to make haste. Their time would come. Then they would strike.

They complemented each other. Carter had contacts. He knew how the bank functioned. He understood the details of the financial world. He knew how delicate the economic balance of the world really was. Falk was the technician who could translate ideas into practical reality.

They spent the evenings together for many months,

refining their plans. During the past 20 years they had been in regular contact.

Carter was jerked out of his thoughts and instinctively reached for the gun under his pillow. But it was only Celine, fumbling with the locks on the kitchen door. He ought to fire her. She made too much noise preparing his breakfast. The eggs were never cooked the way he liked them, and she was ugly and fat. Besides, she was stupid. She could neither read nor write and she had nine children. Her husband spent most of his time – if he wasn't drunk – chatting in the shade of a tree.

Carter had at one time been persuaded that these were the people who would create the new world, but he didn't believe it any longer. So it was just as well to destroy the world, to smash it into bits.

The sun had already swum up over the horizon. And now Tynnes Falk was dead. That which should never have happened, had happened. They had always been aware of the fact that something beyond their control might interfere with their plans. They had built this into their calculations and had taken every possible precaution. But they had never imagined that one of them might die. An unplanned death. When Carter first got that call from Sweden, he had refused to believe it was true. His friend no longer existed. It hurt him and it changed all their plans. And it had happened at the worst possible time – right when they were about to strike. Now he alone was left on the threshold of the great moment. But life always consisted of more than carefully laid plans and conscious decisions. There was always coincidence.

Their great operation had a name in his head: Jacob's Marsh.

On a rare occasion Falk had drunk a lot of wine and

begun speaking of his childhood. He had grown up on an estate where his father was some kind of caretaker. There had been a marsh next to a particular strip of forest. It had been bordered by beautiful, chaotic wild-flower meadows, so Falk had said. He had played there as a child very often, watching the dragonflies and having the best times of his life. He had explained why it was called Jacob's Marsh. A long time ago a man named Jacob had drowned himself there over an unrequited love.

The marsh acquired extra significance for Falk later in life, not least after his meeting with Carter and the realisation that they shared some of their most fundamental understandings of life. The marsh became a symbol for the chaos of life, where the only end was to drown yourself. Or make sure everyone else did.

Jacob's Marsh. That was a good name. Not that the operation needed a name, but it was a way to honour Falk's memory. A gesture only Carter would appreciate.

He stayed in bed a few minutes more and thought about Falk. But when he realised he was getting sentimental he got up, took a shower and went down to the dining room to eat his breakfast.

He spent the rest of the morning in his living room, listening to Beethoven's string quartets until he couldn't stand Celine's clatter in the kitchen a moment longer. Then he went to the beach for a walk. His chauffeur and bodyguard, Alfredo, walked a short distance behind him. Whenever Carter went into Luanda and saw the social disintegration, the heaps of garbage, the poverty and misery, he felt that the action he was taking was justified.

He walked along the ocean and from time to time he looked back at the decomposing city. Whatever rose from the ashes of the fire he was going to start would be better than this.

He was back at the house by 11 a.m. Celine had gone home. He drank a cup of coffee and a glass of water. Then he retired to his study. It had a breathtaking view over the harbour, but he pulled the curtains shut. He liked the evenings best. He needed to keep the strong African sun away from his sensitive eyes. He sat at the computer and went through his daily routine. Somewhere deep inside that electronic world an invisible clock was ticking. Falk had created it from his instructions. It was Sunday, October 12, only eight days away from D-Day.

He had finished his regular checks by 11.15 a.m.

He was on the verge of switching off the computer, when he froze. An icon was flashing from the corner of the screen. The rhythm was two short flashes and one long flash. He took out the manual that Falk had written for him. At first he thought there had to be a mistake. But it was all too true. Someone had just broken through the first layer of security into Falk's computer in Sweden. In that little town, Ystad, which Carter had only ever seen in postcards. He stared at the screen, unable to believe his eyes. Falk had sworn that the system would be impossible to break into. But still someone had done it.

Carter started sweating. He forced himself to remain calm. There were many layers to the security system in Falk's computer, and the innermost core of the program was buried under miles and miles of decoys and firewalls that no-one could penetrate. Even so, someone was trying to get in.

He thought long and hard. He had immediately sent someone to Ystad after hearing of Falk's death. There had been several unfortunate incidents, but until now Carter had felt sure that everything was under control, especially since he had reacted so quickly.

Everything was still under control, he decided, even though he couldn't deny that someone had broken through the first line of defence in Falk's computer and was possibly trying to go further. This needed to be taken care of as soon as possible.

Who could it be? Carter couldn't believe it was one of the policemen he had heard about through his informant, the ones apparently resolving the details of Falk's death and the other events with what appeared to be complacency.

But who else could it be? He found no answer and remained motionless in front of his computer as dusk fell over Luanda. When, finally, he got up from the desk he was still outwardly calm. But a problem had arisen and it was something that needed to be rectified.

He missed Falk more than ever. He typed his message and sent it off into the electronic realm. His answer came back after about a minute.

Wallander was standing behind Martinsson. Modin was sitting at the computer, where an ever-changing matrix of numbers was rushing by on the screen. Then the screen started to settle down. Only the occasional ones and zeroes flashed by. Then it became completely dark. Modin looked at Martinsson, who nodded. He went on tapping commands into the computer and fresh hordes of numbers flashed by. Then they stopped again.

"I have no idea what this is," Modin said. "And I've never seen anything like this."

"Could it be a computation of some kind?" Martinsson said.

Modin shook his head. "I don't think so. It looks like a system of numbers awaiting a command."

It was Martinsson's turn to shake his head. "Can you explain that?" he said.

"It can't be a calculation. There is no evidence of any equation here. The numbers only relate to themselves. I think it looks more like a code."

Wallander was not satisfied. He wasn't sure what he had been expecting, but it wasn't a stream of meaningless numbers.

"Didn't people stop with codes after the Second World War?" he said, but there was no answer from the other two. They kept staring at the numbers.

"It's something to do with the number 20," Modin said.

Martinsson leaned forward, but Wallander's back was hurting and he remained upright. Modin pointed and explained what he meant to Martinsson, who listened with interest. Wallander's thoughts started to drift.

"Could it be something to do with the year 2000?" Martinsson said. "Isn't that when electronic chaos is supposed to break out and all computers are going to go haywire?"

"It's nothing to do with 2000," Robert said stubbornly. "It's the number 20. Furthermore, no computer ever simply goes haywire. Only people do that."

"It will be the 20th in eight days," Wallander said.

Modin and Martinsson kept bouncing ideas back and forth. They called up new numbers on to the screen. Wallander was starting to get impatient.

The phone rang in his pocket. He walked to the door and answered it. It was Höglund.

"I may have found something," she said.

Wallander went into the hall.

"What is it?"

"You remember I told you I was going to root around in Lundberg's life?" she said. "First I was going to talk to his sons. The older one is Carl-Einar. It dawned on me that I had seen that name before. I couldn't remember where."

The name meant nothing to Wallander.

"I started combing through the computer records."

"I thought only Martinsson could do that?"

"Truth be told, I think soon you'll be the only one who *can't* do it."

"What did you find?"

"That Carl-Einar Lundberg was tried for a crime a number of years ago. I think it was while you were on sick leave."

"What did he do?"

"Well, apparently nothing – since he got off – but he was being tried for rape."

Wallander thought for a moment.

"I suppose it's worth looking into," he said, "though I have to admit I can't see how it fits into either Falk's death or Hökberg's."

"I think I'll follow it through," Höglund said.

Wallander went back to the others.

We're not getting anywhere, he thought in a sudden spasm of hopelessness. We don't even know what we're looking for. We're lost.

CHAPTER TWENTY-TWO

Modin was tired and his head ached. He stopped working some time after 6 p.m., but he wasn't giving up. He squinted up at Martinsson and Wallander and said he was more than happy to continue in the morning, but "I need time to think," he said. "I need to consult some of my friends and come up with an approach."

Martinsson arranged for Modin to be driven home.

"Do you think he meant what he said?" Wallander asked Martinsson as they walked into the station.

"That he needed time to think and plan his approach?" Martinsson said. "That's what we do when we run into difficulties. Isn't that what we asked him to do?"

"He sounded like an old doctor who had a patient with unusual symptoms. He would consult with friends, he said."

"He means with other hackers, but comparing it to a doctor and an unusual illness is actually quite an apt simile."

Martinsson seemed to have got over the fact that they still had no official sanction for working with Modin. Wallander thought it as well not to raise the subject again.

Höglund and Hansson were both in. Otherwise the station was pleasantly empty. Wallander thought in passing about the mountain of other work growing on his desk. He told the others to assemble for a quick meeting. Symbolically at least, they were at the end of a working week.

"I talked to one of the dog handlers," Hansson said.

"Norberg. He's getting a new dog actually, since Hercules is almost past it."

"I thought Hercules was dead." Martinsson said.

"Well, he's more or less done for. He's blind, anyway."

Martinsson burst into weary laughter. "That would be something for the papers," he said. "The police and their blind search dogs."

Wallander was not amused. He would miss the old dog, perhaps more than he would miss some of his colleagues when the time came.

"I've been thinking about this business of dog names," Hansson continued. "I can understand calling a dog Hercules, but I still can't get my head around Steadfast."

"We don't have any police dogs by that name, do we?" Martinsson said.

Wallander slammed his fist down on the table. It was the most authoritative gesture at his disposal. "That's enough of that. Now, what did Norberg say?"

"That it was reasonable to assume that objects or bodies that were frozen or had been frozen could stop giving off a scent. Dogs can have trouble finding bodies in winter, when it's very cold."

Wallander proceeded to his next point. "What about the van? Any news?"

"A Mercedes van was stolen in Ånge two weeks ago."

"Where is Ånge?"

"Outside Luleå," Martinsson said.

"The hell it is," Hansson said. "It's closer to Sundsvall."

Höglund went over to the map on the wall. Hansson was right.

"It could be the one," Hansson said. "Sweden is not a big country."

"It doesn't sound right to me," Wallander said. "But there

could be other stolen cars that haven't been reported yet. We'll have to keep an eye on incoming news."

He turned to Höglund for her report.

"Lundberg has two sons who are as unlike each other as could be. Nils-Emil, the one who lives in Malmö, is a janitor in a local school. I tried to get him over the phone. His wife said he was out training with his orienteering club. She was very talkative. It seems that Lundberg's death came as a hard blow to her husband, who is also a regular churchgoer. It's the younger brother who is of more interest to us. Carl-Einar was accused of rape in 1993, but he was never charged. The girl's name was Englund."

"I remember that case," Martinsson said. "It was horrible."

Wallander's only memories from this time were of long walks on the beaches of Skagen in Denmark. Then a lawyer had been murdered and Wallander had returned to his duties, somewhat to his surprise.

"Were you in charge of that investigation?" Wallander said.

Martinsson made a face. "It was Svedberg."

The room fell silent as they thought about their dead colleague.

"I haven't got through all the paperwork yet," Höglund said after a while. "So I don't yet know why he wasn't convicted."

"Nor was anyone else," Martinsson said. "Whoever did it got off. We could never find another suspect. I remember that Svedberg was convinced it was Lundberg. I'd never made the connection with Johan Lundberg."

"Even if we assume that he was guilty as accused," Wallander said, "does that satisfactorily account for the fact that his father was robbed and killed? Or that Hökberg was later burned to death? Or that Falk's fingers were cut off?"

"It was a vicious rape," Höglund said. "You have to at least imagine a perpetrator out there who has been guilty of horrendous violence. The Englund girl was in hospital for a long time. She had severe injuries to the head and to other parts of her body."

"We will look at this more closely," Wallander said. "But I don't think that Carl-Einar Lundberg will turn out to have anything to do with this case. There's something else at work behind all of this, and we don't know yet what it is."

Wallander went on to describe the work that Modin was doing with Falk's computer. No-one made any comment about an unauthorised expert, someone who had served time for advanced computer crime, being brought in.

"I don't really get this," Hansson said. "What do you expect to find in that computer? A confession? An account of everything that's happened? A reason for all this?"

"I don't know if there's anything there that will be of use to us," Wallander said simply. "But we need to know what Falk was up to. From all I know, he was a very odd customer."

Hansson obviously questioned the wisdom of devoting so much time to Falk's computer, but he didn't say so. Wallander saw that the time had come to call the meeting to an end. Everyone was tired and needed to rest.

"We have to continue in this same vein," he started, then interrupted himself and turned to Höglund. "Whatever happened with Hökberg's bag?"

"I'm sorry, I forgot about that," she said. "Her mother said she thought that maybe an address book was missing."

"Maybe?"

"I believe she was telling the truth. The daughter was a very private person. Her mother thinks she remembered her having a small black address book in which she wrote people's phone numbers. She couldn't say for certain. Anyway, it wasn't in the bag."

"If that's true, it's a valuable bit of information. Persson should be able to confirm whether she had such a book." Wallander thought for a while before continuing. "I think we should reassign some tasks. I want Höglund to concentrate on Hökberg and Persson. There has to be a boyfriend out there somewhere, someone who could have given her a lift out of town. Keep looking for any information that can tell us what sort of girl she was and what she did with her time. Martinsson will keep Modin happy. Someone else can check up on Lundberg's son – I'll do that, and I will keep on looking into Falk's life. Hansson can be in charge of keeping the information flowing. Keep Viktorsson informed too, and keep trying to find witnesses and looking for an explanation as to how a body can disappear from a morgue. Last, but not least, someone has to go to Växjö and speak to Persson's father. Just so we can cross that off the list."

Wallander called the meeting to an end and they all stood up. He got out as quickly as he could. It was already 7.30 p.m. He had not had much to eat all day, but he didn't feel hungry. He drove to Mariagatan and scanned the street before unlocking the front door.

For the next hour he cleaned the flat and sorted his laundry. Now and again he stopped in front of the television set and watched the news programme. One item caught his eye. An American general was asked what future wars would look like. They would be fought with computers, he explained. The era of ground troops would soon be over; at least their role would be much smaller.

That made Wallander think of something and, since it was still early, he looked out the number and sat at the phone.

Erik Hökberg answered almost at once. "How is the investigation going?" he said. "We're not doing too well here. We really do need to know what happened to Sonja."

"We're doing all we can."

"But are you getting anywhere? Anywhere nearer to finding who killed her?"

"We don't know that yet."

"How can it be so difficult to find someone who murdered an innocent girl – in a power station, of all places?"

"I'm calling you," Wallander said, "because I need to ask you a question. Did Sonja know how to use a computer?"

"Of course she did. Don't all young people use computers nowadays?"

"Was she interested in them?"

"She mainly surfed the Net, I think. She was pretty adept, but I don't think she was as technically advanced as Emil."

Wallander felt somewhat helpless. Martinsson should have been the one asking these questions.

"You must have been thinking over what happened," he said. "You must have asked yourself why Sonja killed the taxi driver. And then why she in turn was killed."

Erik Hökberg's voice was close to breaking as he answered. "I go into her room sometimes," he said. "I just sit in there and look around. I just don't understand it."

"If you had to describe Sonja to a stranger, how would you do that?"

"I'd say that she was strong-willed. Not always an easy

person to deal with. She would have done well in life."

Wallander thought of the room that had seemed frozen in time. The room of a little girl, not the person her stepfather seemed to be describing.

"Didn't she have a boyfriend?" Wallander said.

"Not that I know of."

"Isn't that strange?"

"Why is it strange?"

"She was 19. And good-looking."

"She never brought anyone home."

"What about phone calls? Did anyone call her a lot?"

"She had her own line. She asked for it when she turned 18. It often rang, but I wouldn't know who was calling."

"Did she have an answering machine?"

"I've checked it. There were no messages left."

"If anyone does call and leave a message, I'd like to have the tape."

Wallander suddenly thought of the film poster in the wardrobe in her room. The only object apart from her clothes that bore witness to the teenager who lived in the room, someone who was on her way to becoming a grown woman. He searched for the title in his mind. *The Devil's Advocate.*

"Inspector Höglund will be in touch with you soon," he said. "She will ask a number of questions and if you are serious about wanting us to find Sonja's killer you'll have to answer in as much detail as possible."

"You don't think we've been helpful enough so far?" Erik Hökberg said, angrily.

Wallander didn't blame him. "No, on the contrary, I think you've been extremely helpful. I won't keep you any longer."

He hung up. The poster lingered in his mind. He looked at the time and saw it was 9.30 p.m. He dialled the restaurant in Stockholm where Linda worked. A distracted man with a heavy accent answered. He said he would find Linda. It took several long minutes for her to come to the phone. When she heard who it was she was furious.

"You can't call me here at this time, you know that. This is our busiest time. You'll get me into trouble."

"I know," Wallander said. "I'm so sorry – just a quick question."

"It had better be quick."

"Have you seen a film called *The Devil's Advocate*, with Al Pacino?"

"Is that what this is about? A film?"

"That's it."

"I'm hanging up."

Now it was Wallander's turn to get angry. "At least answer the question. Have you seen it?"

"Yes, I have," she hissed.

"What's it about?"

"Oh my God! I don't believe this."

"It's about God?"

"In a way. It's about a lawyer who turns out to be the Devil."

"Is that it?"

"Isn't that enough? Why do you need to know this anyway? Are you having nightmares?"

"I'm trying to solve a murder. Why would a 19-year-old girl have a poster of this film on her wall?"

"Probably because she thinks Al Pacino is hot. Or else maybe she worships the Devil. How the hell would I know?"

"Do you have to use that language?"

"Yes."

"Is there anything else to this film?"

"Why don't you see it for yourself? I'm sure it's out on video."

Wallander felt like an idiot. He should have thought of this himself. He could have simply rented the video and not bothered Linda.

"I'm sorry for the interruption," he said.

Her anger had passed.

"It's OK. But I do have to go now."

"I know. Goodbye."

The moment he put the receiver down, the phone rang. He lifted it again with trepidation, fearful of a journalist on the line.

At first he didn't recognise the voice. Then he realised it was Siv Eriksson.

"I hope I'm not catching you in the middle of something," she said.

"Not at all."

"I've been thinking. I've been trying to find something that could help you."

Invite me over, Wallander thought. If you really want to help me. I'm hungry and thirsty and I don't want to sit in this damned flat a minute longer.

"And did you think of anything in particular?"

"Not really. I suppose his wife is the only one who really knew him. Or maybe his children."

Wallander waited to see if she would say anything else.

"I have one memory of him that stands out as unusual. It isn't much. We only knew each other a few years."

"Tell me."

"It was two years ago, in October or the beginning of November. He came here one evening and was very upset. He couldn't hide it. We had a project due, I think it was something for the county. We had a deadline, but I could see that he was very upset and I asked him why. He said he had just seen some teenagers accost an older man who had been a little drunk. When the man tried to brush them away they punched him. He fell and they kicked him as he lay on the pavement."

"Was that it?"

"Yes."

Wallander thought about it. Falk had reacted strongly to a person who was the victim of violence. It was interesting, but he couldn't find a place for it in his picture of the man at the heart of the case.

"Did he intervene in any way?"

"No. It just enraged him."

"What did he say?"

"That the world was chaos. That nothing was worth it any more."

"What was it that wasn't worth it?"

"I don't know. I had a feeling he meant that humankind wasn't worth it any longer. That man's animal nature was taking over, or something like that. When I asked him to explain what he meant he refused, and we never talked about it again."

"How did you interpret his reaction?"

"I felt it was quite natural. Wouldn't you have felt that way?"

Maybe, Wallander thought. But I doubt if I would have reached the same dire conclusion.

Wallander wanted to keep her on the line, but she was bound to see through him.

"I'm glad you called," he said. "Please call me again if you think of anything else. I'll probably call you myself tomorrow."

"I'm doing some programming for a restaurant chain. I'll be in the office all day."

"What will happen with your other projects now?"

"I don't know. I just hope I have enough of a reputation now to survive without Tynnes. If not, I'll have to think of something else."

"Like what?"

She laughed. "Do you need to know for the case?"

"No, I was just curious."

"I might take off and see the world."

Everyone goes away, Wallander thought. In the end it will just be me and all the trash left.

"I've had thoughts like that myself," he said. "But I'm locked in, like most people."

"I'm not locked in," she said cheerfully. "I'm my own woman."

When the conversation was over, Wallander thought about what she had said. "I'm my own woman." She had a point. Just as Åkeson and Widén had done, in their way.

Suddenly he felt very pleased with himself for having sent in the ad to the dating agency. Even though he wasn't expecting an answer, he had done something.

He put on his coat and went to the nearest video shop, on Stora Östergatan. It turned out the shop closed at 9 p.m. on Sundays. He walked on towards Stortorget, the main square, stopping from time to time to look in shop windows.

Where the feeling came from he couldn't say, but suddenly he turned around. No-one was there, apart from a group of teenagers and a security guard. He thought about what Höglund had said, about being careful.

I'm imagining things, he thought. No-one is stupid enough to attack the same police officer twice in a row.

When he got to Stortorget, he turned down Hamngatan and then took Österleden home. The air was crisp. It felt good to be out.

He was back in his flat at 10.15 a.m. He found one can of beer in the fridge and made some sandwiches. Then he sat in front of the television and watched a discussion about the Swedish economy. The only thing he got out of the programme was that the economy was both good and faltering. He nodded off and looked forward to finally getting an undisturbed night's sleep. The case was going to have to get along without him for a few hours.

He went to bed at 11.30 a.m.

He had just fallen asleep when the phone rang.

He counted nine rings before they stopped. Then he pulled the cord out of the socket and waited. If it was one of his colleagues they would try his mobile. He hoped that wouldn't happen.

The mobile on his bedside table rang. It was the patrol officer stationed outside Falk's flat on Apelbergsgatan. His name was Elofsson.

"I don't know how important this is," he said, "but a car has driven past here several times in the last hour."

"Did you get a good look at the driver?"

"That's why I'm telephoning, actually. You remember the orders you gave us." Wallander waited impatiently. "I think he looked Asian," Elofsson said. "But I can't be 100 per cent sure."

Wallander didn't hesitate. The peaceful night he had been looking forward to was already ruined.

"I'll be there."

He hung up and looked at the time. It was one minute past midnight.

CHAPTER TWENTY-THREE

Wallander drove past Apelbergsgatan and parked on Jörgen Krabbes Väg. It took him about 5 minutes to walk from there to Falk's building. The wind had died down. There wasn't a cloud in the sky and it was gradually getting chillier. October in Ystad was always a month that had trouble making up its mind.

The undercover car with Elofsson and his colleague was parked on the other side of the street and about half a block down. When Wallander reached the car, the back door was opened for him and he climbed in. There was a pleasant smell of coffee inside. Wallander thought of all the nights he had spent in cars like this one, fighting the desire to sleep, fighting the cold.

They exchanged some casual remarks. Elofsson's colleague had only been in Ystad for about six months. His name was El Sayed and he came originally from Tunisia. He was the first policeman with an immigrant background to have worked in Ystad. Wallander had been worried that El Sayed would meet with hostility and prejudice. He had no illusions about what his colleagues thought of getting a non-white recruit. As it turned out his fears had been justified. El Sayed had to put up with his share of off-colour jokes and mean-spirited comments. How much of it he noticed and had been expecting, Wallander was still not sure. Sometimes he felt badly that he had never taken the time to invite him over for a meal. No-one else had either. But after a while the young man and his easygoing personality had grown on them and he was becoming part of the group.

"He came from a northerly direction," Elofsson said. "From the Malmö road. At least three times."

"When was he here last?"

"Just before I called you. I tried your regular phone first. You must be a deep sleeper."

Wallander ignored this. "Tell me again, every detail," he said.

"You know how it is. It's only when they go past the second time that you really take notice."

"What was the car?"

"A navy blue Mazda saloon."

"Did he slow down as he went past?"

"I don't know if he did the first time, but he definitely did the second."

El Sayed broke in for the first time. "He slowed down the first time."

This comment clearly irritated Elofsson.

"But he never stopped?"

"No."

"Did he see you?"

"Not the first time. But possibly on his second time around."

"What happened after that?"

"He came back the third time after about 20 minutes, but didn't slow down."

"He may just have been checking that you were still here. Could you see if there was more than one person in the car?"

"We talked about that. We think it was just one person."

"Did you tell your colleagues at Runnerströms Torg?"

"They haven't seen it."

Wallander found that puzzling. If someone was keeping a check on Falk's flat, he would also be interested in his office. He thought about it. The only explanation he could think of was that whoever the person in the car was he didn't know of the existence of the office. Unless the officers on duty there had been sleeping. Wallander didn't want to rule out that possibility at this point.

Elofsson turned and passed Wallander a note with the registration number written on it.

"I take it you've had this number checked out?"

"We tried, but the computer system was down."

Wallander held the note up so that he could read it with the help of the street light. MLR 331. He memorised the number.

"When did they think they'd be back up and running?"

"They couldn't be sure. Maybe by tomorrow morning."

Wallander shook his head. "We need this as soon as humanly possible. When does your shift end?"

"At 6 a.m."

"Before you go home I want you to write up a report on this and give it to Hansson or Martinsson. They'll take care of it."

"What do we do if he comes back?"

"He won't," Wallander said. "Not as long as he knows you're here."

"Should we get involved in any way, if he does come back?"

"No. He hasn't committed a crime, so far as we know. But call me. Use my mobile number."

He wished them luck, then walked back to Jörgen Krabbes Väg. He drove down to Runnerströms Torg. Only one of the officers was asleep. They hadn't been aware of any navy blue Mazdas.

"Keep a close watch," Wallander said, and gave them the registration number.

As he was walking back to his car, he remembered that he still had Setterkvist's keys. He entered the building and walked to the top floor. Before unlocking the door he pressed his ear to it and listened. He walked in and turned on the light, looking around the room in the same way as he had the first time he was there. Was there anything he hadn't noticed that time? Something that he and Nyberg could have overlooked? He found nothing. He sat at the computer and stared at the dark screen.

Modin had talked about the number 20. Wallander had sensed intuitively that the boy was on to something. In the stream of numbers that were a nonsensical jumble to him, and perhaps even to Martinsson, Modin had been able to see a pattern. The only thing Wallander could think of was that October 20 was approaching, and that the number 20 was the first part of the year 2000. But what did it mean? And did whatever it meant have anything to do with the investigation?

Suddenly the phone rang.

Wallander jumped. The sound rang out eerily in the empty room. He stared at the black phone and on the seventh ring he finally lifted the receiver.

He heard static as if it were a long-distance call and he strained to hear something on the other end. Someone was there. Wallander said hello once, then a second time. All he heard was the sound of breathing somewhere inside the buzz of static. Then there was a click and the connection was lost. Wallander hung up. His heart was racing. He had heard that sound before, when he had listened to Falk's messages.

There was someone there, he thought. Someone calling to talk to Falk. But Falk is gone. He's dead.

He thought of another possibility. Someone could be calling to talk to him. Someone who had seen him enter the building and walk up to Falk's flat?

He remembered how he had stopped and turned on the pavement earlier in the evening. As if he was expecting there to be someone behind him, watching him.

His anxiety flared up. Until now he had been able to repress the memory that only a few days ago someone had tried to kill him. Höglund's words came back to him: he should take care.

He got up from the chair and walked to the door. He could hear nothing.

He walked back to the desk. Without thinking, he lifted the keyboard. There was a postcard lying underneath it. He directed the lamp at it and put on his glasses. The card was old and the colours had faded. It was a picture of a tropical bay. There were palm trees, a pier, fishing boats in the water. Behind the shoreline a row of tall buildings. He turned the card over and saw that it was addressed to Tynnes Falk at the Apelbergsgatan address. So much for Eriksson receiving all his mail. Had she lied to him, or did she not know about this other mail? There was no message on the card, just the letter "C". Wallander studied the postmark. The stamp was partly torn off, but he could make out the letters "l" and "d". The other letters probably would be vowels, but he couldn't guess what they were, nor could he decipher a date. There was nothing printed on the card to say where the picture had been taken. Wallander was reminded of an unhappy and chaotic trip he had once taken to the West Indies. The palm trees were the same, but the cityscape didn't look familiar.

He studied the "C" again. The same as the C in Falk's diary. Falk had known who it was, or what it was and had saved the postcard. In this bare room that contained nothing beyond the computer and a blueprint of a power substation, there had been this postcard. Wallander tucked it into his jacket pocket. Then he lifted the computer monitor but there was nothing there. He lifted the phone. Nothing. He looked around for another minute before he turned out the light and left.

He was exhausted when he got back to Mariagatan, but before going to bed he couldn't resist getting out his magnifying glass and studying the postcard again. It didn't tell him anything more.

He went to bed shortly before 2 a.m. and fell asleep at once.

Monday morning Wallander made only a brief stop at the station. He handed the flat keys over to Martinsson and asked him about the car that had been seen the night before. Martinsson already had the report on his desk. Wallander didn't say anything about the postcard. It wasn't that he wanted to keep it to himself, but because he was in a hurry. He didn't want to get bogged down in a long discussion.

Before leaving the station he made two calls. One was to Siv Eriksson. He asked her about the number 20 and about the letter C. She couldn't think of anything, but she said she would be in touch if anything came to her. He told her about the postcard he had found in Falk's office. Her exclamation of surprise was so spontaneous that he didn't doubt it was genuine. Wallander told her what the postcard depicted, but she couldn't shed any light on its provenance.

"Maybe he had even more addresses," she said.

Wallander sensed a note of disappointment in her voice, as if she felt betrayed by Falk.

"We'll look into it," he said. "You could be right about his having other houses."

Wallander realised that the very sound of her voice had cheered him up, but he didn't let himself dwell on it. He made the next call, which was to Marianne Falk. He told her that he would be with her in half an hour.

The next few hours he sat in Mrs Falk's living room and listened to her talk about the man she had been married to. Wallander started at the beginning. When had they met? How had he been in those days? Mrs Falk turned out to have an excellent memory. She rarely faltered or had to pause to gather her thoughts. Wallander had brought his notebook, but he didn't take any notes. He wasn't planning to research what she told him, he was simply trying to get some understanding of the man Falk had been.

Falk had grown up on a farm outside Linköping, she said. He was an only child. On leaving school he had done his military service and then started his studies in Uppsala. He had not been able to decide on any one subject and had taken courses in everything from law to literature. After a year he had moved to Stockholm, to the business school.

That was when they had met. It was in 1972. She was training to be a nurse and had gone to a big party held by a student organisation.

"Tynnes didn't dance," she said, "but he was there. Somehow or other we were introduced. I remember thinking that he seemed boring. It certainly wasn't love at first sight, not from my side. He called a few days after that. I don't know how he got my number. He wanted to see me again, but not for the usual walk or movie. What he suggested surprised me."

"And what was that?"

"He wanted to take me to Bromma, to watch the aeroplanes taking off."

"Did he say why?"

"He liked aeroplanes. We went, and he could tell me everything about the planes that were parked there. I thought he was a little strange. He certainly wasn't how I had imagined the man in my life."

Falk had been persistent according to Marianne, although she had had her doubts.

"He wasn't pushy – physically," she said. "It took him about three months to kiss me. If he hadn't, by that point, I would probably have tired of the whole thing. He was very shy, or at least he pretended to be."

"Why would he pretend?"

"Tynnes was very self-confident when it came down to it. He had a reserved manner, but I think he looked down on most of the rest of humanity, for all that he often claimed the opposite."

A turning point in the relationship came one day in April or May about six months after they had met. They had had no plans to meet that day since Falk had said he had an important lecture at school and she was running errands for her mother. On her way to the railway station, she was forced to stop on the side of the road since a mass of demonstrators was passing by. It was a march to raise awareness of Third World issues. The signs and banners had various aggressive messages about the World Bank and Portuguese colonial oppression. Marianne had come from a stable home with solid Social Democratic values. She had not been caught up by the growing wave of left-wing radicals, nor had she ever detected any such interest in Falk, though he always seemed to have the answer whenever they discussed political issues, and he had clearly enjoyed showing off his political knowledge and superior understanding of political theory. When she caught sight of him that day among the demonstrators she couldn't believe her eyes. She had involuntarily taken a few steps back as he passed her on the street and he never saw her.

Afterwards she had asked him about it. He was furious that she had seen him in the demonstration. It was the first time she had witnessed his temper. But then he had calmed down. She never found out why it had so affected him, but from that day she had known there was a lot more to Falk than met the eye.

"I broke up with him that June," she said. "Not because I had found anyone else. It was just that I didn't believe we were going anywhere. His angry reaction about the demonstration had played a part in that."

"How did he take it?"

"I don't know."

"What do you mean?"

"We had met at an outdoor café in Kungsträdgården. I told him straight out that I wanted to end the relationship and that I didn't think we had a future. He listened to what I had to say and he just got up and left."

"And that was the end?"

"He didn't say a single word. I remember that his face was a complete blank. When I had finished talking he left. He did leave money on the table for our coffees."

"What happened after that?"

"I didn't see him again for several years."

"How long exactly?"

"Four years, I think."

"What did he do during that time?"

"I don't know for sure."

"He vanished without a trace during those four years? Is that what you are saying?"

"It's hard to believe, I know, but about a week after our date in Kungsträdgården I decided I needed to talk to him again. That's when I discovered he had moved out of his student room without leaving a forwarding address. After a few weeks I managed to get in touch with his parents in Linköping, but they, too, had no idea where he had gone. He was gone for four years, and I had no idea where he was. He had withdrawn from the business school. No-one knew anything. And then he turned up."

"When was that?"

"I remember it exactly. It was August 2, 1977. I had just accepted my first nursing position at Sabbatsberg Hospital. And there he was, waiting for me outside the hospital, carrying a big bouquet of flowers. He was smiling. I had gone through a failed relationship over those four years. When I saw him there, it cheered me up. I think I was feeling pretty lost and lonely. My mother had just died."

"You started seeing each other again?"

"He even thought we should get married. He asked me just a few days later."

"But he must have told you what he had been doing the past few years?"

"Actually, he didn't say a word about that. He said he wouldn't ask me about my life if I wouldn't ask him about his. He wanted us to pretend that the past four years had never happened."

Wallander looked closely at her. "Did he look at all different?"

"No. Not apart from the tan."

"He was tanned? Sunburned?"

"Yes. But that was all. It was only by accident that I found out where he had been all that time."

Wallander's mobile rang. He hesitated, but decided to answer. It was Hansson.

"Martinsson gave me this business with the car that was seen last night," he said. "The computer records keep crashing, but at last I've been able to establish that it's a stolen car."

"The car or just the number plate?"

"Probably both, but we are talking number plates here. They were taken from a Volvo that was parked down by the Nobeltorget in Malmö last week."

"Good," Wallander said. "Then Elofsson and El Sayed were right. That car was keeping an eye on things."

"I'm not really sure where to go next."

"Talk to Malmö police about the Volvo. And send out a nationwide alert for the Mazda."

"What crime is the driver suspected of?"

Wallander paused. "That he has something to do with Hökberg's murder. Also that he may have been the one who fired that shot at me."

"He was the one who shot at you?"

"Or been a witness," Wallander answered.

"Where are you right now?"

"I'm with Mrs Falk. I'll call you later."

She was serving him coffee from a beautiful blue-and-white pot. Wallander thought he remembered seeing similar china as a child in his parents' home.

"Why don't you tell me about that 'by accident' part," he said when she sat down again.

"It was about a month after Tynnes had appeared in my life again. He had bought a car and often came to pick me up. One of the doctors I worked with at the hospital saw him one day. The next day he asked me if the man he had seen was Tynnes Falk. When I said yes, he told me he had met him the year before, not in Sweden, but in Africa."

"Where in Africa?"

"In Angola. The doctor had been doing volunteer work, just after Angola had become independent. He had bumped into another Swede in a restaurant late one night. Tynnes had produced his Swedish passport, from which he took out the money to pay his bill. When the doctor saw that, he said hello. They spoke only briefly, but the doctor remembered him. Not least because he thought Tynnes had been so unfriendly to a fellow Swede, as if he didn't want to be recognised."

"You must have asked him what he was doing there?"

"You might think so, but I never did. I meant to, but I suppose it came down to the promise we had made to each other not to ask. Instead, I tried to find out through other channels what he had been doing."

"What other channels?"

"Various relief organisations that had branches in Africa. No-one had any record of him. It was only when I called the Swedish International Development Agency that I got something. They said Tynnes had been in Angola for two months to help with the installation of various radio towers."

"But he was gone for four years," Wallander said. "Not two months."

She didn't reply, perhaps lost in thought. Wallander waited.

"We married and had children," she said finally. "Apart from that chance meeting in Luanda, I had no idea what he had been or what he had done in those four years. And I never asked. It's only now that he's dead that I'm beginning to find out."

She got up and left the room. When she returned she had in her hand something wrapped in a plastic cloth. She put it on the coffee table in front of Wallander.

"After he died I went down to the basement. I knew he had a steel trunk down there. It was locked, but I broke the lock. Apart from this there was nothing but dust."

She nodded for him to open the package. Wallander pulled the plastic cloth aside. Inside was a brown leather photograph album. Someone had written *Angola 1973–1977* on the cover in permanent ink.

Wallander hadn't even opened it when a thought came to him.

"My education isn't what it should be," he said. "What's the capital of Angola?"

"Luanda."

Wallander nodded. He still had the postcard with the letters "l" and "d" on it in his pocket.

What was it that had happened in Luanda? And who was C? He leaned forward and opened the album.

CHAPTER TWENTY-FOUR

The first picture was of a burned-out bus. It was lying by the side of a road which was red, perhaps sand or stained darker with blood. The photograph had been taken from a distance. The bus resembled the body of a dead animal. The handwritten caption read: *North-east of Huambo, 1975*. Wallander turned the page: a group of African women around a waterhole, the landscape parched. The water level was low. There were no shadows on the ground; the picture must have been taken at midday. None of the women was looking at the camera.

Wallander studied the picture. Falk, assuming he was the photographer, had captured these women on film. But it was the dried-up waterhole that was the real focus of the picture. That was the story the photographer was telling, not the lives of the women. Mrs Falk sat quietly on the other side of the room as he turned the pages. He was aware of the ticking of a clock somewhere in the room.

Wallander kept leafing through the shots of villages, war sites and radio towers until he came to a photograph of a group of nine men, a boy and a goat. The goat seemed to have walked into the picture by chance. One of the men was trying to wave it away as the picture was taken. The boy was looking straight at the camera, laughing. Seven of the men were black, two were white. The black men looked cheerful; the white men had serious expressions on their faces. Wallander asked Mrs Falk if she knew who any of the men were. She shook her head. The place name scribbled under the picture was illegible, but it had a date: January 1976. Falk had long been finished with his radio towers by then. Was he on a return trip to make sure the work had been maintained? Or had he stayed on in Angola after the job was done?

Wallander continued through the album until Mrs Falk drew his attention to a picture taken at what seemed to be a party. There were only white people in the group, their eyes red from the flash like nocturnal creatures. There were bottles and glasses on a table. Mrs Falk was pointing out one man with a glass in his hand. It was Falk. The young men around him were cheering and toasting each other, but Falk had a serious expression. He looked thin, dressed in a white shirt buttoned all the way to his throat. The others were in various states of undress, flushed and sweaty. Wallander asked her again if she recognised any of them, but she said no.

Wallander stopped at another picture. It was taken outside what looked like a whitewashed church. Falk was standing against the wall looking at the photographer. For the first time in the album he was smiling, and his shirt was not buttoned to the throat. Who took the photograph? Was it C?

Next page. Wallander leaned in more closely. He recognised a face from an earlier photograph. It was a fairly close shot. A tall man, thin and tanned. His gaze was very determined, his hair cropped short. He looked northern European, possibly German or Russian. Wallander examined the background. There seemed to be a skyline of hills covered in thick green vegetation. In the middle ground, between the hills and the man, was something that looked like a large machine. The construction seemed familiar, but it was only when he held the picture away from himself that he realised what it was. A power substation.

Here is a connection, he thought. Though I have no idea what to make of it. A picture of a man outside a power substation, not unlike the one where Hökberg's body was found. He kept on in the hope of finding more clues, but there was nothing else of interest. There were animal photographs, taken on tourist safaris, presumably in other parts of Africa. But in the last picture he was back again. *Luanda, June 1976*. The thin man again with his close-cropped hair. This time he is sitting on a bench looking out at the ocean. For once Falk had managed to compose a good picture. There were several empty pages at the back of the album, but it didn't look as if anything had been taken out. That was the last one, the image of the man staring out over the sea, and in the background, the same city as in the postcard.

Wallander leaned back in his chair. Mrs Falk gave him a searching look.

"I don't know what these pictures tell us, but I'd like to borrow the album, if I may," he said. "Enlargements of one or two shots could be useful."

She followed him into the hall.

"Why do you think that what he did in those years was so important? It was such a long time ago."

"Something happened there," Wallander said. "I don't know what. But I think that whatever it was stayed with him for the rest of his life."

He put on his coat and shook her hand.

"If you like, we can send a receipt for the loan of the album."

"That won't be necessary." And as Wallander opened the door, she said, "There's one more thing."

Wallander looked at her and waited. She seemed unsure of herself.

"Maybe policemen only want facts," she said. "The thing I've been thinking about is still very unclear even to me."

"Right now anything could be of help."

"I lived with Tynnes for a long time," she said, "and I thought I knew him. What he was doing during those years that he was gone, I don't know, but I always knew there was something else in his life. Since he was so good-natured and he treated me and the children so well, I never bothered digging into it." She stopped abruptly. Wallander waited. "Sometimes I had the feeling I had married a fanatic, a person with two lives."

"A fanatic?"

"Sometimes he had such strange ideas about things."

"For example?"

"About life. About people. About the world. Almost anything. He could suddenly come up with the most violent accusations, not directed at anyone in particular, as if he were sending messages into space almost."

"He never explained himself?"

"I didn't dare ask him about it. It scared me. He would become so filled with hate. And besides, his rages would leave him as quickly as they had come. I had the feeling that they were something he wanted to hide, something that embarrassed him."

Wallander thought carefully. "Did he ever get involved politically?"

"He despised politicians. I don't think he ever voted."

"And he had no ties to any political organisation?"

"No."

"If you think of anything else, please let us know."

Wallander got into his car, putting the album on the passenger seat. He wondered about the man in front of the power substation, whom Falk had met in a faraway land 20 years ago. Was he the one who had sent the postcard, the one who called himself C?

Wallander shook his head. He didn't understand it. Suddenly he felt cold. It was a chilly day. He turned up the heat and drove to the station. His mobile rang as he pulled into the car park. It was Martinsson.

"Trying to crack this code is like scaling a wall," he said. "Modin is doing his best to get over it, but I couldn't tell you what he's actually up to."

"We just have to be patient."

"I take it we pay for his lunch?"

"Keep the receipt," Wallander said. "Give it to me later."

"I'm also wondering if now wouldn't be a good time to get in touch with the National Police computer experts. There's not really any good reason to put it off, is there?"

Martinsson is right, Wallander thought. "We will get in touch with them in good time," he said. "Let's hold off for now."

Irene told him that Gertrud had called. Wallander went to his office and called her back. Wallander sometimes drove out at the weekend to visit her, but it didn't happen often. He felt guilty about it. Gertrud was after all the one who had taken pity on his father in those last difficult years. Without her he would never have lasted as long as he did, but now that his father was gone they didn't really have anything to talk about.

Gertrud's sister answered the phone. She was talkative and had strong opinions on most subjects. Wallander explained that he was short of time and she went to get

Gertrud. It took a long time for her to answer. When she did, it turned out that nothing was amiss. There was no reason for Wallander to have been worried.

"I just wanted to see how you were doing," Gertrud said.

"I'm busy, but otherwise I'm doing fine."

"It's been a while since you were here."

"I know. I'll come and see you as soon as I have more time."

"One day it may be too late," she said. "At my age you never know how much more time you have."

Gertrud was a little over 60. A little young for this kind of emotional blackmail. She was taking after his father in this respect.

"I'll get there," he said in a friendly tone. "Just as soon as I am less busy."

He excused himself, saying that people were waiting to talk to him. He went to the canteen to get some coffee. Nyberg was drinking an unusual kind of herbal tea. For once he seemed rested. His hair, which normally stood on end, was combed into rare order.

"We have no fingerprints," Nyberg said. "The dogs have searched everywhere. But we did do a check on the ones we found in his flat, that is, the ones we're assuming belong to Falk. They don't turn up in our records."

"Send them on to Interpol. By the way, do you know if that covers Angola?"

"How would I know a thing like that?"

"I was just wondering."

Nyberg left. Wallander stole a couple of rusks from Martinsson's private stash and returned to his room. It was already midday. The morning had gone by quickly. The album lay in front of him and he was momentarily unsure of how to proceed. He knew more about Falk now than he had a couple of hours ago, but nothing that satisfactorily clarified his connection to Hökberg.

He pulled the phone towards him and called Höglund. No answer. Nor from Hansson. Martinsson, of course, was still with Modin.

Wallander tried to think what Rydberg would have done. It was easier to imagine his voice. Rydberg would have taken time to think. That was the most important thing a policeman could do besides gathering facts. Wallander put his feet up on the desk and shut his eyes. He went through all the events of the case in his head once again, trying all the time to keep in mind what had happened in Angola all those years ago. He tried various scenarios and thought them through. Lundberg's death. Then Hökberg's. The large power cut.

When he opened his eyes it was with the feeling of being very close to an explanation, but he couldn't seize hold of it.

He was interrupted by the phone. Siv Eriksson was waiting for him in the reception area. He jumped up from his chair, ran his fingers through his hair and went out to see her. She really was an extremely attractive woman. He asked her if she wanted to come back to his office, but she said she had no time. She handed him an envelope.

"Here is the list of clients you asked for."

"I hope it wasn't too much trouble."

"It took a little time, but it was no trouble."

She declined his offer of a cup of coffee.

"Tynnes left some loose threads behind," she said. "I have to attend to them."

"But can you be sure that he had no other project in hand?"

"I don't think he did. Lately he was saying no to most prospective clients. I know that because he asked me to deal with most of them."

"Had that ever happened before? That he turned down so many new jobs?"

"I really couldn't be sure."

"But he offered you no explanation?"

"No. I thought he needed time to rest."

Eriksson walked to a taxi that was waiting for her. When the driver got out to open the door for her Wallander noticed that he was wearing a black armband of mourning.

He went back to his office with her envelope. Many of the companies on her list were unknown to him, apart from two banks, but all, with one exception, were in Skåne. The exception was a company in Denmark. It seemed to Wallander that they manufactured loading cranes. Neither Sydkraft nor any other utility company was on the list.

After a few moments Wallander called the Ystad branch of the North Bank. He had taken out car loans with them on the few occasions he had traded in his old cars for new models. He had come to know a man there called Winberg. He asked to speak to him, but the telephone operator said his line was busy. He left the station and went down to the bank in person. Winberg was busy with a customer. He nodded at Wallander, who sat down and waited. After five minutes he was free.

"I've been expecting you," Winberg said. "Is it time for a new car?"

Wallander was always surprised by how young the bank employees were. The first time he had applied for a loan here Winberg himself had approved it, though he looked hardly old enough to have a driving licence.

"I've come about something else, in fact. Something work-related. The new car will have to wait."

Winberg's smile waned. "Has anything happened here at the bank?"

"If it had I would have spoken to your boss. What I need now is information about your cash machines."

"I'm glad to be of help, but there are some things I can't disclose for security reasons."

Winberg was sounding as bureaucratic as Wallander sometimes did.

"What I'm after is of a technical nature. The first question is very simple: how often does it happen that a machine makes a mistake on a withdrawal or with an account balance?"

"Very rarely, I believe, though I have no exact figures to give you."

"Can I take it that 'very rarely' means that it virtually never happens?"

"Yes."

"And is there any possibility that the date and time printed on a slip would be incorrect?"

"I've never heard of it. I imagine it's not inconceivable, but the odds against it happening would be astronomical. Security and accuracy at the bank, all banks, have to be as good as perfect."

"So one can absolutely rely on what comes out of these machines?"

"Have you had an experience to the contrary?"

"No, but I need answers to these questions."

Winberg opened a drawer in his desk and looked for something. Then he pulled out a cartoon strip of a man being slowly swallowed by a cash machine.

"It never gets quite this bad," he said, smiling. "But it's

a funny image. And when it comes down to it the bank's computers are as vulnerable as all other computerised systems."

There it is again, Wallander thought, this talk of vulnerability. He looked at the sketch and agreed it was good.

"North Bank has a customer by the name of Tynnes Falk," Wallander said. "I need printouts of his bank activities for the past year, which should include his withdrawals at cash machines."

"You'll have to speak to someone higher up," Winberg said. "I couldn't authorise the release of such information, even to you."

"Who should I talk to?"

"Martin Olsson, the manager, is your best bet. He has an office on the second floor."

"Can you see if he's free now?"

Winberg left his desk. Wallander glumly anticipated an extended bureaucratic process before he could reach Olsson, but Winberg escorted him directly to the bank manager. He, too, was surprisingly young. He would do all he could to help Wallander. All he required was an official police request. Once he learned that the customer was deceased, he said the widow could sign in his stead.

"He was divorced," Wallander said.

"A paper from the police is all we need," Olsson said. "I'll see that this is taken care of quickly at our end."

Wallander thanked him and returned to Winberg. "One more question," he said. "Can you check to see if Falk kept a security box here?"

"I don't know if that's allowed," Winberg said.

"Your boss has already cleared it," Wallander lied.

Winberg was gone for a few minutes.

"There's no box in his name," he said when he returned.

Wallander was about to leave, when it occurred to him that he might as well take care of all his business at once.

"You're right, it is time for me to get a new car. Let's do the paperwork now while we're at it," he said.

"How much do you need?"

Wallander thought quickly. He had no other debt right now.

"One hundred thousand should do it. If I qualify for that much."

"No problem," Winberg said, and reached for the appropriate form.

They were finished by 1.30 p.m. Wallander left the bank with the feeling of being rich. When he walked past the bookshop by Stortorget he remembered the book on renovating furniture that he should have collected a couple of days ago. He also remembered he had no cash on him. He turned back and walked to the cash machine next to the post office. There were four people ahead of him in line. A woman with a pram, two teenage girls and an older man. Wallander watched absently as the woman put in her card, took out the cash and then the printed slip. Then he started thinking about Falk. The two girls took out their money, then discussed the amount printed on the slip with great energy. The older man looked around before putting in his card and punching in his code. He put his notes into his wallet and pocketed the printed slip without looking at it.

Then it was Wallander's turn. He took out one thousand kronor and read through the account balance on the slip. Everything seemed to be in order. He crumpled the piece of paper and fed it into the bin next to the machine. Then he froze. He thought about the blackout that had cut the power to most of Skåne. Someone had known exactly which point to hit to affect as many areas as possible. However advanced technology might become, there would always be points of vulnerability. He thought about the blueprint in Falk's office. It could not have been coincidence. Just as it had been no coincidence that the electrical relay was in the morgue. None of what had happened had been coincidence.

Perhaps it was a kind of sacrifice, he thought. There was an altar in Falk's secret chamber, with Falk's face as an object of worship. Perhaps Sonja Hökberg wasn't simply killed but had been sacrificed. To the end that the point of vulnerability would become more evident. A black hood had been pulled down over Skåne and everything had been brought to a halt.

The thought made him shiver. The feeling that he and his colleagues were fumbling around in the dark grew stronger.

He watched the steady stream of people coming to the cash machine. If you can control the power supply you can control this machine, he thought. And God only knows what else you control. Air traffic, trains, the water supply, electricity. All of this can be brought to its knees if you know the right place to strike.

He started walking again. The bookshop would have to wait. He returned to the station. Irene wanted to tell him something, but he waved her away and continued to his office. He threw his coat onto the visitor's chair and reached for his notepad. He wrote out the facts again, this time from the perspective that all that had happened was part of a planned act of sabotage. He thought back to the perplexing fact that Falk had been involved in the release of those minks. Did that gesture foreshadow something bigger, something much more sinister?

He threw the pen down and leaned back in his chair. He was still not convinced that he had found the point that would truly break the case open, but it did offer new possibilities. Lundberg's murder fell outside this scheme of things, but perhaps it was unforeseen, something that had not been planned. That needed addressing. It had, nevertheless, to be the case that Hökberg was killed to keep her quiet. And why were Falk's fingers cut off? To keep something from coming to light.

He kept delving through his material. What happened if they assumed Lundberg's death wasn't part of the larger pattern?

Half an hour later he was less convinced. It was too early to hope that the case would hang together, but he cheered himself up with the thought that he had come a bit further along the road. No doubt, there were more angles from which to view these events, and these would come to light if all of the team persevered.

He had just got up to go to the toilet when Höglund knocked and came in.

"You were right," she said. "Hökberg did have a boyfriend."

"What's his name?"

"More to the point, where is he?"

"Don't you know?"

"It looks as if he's vanished."

Wallander took stock. That visit to the toilet would have to wait.

It was 2.45 p.m.

CHAPTER TWENTY-FIVE

In hindsight, Wallander would feel he had made one of the biggest mistakes of his life that afternoon by listening to what Höglund had to say. As soon as he heard that Hökberg had had a boyfriend, he should have immediately realised that the truth was more complicated. What Höglund had discovered was a half-truth, and half-truths have a tendency to lead you astray. The result was that he didn't see what he should have seen, and it was a costly mistake. In his darkest hours, he would feel that it had cost a person his life. And it could have led to an even greater catastrophe.

That Monday, October 13, Höglund had taken on the job of finding out once and for all if there had been a boyfriend in Hökberg's life. She had brought this up again with Persson, who had persisted in denying that there was one. The only name she gave was Kalle Ryss, with whom Hökberg had been close at an earlier time. Höglund wasn't sure if Persson was telling the truth, but she had not been able to get any further.

Höglund drove to the hardware shop where Ryss worked. They had gone into the storeroom to speak undisturbed. In contrast to Persson, Ryss answered simply and apparently truthfully all Höglund's questions. She thought that, although their relationship had been over for at least a year, he missed Sonja, mourned her death and was frightened by what had happened. He could not shed much light on the direction her life had taken after their break-up. Even though Ystad was not a big town, their paths had not crossed very often. And Ryss usually drove to Malmö at the weekends. That was where his new girlfriend lived.

"But I think there was someone else," he said. "Someone that Sonja was with."

Ryss didn't know much about him except that his name was Jonas Landahl and that he lived all alone in a big house on Snappehanegatan. He didn't know the exact address, but it was by the corner of Friskyttegatan, on the left-hand side if you were coming from town. What Landahl did for a living he couldn't say.

Höglund drove there immediately and saw a beautiful modern house on the left-hand side of the street. She walked through the gate and rang the bell. The house seemed deserted, though she couldn't have said why she thought so. No-one came to the door. She rang the bell several more times, then walked round to the back of the house. She banged on the back door and tried to look in through the windows. When she came back to the front she saw a man in a dressing gown and boots standing outside the front gate. It was a strange sight given the time of day and the cold. He explained that he lived in the house across the street and that he had seen her ringing the doorbell. He said his name was Yngve, but didn't give his last name.

"No-one's home," he said firmly. "Not even the boy."

Their conversation was short but informative. Yngve was apparently a man who liked to keep his neighbours under surveillance. The Landahl family were strange birds in these parts, he said, and had been there about 10 years. What Mr Landahl did he didn't know. They hadn't even bothered to call and introduce themselves when they moved in. They had carried all their possessions and the boy into the house and then shut their doors. He hardly ever saw them. The boy couldn't have been more than 12 or 13 when they arrived, but they often left him alone for long stretches of time. The parents took off on long trips to God knows where. From time to time they came back only to disappear as suddenly as they had come. Neither one of them seemed to hold down a job, but there was always money. The last time he had seen them was some time in September. Then the boy, now a grown man, was alone again. But a few days ago a taxi had come for him and taken him away.

"So the house is empty?" Höglund said.

"There's no-one there."

"When was it the taxi came?"

"Last Wednesday. In the afternoon."

Höglund imagined Yngve sitting in his kitchen with a log of his neighbours' comings and goings and activities in front of him. I suppose it's not unlike watching trains, she thought.

"Do you remember what taxi company it was?" she asked.

"No."

You know perfectly well what company it was, she thought. You may even remember the make of the car and have written down the number plate. But you're not going to tell me because you don't want to admit what I've already found out. That you spy on your neighbours.

"I'd be grateful if you would get in touch with us when he turns up again."

"What's he done?"

"Nothing. We just need to ask him a few questions."

"What about?"

His curiosity knew no bounds. She shook her head and he didn't ask again, but she could tell that he was irritated. It was as if she had breached some unspoken etiquette.

Höglund returned to the station and was lucky enough quickly to find the right taxi company and the driver who had picked up Landahl on Snappehanegatan. The driver came to the police station. His name was Östensson and he was in his thirties.

She asked him about his passenger and he turned out to have a good memory.

"I picked him up just before 2 p.m. I think his name was Jonas."

"Did he give a last name?"

"I think I thought it was a last name. Nowadays people have such strange names."

"And there was only one passenger?"

"Yes. A young man. He was friendly."

"Did he have much luggage?"

"Just one small case on wheels."

"Where did you take him?"

"To the ferry terminal."

"Was he going to Poland?"

"Is there any other destination?"

"What was your impression of him?"

"I didn't have one, really, but he was nice enough."

"Did he seem anxious?"

"No."

"Did he talk?"

"He sat in the back seat and looked out of the window, as far as I remember. But he gave me a tip. I remember that."

Höglund thanked him for his trouble. She decided to get a warrant to search the house on Snappehanegatan.

She spoke to the state prosecutor, who sent over the paperwork she needed. She was just on her way over to the house when the day-care centre called to say that her youngest child was not well, was in fact vomiting. She drove over and took the child home, spending the next couple of hours there, until the child seemed better and her godsend of a neighbour, who often jumped in and helped her in times of need, was available to look after the little one. Now she was back at the station, and Wallander was there too.

"Do we have keys?" he said.

"I thought we would bring a locksmith with us."

"No need. Did the locks look complicated in any way?"

"No, not really."

"Then I'll take care of them myself."

"Just remember that a man in a dressing gown and green boots will be watching us from his kitchen window."

"You'll have to keep him busy, maybe sweet-talk him. Tell him his watchfulness has been a great help and that we would be grateful if he would take special notice of the comings and goings on his street for the next few days. And of course keep everything he finds out to himself. If there's one curious neighbour there could be more."

Höglund laughed. "He's just the type to fall for it," she said.

They drove to Snappehanegatan in her car. As usual he thought she drove too fast and made unnecessarily brusque movements. He was going to tell her about the photograph album, but he couldn't concentrate on anything but his prayers that they would not run into another car.

Wallander walked up to the front door while Höglund went over to the house belonging to the man called Yngve. Just as she had described, he too was struck by a feeling of desolation as he regarded the house. He was about to get the doors open when she returned.

"The dressing-gown man is now part of our undercover team," she said.

"I take it you didn't say we wanted the boy in connection with Hökberg?"

"Who do you take me for?"

"A talented policewoman, of course."

Wallander got the doors open and shut them once they were inside.

"Is anyone here?" Wallander shouted.

The words seemed to be swallowed up by the silence.

They worked their way slowly and deliberately through the house. It was a model of cleanliness and order. Everything in its place, nothing to suggest a hurried departure. There was something almost impersonal about the rooms, as if the furniture had all been bought at the same time and put there only to make the rooms occupied. There was a photograph of a young couple with a newborn baby on the mantelpiece. There was a bare minimum of personal items. An answering machine with a button blinking stood on a table. Wallander pressed it and the messages came on. A computer company reported that his new modem was in. Then there was a wrong number, no message, no name. Then there came the message Wallander had been hoping for. Wallander recognised it immediately, although it took Höglund a few seconds to process it. It was Sonja Hökberg's voice: *I'll call you again. It's important. I'll call you.*

Wallander found the button that saved the message. They played it again.

"So now we know," he said. "Sonja was in touch with the boy who lived here. She didn't even say her name."

"Is this the call we've been looking for? When she escaped?"

"Probably."

Wallander went out into the kitchen, through the laundry room and opened the door to the garage. There was a car. A dark blue VW Golf.

"Call Nyberg," Wallander said. "I want that car gone over with a fine-tooth comb."

"Do you think it's the one that delivered her to her death?"

"It could be. We can't rule that out at any rate."

Höglund got out her phone and started the process of tracking down Nyberg. Wallander used the time to take a look around the second floor. There were four bedrooms, but only two of them, from a swift reconnaissance, looked as though they were lived in. One for the parents, one for the boy. Wallander opened the wardrobe in the parents' room and looked at the clothes hanging in neat rows. He heard Höglund coming up the stairs.

"Nyberg is on his way."

Then she too looked at the clothes. "They have good taste," she said. "And plenty of money, you can tell."

Wallander found a dog's collar and a short leather whip right at the back of the wardrobe.

"Perhaps their tastes run a little to the alternative side," he said thoughtfully.

"It's the in-thing nowadays," Höglund said knowingly. "People think you screw better if you pull a plastic bag over your head and flirt with death."

Her choice of words startled and embarrassed Wallander, but he said nothing.

They continued into the boy's room. It was unexpectedly spartan. There was nothing on the walls or on the bed. There was a computer on a large desk.

"I'll ask Martinsson to take a look at this," Wallander said.

"Do you want me to start it up for you?"

"No, let's hold off."

They went back downstairs. Wallander searched through the slips of paper stuffed into a kitchen drawer until he found what he was looking for.

"I don't know if you noticed this or not," he said, "but there was no name on the front door. That's a little unusual. But here at least is some junk mail addressed to Harald Landahl, Jonas's father."

"Are we going to put out a search for him? I mean the boy."

"Not just yet. We need a little more information first."

"Was he the one who killed her?"

"We don't know. But his departure can be interpreted as an attempt to flee."

They went through more drawers while they waited for Nyberg. Höglund found a number of photographs of what looked to be a newly built house somewhere, probably in the Mediterranean.

"Is that where they keep going?"

"It's not impossible."

"Where do they get their money?"

"The son is still the main focus of our investigation."

The doorbell rang. It was Nyberg and two of his team of technicians. Wallander led them out to the garage.

"Concentrate on fingerprints," he said. "They might correspond with some we've found in other places. On Sonja Hökberg's handbag, for example. Or in the office. Also look for signs placing the car at the power substation. Or that Hökberg has been in it."

"In that case we'll start with the tyres," Nyberg said.

"That will be the fastest. You remember we had one set of tyre marks out there we couldn't account for."

Wallander waited and it only took Nyberg ten minutes to give him the answer he had been hoping for.

"This is the car," Nyberg said after having compared the tread with pictures taken of the crime scene.

"Are you sure?"

"Of course not. There are thousands of tyres out there that are almost identical. But if you look at this back left tyre you'll see that it's low on air and is also worn on the inside since the tyres haven't been balanced properly. That dramatically increases our chances of being right."

"So you are sure."

"As sure as I can be without being 100 per cent certain."

Wallander left the garage. Höglund was busy in the living room. He went to the kitchen. Am I doing the right thing? he thought. Should I send out a description of him right now? A sudden sense of anxiety drove him back upstairs to the boy's bedroom. He sat at the desk and looked around. Then he got up and went over to the wardrobe. There was nothing that caught his eye. He stood on tiptoe and felt around on the upper shelves. Nothing. He returned to the desk and looked at the computer. On an impulse, he lifted the keyboard, but there was nothing underneath. He paused before going to the top of the stairs and calling out to Höglund. They went back into the boy's bedroom together and Wallander pointed to the computer.

"Do you want me to start it up for you?"

"Yes."

"So we're not waiting for Martinsson?"

There was no attempt to conceal the tone of irony in her voice. Perhaps she had been hurt by his earlier insistence that they wait for their colleague. But right now he didn't have time to think about that. How many times had he felt overlooked or humiliated during his years as a policeman? By other police officers, criminals, prosecutors and journalists, and not least by those who were usually referred to as "members of the public".

Höglund sat down and switched on the computer. It made a little noise and the screen slowly came to life. She clicked open the hard drive and various icons emerged.

"What is it you want me to look for?"

"I don't know."

She chose an icon at random and double-clicked on it. In contrast to Falk's computer this one didn't put up any resistance. It dutifully opened the file, the only problem being that the file was completely empty.

Wallander put on his glasses and leaned over her shoulder.

"Try the one called 'Correspondence'," he said.

She clicked on the icon, but the same thing happened. There was nothing there.

"What does it mean?" he said.

"That it's empty."

"Or that it has been emptied. Keep going."

She tried file after file but kept getting the same result.

"It's strange," she said. "There really isn't anything here at all."

Wallander looked around to see if he could find any diskettes. But he couldn't find a single one.

Höglund proceeded to the file that held the information about computer activity.

"The last activity occurred on October 9."

"That was last Thursday."

They looked questioningly at each other.

"The day after he went to Poland?"

"If the neighbourhood spy is to be believed, which I think he is, and the taxi driver too."

Wallander sat down.

"Explain it to me."

"Well, as far as I can see that leaves us with two possibilities. Either he came back. Or someone else has been here."

"And the person who was here could have emptied the computer?"

"Quite easily, considering there was no password and no security barriers."

Wallander tried to draw on the little computer knowledge he had managed to absorb. "Could this person also have removed any trace of such a barrier?"

"Yes, if they had already bypassed it themselves."

"And then emptied the computer at the same time?"

"There would always be prints left behind," she said thoughtfully.

"What do you mean?"

"It's something Martinsson explained to me."

"Tell me."

"You can try to understand it by comparing a computer to a house that has been emptied of its furniture. There are always a few traces left behind. There might be scratches on the hardwood floors, or perhaps there are patches of light and dark left from where the furniture once was."

"Like a wall after the paintings have been taken down," Wallander said. "Lighter patches where they used to be."

"Martinsson used the example of a cellar. Somewhere deep inside the computer there's a space where everything that is supposed to be erased continues to live on. That means that until a hard drive has been destroyed, it is theoretically possible to reconstruct everything that was once on it."

Wallander shook his head.

"I understand what you're saying, though I don't understand how it would be possible," he said. "But what interests me most right now is the fact that someone used the computer on October 9."

Höglund turned back to the monitor.

"Let me just check the games that are on here," she said and started double-clicking on the icons she hadn't yet touched.

"That's funny," she said. "I've never heard of this game, 'Jacob's Marsh'."

When she finished she turned off the computer.

"There's nothing there at all. I just wonder why the icons were left on the desktop."

They searched the room, in the hope of finding some diskettes, but had no luck. Wallander was intuitively convinced that getting to the bottom of the use of the computer on October 9 was a key to unlocking the case. Someone had cleaned out the computer, and the only question was if it was Landahl or someone else.

Finally, they gave up looking and went downstairs. Wallander asked Nyberg to go through the house with a fine-tooth comb after he had finished with the car. Looking in every nook and cranny for diskettes would be his highest priority.

Höglund was on her mobile with Martinsson when he came back into the kitchen. She handed him the phone.

"How is it going over there?"

"Robert has a lot of energy, I'll give him that much," Martinsson said. "He took a lunch break and had a strange kind of quiche, but he was ready to get back to work before I had even had my coffee."

"Any developments?"

"He keeps insisting that the number 20 is significant. It's cropped up in several different contexts. But he's not over the wall yet."

"What do you mean?"

"That's his own terminology. He hasn't cracked the code, though he's sure now it consists of two words. Or possibly a number and a word, though I'm not sure how he knows that."

Wallander told him briefly what they were doing. When the conversation was over, he asked Höglund to go back to the neighbour and confirm the date of Jonas Landahl's departure. He also wanted her to ask if he had seen anyone else on the 9th.

She left and Wallander sat on the sofa to think. But he had not come up with anything when she came back.

"It's pretty disturbing, really," she said. "He keeps a record of everything he sees. Is that all one has to look forward to in retirement? In any case he's absolutely sure the boy left on Wednesday."

"What about the 9th?"

"He didn't see anyone. But of course he can't spend every waking moment at the kitchen window."

"So that doesn't tell us anything," Wallander said. "It could as easily have been the boy as anyone else."

It was 5 p.m. Höglund left to pick up her children. She offered to come back later that night, but Wallander told her to stay at home. He would call her if anything else came up.

He returned to the boy's room for a third time, kneeling to peer under the bed. Höglund had already checked it, but he wanted to see with his own eyes if there was anything there.

Then he lay down on the bed.

Suppose he's hidden something important in this room, Wallander thought. Something he wants to be able to check on when he first wakes up in the morning and when he's going to bed at night. Wallander let his gaze travel along the walls of the room. Nothing. He was about to sit up when he saw that one of the bookcases next to the wardrobe leaned slightly in towards the wall. It was clearly visible from the bed. He sat up, and the angle was no longer apparent. He bent down at the bookcase. Someone had placed a small washer under each side creating a sliver of space beneath. He peered underneath and could just see something there. Using his pencil as a tool, he coaxed the object out and knew what it was before he had a chance to look at it. A diskette. He had his mobile out and was dialling a number even before he made it to the desk. Martinsson answered immediately. Wallander explained where he was and what he had found. Martinsson made a note of the address and said he was on his way. Modin would have to be left unsupervised for a short while.

Martinsson was there within 15 minutes. He started the computer and inserted the diskette. Wallander leaned forward to read the label on the diskette. "Jacob's Marsh". It reminded him of something Höglund had said about the games and he felt a rush of disappointment. Martinsson double-clicked on it. There was only one file on the diskette and it had last been opened on September 29. Martinsson double-clicked on the file.

They were both startled by the text that came up on the screen. "Release the minks."

"What does that mean?" Martinsson asked.

"I don't know," Wallander said. "But we have another connection: Landahl and Falk."

Martinsson stared at him uncomprehendingly.

"Don't you remember? Falk was involved in that animal rights business a while back."

Martinsson remembered.

"I wonder if Landahl was involved. He might have been one of the ones that got away."

Martinsson was still confused. "So this is all about minks?"

"No," Wallander said. "I don't think so. But I think we need to find Landahl very rapidly indeed."

CHAPTER TWENTY-SIX

It was early dawn on October 14 and Carter had just been forced to make an important decision. He had woken in the dark and listened to the noise of the air-conditioning unit. He heard that it was almost time to clean out the mechanism. There was a low hum in the monotone gush of cold air from the machine that shouldn't be there. He had stood up, shaken out his slippers since there could be insects hiding inside, put on his dressing gown and gone down to the kitchen. Carter helped himself to a bottle of the previously boiled water that had spent the night in the refrigerator. Slowly, he drank one large glass and then a second. Then he went upstairs to his study and sat in front of the computer. It was never turned off. It was connected to a large reserve battery in case of a blackout and it was also hooked up to a surge protector that managed the constant ebbs and flows of power from the electrical outlet.

He had a message from Fu Cheng. He read it. For a while he sat motionless in his chair.

The news was not good, not good at all. Cheng had done what he had told him to do, but the police were apparently still trying to break into Falk's computer. Carter was more or less certain that they would never be able to break the codes, and even if they did they wouldn't understand what they were looking at. But there was something in the report that worried him – it was the fact that the police had brought in a young man to help them.

Carter had a healthy respect for young men with glasses who spent a great deal of time in front of their computers. He and Falk had often spoken about these modern-day geniuses. They could break into secure networks, read through and even interpret the most complicated electronic programs.

Cheng had written that he believed this Modin to be one of this breed of young men. Swedish hackers, he said, had broken into the defence systems of other countries. He might be one of the dangerous ones, Carter thought. A modern-day heretic. Someone who won't leave our systems and our secrets alone. In an earlier age a person like Modin would have been burned at the stake.

Carter didn't like it, any more than he had liked any of the developments since Falk's death. Falk had really left him in the lurch. Now Carter was forced to clean up around him and he didn't have time to weigh each decision with due care. Haste had led to mistakes, such as removing Falk's body. Maybe it hadn't been necessary to kill that young woman? But she could have talked. And the police didn't seem to be losing interest.

Carter had seen this kind of behaviour before, just like a person determined to follow a set of tracks leading to the wounded animal hiding in the bush. After a few days he had realised it was the policeman called Wallander who was tracking them. Cheng's analysis had been very clear on the matter. That's why they had tried to take him out. But they had failed, and the man was still tenaciously following their tracks.

Carter got up and walked to the window. No signs of life yet in the city. The African night was full of scents. Cheng was dependable. He was capable of a fanatical loyalty that Carter and Falk had once decided might be useful. The only question now was whether that was enough.

He settled at the computer. It took him a little less than half an hour to list all the possible alternatives. Then he swept his mind clear of any emotion that would distract him from the best possible course of action.

He arrived at his decision in only a few minutes. Carter had identified Wallander's weakness, one that opened a possibility of getting to him.

Every person has his secret, Carter thought. So even this Wallander. Secrets and weaknesses.

He started typing again and heard banging and clattering from the kitchen before he had finished. He read his message three times before he was satisfied and sent it off.

Carter went down to the dining room and ate his breakfast. Every morning he tried to see if he could tell if Celine was pregnant again. He had decided to fire her the next time it happened. He handed her the shopping list he had made the night before. He gave her the money, then unlocked the two front doors. There were 16 different locks to unlock every morning.

Celine left the house. The city had begun to stir. But this house that was built by a Portuguese doctor had thick walls. When Carter returned to his study he had the feeling that he was surrounded by silence, the silence that always existed in the middle of the African din. There was a blinking light on his computer. He had an e-mail.

It was only a week before the electronic tidal wave would wash over the world.

At 7 p.m. on Monday it was as if someone had let the air out of Martinsson and Wallander. That was after they had left the house in Snappehanegatan and returned to the police station.

They had tried to understand what had happened. Did Landahl return to erase all the files on his computer? In that case, why had he left the diskette behind? Was the content on the diskette unimportant? But why then had it been hidden with such care? There were many questions, but no good answers. Martinsson suggested, tentatively, that the perplexing message – "Release the minks" – was an attempt to lead them astray. But what direction was that? Wallander wondered. There seemed to be no direction that was any better than the rest.

They discussed whether or not they should put out an alert for Landahl. Wallander hesitated since they had no real reason to bring him in, at least not until Nyberg had been able to examine the house. Martinsson did not agree with him, and it was at about this time that they were both overtaken by exhaustion. Wallander felt guilty that he couldn't steer the investigation in the right direction. He suspected that Martinsson silently agreed with him on this point.

Modin had been sent home, though he had been willing to work all night. Martinsson started checking the police records for Jonas Landahl. He had focused on descriptions of animal rights activists, but had found nothing. He had turned off his computer and joined Wallander, who was sitting in front of a cup of cold coffee in the canteen.

They had agreed to call it a day. Wallander remained in the canteen for a while, too tired to think, too tired to go home. The last thing he did was try to get in touch with Hansson. Someone finally told him that Hansson had gone to Växjö in the afternoon. Wallander called Nyberg, but he had nothing new to report. The technicians were still working on the car.

On his way home, Wallander stopped at the grocer's. When he was in line to pay he realised he had left his wallet on his desk at work. The checkout girl recognised him and let him take his food on credit. The first thing Wallander did when he got home was write a note to himself in capital letters reminding him to pay his bill the following day. He put the note on the doormat so he wouldn't miss it in the morning. Then he made a spaghetti dinner that he ate in front of the television. For once, the food was quite good. He flipped through the channels and opted for a film, but it was halfway through when he started and he never got into it. That reminded him that there was another film he needed to see. The one with Al Pacino.

He went to bed at 11 p.m. and unplugged the phone. There was no wind and the street lamp outside the window was still. It didn't take long for him to fall asleep.

On Tuesday, he woke up shortly before 6 a.m., feeling well rested. He had dreamed of his father. And about Widén. They had been in a strange landscape filled with rocks. In the dream Wallander had been afraid he was about to lose sight of them. Even I can interpret this dream, he thought. I'm still as afraid of abandonment as I was as a child.

His mobile rang. It was Nyberg. As usual he got straight to the point. He always assumed the person he was calling was fully awake, regardless of what time it was, which never stopped him from complaining about other people calling him at all hours.

"I've just finished work on the garage at Snappehanegatan," he said. "I found something in the back seat of the car that I missed the first time."

"What was it?"

"A stick of gum. It says 'spearmint'."

"Was it stuck to the back seat?"

"It was in its packet. If it had been a piece of chewed gum I would have found it much earlier."

Wallander was already out of bed and halfway across the cold floor to the bathroom.

"Good," he said. "I'll be in touch."

Half an hour later he had showered, dressed and was on his way to the station. His morning coffee would have to wait until he got to the office. He had planned to walk to work, but changed his mind at the last minute and took the car. He tried to quell his guilty conscience. The first person he looked for when he arrived was Irene. But she wasn't in yet. If Ebba was still working she would already be here, Wallander thought. Even though she didn't officially start until 7 a.m. But she would have known intuitively that I needed to speak to her. He realised he was being unfair to Irene. No-one could compare to Ebba. He went to get a cup of coffee in the meantime. He spoke to some of the traffic officers who were complaining about speeding drivers and the rising incidence of driving under the influence. There was going to be a big crackdown today. Wallander listened absently, reflecting that policemen had a tendency to whine. He walked back to the reception area just as Irene was taking off her coat and scarf.

"Do you remember me borrowing some gum from you the other day?"

"I don't think 'borrow' is the right word in that context. I gave it to you, or rather, to that girl."

"What kind was it?"

"A normal brand. Spearmint, I think."

Wallander nodded.

"Was that it?" Irene asked, surprised.

Wallander returned to his office, walking so quickly he almost spilled his coffee. He was in a hurry to confirm this train of thought. He called Höglund at home and heard a child wail in the background when she answered.

"I want you to do me a favour," he said. "I want you to ask Persson what kind of gum she chews. I also want you to ask her if she gave any to Hökberg."

"Why is this so important?"

"I'll explain when you get here."

She called him back after 10 minutes. There was still a lot of noise in the background.

"I talked to her mother. She said Eva chews different kinds of gum. I can't imagine she would lie about something like this."

"So she keeps an eye on what kind of gum her daughter chews?"

"Mothers know a lot about their daughters," she said.

"Or they think they do."

"In some cases."

"What about Hökberg?"

"I think we can assume that the girls would share their gum."

Wallander smacked his lips.

"Why in God's name is this so important?"

"I'll tell you when you get here."

"Everything is such a mess over here," she sighed. "For some reason, Tuesday mornings are the worst."

Wallander hung up. Every morning is the worst, he thought. Without fail. At least all those mornings that you wake up at 5 a.m. and can't get back to sleep.

He walked over to Martinsson's office. No-one there. He was probably with Modin over at Runnerströms Torg. Hansson wasn't in either. Maybe he wasn't back yet from what was probably a completely wasted trip to Växjö.

Wallander sat at his desk and tried to go through the latest findings on his own. They were now almost sure that the blue car over at Snappehanegatan was the vehicle that had taken Hökberg to the power substation. Landahl had probably been the driver, letting her off to be killed, then preparing to take the ferry to Poland.

There were many gaps. Landahl may not have been the driver and he may not have been Hökberg's killer, but he was definitely under suspicion. They needed to speak to him in a hurry.

The computer was an even bigger mystery. If Landahl had not erased what was on it, then someone else did. And how could they account for the hidden diskette?

After a few minutes he came up with a third alternative. Landahl did erase everything on his computer, but someone else also came in later to make sure he had done so.

Wallander turned to a fresh page on his notepad and wrote a list of names:

Lundberg, Hökberg and Persson.
Tynnes Falk.
Jonas Landahl.

There was a connection between all of these people. But there was still no satisfactory motive for any of the crimes. We are still looking for common ground, Wallander thought. We haven't found it yet.

He was interrupted in his thoughts by Martinsson.

"Modin has started his day already," he said. "He insisted on being picked up at 6 a.m. He's a strange bird. He brought his own food with him today. Some funny-looking herbal teas and even funnier rusks. Made from organic ingredients in Bornholm. He also brought a Walkman with him, claiming he works best when he listens to music. I looked at his tapes. Here are the names." He took a slip of paper out of his pocket. "Handel's *Messiah*, Verdi's *Requiem*. What does that tell you?"

"That Modin has good taste in music."

Wallander told Martinsson about the phone calls with Nyberg and Höglund and the fact that they could now be fairly sure that Hökberg had been driven in Landahl's car.

"It may not have been her last car journey, though," Martinsson said.

"I think for now we'll assume it was. We'll also assume that that's why Landahl decided to get away."

"So we put out an alert for him?"

"Yes. Can you arrange it with the prosecutor?"

Martinsson made a face. "Can't Hansson take care of it?"

"He's not in yet."

"Where the hell is he?"

"Someone said he went up to Växjö."

"Why?"

"That's where Persson's alcoholic father is supposed to be."

"And is that really a priority? Speaking to her father?"

Wallander shrugged. "I can't be the only authority on what to prioritise."

Martinsson got up. "I'll talk to Viktorsson, and I'll also see what I can dig up on Landahl. As long as the computers are up."

Wallander detained him for a moment. "What do we know about these groups?" he asked. "These – what do you call them – eco-terrorists?"

"Hansson compares them to motorcycle gangs, since they break into labs and sabotage animal experiments."

"Is that fair?"

"When was Hansson fair?"

"I thought most of these groups espoused non-violence? Isn't it called civil disobedience? Has that gone out of style?"

"As far as I know, most of the time they're non-violent."

"And Falk was involved in this."

"Don't forget that he may not have been murdered."

"But Hökberg was, and so was Lundberg."

"Doesn't that just tell us that we don't have a clue about what's going on?"

"How about Modin – do you think he's going to get anywhere?"

"It's hard to say. I hope so."

"And he still claims the number 20 is important?"

"Yes. He's sure of that now. I only understand about half of what he says, but even that much is persuasive."

Wallander looked at his calendar. "It's October 14 today. That means we have a week left."

"If the 20 refers to a date. We don't know that."

Wallander thought of something else. "Have Sydkraft come up with anything else? They must have finished their internal investigation by now. How could the break-in occur? Why was the gate broken and not the inner door?"

"Hansson is in charge of that. He said that Sydkraft have taken the whole thing very seriously and he expects to see a number of heads roll."

"I wonder if *we* have taken it seriously enough ourselves," Wallander said thoughtfully. "And how did Falk manage to get a hold of the blueprint? And why?"

"Everything is so complicated," Martinsson said. "Naturally we can't dismiss the idea of sabotage. The step from releasing minks to cutting power is perhaps not so great. Not if someone is a fanatic."

Wallander felt his anxiety tighten its grip.

"This thing with the number 20 worries me," he said. "What if it really does stand for October 20? What will happen then?"

"It worries me too," Martinsson said. "But I don't have any answers for you."

Martinsson left the room and Wallander devoted the next two hours to catching up on paperwork and trying to make a dent in the piles that had built up on his desk. The whole time he was searching for a clue he might have overlooked. But he didn't think of anything new.

Later that afternoon they had a meeting. Martinsson had talked to Viktorsson, and Landahl was now officially wanted by the police. The alert had gone out internationally as well. The Polish authorities had responded very quickly and confirmed that Jonas Landahl had entered the country on the day that his neighbour saw him leave Snappehanegatan in a taxi. They had no confirmation as yet of any departure, but something told Wallander that Poland was not where he was.

Nyberg had gone over the car again and sent a number of plastic bags with fibre and hair samples for further analysis. They would not be able to confirm the fact that Hökberg had been in the car until the results came back. The question of the car sparked a heated discussion between Martinsson and Höglund. If Hökberg and Landahl had been going out it would have been natural for her to have been in the car, but that wouldn't prove if it was the car that had taken her to the power substation on the last day of her life or not.

Wallander waited while they argued back and forth.

Neither one was right. Both were tired. Finally the discussion died down of its own accord. Hansson talked about his trip to Växjö, which had been as meaningless as Wallander had suspected. He had also taken a wrong turning on the highway, delaying him even further. By the time he located Persson's father he turned out to be incapably drunk and hadn't been able to give Hansson any interesting information. He had burst into tears each time he said his daughter's name and talked despondently of her future. Hansson had got away as soon as he decently could.

There was no information as yet on the Mercedes van that they were still looking for. Wallander had received a fax from the American Express office in Hong Kong confirming that there was no-one by the name of Fu Cheng at the address indicated on the card. Modin was still wrestling with Falk's computer. After a long and, in Wallander's opinion, unnecessary discussion they decided to wait yet another day before bringing in the computer experts of the National Police.

By 6 p.m. they were exhausted. Wallander looked around at the pale and tired faces at the table. The only thing he could do now was let everyone go home. They would meet again at 8 a.m. the following day. Wallander kept working after the meeting was over but at 8.30 p.m. even he went home. He ate the leftovers of his spaghetti dinner and lay down on his bed to read a book. It was an account of Napoleon's military campaigns and it was incredibly boring. He soon fell asleep with the book open beside him.

The phone rang. At first he didn't know where he was or what time it was. He answered. It was someone from the station.

"One of the ferries approaching Ystad has just contacted us," said the policeman on night duty.

"What's happened?"

"One of the axles for the propellers started malfunctioning and when they located the problem they called us immediately."

"Yes?"

"There was a dead body in the engine room."

Wallander caught his breath. "Where's the ferry?"

"It's half an hour from land."

"I'm going right down."

"Should I notify anyone else?"

Wallander thought for a moment.

"Call Martinsson and Hansson. And Nyberg. We'll meet at the terminal."

"Anything else?"

"Call Chief Holgersson."

"She's at a police conference in Copenhagen."

"I don't care. Call her."

"What should I tell her?"

"That a suspected murderer is on his way back from Poland. But that unfortunately he's coming back dead."

That ended the conversation. Wallander knew that he need to spend no more time worrying about where Jonas Landahl was. Twenty minutes later he met his colleagues by the ferry terminal and waited for the large ship to dock.

CHAPTER TWENTY-SEVEN

As Wallander was climbing down the steep companionway into the engine room he had a strong sense of descending into an inferno. The ferry was docked and the noise from below had died down to an even hum, but he still felt as though there were a hell down there waiting for him. Two white-faced engineers and an equally pale first mate had greeted them and escorted them to the engine room. They had managed to communicate that the body waiting for their inspection in the oily water below had been massacred beyond the point of recognition. Someone, perhaps Martinsson, said that the pathologist was on her way. A fire engine with a rescue crew was on the dockside.

Despite his misgivings, Wallander wanted to be the first to go down. Martinsson was glad to let him. Hansson was still not there. Wallander asked Martinsson to take charge of recording the events surrounding the discovery of the body and asked him to send Hansson below as soon as he arrived.

Then Wallander set off, closely followed by Nyberg. The technician who had discovered the body accompanied them. Once they had reached the lowest deck, he directed them to the stern. Wallander was astonished by the sheer bulk, the space. Finally the technician stopped at another companionway and pointed into the abyss. Wallander started down. While they were still on the ladder, Nyberg stepped on his hand. Wallander cursed from the pain and almost lost his grip. He managed to catch himself. Then they had made it all the way down and there, under one of the two large oily propeller shafts, was the body.

The engineers had not exaggerated. Wallander thought that what he was looking at was no longer human. It was as if a freshly slaughtered animal carcass had been thrown in there. Nyberg groaned. Wallander thought he hissed something about his retirement. Wallander was surprised not to feel the slightest bit queasy. He had been forced to endure so many terrible sights during his career. Car accidents. The remains of people who had died at home and not been discovered for months. But this was among the worst he had experienced. There had been a photograph of Landahl in his bedroom. Now Wallander tried to gauge if this body belonged to the young person he had assumed it must be. But the face was almost completely gone. In its place was a bloody lump without any features.

The boy in the photograph had been blond. The head in front of him, almost completely severed from the body, had only a few tufts of hair that were not matted with oil. They looked fair. That was enough for Wallander, although it didn't prove anything. He stepped aside so that Nyberg could take a closer look. Then Dr Bexell arrived, accompanied by two rescue workers.

"How in the hell did he end up down here?" Nyberg said.

Even though the engine was idling at low speed he had to shout to make himself heard. Wallander shook his head without answering. He felt an almost violent urge to get out of there, to escape this hell as quickly as possible. If only to be able to think clearly. He left Nyberg, the pathologist and the rescue workers and climbed the ladder. He made it all the way up to the deck, walked into the fresh air and took some deep breaths. Martinsson turned up from somewhere and asked him how it was.

"Worse than you can imagine."

"Was it Landahl?"

They hadn't talked openly about this possibility until now, but clearly it had been in Martinsson's mind too.

"It's impossible to be sure," Wallander said. "But I believe it's him."

Then he tried to muster his organisational skills. Martinsson had found out that the ferry was not scheduled to leave again until the following morning. That would give them enough time to finish the forensic investigation and remove the body.

"I've asked for a list of passengers," Martinsson said. "But there was no record of a Jonas Landahl, not for this trip."

"But he was on board today," Wallander said firmly. "Whether or not he appears on the list. He may have used a different name. We'll need a printout of that list and the names of all the crew. Then we'll see if there isn't a name that looks familiar or is a version of Landahl."

"You're ruling out the possibility that it was an accident?"

"Oh yes," Wallander said. "It's about as much of an accident as what happened to Hökberg. And it's the same people."

He asked if Hansson had arrived. Martinsson said he was taking statements from the engineers.

The ferry seemed completely deserted. A small cleaning crew was working on the broad staircase that connected the different levels of the ship. Wallander directed Martinsson into the large cafeteria. There wasn't a single person to be seen, but there were noises coming from the kitchen. Through the portholes they saw the lights of Ystad.

"See if you can get hold of some coffee," he said. "We need to talk."

Martinsson walked into the galley. Wallander sat down. What did it mean that Landahl was dead? He was slowly coming up with two different theories that he wanted to discuss with Martinsson.

A man in a uniform appeared at his side. "Why haven't you disembarked?" he said.

Wallander looked at the man, who had a long beard and a ruddy complexion. There were several gold stripes on his epaulettes. This is a large ferry, he thought. Not everyone knows about what happened down in the engine room.

"I'm a police officer," Wallander said. "Who are you?"

"I'm third mate on this ship."

"That's good," Wallander said. "Go and have a word with your captain or the first mate and they'll put you in the picture."

The man hesitated, but then seemed to make up his mind that Wallander was telling the truth and was not a lingering passenger to be dealt with. He hurried away just as Martinsson came out of the galley with a tray.

"They were eating," he said when he sat down. "They hadn't heard anything about what happened, though they had of course noticed that the ferry cut back on power for part of the trip."

"The third mate came to toss me ashore," Wallander said. "He didn't know anything either."

"Have we made a big mistake?"

"In what way?"

"Shouldn't we have detained everyone for a while? At least until we could have checked the names on the list and all the cars."

Martinsson was right, but that kind of an operation would have required more manpower than they could possibly have mustered at short notice. Wallander also doubted that they would have had any results.

"Maybe," he said. "But we should focus on the situation as it is."

"I dreamed about going to sea when I was younger," Martinsson said.

"Me too," Wallander said. "Doesn't everyone?"

Then he dived right in. "We have to come up with an interpretation," he said. "We had begun to suspect that Landahl was the one who drove Hökberg to the power substation and then killed her there. And that that was why he later ran away from Snappehanegatan. Now he, too, is killed. The question is simply how does this change the picture?"

"You remain convinced that it couldn't have been an accident?"

"Is that what you think it was?"

Martinsson shifted slightly.

"As I see it, there are two conclusions that can be drawn," Wallander said. "The first is that Landahl did kill Hökberg for some reason that we still don't know, although we suspect it has to do with keeping something quiet. Next, Landahl takes off to Poland. Whether he is driven by panic or pursuing a deliberate plan, we don't know. But then he is killed, possibly as a kind of revenge. Perhaps because he in turn has become a liability for someone else."

Wallander paused but Martinsson didn't say anything. Wallander continued.

"The other possibility is that an unknown person killed first Hökberg and now Landahl."

"How does that account for Landahl's quick getaway?"

"When he found out what happened to Hökberg he was scared. He fled, but someone caught up with him."

Martinsson nodded. It seemed to Wallander that they were thinking along the same tracks now.

"Sabotage and death," Martinsson said. "Hökberg's body is used to cause a huge blackout in Skåne. Then Landahl's body is thrown down into the propeller shafts of the Poland ferry."

"Do you remember what we talked about a little while ago?" Wallander said. "We put it this way: first the minks were released, then there was the blackout and now a murder on the ferry. What's next?"

Martinsson shook his head despondently. "It doesn't make sense," he said. "I can understand releasing the minks, that a group of animal rights activists plan and execute that task. I can perhaps even see some logic to the blackout – someone wants to demonstrate the crucial weaknesses built into our society. But what would be the point of causing chaos in the engine room of a ferry?"

"It's like a game of dominoes. If one piece falls, the rest will follow suit. The first piece to fall was Falk."

"What about Lundberg? How do you fit his killing into your scheme of things?"

"That's just the problem. I can't get it to fit and therefore I've started thinking something else."

"That Lundberg's death is incidental to the rest of the events?"

Martinsson could think quickly when he tried.

"Do you mean that we should separate these two sequences of events? Even though Hökberg figures so prominently in both?"

"That's just it," Wallander said. "What if her role in the

sequence of events is much less important than we have thought?"

At that moment Hansson came into the cafeteria. He cast a longing glance at their coffee. Right behind him was a grey-haired, pleasant-looking man with many stripes on his epaulettes. He turned out to be the captain. Wallander got to his feet and introduced himself. When Captain Sund spoke, it was clear he was not from Skåne.

"Terrible things," he said.

"No-one has seen anything," Hansson said. "Even though you would think someone would have noticed the victim on his way down to the engine room."

"So there are no witnesses?"

"I spoke to the two engineers who were on duty on the trip over from Poland. Neither one of them saw anything."

"And the doors to the engine room aren't locked?" Wallander asked.

"Our security measures don't allow it. But they are clearly marked with signs that say 'No entry'. Everyone who works in the area knows to keep an eye out for stray passengers. Sometimes, when people have had a bit too much to drink, they wander. But I never thought anything like this could happen."

"I take it that all the passengers are gone by now," Wallander said. "Is there by any chance a car that hasn't been claimed?"

Sund sent out a message on the radio in his hand. A crew member down on the car deck answered.

"All vehicles have been claimed," Sund said. "The car hold is completely empty."

"What about the cabins? Is there any unclaimed luggage?"

Sund went off in search of an answer. Hansson sat

down. Wallander noted that Hansson had been unusually careful in his questioning of the crew.

When the ferry left Swinoujscie the captain had estimated that the trip to Ystad would take about seven hours. Wallander asked if any of the engineers could pinpoint a time when the body must have slipped into the axles. Could it have happened even before the ferry left Poland? Hansson had thought to ask this question and could report that yes, the body could indeed have been there at the very start of the trip.

There wasn't much to add. No-one had seen anything unusual, let alone noticed Landahl. There had been 200 or so passengers on board, most of them Polish truckers. There had been a delegation from the Swedish cement industry, returning from an investment conference.

"We need to know if Landahl was travelling alone or with someone," Wallander said when Hansson finished. "That's important. Plus, we need a photograph of him. Then someone will have to take the boat there and back tomorrow and see if anyone recognises him."

"I hope that someone isn't me," Hansson said. "I get seasick."

"Find someone else," Wallander said. "What I need you to do right now is go up to Snappehanegatan and get that photograph. Check with the boy who works in the hardware shop that it's a decent likeness."

"You mean Ryss?"

"That's the one. He must have bumped into his successor at some point."

"The ferry leaves at 6 a.m. tomorrow."

"So you'll have to take care of all this by then," Wallander said patiently.

Hansson set off. Wallander and Martinsson remained in the cafeteria for a while longer. Dr Bexell came in after a while and sat down with them. She looked far from well.

"I've never seen anything like this," she said. "First a young woman's body burned by God knows how many millions of volts, and now this."

"Can you confirm that the victim is a young man?" Wallander said.

"Yes, it's a young man."

"Can you give us a cause of death? A time?"

"Of course not. You saw what kind of shape he was in. The boy was completely mangled. One of the rescue workers was as sick as a cat. And I don't blame him."

"Is Nyberg still there?"

"I think so."

Dr Bexell left. Captain Sund still had not returned. Martinsson's mobile started to vibrate. It was Holgersson calling from Copenhagen. Martinsson stretched the phone out to Wallander, but he shook his head.

"You talk to her."

"What should I tell her?"

"Tell her the facts. What else?"

Wallander got up and started pacing up and down the empty cafeteria. Landahl's death had closed an avenue that had seemed promising. But what kept working its way to the forefront of his mind was the idea that his death might have been avoided, if it was that Landahl had fled not because he was the killer but because he was frightened of someone else, who was.

Wallander chastised himself. He hadn't been thinking clearly enough. He had simply jumped to the easiest conclusion without keeping other theories in mind. And now Landahl was dead.

Martinsson finished his conversation and put his phone away. Wallander returned.

"I don't think she was 100 per cent sober, to tell you the truth," he said.

"She's at a police conference," Wallander said. "But at least now she knows what our evening has been like."

Captain Sund returned.

"There is one bag that was left behind in one of the cabins," he said.

Wallander and Martinsson got up as one from their chairs. They followed the captain through a myriad of corridors until they came to a cabin with a woman wearing the company uniform posted outside. She was Polish and spoke poor Swedish.

"According to our records this cabin was booked by a passenger called Jonasson."

Wallander and Martinsson exchanged glances.

"Is there anyone who can give us a description of him?"

It turned out that the captain spoke excellent Polish. He translated the question for the woman who listened and then shook her head.

"Did he share the cabin with anyone?"

"No."

Wallander went in. The cabin was narrow and windowless. Wallander shuddered at the thought of having to spend a stormy night in such quarters. On the bed that was attached to the wall there was a small suitcase with wheels. Martinsson handed him a pair of rubber gloves which he put on. He opened the case. It was empty. They searched the room for about ten minutes but without results.

"Nyberg will have to take a look in here," Wallander said when they had given up. "And the taxi driver who took Landahl to the ferry might be able to identify the bag."

Wallander went back out into the corridor. Martinsson made arrangements for the cabin to be kept out of bounds until further notice. Wallander looked at the doors to the cabins on either side. There were used sheets and towels outside each one. The numbers on the doors were 309 and 311.

"Try to find out who was in the cabins on either side," Wallander said. "They may have heard something or even seen someone come or go."

Martinsson wrote it down in his notebook, then started speaking in English to the Polish woman. Wallander had often been envious of Martinsson's proficiency in that language. Wallander spoke it badly. Linda had often teased him about his poor pronunciation, especially when they travelled together. Captain Sund escorted Wallander back to the upper deck.

It was almost midnight.

"Would it be in order for me to offer refreshments of a stronger nature after this ordeal?" Sund said.

"Unfortunately not," Wallander said.

A call came through on Sund's radio. He excused himself. Wallander was glad to be left alone. His conscience kept gnawing at him. Would Landahl have had a chance if Wallander had made different assumptions from the beginning? He knew that he would just have to live with his conscience on this score.

Martinsson joined him after 20 minutes.

"There was a Norwegian called Larsen in room 309. He's probably on the road to Norway as we speak, but I have his home number. In 311, there was a couple who live in Ystad, a Mr and Mrs Tomander."

"Talk to them first thing in the morning," Wallander said. "That may give us something."

"I saw Nyberg on the way up, by the way. He was covered in oil up to his waist. But he promised to take a look at the cabin once he had put on clean clothes."

"I don't know that we can do much else tonight," Wallander said.

They walked together through the deserted ferry terminal where a few young men were sleeping curled up on benches. The ticket office was closed. They stopped when they reached Wallander's car.

"We have to go through everything again tomorrow morning," Wallander said. "At 8 a.m."

Martinsson studied his face. "You seem nervous."

"That's because I am. I'm always nervous when I don't understand what's going on."

"How is the internal investigation going?"

"I haven't heard anything. No journalists have tried to call either, but that may be because I keep my phone unplugged most of the time."

"It's too bad when these things happen," Martinsson said.

Wallander sensed a double meaning in his words. He was on his guard immediately, and angry.

"What does that mean exactly?"

"Isn't it what we're always afraid of? That we're going to lose control and start lashing out at people?"

"I slapped her. End of story. I did it to protect her mother."

"I know," Martinsson said. "But still."

He doesn't believe me, Wallander thought after he sat down behind the wheel. Maybe no-one does. The insight came as a shock. He had never before felt truly betrayed or at least abandoned by his closest colleagues. He sat there without turning on the engine. The feeling even overshadowed the image of the young man crushed in the propeller shaft.

For the second time in a week he felt hurt and bitter. I'm leaving, he thought. I'll hand in my resignation first thing in the morning and then they can shove this whole investigation up their backsides.

He was still upset when he got home. In his mind he continued a heated discussion with Martinsson. It was a long time before he fell asleep.

They met at 8 a.m. the next day. Viktorsson joined them, and Nyberg, who had oil under his fingernails still. Wallander was in a better mood this morning. He was not going to resign, nor would he confront Martinsson. First he would wait for the results of the internal investigation. Then he would wait for the right moment to tell his colleagues what he thought of them and their lack of faith in him.

They talked at length about the discovery of last night. Martinsson had already spoken to Mr and Mrs Tomander, but neither of them had seen or heard anything from the next-door cabin. The Norwegian, Larsen, had not yet reached home, but his wife assured Martinsson he would be back by mid-morning.

Wallander set out his two theories regarding Landahl and no-one had any quarrel with them. The discussion proceeded calmly and methodically, but Wallander sensed that beneath the surface everyone was impatient to get on with their own jobs.

When they finished, Wallander had decided to concentrate his energies on Falk. He was more than ever convinced that everything started with him. Lundberg's murder had to be put on one side for now and its exact connection with the rest of the events remained to be determined. The questions Wallander kept returning to were very simple. What dark forces had been set in motion when Falk had died during his late-night walk? Had he died from natural causes? Wallander spent the next few hours calling the coroner's office in Lund and talking again to the pathologist who had performed the autopsy on Falk. He called Enander again, Falk's doctor who had visited Wallander at the police station. As before, there was no consensus. But by lunchtime, when Wallander was suffering acute pangs of hunger, he was convinced that Falk had died a natural death. No crime had been committed, but this sudden death in front of a cash machine had set a certain course of events in motion.

Wallander pulled over a sheet of paper and wrote the following words: *Falk. Minks. Angola.* He looked at what he had written, then added: *20.* The words formed an impenetrable matrix. What was it that he was unable to perceive?

To assuage his sense of irritation and impatience, he left the station and took a walk. He stopped at a pizzeria for his lunch. Then he returned to his office and stayed there until 5 p.m. He was on the verge of giving up. He couldn't see a motive or logic behind any of the events. He was about to get a cup of coffee when the phone rang. It was Martinsson.

"I'm at Runnerströms Torg," he said. "We've done it at last."

"What?"

"Modin got through. He's in. And there are some strange happenings on the screen."

Wallander threw down the receiver. At last, he thought. We have finally broken through.

CHAPTER TWENTY-EIGHT

Wallander did not think to look around as he got out of his car. If he had, he might have caught a glimpse of the shadow retreating into the darkness further up Runnerströms Torg. He would then have known that someone was watching the flat. The undercover cars posted on Apelbergsgatan and Runnerströms Torg had not been a deterrent.

He locked his car and hurried into the building, eager to see for himself the strange things that Martinsson said were happening on Falk's computer. Wallander was surprised to see that Martinsson had brought in the kind of folding chair that people used on camping trips. There were two new computers in the room. Modin and Martinsson were mumbling and pointing at the screen in front of them. Wallander could almost feel the intense concentration emanating from them. He greeted them without getting much of a reply.

The screen really did look different now. The chaotic swarms were gone, replaced by more orderly, fixed arrangements of numbers. Modin had removed his headphones. His hands wandered back and forth between the three keyboards like a virtuoso playing different instruments at the same time. Wallander waited. Martinsson had a pad in his hands and from time to time Modin dictated something. Modin was obviously running the show. Ten minutes had passed before it was as if they suddenly became aware of Wallander's presence. Modin stopped typing.

"What's happening?" Wallander said. "And why are there now three computers?"

"If you can't get over the mountain, you have to go around it," Modin said. His face was shiny with sweat, but he looked happy.

"It's best if Robert explains," Martinsson said.

"I never did manage to find out what the password was," Modin said. "But I brought in my own computers and connected them to Falk's. That way I could get in through the back door."

Wallander knew computers had windows, but he had never heard about there being doors.

"How does that work?"

"It's hard to describe without getting technical. Moreover, it's kind of a trade secret. I'd rather not get into it."

"OK, let it go. What have you found?"

Martinsson took over. "Falk was connected to the Internet, of course, and in a file with the bizarre name 'Jacob's Marsh' we found a long row of phone numbers, apparently in a particular order. At least that was what we thought. No more codes. There were two columns, one consisting of names, and then a long number. Now we're trying to work out what these are."

"In point of fact, there are both phone numbers and codes in there," Modin said. "And there are long number combinations that serve as code names for institutions in various parts of the world. There are codes for the USA, some in Asia, some in Europe, even one each in Brazil and Nigeria."

"What sort of institutions are we talking about?"

"That's what we're trying to find out," Martinsson said. "But there's one that Robert recognised right away. That was why we called you."

"What was it?"

"The Pentagon," Modin said. Wallander couldn't make up his mind whether it was a note of triumph or of fear in Modin's voice.

"What does that tell you?"

"We don't know yet," Martinsson said. "But there is a hell of a lot of classified, some of it perhaps illegally obtained, information stored in this computer. It might mean that Falk had hacked his way into these institutions."

"I can't help feeling that someone who thinks the same way I think has been working on this computer," Modin said suddenly.

"Let me get this clear," Wallander said. "Falk was breaking into other people's computer networks, is that it?"

"That seems to be the case."

"And what could he have been using all this classified information for?" he asked.

"It's too early to say," Martinsson said. "First we have to identify more of these sources, then we may get a clearer picture. But it will take time. Every stage is complicated, because Falk arranged it very deliberately so that no-one from outside would be able to see what he was doing."

He got up from his folding chair. "I have to go home for a while," he said. "It's Terese's birthday. But I'll be back soon." He handed Wallander the pad.

"Give her my congratulations. How old is she?"

"Sixteen."

Wallander remembered her as a little girl. He had been to her fifth birthday party. She was two years older than Persson.

Martinsson paused at the door. "I forgot to tell you that I talked to Larsen," he said.

It took Wallander a few seconds to place the name.

"He had the cabin next door to Landahl," Martinsson said. "The walls were thin, so he heard him, but he never saw him. Larsen says he was tired and slept most of the way from Poland."

"What did he hear?"

"Voices, but nothing to suggest any trouble or a fight. He couldn't be sure how many people were there."

Wallander sat down gingerly on the folding chair. Modin kept working. Wallander realised the futility of his asking more questions. This new age of electronic development would soon demand a whole new breed of police officer. As always, for the time being, criminals were way ahead.

Modin hit "enter" and leaned back in his chair. The modem next to the monitor started blinking.

"What are you doing now?" Wallander said.

"I'm sending an e-mail to see where it ends up. But I'm sending it from my own computer."

"But weren't you using the keyboard for Falk's?"

"I've connected them."

Modin jumped up and leaned towards the monitor. Then he started typing again. Suddenly everything on the screen went blank. Then the numbers came back. Modin furrowed his brow.

"What's happening?"

"I don't know, but I was denied access. I have to cover my tracks. Give me a couple of minutes."

The typing continued. Wallander was getting impatient.

"One more time," Modin mumbled.

Then something happened that made Modin jump up again. He stared for a long time at the screen.

"The World Bank," he said at last.

"What do you mean, the World Bank?"

"That is one of the institutions Falk has access to. If I'm

right, the code here is for a branch that deals with global finance inspections."

"The Pentagon and the World Bank," Wallander said. "We're not talking corner shops."

"It's time I had a little conference with my friends," Modin said. "I've asked them to be on alert."

"Where are these friends?" Wallander said.

"One lives in Rättvik, the other in California."

Wallander realised that it was high time he got in touch with computer experts at the National Crime Division. He played out bruising scenarios in store. He had no illusions about the risk he was running: he would be fiercely criticised for recruiting Modin, however skilled he had turned out to be.

While Modin was communicating with his friends, Wallander paced the room. He was thinking about the case, but his thoughts kept reverting to the feeling that his colleagues mistrusted him. Perhaps this extended beyond the incident with Persson; perhaps they thought he was over the hill? Did they think it was time for Martinsson to take charge?

He was hurt and racked with self-pity. But anger pounded in his veins. He wasn't going to give up without a fight. He had no exotic place in the wings where he could start a new life. He had no stud to sell. All he had to look forward to was a state pension, and a meagre one at that.

The typing behind him had stopped. Modin got up from his chair and stretched.

"I'm hungry," he said.

"What did your friends say?"

"We're taking an hour's break to think. Then we'll talk again."

Wallander, too, was hungry. He suggested they go out for a pizza. Modin seemed insulted by the suggestion.

"I never eat pizza," he said. "It's not healthy."

"What do you eat?"

"Bean sprouts."

"Nothing else?"

"Pickled egg is good."

Wallander wondered if there was any restaurant nearby, let alone in Ystad, that offered a menu that would appeal to Modin. Modin looked through the plastic bags of food that he had brought with him, but there seemed to be nothing there that caught his fancy.

"A plain salad will do," he said.

They left the building. Wallander asked Modin if he wanted them to drive, but he preferred to walk. They went to the only salad bar Wallander knew of in Ystad. Wallander ate heartily, but Modin scrutinised every leaf of lettuce and every vegetable before chewing it. Wallander had never seen a person who ate so slowly. He tried making conversation with Modin, but the latter answered only in monosyllables. After a while Wallander realised he was still obsessed with the figures and patterns in Falk's computer.

They were back at Runnerströms Torg before 8 p.m. Martinsson was not back. Modin sat at the computer to reconnect with his friends. Wallander imagined that they must look exactly like the young man beside him.

"No-one has traced me," Modin said after he had performed some operations far too complex for Wallander to follow on the computer.

"How can you tell?"

"I just see it."

Wallander shifted on the folding chair. It really is like being on a stalking expedition, he thought. We're out stalking electronic elk. We know they're there. But we don't know what direction they're going to come from.

Wallander's mobile rang. Modin flinched.

"I hate mobile telephones," he said with distaste.

Wallander went out to the landing. It was Höglund. Wallander told her where he was and what Modin had managed to extract from Falk's computer.

"The World Bank and the Pentagon," she said. "Two of the world's most powerful institutions."

"We don't know what it all means yet," Wallander said. "But why did you call?"

"I decided that I needed to talk to that man Ryss again. He was, after all, the one who led us to Landahl, and I'm becoming more than ever convinced that Persson knew very little about the friend she claims to have worshipped. In any case we know she's lying."

"What did he say? His name is Kalle, isn't it?"

"Kalle Ryss. I wanted to ask him why he and Hökberg broke up. He wasn't expecting that question and he plainly didn't want to answer it, but I wouldn't back off. But he said something interesting. He said he broke up with her because she was never interested."

"Interested in what?"

"In sex, of course."

"He told you this?"

"Yes, and once he started the whole story came pouring out. He fell in love with her the moment he first saw her, but soon after they started going out it was obvious that she had no interest in sex. Eventually he tired of her. But it's the reason for her lack of interest that's important."

"What was it?"

"Hökberg had told him that she had been raped a few years ago. She was still traumatised by the experience."

"Sonja Hökberg was raped?"

"According to him she was. I checked our files, but I didn't find any case that involved Hökberg."

"Did it happen in Ystad?"

"Apparently. So I started putting two and two together."

Wallander saw where she was heading. "Lundberg's son. Carl-Einar?"

"It's only a theory, but I think it holds water."

"What do you think happened?"

"This is what I was thinking: Carl-Einar Lundberg has been on trial for a nasty rape case. He was acquitted, but there were several pointers to his having been guilty. In which case nothing would prevent him from having committed an earlier rape. But Sonja Hökberg never went to the police."

"Why not?"

"There are many reasons why a woman doesn't go to the police in such a case. You should know that."

"So what's your conclusion?"

"It's bizarre, I admit, but I think it's possible to see Lundberg's murder as a revenge on his son."

"That gives us a motive. And it also tells us something about Hökberg that perhaps we did not know before."

"What is that?"

"That she was stubborn. And you said her stepfather described her as a strong person."

"I'm not entirely convinced. How did the girls know that the father would be the one driving the taxi? And how would she have known he was Carl-Einar's father?"

"Ystad is a small town. We don't know how Hökberg reacted to the rape. She could have been consumed by the idea of vengeance. Rape affects the victims very deeply. Some withdraw and turn inward, but some are possessed by violent dreams of revenge."

What Höglund had discovered conformed to his own idea that Lundberg's murder was incidental to the central chain of events involving Falk.

"See how soon you can find out if Persson knew any of this," he said.

"I will. And we need to find out if Hökberg ever came home with bruises. The rape that Carl-Einar Lundberg was accused of was violent."

She said she would call if she found anything else. Wallander put his phone in his pocket, but stayed on the unlit landing. A thought was bubbling up from his unconscious. Why did Hökberg escape from the police station? They had not looked closely into that question. They had simply settled for the most obvious answer: that she had seized the chance to run from punishment and to avoid responsibility. After all, she had confessed to the crime. But now Wallander saw another way to look at it. Hökberg may have left because she had something else to hide. The only question was what. Wallander instinctively sensed that he was getting closer to something important. But there was still something missing, a connection he was trying to make.

Then he thought of what it was. Sonja Hökberg could have left the station in the vain hope of getting away. So far so good. But somewhere out there waiting for her was someone less concerned that she had just confessed to killing Lundberg than that she might tell the police something else while she was there. Something concerning a matter very different from personal revenge.

This works, Wallander thought. This way Lundberg fits with everything else and there's a reasonable explanation for what follows. Something had to be kept quiet, something Sonja might have told us had she lived. She is killed to keep her quiet. But her killer is done away with in turn. Just as Modin sweeps away any traces of himself in the computer, someone has been trying to clean up.

What had transpired in Luanda? he thought again. Who is "C"? And to what does the number 20 refer?

Höglund's idea had cheered him up. He returned to Modin's side with renewed energy.

Fifteen minutes later Martinsson returned. He described the cake he had just eaten in detail, while Wallander listened impatiently. Then he asked Modin to bring Martinsson up to speed on what they had discovered while he was gone.

"The World Bank?" Martinsson asked. "What does that have to do with Falk?"

"That's what we have to find out."

Martinsson removed his coat, sat down on the folding chair and rubbed his hands together. Wallander summarised his conversation with Höglund. Martinsson could see the importance of the discovery.

"That gives us a way in," he said when Wallander had finished.

"It gives us more than that," Wallander said. "We're finally starting to make sense of this."

"I've never seen a case like this," Martinsson said. "There's still much we can't account for. We don't know why the electrical relay was placed in the morgue. We don't know why Falk's body was removed. I just don't think cutting off his fingers was the driving motive."

"We'll do what we can to fill in the gaps," Wallander said. "I'm going back to the station. But let me know if anything happens."

"We'll keep going until 10 p.m.," Modin said. "But then I need to sleep."

Once on the street, Wallander felt at a loss. Should he

push himself for a few more hours? Or should he head straight home?

He decided to do both. There was no reason he couldn't work at the kitchen table. All he needed was time to digest what Höglund had told him. He got into his car and drove home.

He sat down at the table and spread out his notes. Höglund's theory was on his mind and he wanted to go through the case methodically. At 11 p.m. he finally went to bed.

The gaps are still there, he thought. But it still seems that Höglund's insight has brought us forward.

He fell asleep almost immediately.

Modin packed up his computers on the dot of 10 p.m. and Martinsson drove him home. He would pick him up at 8 a.m. the following day.

His parents had already gone to bed. The house was silent. But Modin did not go to bed after Martinsson left. Although the memory of what happened after he broke into the Pentagon system was still raw, the temptation was too great. Besides, he had learned his lesson, he knew now to erase all his tracks.

Martinsson hadn't been watching when Modin copied some of the material he had accessed in Falk's computer. He hooked up his computers and started going through those files again, looking once more for clues and openings, new ways to climb the firewall.

A storm front came in over Luanda.

Carter had spent the evening reading a report that criticised the International Monetary Fund's operations in some East African countries. The criticisms were well formulated and devastating. Carter could not have done the job better himself, but he remained convinced of the necessity of what he had planned. There was no alternative at this point. If the world's financial systems remained as they were, there could be no true reform.

He put the report down and from the window watched the lightning dance across the sky. His night-time guards huddled under their makeshift rain shelter.

The air-conditioning unit in the study droned loudly. He was on his way to bed, but something led him to his desk. He knew at once that someone was trying to break into the server. But this time it was different. After a while he saw what it was. Whoever it was had become careless.

Carter dried his hands on a handkerchief. Then he began the pursuit of the person who was threatening to uncover his secret.

CHAPTER TWENTY-NINE

Wallander stayed at home until nearly 10 a.m. on Thursday. He had woken early, feeling fully rested. His joy at having been able to sleep undisturbed for a whole night was so great that it gave him a guilty conscience. He often wondered where his overdeveloped work ethic had come from. His mother had been a housewife who had never regretted not being free to work away from home. At least she had never complained about it.

His father had certainly never opted for extra work. Wallander had occasionally spied on him and was surprised by how little time he spent at his easel. Sometimes he had been reading a book and sometimes he had been fast asleep on the old mattress in a corner of the studio. Or he had been playing solitaire at the rickety old table. Wallander was beginning to look a lot like his father, but on the inside he was driven by a constant state of unrest and dissatisfaction, demons he had never seen in either of his parents.

He had called the station at 8 a.m. The only person he could get through to was Hansson. Everyone else was busy with their investigative tasks. He told Hansson to postpone their meeting until the afternoon. Then he went down to the laundry room to sign up ahead and found that all the morning hours were free. He had booked the next two hours and went back to collect his dirty washing.

The letter arrived while he was loading his clothes into the washing machine. It was on the floor in the hall. There was no stamp, no return address on the envelope. His name and address were handwritten. He put it on the kitchen table supposing that it must be some kind of invitation. He hung his bedclothes on the balcony to air. It was getting colder again, but there was no frost. He only opened the letter when it was time for his second cup of coffee. There was a second envelope inside with no name on it. He read the letter. At first he couldn't make any sense of it, but then it dawned on him that he had received a reply to his ad. He put the letter down, walked once round the table, then read it again.

The woman who had written to him was called Elvira Lindfeldt. She had not included a photograph of herself, but Wallander decided she must be very beautiful. Her handwriting was elegant and firm, no fussy loops or twiddly bits. The dating agency had forwarded his ad and she had found it interesting. She was 39 years old and divorced. She lived in Malmö, and worked for a shipping company called Heinemann & Nagel. She ended her letter by giving her phone number and saying she hoped to hear from him soon. Wallander felt like a ravenous wolf who had at last succeeded in bringing down his prey. He was tempted to call her straight away. But then he controlled himself and decided he should throw the letter away. The meeting was doomed. She would be disappointed because probably she imagined him to be different.

Furthermore, he had no time for this. He was in the throes of the most complicated investigation he had ever led. He walked round the table a few more times. Then he realised the absurdity of ever having written to the dating agency. He took the letter, tore it into pieces and threw it in the bin. Then he sat down to think about the case. Before driving to the station, he put his laundry in the dryer. The first thing he did when he got to his office was write himself a reminder to collect his laundry when he went home. He met Nyberg striding down the corridor with a plastic bag.

"We're going to be getting some results in today," he said. "Among other things we've been cross-checking a number of fingerprints."

"Do you have a better idea of what happened in the engine room?"

"I don't envy the pathologist, I'll tell you that. The body was so crushed there wasn't a whole piece of bone in there. Well, you saw it, you know what it looked like."

"Hökberg was probably already unconscious or even dead by the time she was thrown against the high-voltage wires," Wallander said. "Do you think that was the case with Landahl? If it was Landahl."

"Oh, it was him," Nyberg said.

"How do you know that?"

"He was identified by an unusual birthmark above one of his ankles. The parents have been contacted."

"Good. Then that's taken care of," Wallander said. "First Hökberg, then her boyfriend."

Nyberg raised his eyebrows. "I was under the impression that you thought he had killed her? That could suggest he committed suicide. Although I admit it's a pretty horrendous way to die."

"There are other possibilities," Wallander said. "But the key thing for now is we've established who he was."

Wallander returned to his office. He had just taken off his coat and was beginning to regret having thrown Elvira's letter away when the phone rang. It was Holgersson. She wanted to see him straight away. He approached her office with a sense of dread. Normally he enjoyed his discussions with her, but ever since she had openly displayed her mistrust of him a week ago, he had been doing his best to avoid her. As he had anticipated, the atmosphere was far from relaxed. Holgersson was sitting at her desk and her trademark smile was forced. Even as he sat down, Wallander felt his anger bubbling up in anticipation of whatever was about to come his way.

"I'm going to get right to the point," she said. "The investigation into allegations made against you by Eva Persson and her mother is now under way."

"Who's in charge?"

"A man from Hässleholm."

"A man from Hässleholm? That sounds like the name of a bad television series."

"He's a highly regarded officer. I also need to inform you that you have been reported to the Justice Department ombudsman. And not just you. We have both been reported."

"Did you slap her too?"

"I'm responsible for the conduct of my officers."

"Who filed the report?"

"Persson's lawyer, Klas Harrysson."

"Thanks for letting me know," Wallander said and got up. He was furious now. The energy from the morning was draining from his body, and he didn't want it to go.

"I'm not finished."

"We have a homicide investigation on our hands."

"I spoke to Hansson earlier. I am aware of how it's going."

He said nothing about having talked to her, Wallander thought. Are all my colleagues going behind my back?

He sat down heavily.

"This is a difficult situation," she said.

"Not really," Wallander said, interrupting her. "What

happened between Persson, her mother and me happened exactly as I told you. I haven't changed a syllable of my account of it since it happened. You should be able to tell that I don't flinch or get nervous when you press me on details. What makes me mad as all hell, however, is that you don't believe me."

"What do you expect me to do?"

"I want you to believe me when I tell you something."

"But the girl and her mother have a different story. And there's two of them."

"There could be a hundred of them and it wouldn't change an iota. You should believe me, not them. They have a reason to lie."

"So do you."

"I do?"

"If you hit her without provocation."

Wallander got up a second time, this time more forcefully. "I won't even dignify that remark with an answer. It's a gross insult." She started to protest, but he interrupted her. "Is there anything else?"

"I'm still not finished."

Wallander remained where he was. The situation was almost unbearably tense. He was not going to back down, but he wanted to get out of the room as rapidly as possible.

"The situation is sufficiently serious for me to have to take action," she said. "For as long as the investigation is in progress I have to suspend you."

Wallander heard her words and knew what they meant. Both Svedberg and Hansson had been suspended. In Hansson's case, Wallander had been convinced that the allegations were false. In Svedberg's case, he hadn't been so sure, but Svedberg's word had later been corroborated. But in neither case had he supported Björk, who was chief then, in his decision to suspend his colleagues. It seemed to him to be taking sides against them before the investigation had even begun.

Suddenly his anger left him. He was completely calm.

"You do as you like," he said. "But if you suspend me I shall resign with immediate effect."

"That sounds like a threat."

"I don't care what the hell it sounds like. It's simply a fact. And don't think you can count on me coming back when the investigation proves that they were lying and I was telling the truth."

"I wish you would cooperate instead of threatening me with your resignation."

"I have been a police officer for a very long time," Wallander said, "and I know perfectly well that the step you say you are obliged to take is not in the regulations. There's someone higher up who's nervous about that picture in the paper and who wants an example made of me, and you are choosing to go along with it."

"It's nothing like that," she said.

"That's exactly what it's like. When were you planning to suspend me? As soon as you dismissed me from this meeting?"

"The man from Hässleholm has undertaken to work quickly. Since we are up to our ears in a case I was going to put it off."

"Why bother? Let Martinsson take charge. He'll do an excellent job."

"I thought we would finish the week as we are."

"No," Wallander said. "Nothing is as we are right now. Either you suspend me now or you don't do it at all."

"Why do you have to resort to these threats? I thought we had a good working relationship."

"I thought so too. But clearly I was wrong."

They were silent.

"So how is it going to be?" Wallander asked. "Am I suspended or am I not?"

"You are not suspended," she said. "At least not right now."

Wallander marched out of her office. He realised he was drenched in sweat. He locked his office door behind him, and the full force of his emotions assailed him. He wanted no more than to write his resignation, clear out his office and leave the station for good. The afternoon meeting, and every future meeting, would have to take place without him. He was never coming back.

At the same time something inside him resisted the furious urge. If he left now, it would look as if he was guilty. That way the verdict of the investigation wouldn't have much impact. He would be forever tainted.

Slowly he arrived at his decision. He would go on working for now, but he would inform his colleagues of the situation. The vital thing was that he had let Holgersson know how things stood. He did not intend to toe the line on this or to ask for mercy.

He began to calm down. He opened his door wide and got on with his work. At noon he went home and took his clothes out of the dryer. He picked out the pieces of Elvira's letter from the bin. He didn't have a very good reason for doing that; perhaps it was because she had nothing to do with the police.

He had lunch at István's restaurant and chatted with one of his father's friends who was there. He returned to the station shortly after 1.30 p.m.

He walked in, feeling somewhat on edge. Holgersson could have changed her mind since their meeting and decided to suspend him after all. He didn't know how he would react to this. He couldn't even begin to imagine what his life would look like after that. Secretly he found the idea of handing in his resignation appalling. But there were only a few unimportant messages waiting for him. Holgersson had not tried to reach him. Wallander took a few deep breaths and then called Martinsson. He was at Runnerströms Torg.

"We're working slowly but surely," he said. "He's managed to break a couple more codes." Wallander could hear the rustling of paper. Then Martinsson came back on the line. "We have a connection to a stockbroker in Seoul and to a British firm, called Lonrho. I contacted a person in Stockholm who was able to tell me that Lonrho was originally an African company that was involved in illegal operations in Southern Rhodesia during the time of sanctions."

"What are we supposed to deduce from this?" Wallander broke in. "A stockbroker in Korea? And this other company, whatever its name is. How does it relate to Falk and our investigation?"

"We're trying to work it out. Modin says there are about 80 companies entered into this program. But it will take us a while to find out what the connections between them are."

"But if you had to speculate, what would you say?"

Martinsson chuckled. "I see money."

"Anything else?"

"Isn't that enough?"

"Who knows," Wallander said. "Perhaps the key player in all of this isn't Falk but the cash machine where he died."

Martinsson laughed. Wallander suggested that they meet at around 3 p.m.

After the conversation ended, Wallander thought about Elvira Lindfeldt. He tried to imagine what she could look like, but he kept finding himself thinking of Baiba. And Mona. And a glimpse of a woman he had met once at a roadside café outside Västervik.

He was interrupted in his thoughts by Hansson, who appeared in the doorway. Wallander felt guilty, as if his thoughts were written on his face.

"All the keys are accounted for," Hansson said.

Wallander couldn't think what he was talking about, but he didn't say anything because he felt sure that he should know.

"I have a fax from Sydkraft," he said. "All people who had keys to the substation can account for them."

"Good," Wallander said. "It's always a help to be able to strike something off our list."

"Unfortunately, I haven't been able to trace the Mercedes van."

Wallander leaned back in his chair. "You can put that aside for now. We'll get to it eventually, but there are more important tasks."

Hansson nodded and wrote something in his notebook. Wallander told him about the 3 p.m. meeting.

Putting aside his thoughts of Elvira and her appearance, he got back to his paperwork and also thought about what Martinsson had said. The phone rang. It was Viktorsson, asking how the case was going.

"I thought Hansson was keeping you abreast of all developments."

"But you are in charge."

Viktorsson's comment surprised Wallander. He had been sure that Holgersson had arrived at her decision to suspend him in consultation with Viktorsson, but he was pretty sure that Viktorsson was not being disingenuous when he said that Wallander was in charge. Wallander instantly warmed towards him.

"I can see you tomorrow morning."

"I'm free at 8.30 p.m."

Wallander made a note of it. Then he spent another half-hour preparing for the meeting. At 2.40 p.m. he went to get more coffee, but the machine was broken. Wallander thought once more about Erik Hökberg's observation about the vulnerability of society. That gave him a new idea. He went back to his office to give Hökberg a call. He answered at once. Wallander gave him what details he could about the latest developments and asked him if the name Jonas Landahl meant anything to him. Hökberg said no, definitely no. Wallander was surprised.

"Are you absolutely sure?"

"The name is unusual enough that I would have remembered it. Was he the one who killed Sonja?"

"We only know that they knew each other and we have some information which indicates that they may even have been more than just friends."

Wallander wondered if he ought to raise the subject of rape, but decided that it wasn't something they should discuss over the phone. Instead, he moved on to the question he had been wanting to ask.

"When I was out to see you last, you told me about your computer transactions. I came away with the impression then that there were no limits really to what you could do."

"That's right. If you connect to the large databases around the world then you're at the centre of things, wherever you are yourself."

"You could do business with a stockbroker in Seoul if you felt like it."

"Yes, indeed."

"What would I need to know in order to do that?"

"First, you would need his e-mail address. Then the security systems have to match up. He has to be able to see who I am, and vice versa. Otherwise there are no real problems. None of a technical nature, at any rate."

"What would those be?"

"Each country has its own set of laws and regulations governing trade. You would have to know what those are, unless you are operating illegally."

"Since there is so much money involved, the security measures must be damned stringent. Could they, do you think, be cracked?"

"I'm not the right man to answer those questions. But as a police officer you should know that anyone with a strong enough desire can do almost anything. What is it people say? If you really wanted to kill the President of the USA, you could do it. But I'm getting curious as to why you're asking me these questions."

"You impressed me as having a great deal of technical expertise."

"Only on the surface. The electronic world is so complicated and is changing so fast that I doubt there's anyone out there who understands it completely. Or who has control over it."

Wallander said he would be in touch with him soon. Then he went to the conference room. Hansson and Nyberg were there already. They were complaining about the coffee machine breaking down more and more often these days. Wallander nodded to them and sat down just as Höglund and Martinsson arrived. Wallander had not yet decided whether to begin or to end by describing his meeting with Holgersson. He decided to wait. His hard-working colleagues were involved in a tough enough investigation as it was, and he shouldn't burden them more than was absolutely necessary.

They began by discussing the events surrounding Landahl's death. There were no eyewitness accounts. No-one had seen him on the ferry, no-one had seen him make his way to the engine room.

"I find it very strange," Wallander said. "No-one saw him, either when he paid for his cabin or anywhere on the ship. No-one saw him enter the restricted area leading to the engine room. It makes no sense."

"He must have travelled with someone," Höglund said. "I spoke to one of the engineers before I got here and he said it would have been impossible for Landahl to squeeze himself into the propeller shaft on his own."

"So he must have been forced into that position," Wallander said. "Which means that now we have two people who managed to find their way into the engine room without being seen. And one who made his way back. We can draw a conclusion from this, which is that Landahl must have gone willingly with this person. If he had been dragged there someone would be bound to have noticed, and it would have been hard for the killer to force Landahl down those ladders."

They talked through various aspects of the case until 6 p.m., at which time Wallander decided that they were no longer being productive. Everyone was worn out. Wallander decided not to mention his conversation with Holgersson. He simply didn't have the energy.

Martinsson went back to Runnerströms Torg. Hansson brought up the point that Modin should probably be compensated in some way. Nyberg yawned. He still had oil under his fingernails. Wallander talked for a few more minutes with Hansson and Höglund in the corridor. They assigned some of the tasks that remained. Then Wallander went to his office and closed his door.

He stared at the phone for a long time without understanding his hesitation. Finally he dialled Elvira's number.

She answered after the seventh ring. "Lindfeldt."

Wallander put the phone down, waited a few minutes, and then dialled her number again. This time she answered immediately. He liked the sound of her voice.

Wallander said who he was and they chatted for a few minutes. It was apparently quite windy in Malmö, more so than in Ystad. Elvira also complained that many of her colleagues at work were coming down with colds. Wallander agreed. Autumn was always a difficult time that way. He was recovering from a sore throat himself.

"It would be nice to get together sometime," she said.

"I'm not a big believer in dating agencies," he said, regretting it as soon as the words left his mouth.

"It's really no better or worse than any other way to meet people," she said. "We're both adults, after all."

Then she said another thing that surprised him. She asked him what he was doing that evening. She suggested that they meet in Malmö. I can't, Wallander thought. This is far too fast and I have work to do, but then he said yes. They agreed to meet at 8.30 p.m. in the Savoy bar.

"We'll skip the carnations," she said. "I am sure we'll be able to pick each other out."

Wallander wondered what he was getting himself into, but he was also excited. It was 6.30 p.m. He had to get ready.

CHAPTER THIRTY

Wallander parked outside the Savoy at exactly 8.27 p.m. He had driven much too fast from Ystad because he thought he would be late. He had taken so long deciding what he was going to wear. He picked a clean but unironed shirt from a pile of washed clothes and then couldn't settle on which tie. Finally, he decided against wearing one at all. And his shoes needed polishing. The result was that he left the flat later than he had planned.

Hansson had also called him as he was cleaning his shoes, and asked him if he knew where Nyberg was. Wallander had not discovered why he needed to know so badly. He had kept his answers so brisk that Hansson had asked him if he was pressed for time. Wallander had been so cold that Hansson had asked no further questions. When he was about to leave, the phone rang again. This time it was Linda. There was a lull at the restaurant and her boss was on holiday, so she thought she would come and stay with him. Wallander nearly told her where he was going. Linda was the one, after all, who had encouraged him to get into this in the first place. She gathered straight away that he was in a hurry. Wallander could never put anything past her, but nevertheless he tried to convince her that he was on his way to attend to police business. They arranged that she would call the next evening.

Once on the road, Wallander realised that he was almost out of petrol. He might make it to Malmö, but he didn't want to take a chance on it. He stopped at a petrol station outside Skurup and was worried that he might not be there on time. He still bore the scar of the time he had been 10 minutes late for a date with Mona and she had simply left.

But he did make it in time. He sat in the car for a moment and looked at his face in the mirror. He was thinner now than a few years ago and his features were more sharply defined. She wouldn't know that he had his father's face. He closed his eyes and took a few deep breaths. He forced all his expectations away. He wasn't likely to be disappointed, but she probably would be. They would meet in the bar, have a drink and that would be it. He would be in his bed by midnight. When he woke up the next day he would have forgotten her already and also be confirmed in his suspicions that this dating agency business was not for him.

He sat in the car until almost 8.40 p.m., then got out and walked across the street to the Savoy.

They saw each other at the same time. She was at a table in the far corner. Apart from a few men at the bar there were not many guests, and she was the only woman alone. Wallander caught her gaze and she smiled. When she stood up to greet him he saw that she was very tall. She was wearing a dark blue suit. Her skirt came to just above her knees and he saw that she had beautiful legs.

"Am I right?" he said, as he stretched out his hand.

"If you are Kurt Wallander, I am Elvira."

He sat down across the table from her.

"I don't smoke," she said. "But I do drink."

"So do I," Wallander said. "But not tonight. I'm driving, so I'll have to stick to mineral water."

He craved a glass of wine. Or better still, several glasses.

But since that time many years ago when he had been stopped by his colleagues Peters and Norén after having had one or two too many he had been very careful. They had said nothing, but Wallander knew he had been so drunk that it would have meant immediate dismissal if they had. It was one of the ugliest memories of his career. He couldn't risk anything like that again.

The waiter came to the table and took their order. Elvira ordered another glass of white wine.

Wallander felt self-conscious. Since he was a teenager he had had the idea that he looked best in profile. Now he turned his chair sideways to the table.

"Do you not have room for your legs?" she asked. "I can pull the table over if you like."

"Not at all," Wallander said. "I'm fine." What the hell do I say now? he wondered. Do I tell her I fell in love with her from the moment I stepped in the room? Or rather when I first read her letter?

"Have you ever done this before?" she said.

"Never."

"I have," she said, cheerfully. "But it's never led to anything."

Wallander noticed that she was very direct, in contrast to himself. He was still chiefly concerned about the angle at which he was sitting.

"Why didn't it work out before?"

"Wrong person, wrong sense of humour, wrong attitude, wrong expectations. Some have been pompous or had too many drinks. A lot can go wrong."

"Perhaps I've already done something wrong too?"

"You look nice enough," she said.

"That's a word only rarely applied to me," he said. "But I suppose I'm no ogre."

At that moment he thought of the picture of Persson that had appeared in the papers. Had she seen it? Did she know he was accused of assaulting a juvenile? But it never came up in their conversation. Wallander began to believe that she hadn't seen it. Perhaps she didn't read the evening papers. Wallander sat nursing his mineral water and longed for something stronger. She went on drinking wine. She asked him what it was like to be a policeman and Wallander tried to answer her questions truthfully. But he noticed that he kept touching on the tougher aspects of his work, as if he were trying to elicit her sympathy.

Her questions were well considered, sometimes unexpected. He had to keep his wits about him to give her meaningful answers.

She told him about her own work. The shipping company she worked for did a lot of moving of household goods for Swedish missionaries who were either setting off abroad or coming home. He began to realise that she held a position of some responsibility since her boss was often away on business. She obviously enjoyed her work.

The time flew by. Shortly after 11 p.m. Wallander was in the middle of telling her about his failed marriage with Mona. She listened attentively, seriously but also supportively.

"And afterwards?" she said, when his story trailed off. "You have been divorced for some time now. There must have been someone else."

"I've been alone for long periods of time," he said. "For a while I was seeing a woman from Latvia, from Riga. Her name was Baiba. I had high hopes of the relationship and I thought she shared those hopes. But it didn't work out."

"Why not?"

"She wanted to stay in Riga, and I wanted to stay here. I had made all kinds of plans. We were going to live in the country, start over."

"Perhaps your dreams were too ambitious," she said. "You got burned."

Wallander had the feeling that he had talked too much, that he had said too much about himself and perhaps about Mona and Baiba. But the woman was easy to confide in.

She told him her own history. It was much the same as his, except that in her case it was two failed marriages rather than one. She had one child from each of them. She said nothing explicit, but Wallander had the impression that her first husband had been physically abusive. Her second husband had been Argentinian and she told him with equal measures of insight and irony how his passionate nature which at first had been a breath of fresh air had finally become stifling.

"He vanished two years ago," she said. "The last I heard he was in Barcelona, penniless. I helped him with his ticket back to Argentina. I haven't heard from him for a year. His daughter, of course, is distraught."

"How old are the children?"

"Alexandra is 17, Tobias 21."

They paid their bill at 11.30 p.m. Wallander wanted to treat her, but she insisted on splitting it.

"It's Friday tomorrow," Wallander said once they were out on the street.

"I've never been to Ystad. Isn't that odd?"

Wallander wanted to ask if he could call her. He didn't really know what he was feeling, but she seemed not to have found too many faults in him yet. For now that was plenty.

"I have a car," she said. "I could even take the train. Do you have any time?"

"I'm up to my neck in a difficult homicide case right now," he said. "But even policemen need time off occasionally."

She lived in a Malmö suburb, towards Jägersro. Wallander offered to give her a lift, but she said she wanted to walk for a while and then would take a taxi.

"I take as many long walks as I can," she said. "I hate jogging."

"Me too," Wallander said.

But he had said nothing about his diabetes, the reason he was now an avid walker.

They shook hands and said good night.

"It was nice to meet you," she said.

"Yes," Wallander said, "same here."

He watched her until she had rounded the corner of the hotel. Then he drove back to Ystad. He put on a cassette of arias by the tenor Jussi Björling. Music filled the car. As he passed the turning to Stjärnsund where Widén's ranch was he reckoned that his recent sting of jealousy was not as strong any more.

It was almost 1 a.m. by the time he parked the car. He walked up to his flat and sat down on the sofa. It had been a long time since he had felt as happy as he did this evening. The last time must have been when he had begun to sense that Baiba reciprocated his feelings. He went to bed without even thinking about the case.

Wallander arrived at the station on Friday morning with explosive energy. The first thing he did was to cancel the surveillance on Falk's flat on Apelbergsgatan. He did, however, want the surveillance at Runnerströms Torg to continue. Then he walked over to Martinsson's office. It was empty. Hansson was not in yet either. But he bumped into Höglund in the corridor. She looked unusually tired and grumpy. He ought to say something encouraging, but he could not find the words.

"Hökberg's address book still hasn't turned up," she said. "The one she carried in her bag."

"Have we established that she had one?"

"Persson has corroborated Hökberg's mother's claim. It was a small, dark blue book with a rubber band around the middle."

"Then we're assuming that whoever killed her and threw away the handbag had first pinched the book?"

"It seems plausible."

"The question is: what phone numbers were in there? And what names?"

Höglund shrugged. Wallander looked more closely at her.

"How are things with you anyway?"

"Things are as they are," she said. "But they sure as hell could be better."

She went into her office and closed the door. Wallander hesitated but then knocked at her door. When he heard her voice, he went in.

"We have one or two other things to discuss," he said.

"I know. I'm sorry."

"Don't be."

He sat down. As usual her office was perfectly tidy.

"We have to sort out this business of the rape," he said. "I haven't spoken to Hökberg's mother yet. I have a meeting with Viktorsson at 8.30 a.m., but then I'm going to their house. I take it she's back from her sister's?"

"They're planning the funeral. It's very hard on them."

Wallander got up. "What's going to happen to Persson?" he asked.

"I don't know."

"Even if she manages to lay the blame on Hökberg, her life has been destroyed."

Höglund made a face. "I don't know if I would go that far. Persson seems like one of those people who can let everything run over her and not let it get to her. How you get like that, I can't imagine."

Wallander thought about what she had said. Perhaps he would understand it better later.

"Have you seen Martinsson?" he said, as he was leaving.

"I saw him come in."

"He wasn't in his office."

"I saw him go into Lisa's office."

"I didn't think she was ever in this early?"

"They had a meeting."

Something in her voice made him stop. She saw his hesitation and seemed to make a decision. Then she gestured for him to come back and close the door.

"A meeting about what?"

"Sometimes you really surprise me," she said. "You see and hear everything. You're a great policeman and you know how to keep your investigative team motivated. But at the same time it's as if you see nothing that's going on around you."

Wallander felt something cramp up in his gut, but he said nothing, just waited for her to go on.

"You always speak well of Martinsson, and he always follows where you lead. You work well together."

"I'm forever worried that he's going to get fed up and leave."

"He won't, believe me."

"It's what he always tells me. And it would be a shame. He is a good police officer."

She looked squarely at him. "I shouldn't be telling you this, but I will anyway. You trust him far too much."

"What do you mean?"

"I mean that he's going behind your back. What do you think is going on in Lisa's office right now? They may very well be talking about it being high time for some changes around here. Changes that would be to your detriment but not to Martinsson's."

Wallander couldn't believe it. "How do you mean 'going behind my back'?"

She threw her letter opener across her desk in annoyance.

"It took me a while to see it," she said. "But Martinsson is smart. He's manipulative, and good at it. He complains to Lisa about the way you're handling this investigation."

"He tells her I'm incompetent?"

"I don't think he would express himself so bluntly. He rather implies certain deficiencies: weak leadership, strange priorities. He went straight to Lisa when you brought in Modin, for example."

Wallander was amazed. "I can't believe this."

"You should. But I hope you understand that I'm telling you this in confidence."

Wallander nodded. His stomach was hurting now.

"I just thought you should know. That's all."

Wallander looked at her. "Do you agree with him?"

"If I did I would tell you to your face. Not go behind your back."

"What about Hansson? Nyberg?"

"This is Martinsson's game. No-one else's. He's going after the throne."

"But what about his endless complaints about work? He doesn't even know if he wants to stay in the force."

"Aren't you the one who's always telling us to look past the surface to the very bottom? You always take Martinsson at face value. But I can tell you, I've seen what's underneath, and I don't like what I see."

Wallander felt almost paralysed. The energy and joy he had felt when he woke this morning had evaporated. Inside him, anger was starting to bubble up.

"I'm going to get him for this," he said. "I'm going to confront him right now and see what he has to say for himself."

"That is not a good idea."

"How am I supposed to keep working with someone like that?"

"I can't tell you. But you have to wait for a better opportunity to confront him. If you say anything now, you'll just give him more reason to complain about you being unbalanced. He also thinks that the slap you gave Persson was no coincidence."

"Maybe you know that Lisa is thinking of suspending me."

"It wasn't Lisa's idea," Höglund said grimly. "It was Martinsson's."

"How do you know all this?"

"He has a weakness," she said. "He trusts me. He thinks I'm on his side, even though I've told him that he should stop going behind your back."

Wallander got up from the chair.

"Don't do anything rash," she said. "Try to think of this information as having one up on him. Save it for when the time comes."

She was right. Wallander went back to his office. His

anger was tainted with sadness. He could have believed it about almost anyone but Martinsson. Not Martinsson. He was interrupted in his thoughts by the phone. It was Viktorsson, calling to see where he was since he hadn't turned up for the meeting. Wallander walked over to the prosecutors' department, nervous about running into Martinsson. But he had probably already left to be at Modin's side in Falk's office.

The conversation with Viktorsson did not take long. Wallander forced himself to put all other thoughts aside and focus on the case. He told Viktorsson where they thought they were and what direction they were planning to take. Viktorsson asked a few questions, but he raised no objections.

"What do you expect to find in Falk's computer?"

"I don't know, but I believe it may help us unravel the motive."

"Did Falk commit any kind of a crime?"

"Not as far as we know."

Viktorsson scratched his head. "Do you know enough about these things? Shouldn't specialists from the National Police be brought in?"

"We have a local expert working with us. But we have decided to be in touch with Stockholm."

"I would urge you to do that as soon as possible. They can be touchy about these kinds of things. Who is this local expert?"

"His name is Robert Modin."

"And he's very good?"

"Better than most."

Wallander realised he should tell Viktorsson the truth about Modin's criminal past, but before he had gathered himself to do so the moment was past. Wallander had in effect chosen to safeguard the investigation rather than himself. He had taken the first step on a path that could lead straight into personal disaster. Even if he escaped suspension for the business with Persson, this could settle it, and Martinsson would have more than enough grounds to crush him.

"I take it you have been informed about the internal investigation that is now under way?" Viktorsson said abruptly. "The girl's lawyer has filed a complaint with the Justice Department ombudsman on top of charging you with assault."

"That picture tells a lie," Wallander said. "Whatever anyone says, I was simply protecting the mother."

Viktorsson didn't answer. Is there anyone who believes me? Wallander thought. Anyone?

Wallander left the station at 9 a.m. He drove to the Hökbergs' house. He had not called them to say he was coming. What mattered was to get away from the station for a while. He wouldn't now run into Martinsson, but it would happen sooner or later, and he didn't trust his ability to control himself.

As he got out of his car his mobile rang. It was Siv Eriksson.

"I'm sorry to have to bother you," she said.

"No problem."

"I'm calling because I need to talk to you."

He suddenly heard that she was upset. He pressed the phone closer to his ear and tried to turn out of the wind.

"Has anything happened?"

"I don't want to talk about it over the phone. I'd be grateful if you could come as soon as possible."

It must be urgent. He said he would drive over straight away. The conversation with Hökberg's mother would have to wait. He drove back to Ystad and parked in Lurendrejargränd. The sharp east wind was making it much colder in Skåne. Wallander pressed the bell to her flat. She buzzed him in and was on the landing to meet him. He could see that she was frightened. As they walked into the living room, she stopped to light a cigarette. Her hands were shaking.

"What happened?" he asked.

It took several tries to light her cigarette. She inhaled deeply, then stubbed it out.

"I often go to see my mother," she said. "She lives in Simrishamn and I went there yesterday. It got late and I decided to spend the night. When I got back this morning I saw what had happened."

She stopped and walked into her study. Wallander followed her. She pointed to her computer.

"I had just sat down to work, but when I turned on the computer nothing happened. At first I thought the computer had been unplugged, but then I realised what had happened."

She pointed to the screen.

"I don't follow you," Wallander said.

"Someone has deleted all my files," she said. "My hard drive is empty. But it gets worse."

She walked over to a cabinet and opened the doors.

"Every one of my back-up disks is gone. Nothing is left. Nothing. I even have a reserve hard drive. That's gone too."

Wallander looked around. "So someone broke into your flat last night?"

"But there are no signs of it. And how did they know I wasn't going to be here?"

"Did you leave a window open? Were there any marks on the front door?"

"No, I checked."

"Does anyone else have the keys to your flat?"

Her answer came slowly. "Yes and no," she said. "I gave Tynnes a spare key."

"Why did you do that?"

"So he would have access to my flat when I was away. In case anything happened. But he never used them, as far as I know."

Wallander nodded. He understood why she was so upset. Someone had used her spare keys when she was away, and the only person who had had those keys was dead.

"Do you know where he kept them?"

"He said he was going to keep them in his flat on Apelbergsgatan."

Wallander nodded. He thought about the man who had tried to shoot him. Perhaps he had finally been given the answer to what the man had been looking for. The keys to Siv Eriksson's flat.

CHAPTER THIRTY-ONE

For the first time since the investigation began, Wallander felt that he had a clear picture. After checking the front door and all the windows of the flat he was sure that Eriksson was right. The person who had cleaned out her computer had used keys to get in. Furthermore, someone had been watching her and waiting for the right moment to strike.

They returned to the living room. She was still upset and lit another cigarette which she also stubbed out straight away. Wallander decided to wait a while before calling in Nyberg. There was something else he wanted to clarify first. He sat down.

"Do you have any idea who might have done this?"

"No. It's utterly incomprehensible."

"Your computer equipment must be pretty valuable, but the burglar didn't come for that. He wanted only what was inside."

"Everything is gone," she said. "Everything. All my work."

"You must have had a password."

"Of course I did."

"So the burglar knew what it was?"

"Or was able to get around it somehow."

"No ordinary burglar. It was someone very skilled with computers."

"I haven't even been able to think that far," she said. "I'm too distraught."

"That's understandable. What was your password?"
"'Cookie' – it was my nickname as a child."
"Did anyone else know it?"
"No."
"Not even Falk?"
"No."
"Are you sure?"
"Yes."
"Was it written down anywhere?"
"No."
"Are you sure?"
She paused before she replied. "Yes."
Wallander sensed that they were honing in on a crucial point. He advanced carefully. "Did anyone else know about this nickname?"
"My mother, of course, but she's basically senile."
"No-one else?"
"I have a friend who lives in Austria. She knows it."
"Do you exchange letters with her?"
"Yes. But the past few years it's been mainly e-mail."
"Do you sign those with your nickname?"
"Yes."
Wallander sat back and took a minute to think.
"I don't know how this works," he said, "but I suppose those letters are stored in your computer."
"Yes."
"So if someone accessed them they would have been able to see your nickname, and perhaps guessed it might have been used as a password."
"That's impossible. They would need the password up front to gain access to my letters."
"But someone did manage to break into your computer and delete your files," Wallander said.

She shook her head obstinately. "Why would anyone do that?"

"You're the only person who can answer that question. It's a crucial question, as I hope you realise. What did you have in your computer that someone must have wanted?"

"I never worked with classified information."

"This is very important. You have to think carefully."

"You don't have to remind me."

Wallander waited. She looked as though she were thinking hard.

"There was nothing," she said finally.

"Perhaps there was something there that you didn't realise was valuable?"

"And what would that have been?"

"Again, only you can tell me."

Her voice was firm when she answered him. "I pride myself on keeping all areas of my life, particularly my work, in meticulous order," she said. "I am forever cleaning and sorting files. And I never worked on especially advanced projects, as I told you."

Wallander also thought hard before proceeding. "Did Falk ever come over and use your computer?"

"Why would he do that?"

"I have to ask. Could he have come here without your knowledge? He had keys to your flat."

"I would have noticed it. It's hard to explain without getting too technical."

"I see. But Falk was very good at these things. Isn't it possible that he could have erased all trace of what he had done? It's so often a question of who is better at staying one step ahead – the intruder or the investigator."

"I can't see what would be the point of his using my computer."

"Perhaps he wanted to hide something. The cuckoo hides his eggs in other birds' nests."

"But why?"

"We don't know why. It may also simply be that someone *thought* he had hidden something here. And now that Falk is dead they need to make sure there isn't something here that you would eventually discover."

"Who are these people?"

"That's what I want to know."

This is what must have happened, Wallander thought. There is no other reasonable explanation. There's a lot of frenetic cleaning going on around this town. Something needs to be kept secret at all costs.

He repeated the words in his head. Something needs to be kept secret at all costs. That was the case in a nutshell. If they could find the secret, the case would solve itself.

Wallander sensed that he was running out of time.

"Did Falk ever talk of the number 20?" he asked.

"Why? Is that important?"

"Just answer the question, please."

"Not as far as I remember."

Wallander got out his mobile and called Nyberg. There was no answer. He called Irene and asked her to find him.

"I'll be sending over a forensic team," he said. "I'd be grateful if you could not touch anything in your study. They might find some fingerprints."

Eriksson escorted him to the door. "I don't know what I'm going to do," she said desperately. "Everything is gone. My whole career has vanished overnight."

Wallander didn't know how to comfort her. He recalled Erik Hökberg's words about society's vulnerability.

"Was Falk a religious man?" he said.

Her surprise was genuine. "He never said anything to suggest such a thing."

Wallander promised to be in touch. When he came down to the street he was at a loss. The person he most needed to talk to was Martinsson, but the question was: should he take Höglund's advice? He wanted to confront him with what she had told him. Then he was smitten by fatigue. The betrayal was so hurtful and unexpected. He still hardly accepted it, but deep down he knew it must be true.

Since it was still early, he decided to wait. Perhaps his anger would subside over the course of the day. First he would go back to the Hökbergs. Then he remembered something that he had forgotten to do. He stopped outside the video shop that had been closed when he came here last. He was going to rent the film with Al Pacino that he wanted to see. He then continued on to the Hökberg house and stopped outside. Just as he was about to ring the bell the door opened.

"I saw you pull up," Erik Hökberg said. "You were here about an hour ago, but you didn't call in."

"Something came up that I had to attend to."

They went inside. The house was quiet.

"Actually, I came to speak to your wife."

"She's resting in the bedroom upstairs. Or crying. Or both."

Erik Hökberg's face was ashen. His eyes were bloodshot.

"My son is back in school," he said. "I think it's the best thing for him."

"We still don't know who killed Sonja," Wallander said. "But we're optimistic that we're closing in on whoever is responsible."

"I have always been against the death penalty," Hökberg

said. "But I don't know about that any more. Just promise not to let me get close to whoever did this. I don't know what I would do to him."

He went upstairs to get his wife. Wallander walked around the living room while he waited. The silence was oppressive. It took almost a quarter of an hour, then he heard footsteps on the stairs. Hökberg came down alone.

"She's very tired," he said. "But she'll be down shortly."

"I'm sorry that this conversation can't wait."

"We understand."

They waited for her in silence. Then she turned up, barefoot and wearing black. Beside her husband she looked very small. Wallander shook her hand and expressed his condolences. She wobbled slightly then sat down. She reminded Wallander of Anette Fredman. Here was yet another mother who had lost a child. He wondered how many times he had found himself in this situation. He had to ask questions that would be salt in already painful wounds.

This situation was perhaps worse than many of the others. Sonja Hökberg had not only been the victim of murder. Now he was about to confront them with the idea that she may also have been raped on an earlier occasion. He groped around for a way to begin.

"To find Sonja's killer we have delved into the past. There is one particular incident that has come to our attention and that we need more information about. Probably you are the only people who can give us that information."

Hökberg and his wife watched him intently.

"Can we look back about 3 years?" Wallander said. "Sometime in 1994 or 1995. Did anything unusual happen to Sonja during that time?"

Ruth, Sonja's mother, spoke very quietly. Wallander had to lean forward to catch her words.

"What kind of thing are you looking for?"

"Did she ever come home looking as if she had been involved in an accident? Did she have unexplained bruises?"

"She broke her ankle once."

"Sprained," Erik Hökberg said. "She didn't break her ankle. She sprained her ankle."

"I'm thinking more of bruises on her face and body. Did that ever happen?"

Ruth Hökberg jumped in. "My daughter was never naked in the house."

"She may have been extremely upset or depressed during this time," Wallander said.

"She was a moody girl."

"So neither one of you can think of anything unusual along these lines?"

"I don't even understand why you're asking these questions."

"He has to," Erik Hökberg said. "It's his job."

Wallander was grateful for this.

"I don't remember her ever coming home with bruises."

Wallander decided he couldn't keep going around in circles.

"We have information to indicate that Sonja was raped at some point during this time. She never reported it."

Ruth flinched as if she had been burned. "It's not true."

"Did she ever speak of it?"

"That she had been raped? Never." She started laughing helplessly. "Who said this? It's a lie. It's nothing but a lie."

Wallander had the feeling that she was withholding something. Perhaps she had suspected something of the kind. Her protestations were unconvincing.

"The information we have is quite compelling."

"Says who? Who is spreading these lies about Sonja?"

"I am afraid I can't tell you that."

"Why not?" Erik Hökberg blurted out.

"It's standard practice during investigations of this nature."

"Why is it?"

"For now it has to do with making sure the source remains protected."

"What about my daughter?" Ruth screamed. "Who is protecting her? No-one. She's dead."

The situation was getting out of hand. Wallander regretted not letting Höglund handle this questioning. Hökberg calmed his wife, who was sobbing. It was a horrible scene.

After a while he went on. "But she never talked about having been raped?"

"Never."

"And neither of you noticed anything out of the ordinary in her behaviour?"

"She was a hard person to gauge."

"In what way?"

"She kept to herself. She was often in a bad temper, which I suppose is normal for teenagers."

"Was she angry with you?"

"Mostly with her younger brother."

Wallander thought back to the only conversation he had ever had with the girl. She had complained then that her brother always got into her things.

"Let's go back to the years 1994 and 1995," Wallander said. "She had returned from England. Did you notice any sudden change at that time?"

Erik got up from his chair so violently that it fell backwards. "She came home one night, bleeding from her mouth and her nose. It was in February 1995. We asked her what had happened, but she wouldn't say. Her clothes were dirty and she was in shock. We never found out what happened. She said she had fallen. It was a lie of course. I realise that now, now that you come here and tell us she'd been raped. Why do we have to keep lying about this?"

Ruth started crying again. She tried to say something, but it was unintelligible. Hökberg gestured to Wallander to follow him to the study.

"You won't get anything more from her."

"I only have a few more questions."

"Do you know who raped her?"

"No."

"But you suspect someone?"

"Yes, but I can't give you a name."

"Was he the same person who killed her?"

"I doubt it. But anything you can tell me may help to clarify the events that led to her death."

"It was towards the end of February," Hökberg said, after a pause. "It snowed all day. By evening everything was white. And she came home bleeding. In the morning you could still see her blood on the snow."

Suddenly it was as if he was overcome by the same helplessness as his wife crying in the room next door.

"You have to get him. A person who can do something like this deserves whatever's coming to him."

"We will get the person who is responsible," Wallander said, "but we need your help."

"You have to understand my wife," Hökberg said. "She's lost her daughter. How is she supposed to react to being told that Sonja was also raped?"

Wallander understood. "So it was the end of February

1995. Do you remember anything else? Did she have a boyfriend at the time?"

"We never knew who she associated with."

"Did any cars ever stop outside the house? Did you ever see her with a man?"

Anger flashed in Hökberg's eyes. "A man? I thought you were talking about boyfriends?"

"That's what I meant."

"It was a grown man who did this to her?"

"I repeat: I can't give you that information."

Hökberg lifted his hands defensively. "I've told you all I know. I should get back to my wife."

"Before I leave I'd like to take a look in Sonja's room again."

"You'll find it just as it was the last time. We haven't changed anything."

Hökberg went into the living room and Wallander went upstairs. When he walked into the room he had the same feeling as before. It was not the room of a 19-year-old girl. He opened the wardrobe door to look at the poster. It was still there. *The Devil's Advocate.* Who is the Devil? he thought. Tynnes Falk worshipped his own image. And Sonja Hökberg has a picture of the Devil in her bedroom. But he had never heard rumours of Satan worshippers in Ystad.

He shut the wardrobe door and was about to go downstairs when a boy appeared in the doorway.

"What are you doing here?" he said.

Wallander told him who he was. The boy looked at him, suspiciously.

"If you're police, you should be able to get the man who killed my sister."

"We're trying," Wallander said.

The boy didn't move. Wallander couldn't decide if he seemed scared or simply curious.

"You're Emil, aren't you?"

The boy said nothing.

"You must have liked your sister."

"Sometimes."

"Only sometimes?"

"Isn't that enough? Do you have to like people all the time?"

"No, you don't."

Wallander smiled, but the boy didn't smile back.

"I think I know one time when you liked her," Wallander said.

"When was that?"

"A couple of years ago. She came home and was hurt."

The boy shifted his feet. "How do you know that?"

"I'm a policeman," Wallander said. "I have to know. Did she ever tell you what happened?"

"No. But someone hit her."

"How do you know that if she didn't tell you?"

"I'm not saying."

Wallander thought that if he pushed too hard the boy might clam up.

"You asked me just now if I was going to find the man who killed your sister. If I'm going to be able to do that, I need your help. The best thing you can do right now is to tell me how you know that someone hit her."

"She made a drawing."

"She drew?"

"She was good at it, but she never showed anyone. She drew pictures and then tore them up. But I went into her room sometimes when she wasn't here."

"And you found something?"

"She drew a picture of what happened."

"Did she say that?"

"Why else would she draw a picture of someone hitting her on the nose?"

"Do you still have the picture?"

The boy left the room. After a few minutes he came back with a pencil drawing in his hand.

"I want it back."

"Promise."

Wallander took the drawing to the window. It was a disturbing picture. He saw that Sonja was good at drawing. He could recognise her face. But it was the man who dominated the picture. He loomed over her and his fist hit her nose. Wallander studied the face. If it was as accurate as her self-portrait they ought to be able to identify him from this drawing. Something on the man's wrist also caught his attention. At first he thought it was a bracelet. Then he saw that it was a tattoo.

Wallander was suddenly in a hurry.

"You did the right thing when you kept this drawing," he told the boy. "I promise you'll get it back."

The boy followed him down the stairs. Wallander carefully folded the paper and put it in his inside pocket. There were still the sounds of sobbing coming from the living room.

"Is she always going to be like that?" the boy said.

Wallander felt a lump in his throat. "It will take time," he said. "But it will get better."

Wallander didn't go in to say goodbye. He touched the boy's head and softly closed the front door behind him.

Wallander tried to reach Höglund on his mobile but there was no answer. He called Irene who told him Höglund had had to go home. One of her children was sick.

Wallander didn't have to think twice. He drove to her house on Rotfruktsgatan. It had started to rain. He folded his arms over his chest to make sure no rain would penetrate his coat and reach the drawing. Höglund opened the front door with a child on her arm.

"I wouldn't have bothered you, but this is important," he said.

"It's OK," she said. "She's a bit feverish, and my neighbour can't take her until later."

Wallander went in. It had been a while since he was last here. In the living room he saw that the Japanese masks had gone from the walls. She followed his gaze.

"He took his mementos with him," she said.

"Does he still live in town?"

"He moved to Malmö."

"Are you going to stay here?"

"I don't know if I can afford it."

The girl in her arms was almost asleep. Höglund put her gently down on the sofa.

"In a moment I'm going to show you a drawing," Wallander said. "But first I need to ask you something about Carl-Einar Lundberg. I know you haven't met him, but you've seen pictures of him and read the case files on him. Can you recall if there was any mention of a tattoo?"

She didn't need time to think. "He had a snake design on his right wrist."

Wallander smacked his hand down on the coffee table. The child jerked awake and started crying, but soon stopped and went back to sleep. At last they had reached a conclusion that held water. He took the drawing out, unfolded it and passed it to her.

"That's Carl-Einar, no question. Where did you get hold of it?"

Wallander told her about his encounter with Emil, and learning of his sister's hidden talent for drawing.

"I'm not sure if we will ever be able to make a charge stick," Wallander said. "But that's not the most important thing right now. What we've done is to prove your theory. It's no longer only a working hypothesis."

"All the same, it's difficult to believe that she would kill his father."

"Keep in mind that there may be other factors we still don't know about. But we can lean on Lundberg and see what we get. We're going to assume she killed his father out of revenge. And Persson may not be lying when she said that Hökberg was the one who did both the stabbing and the hitting. Persson is a riddle unto herself that we'll have to attend to later."

They pondered in silence these latest developments. Finally, Wallander said: "Someone became worried that Hökberg was going to tell us something. So we have three questions we need answers to: what was it she knew? What did it have to do with Falk? Who was the person who became worried?"

The little girl on the sofa began to whimper. Wallander took that as his cue to leave.

"Have you seen Martinsson since this morning?" Höglund said.

"No, but I'm going there now. Don't worry, I'm planning to take your advice. I won't say a word."

Wallander hurried to his car. He drove to Runnerströms Torg in the pouring rain.

He sat in his car for a long time, summoning his energy. Then he walked into the building to face Martinsson.

CHAPTER THIRTY-TWO

Martinsson greeted Wallander at the door with his widest smile.

"I've been trying to call you," he said. "Things are happening."

Wallander had gone into Falk's office with a great deal of pent-up aggression in his body. He was itching to punch Martinsson in the face. But Martinsson smiled and immediately led the conversation to the news of their morning's work. Wallander was somewhat relieved. It gave him breathing space. Time enough for him to have it out with Martinsson later. Besides, Martinsson's smile gave him pause. What if Höglund had misunderstood Martinsson's intentions? Martinsson may have had other matters to discuss with Holgersson. Höglund may also have taken some of his comments the wrong way. Yet in his heart he knew that she had not exaggerated the situation. She had said what she did because she was also upset by it.

Wallander walked around the table to say hello to Modin.

"Tell me what's happened," he said.

"Robert is breaking through one layer of defence after another," Martinsson said with satisfaction. "We're getting deeper and deeper into the strange and fascinating world inside Falk's computer."

Martinsson offered Wallander the folding chair, but he

declined it. Martinsson checked his notes while Modin took a sip of what looked like carrot juice.

"We've identified four more institutions in Falk's network. The first is the National Bank of Indonesia. Don't ask me how Robert managed to confirm that. He's a wizard when it comes to getting around security."

Martinsson kept flipping the pages.

"Then there's a bank in Liechtenstein called Lyder Bank. It gets somewhat harder after this. If we're right, then the next two companies are a French telecommunications firm and a commercial satellite company in Atlanta."

Wallander furrowed his brow. "What do you make of it?"

"Our previous theory, that it's all about money, still stands as far as I'm concerned. But it's not clear yet how the telecom company or the Atlanta satellites are involved."

"Nothing is here by coincidence," Modin said, curtly.

Wallander turned towards him. "Try to explain it to me in a way I'll understand."

"OK. Everyone arranges their bookshelves in their own way. Or their folders, or whatever. After a while you learn to see people's patterns even in their computers. The person who worked on this one was very deliberate. Everything is tidy. There is nothing superfluous. But it also isn't arranged in any obvious fashion, like in alphabetical order, or numerical sequences."

Wallander interrupted him. "Say that again."

"Well, usually people arrange things alphabetically or in numerical order. A comes before B comes before C. One comes before two and five before seven. But here, there isn't any of that."

"What's the pattern, then?"

"Something else entirely."

"Do you see another kind of pattern?"

Modin pointed to the screen. Wallander and Martinsson leaned forward.

"Two components turn up repeatedly," Modin said. "The first one I discovered was the number 20. I tried to see what would happen if I add a few zeroes or change the order round. If I do that, something interesting happens."

He pointed to the digits on the screen: a two and a zero.

"See what happens when I do this." Modin typed something and the numbers were highlighted. Then they disappeared.

"They're like frightened animals that run and hide," Modin said. "It's as if I were shining a bright light on them. They rush back into the darkness. But after a while they come out again, and always in the same place."

"So how do you interpret this?"

"That they're important somehow. There's also another component that behaves in this way."

Modin pointed to the screen again, this time to the initials "JM". "They do the same thing," he said. "If you try to home in on them, they disappear."

Wallander nodded.

"They turn up all the time," Martinsson said. "Every time we identify a new institution on the list, they're there. But Robert has found something else."

Wallander stopped them so he could polish his glasses.

"If you leave them alone," Modin said, "you start to see after a while that they move around."

He pointed to the screen again.

"The first company we identified was the first on the list," he said. "And here the nocturnals are at the top of the column."

"Nocturnals?"

"That's what we are calling them," Martinsson said. "We thought it was fitting."

"Keep going."

"The second item we managed to identify a bit further down the list, in the second column. Here the nocturnals have moved to the right and lower. If you continue through the list you'll see that they move according to a strict pattern. They move towards the right-hand bottom corner."

Wallander stretched his back.

"This still doesn't tell us what they're doing."

"We're not quite done," Martinsson said. "This is where it gets really interesting."

"I've found a time element," Modin said. "The nocturnals change their co-ordinates with time. That means there's an invisible timekeeper in here somewhere. I amused myself by constructing a calculation. If you assume that the upper left corner is zero and there are 74 identities in the network and that the number 20 refers to October 20, then you see the following . . ." Modin typed until a new text emerged on the screen. Wallander read the name of the satellite company in Atlanta. Modin pointed to the last two components.

"This is number four from the end," he said. "And today is October 17."

Wallander nodded slowly. "You mean the pattern will reach some sort of high point on Monday? That the 20th represents some kind of end point for these nocturnals?"

"It seems possible."

"But what about the other component? This JM? What does it mean if we take the 20 to refer to the date?"

No-one had an answer to that question.

"What happens on Monday, October 20?"

"I don't know. But I can tell you that some kind of countdown is under way."

"Maybe we should just pull the plug."

"It wouldn't help. This is just a monitor," Martinsson said. "We can't see the network clearly and we don't know if one or more servers are involved."

"Let's assume the countdown is for a bomb of some kind," Wallander said. "Where, if not from here, is it being controlled?"

"We don't know."

Wallander suddenly had the feeling they were on the wrong track. Was he misguided in his assumption that the answer to the whole case lay in Falk's computer? Wallander hesitated. The doubt that had come over him was very strong.

"We have to rethink this," he said. "From the beginning."

Martinsson looked shocked. "Do you want us to stop?"

"I mean we have to rethink this. There have been some developments you aren't aware of."

They walked onto the landing. Wallander told him about Carl-Einar Lundberg. He felt uncomfortable in Martinsson's presence now, but did his best to hide his feelings.

"We should move Hökberg's role out of the centre," he said. "I'm convinced now that she died because someone was afraid of what she could tell us."

"And how do you explain Landahl's death?"

"They had been in a relationship. Perhaps she had told him what she knew, and this had something to do with Falk."

He also told him what had happened in Eriksson's flat.

"That seems to contradict our ideas," Martinsson said.

"We don't yet know why the electrical relay turned up in the morgue, or why Falk's body was removed. There's an air of desperation in all of this, combined with an extreme ruthlessness. Why would people behave in this way?"

"Maybe they're fanatics," Martinsson said. "The only thing that matters to them is what they believe in."

Wallander gestured towards Falk's office. "Modin has done a great job, but the time has come for us to bring in a specialist from the National Police. We can't take any risks if we are facing a countdown to Monday."

"So Robert is finished here?"

"Yes. I want you to contact Stockholm immediately. Try to get someone down here today."

"But it's Friday."

"I don't care. Monday is just around the corner."

They went back in. Wallander congratulated Modin on his excellent work and told him he was no longer needed. Modin was clearly disappointed, but he didn't say anything. He just went back to the computer to finish up.

Wallander and Martinsson turned their backs to him and started discussing the matter of his payment in low tones. Wallander said he would deal with it. Neither one of them noticed that Modin had copied the remaining material on to his computer. They said goodbye outside in the rain. Martinsson was going to drive Modin home. Wallander shook his hand and thanked him.

Then he drove to the station. He thought about the fact that Elvira Lindfeldt was coming from Malmö that evening. He was both excited and nervous. But before then he had to sit down with the others to rethink the case. Hökberg's rape had dramatically altered the significance of certain events.

When Wallander walked in through the front doors he saw that someone was waiting in reception. The man came over and introduced himself as Rolf Stenius. The name was familiar to Wallander, but he couldn't place it until the man explained that he was Falk's accountant.

"I should have called you before coming down here," Stenius said. "But I happened to be in town for another meeting and thought perhaps I'd drop in."

"It's not a good time," Wallander said. "But I can spare a couple of minutes."

They went to his office. Rolf Stenius was a gaunt man, about his own age, with thinning hair. Wallander remembered seeing in a memo that Hansson had been in contact with him. Stenius took a plastic folder from his briefcase.

"I had already been told the sad news of Falk's death when the police contacted me."

"Who told you?"

"Falk's ex-wife."

Wallander nodded for him to continue.

"I've made a spreadsheet for you of the past two years, and also included other things that may be of interest to you."

Wallander accepted the plastic folder without looking at it.

"Was Falk a rich man?"

"That depends on what you mean by rich. He had about ten million kronor."

"Then, in my book, he was rich. Did he have any outstanding debts?"

"Nothing of any consequence. His operating costs were also quite low," Stenius said.

"His income came from his various consulting projects. Is that correct?"

"I've given you all the information in this folder."

"Was there any one project that was significantly more lucrative than the others?"

"Some of his projects in the US paid very well, but nothing really out of the ordinary."

"What kind of projects were those?"

"Among other things he worked for a national advertising chain. Apparently he helped improve their graphic design program."

"What else?"

"He worked for a whisky importer by the name of DuPont. He made some kind of advanced warehouse storage program."

"Did his revenues grow less rapidly in the past year?"

"I don't think one could say that. He always made wise investments and never put all his eggs in one basket. He had money in Swedish and other Scandinavian and American funds. He kept a good amount of cash on hand, and he invested in several reputable companies. Ericsson, for example."

"Who handled his stock market account?"

"He did that himself, mostly."

"Did he have any interests in Angola?"

"Where did you say?"

"Angola."

"Not that I know of."

"Could he have had such interests without your knowing about it?"

"Of course. But I don't think so. Falk was a very honest man. He felt strongly about paying his taxes. When I suggested he think about moving his assets abroad so as to achieve a more favourable tax rate he was very upset."

"In what way?"

"He threatened to get a new accountant."

Wallander felt tired.

"Thank you," he said. "I'll look through these papers as soon as I have a chance."

"It's a sad affair," Stenius said, and closed his briefcase. "Falk was a good man. Overly reserved, perhaps, but amiable."

Wallander escorted him back to reception.

"Did you have regular meetings with Falk?"

"I took care of most of the business over the phone."

"So you didn't have to meet in person?"

"It's often sufficient to circulate documents and have people sign them in their own time."

Stenius left the station, unfurling his umbrella as he went. Wallander returned to his office and wondered if anyone had had a chance to speak to Falk's children. We don't even have time for the most important tasks, he thought. We're working our fingers to the bone, but the justice system is degenerating into a crumbling warehouse of unsolved cases.

At 3.30 p.m., the investigative team gathered for a meeting. Nyberg sent his apologies. Höglund reported that he was suffering from vertigo. They speculated gloomily who among them would be the first to suffer a heart attack. Then they launched into the discussion about Hökberg's rape and its possible consequences for the case. Wallander insisted that Carl-Einar Lundberg be brought in for questioning as soon as possible and looked over to Viktorsson, who nodded his assent. Wallander also asked Höglund to find out if Lundberg senior had been involved in any way.

"You think he had been after her too?" Hansson said. "What kind of a family is that?"

"We have to know all the facts," Wallander said.

"I can't swallow the theory of a revenge by proxy," Martinsson said. "I'm sorry, but that just seems too far-fetched to me."

"We're not discussing how we feel about these things," Wallander said. "We're talking about facts."

His voice was sharper than he intended. He saw that the others round the table had noticed it. He hurried on in a more friendly tone.

"What about the National Police and their computer specialists? What did they say?"

"Well, they whined when I insisted that someone come down right away, but someone will be here by 9 a.m. tomorrow."

"Does this someone have a name?"

"His name is actually Hans Alfredsson."

Everyone burst out laughing. Hans, or rather Hasse, Alfredsson was a legendary Swedish comedian. Martinsson volunteered to meet his plane at Sturup.

"Do you think you'll be able to show him what's been done so far?" Wallander said.

"Yes. I made plenty of notes while Modin was working."

They finished the meeting by talking about Jonas Landahl. Hansson had already contacted his parents and received information over the phone that enabled them to identify the body. The couple had been in Corsica and were now on their way home. Nyberg had sent Höglund a memo in which he stated that Sonja Hökberg had indeed been in Landahl's car, and that the car had been at the substation that night. They now knew that Landahl had no previous record, but that did not mean that he had not been involved in the releasing of the minks at the farm in Sölvesborg, when Falk had been apprehended.

It was almost 6 p.m. Wallander felt they were not going to get any further and ended the meeting. They would meet again on Saturday. Wallander was now in a hurry. He needed to clean the flat and get himself ready before Elvira arrived. But he went to his office and called Nyberg. It took so long for him to answer that Wallander was getting worried. Finally he answered, furious as usual, and Wallander was able to relax. Nyberg said he was feeling better and would be at work the following day.

Wallander had just managed to tidy up in his flat and change his clothes when the phone rang. Elvira was calling from her car. She had just passed the exit to Sturup. Wallander had booked a table at a fancy Ystad restaurant. He gave her the directions to the main square where they arranged to meet. He put the receiver down so clumsily that it fell to the floor. He picked it up again, cursing, when he suddenly remembered that he and Linda had agreed to talk this evening. He thought for a while and then decided to leave the number of the restaurant on his answerphone in case anyone needed to reach him. There was a chance that a journalist would call, but he decided that it was only a small one. Interest in the scandal seemed to have died down.

He left the car at home and walked. It had stopped raining and the wind had also died down. Wallander was feeling a twinge of disappointment. She had taken the car and not the train. That meant she was planning to return to Malmö this evening. But his hopes were unreasonable. He concentrated on the fact that for once he was going to have the pleasure of dining with a beautiful woman.

He stopped outside the bookshop on the main square and waited. After about 5 minutes he saw her come walking along Hamngatan. He felt suddenly shy, and was baffled by her directness. While they were walking up Norregatan to the restaurant he felt her take his arm. They were passing the building where Svedberg had lived. Wallander stopped and told her about what had happened here. She listened attentively.

"How do you feel about it now?" she said.

"I don't know. It's like a bad dream. Something I can't accept really happened."

The restaurant was small and had only been open about a year. Wallander had never been there, but Linda had recommended it. Wallander had been expecting it to be full, but only a few tables were taken.

"Ystad is hardly a bustling metropolis," he said, by way of an apology. "But the food is supposed to be good."

A waitress whom Wallander recognised from the Continental Hotel showed them to their table.

"You took the car," Wallander said, studying the wine list.

"Yes, I thought I'd drive back."

"Then I'll be drinking the wine today."

"What do the police say about blood alcohol levels?"

"That it's best not to have any alcohol at all if you're planning to drive. But I think one glass is fine with a meal. If you like we can go up to the station after dinner and give you a breath test."

The food was excellent. Wallander finished his first glass of wine and pretended to hesitate before ordering another. The conversation so far had been mainly about his work. For once, he was enjoying it. He told her how he had been a very junior policeman in Malmö and been almost stabbed to death. She asked him about the cases he was involved in now and he was persuaded that she knew nothing about the picture in the paper. He told her about the strange death at the power substation, about the man who had been found at the cash machine and the boy who had been thrown between the propeller shafts on the Poland ferry.

They had just ordered coffee when the door to the restaurant opened. It was Modin. Wallander spotted him immediately. When Modin saw that Wallander was not alone he seemed to hesitate, but Wallander gestured for him to come over. He introduced Modin to Elvira. Wallander saw that he looked worried. He wondered what had happened.

"I think I've found something," Modin said.

"If you need to speak privately, I can leave," Elvira said.

"There's no need."

"I asked my dad to drive me from Löderup," Modin said. "I found out where you were from your answerphone."

"You said you thought you had something?"

"It's hard to explain without the computer in front of me, but I think I've managed to crack the last codes."

Modin looked sure of himself.

"Call Martinsson first thing tomorrow," Wallander said. "I'll tell him in advance of this development."

"I'm pretty sure I'm right."

"There was no need for you to come all this way," Wallander said. "You could have phoned me."

"I get a little carried away sometimes."

Modin nodded nervously in Elvira's direction. Wallander thought he should ask him more closely about the new breakthrough, but decided it could wait until the next day. He wanted to be left alone right now. Modin understood. He walked out again. The conversation had taken two minutes.

"He's a very talented young man," Wallander said as he left. "He's a computer buff and he's helping us with part of our investigation."

Elvira smiled. "He seemed like a nervous type. But I'm sure he's very good at what he does."

They left the restaurant around midnight and walked slowly back to Stortorget. Her car was parked on Hamngatan.

"I've had a wonderful time," she said when they said goodbye.

"You're not tired of me yet?"

"No. What about you?"

Wallander wanted her to stay longer, but he knew he had to let her go. They said they would talk again over the weekend. He gave her a hug. She left, and Wallander made his way home. Suddenly he stopped in the middle of the street. Is it possible? he thought. Have I really met someone? He walked on to Mariagatan and fell asleep shortly after 1 a.m.

Elvira Lindfeldt drove towards Malmö through the darkness. Short of Rydsgård she pulled into a parking space by the side of the road. She dialled a number in Luanda. She tried three times before she got through. It was not a good connection. When she heard Carter on the line, she came straight to the point.

"Fu Cheng was right. The person who is killing our system is called Robert Modin. He lives outside Ystad in a village called Löderup."

She repeated it until she was sure that he understood what she had said, and then the connection was broken.

She drove back onto the main road and continued on to Malmö.

CHAPTER THIRTY-THREE

Wallander called Linda on Saturday morning. He had woken at dawn but had managed to get back to sleep until shortly after 8 a.m. When he had finished breakfast, he called her flat in Stockholm. He woke her up. She asked him why had he not been at home the evening before. Twice she had called the number he had left on the answering machine, but it had been engaged both times. Wallander decided to tell her the truth. She listened without interrupting him.

"I never would have thought," she said, "that you had enough brains in your thick head to take my advice for once."

"I had my doubts."

"But not any more?"

She asked about Elvira and they talked for a long time. She was happy for him, though he kept trying to play it down. It was too early to read something into it. For now, it was enough not to have spent another Friday night alone.

"That's not true," she said. "I know you. You're hoping this will turn out to be the real thing. So am I." Then she changed the subject. "I want you to know that I saw that picture in the paper. It was a bit of a shock. Someone at the restaurant showed it to me and asked if that was my dad."

"What did you say?"

"I thought about saying no, but I didn't."

"That was nice of you."

"I simply made up my mind it couldn't be true."

"It isn't."

He told her what had actually happened, and about the internal investigation. He told her he was confident the truth would come out.

"It's important for me to hear this right now," she said. "It's very important right now."

"Why?"

"I can't tell you why. Not yet."

Wallander's curiosity was piqued. During the past few months he had begun to suspect that Linda's plans for the future had taken a new turn. But in what direction he had no idea. If he ever raised the subject, she always changed it. They ended their conversation by talking about when she was next coming to Ystad. She thought she could make it in mid-November, but not before.

Wallander put the phone down and wondered if she would ever get a real job and think of settling in Ystad. She's got something on her mind, he thought. But for some reason she won't tell me what it is.

It was pointless trying to guess what she was up to. He looked at the time. It was 8.20 a.m. Martinsson would soon be picking up Alfredsson, the computer specialist from Stockholm. Wallander thought about how Modin had turned up so unexpectedly at the restaurant the night before. He had seemed very sure of his discovery. Wallander should let Martinsson know, but something inside him stopped him from having more contact with Martinsson than absolutely necessary. He had lingering doubts about what Höglund had told him, doubts which were caused mainly because he wanted it to be untrue. To lose

Martinsson as a trusted friend would create an impossible work environment. The betrayal would be too hard to bear. He believed he had trained Martinsson the way Rydberg had trained him, but Wallander had never been tempted to or had any wish to overthrow Rydberg's authority.

The force is a wasp's nest, he thought angrily. Nothing but envy, gossip and intrigue. I've always liked to imagine that I remained above it all, but now it seems I've been pulled into the very maelstrom. I'm a leader whose successor is getting impatient.

Overcoming his reluctance, he called Martinsson on his mobile. After all, Modin had forced his father to drive him in all the way from Löderup the night before. They had to take him seriously. He may have already been in touch with Martinsson, but if not, Wallander's call could be important. Martinsson had just parked and was on his way to the terminal. Modin had not yet contacted him. Wallander briefly explained the situation.

"It seems a little strange," Martinsson said. "How could he have thought of this when he didn't have access to the computer any more?"

"You'll have to ask him that."

"He's wily," Martinsson said. "I wouldn't put it past him to have copied some of that material onto his own computer."

Martinsson said he would call Modin, and they agreed to be in touch again in the afternoon.

Wallander felt that Martinsson sounded absolutely normal. Either he's much better at this game of deception than I could have imagined, he thought, or else what Höglund told me isn't right.

Wallander got to the station at 8.45 a.m. When he reached

his office there was a message on his desk. *Something has come up* he read in Hansson's jerky handwriting. Wallander sighed over his colleague's inability to communicate more effectively. "Something" was his trademark. The question was always what this "something" referred to.

The coffee machine in the canteen had been fixed. Nyberg was eating his breakfast. Wallander sat across from him.

"If you ask me about my vertigo, I'm leaving," Nyberg said.

"I'll pass then."

"I feel fine," Nyberg said. "I just wish retirement would hurry up and get here. Even though the money will be wretched."

Wallander knew it wasn't true. Nyberg was tired and worn out, but he was probably just afraid of being retired.

"Is there any word from the coroner's office on Landahl?"

"He died around 3 hours before the ferry arrived in Ystad. I guess that means whoever killed him was still aboard. Unless he jumped ship, of course."

"That was a mistake on my part," Wallander admitted. "We should have checked the passengers before allowing them to disembark."

"What we all should have done was choose a different career," Nyberg said.

Wallander decided it was best to leave him alone. This was an easy choice since he never had to direct him in any way. Nyberg was thorough and well organised and could always judge which aspects of a case were most urgent and which could wait. He got up.

"I've been thinking," Nyberg said.

Wallander waited, all ears. Nyberg had an uncanny

ability to come up with crucial observations. More than once he had helped to turn a case completely around.

"What have you been thinking?"

"About that relay in the morgue. About the handbag by the fence. And the body with the missing two fingers put back at the cash machine. We've been trying to find a meaning in all of this, to get the bits to fit into a pattern. Isn't that right?"

Wallander nodded.

"We've been trying. But it's not going very well. At least not so far."

Nyberg scraped up the rest of his muesli from his bowl before going on.

"I talked to Höglund yesterday. She filled me in on what you talked about at the meeting. Apparently you had stressed the double meaning in the events of this case. You said there was both something deliberate and accidental about the events. Is that right?"

"Something like that."

"Well, what happens if we take this a stage further and assume that there is both planning and coincidence at work here?"

Wallander had nothing to say and waited for Nyberg to go on.

"So I had an idea. What if we are overinterpreting what's happened? First, we suppose that the murder of the taxi driver is much less significant than we thought. What if that is true about the other things as well? What if much of what has happened is meant to lead us astray, as it were?"

"What are you thinking of specifically?"

"For a start, this relay."

"Are you saying that Falk had nothing to do with Hökberg's murder?"

"No. But I believe that someone wants us to think that Falk had more to do with it than he did."

Wallander was getting very interested.

"Or his body turning up again. What if we assume that it doesn't mean anything? Where does that get us?"

Wallander thought about it. "It leaves us in a swamp. We don't know where to put our feet to reach solid ground."

"A good image," Nyberg said approvingly. "I didn't think anyone would ever be able to top Rydberg as far as apt analogies went, but I wonder if you aren't even sharper than he was. We're wading our way through a swamp, exactly where someone wants us to be."

"And we need to find our way back to solid ground?"

"Take the business of the fence. We've been driving ourselves nuts trying to work out why the outer gate was forced and the inner door was unlocked."

Wallander could see what Nyberg was driving at, and it irritated him that he hadn't picked up on this himself. "So whoever unlocked the door later damaged the outer gate simply to confuse us. Is that what you mean?"

"It looks like the best explanation to me."

"I'm embarrassed I haven't seen this myself until now," Wallander said.

"You can't think of everything yourself."

"Are there any other aspects we should ignore?"

"No. We only need to proceed cautiously and weigh up each development. Decide if it's important or not."

Nyberg stood up, signalling the end of the conversation. He walked over to the sink to wash his plate. The last thing Wallander heard before leaving the canteen was Nyberg complaining about the worn-out bristles on the brush.

Wallander paused at Hansson's office. His door was open

and he was filling in his betting slips. Wallander knocked to give him a moment to put them away before he walked in.

"I saw your note," he said.

"The Mercedes van has turned up," he said.

Wallander leaned against the doorpost while Hansson searched through his ever-increasing piles of paper.

"I did as you said and went through the records again yesterday. A small car-rental company in Malmö finally reported a stolen vehicle. A dark blue Mercedes van which should have been returned on Wednesday."

"What was the name it was rented under?"

"You'll like this," Hansson said. "It was a man named Fu Cheng."

"Who paid with American Express?"

"Exactly."

Wallander nodded grimly. "He must have given them a local address."

"Hotel St Jörgen, but the company checked and they have no guest of that name."

Wallander frowned. "That's strange. You wouldn't think this Fu Cheng would risk being shown up like that."

"There's a possible explanation," Hansson said. "There *was* a man of Asian appearance staying at the St Jörgen, name of Andersen and he came from Denmark. The car company checked his description with the hotel staff and are convinced it was the same man."

"How did he pay for his room?"

"Cash."

"He would have to have given them a home address."

Hansson searched for another piece of paper in his pile. A betting slip fell to the ground without his noticing and Wallander kindly ignored it.

"Here we are. An address in Vedbaek."

"Has anyone checked it out?"

"The car company has been extremely persistent. No doubt the van was a valuable asset. The street he wrote down doesn't exist."

"And that's where the tracks stop," Wallander said.

"Do we keep looking for the van?"

Wallander didn't take long to make up his mind. "Hold off on that for now. You have more important things to do. We'll get back to it."

Hansson gestured towards the heaps of paper. "I don't know how we're to get all this other stuff done at the same time."

Wallander didn't have the energy for yet another discussion of chronic police understaffing.

"We'll talk later," he said and left. He cast a quick eye over the latest papers to have landed on his desk, then took his coat and prepared to go to check on Alfredsson. He was curious as to how the meeting with Robert Modin would go. But after he got behind the wheel he did not immediately start the engine. His thoughts turned to his dinner with Elvira. It was a long time since he had felt so good. It was hard to believe it was true. But Elvira was real. She was no mirage.

He couldn't resist the impulse to call her up. He took out his mobile and dialled the number he had already memorised. She answered after the third ring. She said she was happy to hear from him, but Wallander felt sure he had interrupted her. He couldn't put his finger on it, but there was something there. A wave of unexpected jealousy came over him, but he kept it out of his voice.

"I wanted to thank you again for coming over here last night."

"Oh, there's no need, but it's sweet of you."

"Was the drive home all right?"

"I almost ran over a rabbit, but apart from that it was fine."

"I'm in my office and I was trying to imagine what you do on Saturday mornings. But I must be disturbing you."

"Not at all. I was cleaning my flat."

"This is probably not a good time, so I won't keep you. But I wonder if you have any time to get together this weekend?"

"Tomorrow would be best for me. Could you call back this afternoon?"

Wallander promised to do so.

Afterwards he sat and stared at the phone. He had disturbed her, he could hear it in her voice. I'm imagining things, he thought. I once made that mistake with Baiba. I even went to Riga without warning her, to see if my suspicions were justified. But there wasn't another man in her life. I was wrong.

He would have to take her at her word. She was busy cleaning up, nothing more. When he called in the afternoon she would be back to normal.

Wallander drove to Runnerströms Torg. He sat in the car, lost in thought, until someone knocked on the window. He jumped. It was Martinsson, smiling and holding up a bag of pastries. Wallander felt almost happy to see him. Normally he would have discussed the events of the day, but he said nothing as he got out of the car.

"Were you napping?"

"I was thinking," Wallander said, curtly. "Is Alfredsson here?"

Martinsson laughed. "The funny thing is that he actually

looks like his namesake. But that's just the surface. I don't think he's much of a comedian at heart."

"Is Modin here too?"

"I've arranged to pick him up at 1 p.m."

They crossed the street and climbed the stairs. There they paused.

"Alfredsson is a thorough sort," Martinsson said. "I'm sure he's good. He's still working his way through what we've done so far. His wife keeps calling every so often and chastising him for not being at home."

"I'm just going to say hello," Wallander said. "Then I'll leave you two alone until Modin gets here."

"What was it he claimed to have done, by the way?"

"I don't know exactly, but I think he said he had broken the rest of the codes."

They walked in. Martinsson was right. Alfredsson bore an uncanny resemblance to the comedian. Wallander couldn't help smiling. It lifted his mood.

"We're grateful you could come down here at such short notice," Wallander said.

"I wasn't aware I had a choice," Alfredsson said, sourly.

"I've bought some pastries," Martinsson said. "That may help a little."

Wallander decided to leave immediately. It was only when Modin was in place that it would be worth his while.

"Call me when Modin gets here," he said to Martinsson. "I'll come back then."

Alfredsson exclaimed from his chair in front of the computer. "There's a message for Falk," he said.

Wallander and Martinsson went over to take a look. A small icon indicated that there was mail. Alfredsson retrieved it.

"It's for you," he said, surprised, and looked at Wallander.

Wallander put on his glasses and read the message. It was from Modin: *They have traced me. I need help. Robert.*

"Damn," Martinsson said. "He said he always covered his tracks!"

Not another one, Wallander thought helplessly. I can't cope with another one. He was already on his way down the stairs with Martinsson at his heels.

It was pouring with rain. Martinsson's car was closer. Wallander put the police light on the roof.

They sped out of Ystad. It was 10.30 a.m.

CHAPTER THIRTY-FOUR

After the hair-raising drive to Löderup, Wallander finally met Robert's mother. She was overweight and seemed very nervous. She had plugs of cotton wool in her nostrils and was lying on the sofa with a damp towel on her forehead.

Modin's father had opened the front door as they pulled into the driveway. Wallander searched in vain for his first name. He looked over at Martinsson.

"Axel Modin."

They ran across the yard to get out of the heavy rain and the first thing Axel Modin said was that Robert had taken the car. He said this over and over again.

"The boy took the car. He doesn't even have a licence."

"Does he know how to drive?" Martinsson said.

"Hardly. I've tried to teach him. I have no idea how I got such an impractical son."

But he knows his way around a computer, Wallander thought. However you explain that.

Once they were inside, Axel Modin said in a low voice that his wife was in the living room.

"She has a nose bleed," he said. "She always gets one when she is upset."

Wallander and Martinsson walked in to meet her. She started to cry when she heard that they were from the police.

"We'd better sit in the kitchen," Axel Modin said. "That way we won't disturb her. She gets anxious."

Wallander sensed a note of sadness in his voice as he spoke of his wife. Axel closed the kitchen door part of the way. During their conversation Wallander had the feeling that he was listening for any sound from the living room.

He offered them coffee and they both said no. They shared a feeling of urgency. During the drive out to Löderup Wallander had grown increasingly worried. He wasn't sure what was going on, but he knew that the boy could be in real danger. Already they had two young people dead in the case and Wallander couldn't bear the prospect of it happening a third time.

While they had been speeding down the main road towards Löderup, Wallander had been too nervous about Martinsson losing control on the wet surface to say anything, but once they reached the minor roads and he was forced to slow down Wallander started asking questions.

"How could he have known that we were in Falk's office? And how did he have Falk's e-mail address?"

"He probably tried to call you first," Martinsson said. "Is your phone on?"

Wallander looked. He had turned it off. He swore.

"He must have guessed that we were there," Martinsson said. "And of course he simply memorised Falk's address. There's nothing wrong with his mind."

Now they were sitting in the kitchen.

"We got what amounts to an SOS from Robert," Wallander said.

Axel Modin stared at him. "An SOS?"

"He sent us an e-mail. But the most important thing is that you tell us what happened at this end."

"I don't know anything," Axel Modin said. "I didn't even know you were coming here. But I did notice that he's been up late these past couple of nights. I don't know what he's been up to, but I know it has to do with those damned computers of his. Today when I woke around 6 a.m. he was still at it. He can't have slept at all. I knocked on his door and asked if he wanted a cup of coffee. He said yes. He came down after about half an hour, but didn't say anything. He seemed completely bound up in his thoughts."

"Was that typical of him?"

"Yes, it didn't surprise me. I could see in his face that he hadn't slept."

"Did he say anything about what he was doing?"

"No, he didn't. It wouldn't have done any good. I'm an old man and I don't understand the first things about computers."

"And then what happened?"

"He drank the coffee, had a glass of water and went back upstairs."

"I didn't think he drank coffee," Martinsson said. "I thought he was very particular about his diet."

"Coffee is the big exception. But you're right. He's vegan, he says."

Wallander wasn't sure what the parameters for a vegan were. Linda had tried to explain it all to him once and had mentioned things such as environmental consciousness, buckwheat and bean sprouts. But it was beside the point now. He pressed on.

"So Robert goes back to his bedroom. What time was that?"

"About 6.45 a.m."

"Were there any telephone calls this morning?"

"He has a mobile. I can't hear it."

"So what happened then?"

"At 8 a.m. I went upstairs with breakfast for my wife.

When I walked past his door I didn't hear anything. I actually stopped and tried to hear if he might have gone to bed."

"Do you think he had?"

"It was quiet and I think he was lying in bed. But I don't think he was sleeping. It seemed to me that he was thinking."

Wallander wrinkled his nose. "How could you know that?"

"I can't, of course. But I don't think it's so hard to tell if a person behind a closed door is thinking with great concentration. Don't you think you can sense it?"

Martinsson nodded in an understanding manner that irritated Wallander. The hell you would be able to tell if I had the door closed and was thinking hard, he thought to himself.

"Let's move on. You gave your wife breakfast in bed."

"Not in bed, actually. She has a little table in the bedroom. She's often unsettled in the morning and needs a bit of time to herself."

"And then?"

"I went back to the kitchen to wash the dishes and feed the cats. And the chickens out back. We have a couple of ducks as well. Then I went to the letter box and got the paper. I had some more coffee and read the paper."

"And all this time you didn't hear anything from upstairs?"

"No. It was after this that it happened."

Axel Modin got up and walked over to the door. He pushed it closer, then came back to the table.

"I heard Robert's door open with a bang. He came down the stairs at an incredible speed. I only had time to stand up before he reached the kitchen. He looked completely in shock, as if I was a ghost. Before I had time to say anything he ran into the hall and locked the front door. Then he came back and asked me if I had seen anyone. He screamed it at me."

"That was what he said? 'Have you seen anyone?'"

"Right. He was beside himself. I asked him what was the matter, of course. But he didn't listen. He was looking out of the window, here in the kitchen and then in the living room. My wife started shouting from upstairs. She was frightened by the noise. It was pretty hectic in here for a few minutes, I can tell you."

"What happened next?"

"When he came back to the kitchen he had my shotgun and he ordered me to get the cartridges for it. That scared me and I asked him again what had happened, but he wouldn't say. He just wanted the cartridges. But I didn't give him any."

"Then what happened?"

"He threw the shotgun on the sofa in there and grabbed the car keys. I tried to stop him, but he pushed me aside and ran out."

"What time was it?"

"I don't know. My wife was at the head of the stairs screaming and I had to take care of her. But it would have been about 8.45 a.m."

Wallander looked at the time. He had sent his e-mail asking for help and then he had left. Wallander stood up.

"Did you see which way he went?"

"He went north."

"One other thing. Did you see anyone when you went out to get the paper? Or when you fed the chickens?"

"Who would I have seen? And in this weather?"

"There may have been a car parked somewhere. Or a car driving past."

"There was no-one here."

Wallander nodded to Martinsson. "We have to look at his room," Wallander said.

Axel Modin had buried his face in his hands. "Can someone explain to me what's going on?"

"Not right now," Wallander said. "But we're going to try to find your son."

"He was frightened," Axel Modin said softly. "I have never seen him so frightened. He was as frightened as his mother sometimes gets."

Wallander and Martinsson went upstairs. Martinsson pointed to the shotgun leaning against the banister. The flickering screens of two monitors greeted them in Robert's room. There were clothes all over the floor and the waste-paper basket next to the desk was overflowing.

"What was it that happened shortly before 9.00 this morning?" Wallander said. "Something scared him. He sent us the e-mail and then ran. He was desperate, literally afraid for his life. He wanted the shotgun for protection. He looks out the windows and then takes the car."

Martinsson picked up the mobile that was lying next to the computers. It was switched off.

"Maybe someone called," he said. "Or else he may have made a call himself and was told something that frightened him. Too bad he didn't take the phone with him when he left."

"If he sent us an e-mail, he may also have received one. He told us that someone had traced him and that he needed our help."

"But he didn't wait for us."

"Either something else happened after he e-mailed us, or he seriously didn't want to wait any longer."

Martinsson sat at the desk. "We'll leave that one

for now," he said, referring to the smaller of the two computers.

Wallander didn't ask how Martinsson could determine which of the two was more important. For the time being he was dependent on his expertise. Wallander didn't like it when one of his colleagues knew more than he did.

While Martinsson started typing on the keyboard Wallander looked around the room. The rain was whipping against the window. On one wall there was a large poster with a carrot on it. It was the only thing that stood out in a room devoted to the electronic sphere. There were computer books, diskettes and cables. Some of the computer cords were wrapped round each other like a nest of vipers. There was a modem, a printer, a television and two video recorders. Wallander walked over to the desk and bent down. What could Robert have seen through this window as he was sitting at the desk? There was a road far in the distance. He could have seen a car, Wallander thought. He looked around the room again, lifting things carefully until he found a pair of binoculars under some papers. He focused them on the distant landscape. A raven flew across his line of vision, close to the house, and Wallander flinched involuntarily. Otherwise there was nothing. A tumbledown fence, trees, and a narrow road that snaked through the fields.

"How's it going?" he said.

Martinsson mumbled something. Wallander put on his glasses and looked at the pieces of paper closest to the computers. Robert Modin's handwriting was hard to read. There were some half-finished equations and phrases, without beginning or end. The word "delay" occurred several times. Sometimes it was underlined, other times it appeared with a question mark beside it. Wallander kept looking.

On another page Robert had written "Completion date of programming?" and then: "Insider necessary?" A lot of question marks, Wallander thought. He's been searching for answers just as we have.

"Look here," Martinsson said, suddenly. "He got an e-mail. Then he sent his message to us."

Wallander leaned in and read the message. *You have been traced*. Nothing else.

"Was there anything later?" Wallander said.

"No messages since then."

"Who sent the message?"

"The source is hidden behind all these scrambled codes. This is someone who didn't want to say who he was."

"But where did it come from?"

"The server is Vesuvius," Martinsson said. "We can certainly have it traced, but it may take a while."

"You don't think it's here in Sweden?"

"I doubt it."

"Vesuvius is a volcano in Italy," Wallander mused. "Can that be where it came from? What happens if we reply to the message?"

"I'm not sure. We can try." Martinsson prepared a return message. "What do you want the text to say?"

Wallander thought about it.

"'Please repeat your message,'" he said. "Try that."

Martinsson nodded approvingly and wrote the message in English.

"Should I sign it?"

"Yes. 'Robert Modin.'"

Martinsson hit "send" and the reply went into cyberspace. Almost at once a message came up on the screen saying that the address was unknown.

"You'll have to tell me what you want me to do next,"

Martinsson said. "What should I look for, do you think? Where Vesuvius is, or something else?"

"Send a message to someone over the Internet asking about this server," Wallander said. "Ask if anyone knows where to find it." But then he changed his mind. "Put the question this way. Is the server Vesuvius based in Angola?"

Martinsson was taken aback. "Are you still thinking about that postcard from Luanda?"

"No, I think the postcard is incidental. But I think Falk met someone in Luanda a number of years ago and that it was a turning point in his life. I don't know what happened there but I'm sure it's important. Crucial, in fact."

Martinsson looked hard at him. "Sometimes I think you put too much stock in your intuition, if you'll pardon my saying so."

Wallander had to work hard to control himself. Rage at Martinsson boiled up inside him, but he took a deep breath. They had to focus on Modin. But Wallander did file away what Martinsson had said, word for word. He had a long memory, as Martinsson was going to learn first-hand. But for now he had an idea he wanted to try out.

"While Robert was working for us, he sometimes consulted a couple of friends online," Wallander said. "One in California and one in Rättvik. Did you ever make a note of their e-mail addresses?"

"I wrote everything down," Martinsson said in a hurt voice. Wallander assumed he was upset because he hadn't thought of it himself.

Wallander cheered up. "They won't hold anything against us asking about Vesuvius," he said. "Make it clear that we're asking on Robert's behalf. While you do that I'm going to start looking for him."

"What does this message mean anyway?" Martinsson said. "He didn't manage to clean up after himself. Is that it?"

"You're the specialist," Wallander said. "Not me. But I have a feeling that has only been growing stronger. You will no doubt correct me if I'm wrong – and this feeling has nothing to do with my intuition, only with facts – but I feel as if the people we are dealing with are supremely well informed of our activities."

"We know someone has been observing our activities at Apelbergsgatan and Runnerströms Torg. You almost ran into him, in fact. When he took a shot at you."

"That's not it. I'm not talking about this person, who may or may not be called Fu Cheng. What I'm getting at is that it almost seems as if they have a mole inside the station."

Martinsson burst out laughing. Wallander couldn't tell if it was mocking or not.

"You're not serious! You don't think one of us is mixed up in this, do you?"

"No, I don't. But I'm wondering if there might be another kind of leak."

Wallander pointed at the computer. "What I'm wondering is if someone has been doing the same thing we were doing with Falk's computer. Breaking in to get secret information."

"The national records are exceedingly well secured."

"But what about our individual computers? Are they so watertight that someone with the expertise and enough drive couldn't break into them? You and Höglund write all your reports on them. I don't know about Hansson. I do it some of the time. Nyberg tussles with his machine. The coroner's report comes both in a hard copy and electronically. What would happen if someone had a way in and was watching everything that came into our computers? Without us being aware of it?"

"It isn't plausible," Martinsson said. "Our security is too good."

"It's just a thought," Wallander said. "One of many."

He left Martinsson and walked down the stairs. Through the half-open door to the living room he could see Axel Modin put an arm round his giant wife, who still had cotton wool in her nostrils. It was an image that filled him with pity and, mysteriously, with joy. Which feeling dominated, he wasn't sure. He knocked gently on the door.

Axel Modin came out.

"Can I use your phone?" Wallander said.

"Do you know what happened? Why Robert is so afraid?"

"We're still trying to discover that. But there is nothing to worry about."

Wallander said a silent prayer that his words would turn out to be true. He sat by the phone in the hall. Before lifting the receiver he reflected on what needed to be done. The first thing he had to address was whether or not there really was cause for alarm. The e-mail to Robert was real enough, for all that the source was hidden. And so far the case was characterised by secrecy and silence, and by people who did not hesitate to kill.

Wallander decided that the threat to Robert was real. He couldn't take the chance of being wrong. He lifted the receiver and called the station. He was lucky enough to get on to Höglund right away. He told her what was going on and asked her to send patrol cars to search the area around Löderup. Since Robert was an unpractised driver he had probably not managed to get far. Perhaps he had already caused or been in an accident. Wallander called out to Axel Modin to give him the registration number as well as a description of the car. Höglund said she would take care of it. Wallander put the phone down and walked back up the stairs. Martinsson hadn't heard anything from Modin's hacker friends.

"I need to use your car," Wallander said.

"The keys are in the ignition," Martinsson said without taking his eyes off the screen.

Wallander decided to take a look at the road that ran through the fields and that Robert could see through his window. Probably there was nothing there, but Wallander wanted to be sure. He drove out on to the road and started looking for the turn-off. He drove too fast on the muddy surface between the fields, but it was Martinsson's car and it was a way to take another small revenge. He stopped when he got to the point he had found through the binoculars. He got out and looked around. The rain was almost gone now and a thick fog was rolling in. If Martinsson looked up he would be able to see his car and its driver. Wallander looked down at the road and saw that another car had been there. He thought he could tell where it had stopped nearby, but the tracks were not easy to read. The rain had all but washed them away. But someone probably stopped here, he thought.

Wallander felt uneasy. If someone had been keeping an eye on the house from here, he would have seen Modin leave in the car.

He felt the sweat start to break out over his body. It's my responsibility, he thought. I should never have got him mixed up in this. It was too dangerous and I was irresponsible.

He had to force himself to stay calm. Modin had

panicked and wanted a gun. Then he had decided to leave in the car. The question he had to answer was: where had the boy gone?

Wallander looked around one more time then drove back to the house through the thickening fog. Axel Modin met him at the door and raised his eyebrows.

"I haven't found Robert," Wallander said. "But we are looking and there's no need to be concerned."

Axel Modin did not believe him – Wallander could see it in his face – and he looked away. There was no sound from the living room.

"Do you have any idea where he may have gone?" Wallander said.

Axel Modin shook his head. "None at all."

"But he had friends. When I came here that first night he had been at a party."

"I've called all his friends. No-one has seen him. They promised to let me know if they did."

"You have to think hard," Wallander said. "He's your son. He's scared and he took off in your car. What would he think of as a safe hiding place?"

"He likes to walk on the beach," Modin said doubtfully. "Down by Sandhammaren or on the fields around Backåkra. I don't know of anywhere else."

Wallander was also doubtful. A beach was too open, no better than a field. There was the fog of course. A better hiding place than a Skåne fog was hard to imagine.

"Keep thinking," Wallander said. "You may be able to remember something else, some hiding place from his childhood."

He called Höglund. The patrol cars had been dispatched. The Simrishamn police had been alerted. Wallander told her about Sandhammaren and Backåkra.

"I'm going to Backåkra," he said. "Get a car to Sandhammaren."

Höglund said she would and that she was coming out to Löderup. Wallander was hanging up as Martinsson came running down the stairs.

"Rättvik got back to me," he said. "You were right. Vesuvius is registered in Luanda."

Wallander nodded. He was not surprised by the news, but it ratcheted up his anxiety.

CHAPTER THIRTY-FIVE

Wallander stood in the hall staring at Martinsson and felt his fear increase as the seconds ticked by. The only thing he was sure of was that they had to find Modin before it was too late. Images of Hökberg's scorched body and Landahl's butchered remains swept in front of his eyes. Wallander wanted to dash into the fog and start searching. But the situation was still unclear. Modin was out there somewhere, terrified. Landahl, too, had fled, but someone had caught up with him. And now Modin was in the same situation.

Martinsson had discovered that some Brazilian entrepreneurs were responsible for the installation and upkeep of the server Vesuvius. But they had not yet identified the source of the message to Modin, even if Wallander suspected it to be "C", whoever that was, or maybe "C" was more than one person.

Martinsson returned to the computers. Wallander had encouraged him to keep talking to Modin's friends in Rättvik and California. They might know of a possible hiding place.

Wallander walked to the window and looked out. A strange silence seemed to accompany the fog. Wallander had never experienced it anywhere except here in Skåne in October and November, before winter struck. The landscape seemed to be holding its breath when the fog came in.

Wallander heard a car pull up. He opened the front door. It was Höglund. She introduced herself to Axel Modin while Wallander walked to the stairs and asked Martinsson to come down. They sat around the kitchen table. Axel Modin hovered in the background, attending to his wife and her debilitating anxiety.

For Wallander nothing else mattered now except finding the boy. It was not enough that they put patrol cars on the job, they needed to send out a regional alert. All neighbouring police districts should be involved in the search. Wallander gave this task to Martinsson.

"He fled in a state of panic. We have no idea where he is," Wallander said. "We can't know the seriousness of the threat against him and we don't know if his movements were being watched, but that is what we're going to assume is the case."

"They're very good, whoever they are," Martinsson said from the doorway with the telephone receiver pressed against his ear. "I know how conscientious he was about erasing his tracks."

"That can't have been enough," Wallander said. "Especially if he copied material and kept working on it through the night after he got home. After he had said goodbye to us."

"I have found nothing to confirm that," Martinsson said. "But you may be right."

Once Martinsson had seen to the regional alert, they decided to establish their temporary headquarters at the house. It was possible that Modin would contact his father. Höglund would go to Sandhammaren with two patrol cars, while Wallander went to Backåkra.

On the way out to the cars Wallander noticed that Höglund was carrying her gun. Once she had gone

Wallander went back to the house. Axel Modin was sitting in the kitchen.

"I'd like the shotgun," Wallander said. "And some cartridges." Wallander could see the fear flare up in the man's face. "It's just a precautionary measure," he said.

Modin got up and left the kitchen. When he came back he had the shotgun and a box of cartridges with him.

Wallander was back in Martinsson's car, driving to Backåkra. Cars were crawling along. Headlights emerged from the fog and were swallowed up again. The whole time he was racking his brains to work out where Modin might have gone. Had he left without a thought in his head, or had he had a plan? Wallander realised he wasn't going to get anywhere. He didn't know the boy well enough.

He almost missed the turning to Backåkra. He increased his speed a little, though he was on a narrower road. He didn't expect to meet other cars here. The grounds as well as the house were owned by the Swedish Academy, the élite group of writers and intellectuals responsible for awarding the Nobel Prize for Literature every year. It was probably deserted at this time of year. He found his way into the car park and got out, taking the shotgun with him. He heard a foghorn in the distance, and he could smell the sea. Visibility was minimal. He walked around the car park but there was no other car. He walked to the house and round its outer buildings, but it was all thoroughly secured. What am I doing here? he wondered. If there's no car, then there's no Robert either. But something drove him on towards the fields. He went to the right, where he knew he would find the small meditation garden. A bird squawked nearby. The fog made it impossible to judge distances. He reached the ring of stones that bordered the garden. He could hear the sea clearly now. No-one was there and no-one seemed to have been there either. He got out his phone and called Höglund. She was in Sandhammaren. No sign of Modin's car there either.

"The fog is very localised," she told him. "Air traffic is normal at Sturup. A bit north of Brösarp everything is clear."

"I don't think he's gone that far," Wallander said. "He's still in the area, I'm sure of it."

He ended the conversation and started back. Suddenly something caught his attention. He listened. A car was approaching. He concentrated intensely. Modin had gone off in a Golf. But the engine noise of this car was different. He loaded the shotgun. Then he pressed on. The engine stopped. Wallander waited. A car door was opened, but not closed. Wallander was sure it was not Modin. Perhaps it was a caretaker coming to see to the place. Or to find out who it was who had just arrived, to make sure it was not a burglar. Wallander thought about getting closer, but his instinct warned him not to. What it was, he couldn't say. He left the path he was on and made a wide circle back, heading towards the far end of the car park. From time to time he stopped. I would have heard someone unlock the door and enter the house, he thought. But it's too quiet out there. Much too quiet.

He was directly behind the house. He took a few steps back and it disappeared into the grey fog. Then he walked towards the car park. He climbed over the fence with some difficulty. Then he slowly reconnoitred the car park. It was harder than before to see his way. He thought that it was probably a bad idea to get too close to Martinsson's car. Better to go round it. He stayed close to the fence so he wouldn't lose his bearings.

He stopped when he had reached the entrance. There was the car. Or rather, the van. At first he wasn't sure what it was, but then it dawned on him: it was a dark blue Mercedes van.

He took a few quick paces back into the fog and listened. His heart was beating fast. He undid the safety catch on the shotgun. The driver's door was standing open. He stood stock still. This was undoubtedly the van they had been looking for. The one that had brought Falk's body back to the cash machine. And here it was, out in the fog looking for Modin.

But Modin isn't here, Wallander thought.

Then he realised that it could be him they were looking for. If they had seen Modin drive away they could have been watching him too. He replayed his drive here. No car had overtaken him, but had there been headlights in his rear-view mirror?

His mobile rang in his pocket. Wallander jumped and answered as quickly as he could with a low voice. It wasn't Martinsson or Höglund. It was Elvira Lindfeldt.

"I hope I'm not disturbing you," she said. "But I wonder if we could set a date for tomorrow. That is, if you'd still like to."

"I'm a bit busy right now," Wallander said.

She asked him to speak up, saying it was hard to hear him.

"Can I call you back?" he asked. "I'm tied up right now."

"I really can't hear you very well," she said.

He raised his voice as far as he dared. "I can't talk now. I'll call you back."

"I'm at home," she said.

Wallander switched off his phone. This is insane, he thought. She won't understand. She will think I'm avoiding her. Why did she have to pick this time to call, for heaven's sake?

Then he had a thought that made his head spin. He couldn't imagine where it had come from and he brushed it aside before it had a chance to take hold. But it had been there, like a dark undercurrent in his mind. Why did she call now? Was it a mere coincidence?

It was an unreasonable thought and it was a symptom of his exhaustion and the growing sense of being the object of his colleagues' conspiracies to get rid of him. He stared at the mobile before putting it back. He would call her back as soon as this was over. He was putting the phone into his pocket when it slipped his grasp. He bent to try to catch it before it fell onto the wet ground.

That saved his life. In the same instant there exploded a terrific noise above and behind him. He abandoned the phone and raised his shotgun. Something was moving in the fog. Wallander dropped to the ground and crawled away as fast as he could. His heart was beating wildly. Someone had fired a gun at him and he didn't know from where. He must have heard my voice, Wallander thought. He heard me and was creeping up towards me. If I hadn't dropped the phone, I would be dead now. The thought terrified him. The shotgun shook in his hands. He didn't know where his phone was nor the car. He lost all sense of direction as he crawled. He only wanted to get away, but when he had put enough distance between him and where the shot had just missed him, he forced himself to kneel on one knee with the shotgun at the ready, and waited. The man was there, but there was no sound. Wallander tried to see through the thick white mass and strained his ears. Perhaps he shouldn't stay. He wanted to leave. He made up his mind. He fired into the air. The bang was deafening and he ran a few metres to one side, then stopped and listened. He reloaded. He was close to the fence and knew which way to go to get out of the car park.

Then there was a new sound. Sirens were rapidly approaching. Someone heard that first shot, he thought. There are plenty of police on the roads right now. He ran along the fence towards the entrance. Now he had a leg up on his opponent, and that feeling was transforming his fear to rage. He had been shot at for the second time in a few days. But he also tried to think clearly. The Mercedes van was still there, and there was only one way out of the car park. If the man dared to take the vehicle it would be easy to get him. If he fled on foot it would be much harder.

Wallander reached the entrance and ran down the road. The sirens were closer now, signalling one, maybe even two or three, patrol cars. Hansson was in the first car. Wallander had never been so glad to see him.

"What's happening here?" Hansson shouted. "We got a report of guns fired in the area. And Höglund said you were down here."

Wallander tried to explain what had happened as succinctly as possible. "No-one goes down there without proper protection," he finished. "We mainly need dogs, but first we have to be prepared for the possibility that he tries to shoot his way out."

They put on their vests and helmets and quickly erected a barrier. Then Höglund arrived, closely followed by Martinsson.

"The fog is going to lift very soon," Martinsson said. "I've talked to the National Weather Service."

They waited on the road outside the car park. It was 1 p.m. on Saturday, October 18. Wallander had borrowed Hansson's phone and walked off to one side. He dialled

Elvira's number, but he changed his mind and hung up before she answered.

The fog didn't lift until 1.30 p.m., but then it dispersed in a matter of minutes and the sun came out. There were the van and Martinsson's car. No-one was to be seen. Wallander walked over and retrieved his mobile.

"He must have taken off on foot," he said.

Hansson called Nyberg. He would come as quickly as possible. They searched the van, but found nothing that told them anything about its driver.

"Did you catch sight of him at all?" Höglund said. It irritated Wallander and made him defensive. "No," he said. "I didn't see him, and you wouldn't have been able to either."

She was taken aback. "It was just a question," she said, shortly.

We're all tired, Wallander thought. She and I both. Not to mention Nyberg. Martinsson might be the exception since he had the energy to sneak around the police station and talk behind people's backs.

Two dog units had been set off and were searching the area. They immediately picked up a scent leading down to the water. Nyberg arrived with his forensic technicians. There was still no trace of Modin.

"I want fingerprints," Wallander said. "That's the main thing. I want to know if anything matches what we found at Apelbergsgatan or Runnerströms Torg. Or the power substation and Hökberg's handbag. Don't forget Eriksson's flat."

Nyberg took a quick look into the van. "I'm so grateful every time I'm called out to look at something that doesn't include mutilated bodies," he said. "Or so much blood that I have to put on waders."

The dog units came back at 3 p.m. They had lost the trail some way along the coast.

"Everyone looking for Robert Modin should also be keeping an eye out for a man with an Asian appearance," Wallander said. "But it's important that he not be directly approached. This man is armed and dangerous. He's been unlucky twice, but he won't be a third time. We should also remain alert to reports of stolen cars."

Wallander gathered the members of his team. The sun was shining and there was no wind. He led them to the meditation garden.

"Were there any police during the Bronze Age?" Hansson said.

"Very likely," Wallander said. "But I doubt if there was a justice department breathing down their necks."

"They played horns," Martinsson said. "I was at a concert recently at the Ales Stenar. They tried to re-create prehistoric music. It sounded like foghorns."

"Let's focus on the situation at hand. The Bronze Age will have to wait," Wallander said. "Modin receives a threat on his computer and he takes off. He has been gone for six and a half hours. Somewhere out here is a person looking for him, but we may assume that this person is after me too. And that naturally extends to all of you also." He looked around at them. "We need to ask ourselves why, and I can only find one reasonable explanation. He, or someone, is worried that we know something. And even worse, this person or these persons worry that we are in a position to prevent something from occurring. I am convinced that everything that has happened has been a consequence of Falk's death, and has to do with whatever is in his computer."

He paused and looked at Martinsson. "How is Alfredsson getting on?"

"I spoke to him last more than 2 hours ago. At that point he could only tell us what Modin had told us, that there is some kind of a ticking time bomb built into the program. Something is going to happen. He was going to apply various probability calculations and reduction programs to see if he could isolate a pattern. He is also in contact with Interpol computer specialists to see if any other countries have experience with this kind of thing. To my mind, he's thorough and he knows what he's doing."

"Then we'll leave it in his hands," Wallander said.

"But what if something is really going to happen on the 20th? That's on Monday. It's less than 34 hours away," Höglund said.

"Quite honestly, I don't know what to tell you," Wallander said. "But we know it's important to these people who are prepared to commit murder to protect its secret."

"Surely it has to be an act of terrorism?" Hansson said. "Shouldn't we have contacted the National Guard a long time ago?"

Hansson's suggestion was greeted with hearty laughter. Neither Wallander nor any of his colleagues had the slightest confidence in the Swedish National Guard. But Hansson was right, and Wallander should have thought of it since he was leading the investigation. His was the head on the block, and it would roll if a situation developed which the National Guard could have played a role in preventing.

"Call them," Wallander told Hansson. "If they stay open for business during the weekend."

"What about the blackout?" Martinsson said. "It seems that whoever is behind this has developed a sophisticated knowledge of power stations. Could there be a plan to knock out the power grid?"

"We can't rule out anything," Wallander said. "But that

reminds me: the blueprint we found in Falk's office – have we found out how it got there?"

"According to Sydkraft, the original was in Falk's office and a copy had been left in its place in their files," Höglund said. "They gave me a list of people who would have had access to these files. I gave it to Martinsson."

Martinsson made an embarrassed gesture. "I haven't had time," he said. "I'll feed it through our records as soon as I get a chance."

"That is now a priority," Wallander said. "It could give us something."

A soft wind had started blowing cold air across the fields. They talked about the priorities at hand, then Wallander delegated them. Martinsson was the first to leave. He was going to take Modin's computers to the station, as well as cross-check the names that Sydkraft had sent them. Wallander put Hansson in charge of the search for Modin. Wallander felt the need to talk through the situation with someone, in this case Höglund. Ordinarily he would have chosen Martinsson, but now that was unthinkable.

Wallander and Höglund started back towards the car park together.

"Have you talked to him yet?" she said.

"No. It's more important to concentrate on finding Modin and the cause of all this."

"You've just been shot at for the second time this week. I don't understand how you can take it so well."

Wallander stopped and looked at her. "Who says I'm taking it well?"

"You give that impression."

"Well, it is false."

They kept walking.

"Tell me how you see the case now. Take your time.

How would you describe it to someone? What can we expect next?"

She swept her coat tightly around her. She was freezing.

"I can't tell you any more than you already know."

"But you'll tell me in your way. And if I hear your voice at least I won't be hearing my own thoughts for a while."

"Hökberg was definitely raped," she said. "I see no other reason for what she did. If we were to keep digging into her life, we would find a young woman consumed by hatred. But she is not the stone that is thrown into the water, she is one of the outer rings. I think perhaps timing is the most important factor in her case."

"What do you mean by that?"

"What would have happened if Falk had not died so close to the time she was arrested? Let's say a few weeks had gone by, and say it wasn't so close to October 20."

Wallander nodded. So far her thinking was right on track. "The fact that it is close to some important event in time leads to hasty and unplanned actions. Is that what you mean?"

"The perpetrators have no margins for error. Hökberg is being held by the police. Someone is afraid of what she can tell us. Specifically, something she may have heard from her friends, first and foremost Jonas Landahl, who is later also killed. All of these events are part of an attempt to keep secret something that is inside a computer. The nocturnals, as Modin apparently called them, want to keep doing their work in the dark. If one disregards some loose details, I think this about sums it up. It then also makes sense that Modin was threatened. And that you were attacked."

"Why me? Why not any other police officer?"

"You were in the flat when they came the first time.

You have all the time been out in front leading this investigation."

They kept walking in silence. The wind was gusting now. Höglund hunched her shoulders against it.

"There's one more thing," she said, "that we know, but that they don't know."

"What's that?"

"That Hökberg never told us anything. In that sense she died a pointless death."

Wallander nodded. She was right.

"I keep wondering what could be in that computer," he said after a while. "The only thing that Martinsson and I have come up with is that it has something to do with money."

"Perhaps there's a big bug in the works? Isn't that the way it's done nowadays? A bank computer goes haywire and starts transferring money into the wrong account."

"Maybe. We just don't know."

They had reached the car park. Höglund opened her mouth to say something when they both saw Hansson running towards them.

"We've found him!" Hansson shouted.

"Modin or the man who shot at me?"

"Modin. He's in Ystad. One of the patrol cars spotted him as they were driving back to change shifts."

"Where was he?"

"Parked at the corner of Surbrunnsvägen and Aulingatan. By the People's Park."

"Where is he now?"

"At the station."

Wallander saw the relief in Hansson's face.

"He's OK," Hansson said. "We got to him first."

"Yes, it seems like it."

It was 3.55 p.m.

CHAPTER THIRTY-SIX

The call that Carter had been waiting for came at 5 p.m. It was a bad connection and it was difficult to understand Cheng's broken English. Carter thought that it was like being transported back to the 1980s when communications between Africa and the rest of the world were still very poor. He remembered a time when it was a challenge to do something as simple as send or receive a fax.

But in spite of the static Carter had managed to hear Cheng's message. When the call was over, Carter had walked into the garden to think. He had difficulty controlling his irritation. Cheng had not lived up to expectations, and nothing infuriated him more than people not being able to handle the tasks that he had given them. This latest report was unsettling and he knew he had to make an important decision.

The heat after he left the air-conditioned house was oppressive. Lizards ran to and fro under his feet. The sweat was already trickling down inside his shirt, but it was not from the heat. It was from the anxiety he felt inside. Carter had to think clearly and calmly. Cheng had failed him, but his female watchdog was doing a better job. Nonetheless, she had her limits. He knew he had no choice now, and it was not too late. There was a plane leaving for Lisbon at 11 p.m. That was in six hours. I can't take any more chances, he thought. Therefore I have to go.

The decision was made. He went back inside and sent

the necessary e-mails. Then he called the airport to book his flight.

He ate the dinner that Celine had prepared. Then he showered and packed. He shivered at the thought of having to travel to the cold.

At 11.10 p.m. the TAP plane for Lisbon took off from Luanda airport. It was only ten minutes late.

Modin had been set up in Svedberg's old office. It was now mainly used by officers on temporary assignments. He was drinking a cup of coffee when Wallander came in. Modin smiled uncertainly when he saw Wallander, but Wallander could still see the fear underneath.

"Let's go into my office," he said.

Modin took his cup of coffee and followed him. When he sat down in the chair across from Wallander's desk the armrest fell off. He jumped.

"That happens all the time," Wallander said. "Leave it."

He sat down himself and cleared all the paperwork from the middle of his desk.

"I'm going to present you with a hypothesis. I think that when we weren't looking you copied some material from Falk's computer and transferred it to your own. What do you think of that?"

"I want to speak to a lawyer," Modin said firmly.

"We don't need lawyers," Wallander said. "You haven't actually broken any laws. At least, not as far as I know. But I need to know exactly what you did."

Modin didn't believe him.

"You're here now so that we can protect you," Wallander said. "Not for any other reason. You are not being held here on charges. We don't suspect you of anything."

Modin seemed still to be weighing Wallander's words. "Can I have that in writing?" he said, at last.

Wallander stretched out for a pad of paper and wrote a guarantee for him. He signed it and wrote the date.

"I don't have a stamp," he said. "But this ought to work."

"It's not good enough," Modin said.

"It will have to do," Wallander said. "This is between you and me. I would accept it, if I were you. If you don't, there's always the chance I'm going to change my mind."

Modin realised he meant business.

"Tell me what happened," Wallander said. "You received a threatening e-mail on your computer. I've read it myself. Then you looked up and saw that there was a vehicle parked on that little road that goes between the fields behind your house. Is that right?"

Modin looked at him in astonishment. "How can you know all that?"

"I just know," Wallander said. "You were frightened and you left. The question is: why were you so frightened."

"They had traced me."

"So you weren't careful enough at crossing out your every step? Did you make the same mistake as last time?"

"They're very good."

"But so are you."

Modin shrugged.

"The problem is that you started taking chances, isn't that so? You copied material from Falk's computer on to your own and something happened. The temptation was too great. You kept working on the material through the night, and somehow they caught on to you while you weren't looking."

"I don't know why you keep asking if you already know everything."

Wallander decided to make his point. "You have to understand how serious this is."

"Of course I do. Why would I have tried to get away otherwise? I don't even have a driving licence."

"Then we see eye to eye on this much. You realise you're involved in a very dangerous business. From now on you need to do as I say. By the way, has anyone brought you any food?" he asked. "I know you have unusual food preferences."

"A tofu pie would be nice," Modin said. "And some carrot juice."

Wallander called Irene. "Could you get us a tofu pie and a carrot juice, please?"

"Can you repeat that?"

Ebba would not have asked any questions, Wallander thought. "Tofu pie."

"What on God's earth is that?"

"Food. It's vegetarian. Please try to get it as quickly as you can."

He hung up before Irene had a chance to ask anything else.

"Let's start by talking about what you saw from your window," Wallander said. "At some point you discovered a car out there."

"There are never any cars on that road."

"You took out your binoculars for a closer look."

"Everything I did you already know."

"No," Wallander said. "I know part of it. What did you see?"

"A dark blue car."

"Was it a Mercedes?"

"I don't know the first thing about cars."

"Was it big? Did it look like a van?"

"Yes."
"And there was someone standing next to the car?"
"That was what scared me. When I looked through the binoculars I saw a man who was looking at me with some binoculars of his own."
"Could you see his face?"
"I was pretty scared."
"I know. What about his face?"
"He had dark hair."
"What was he wearing?"
"A darkish raincoat. I think."
"Did you see anything else? Had you ever seen him before?"
"No. And I don't remember noticing anything else."
"You left. Could you tell if he followed you?"
"I don't think he did. There's a tiny road just a little bit past our house. I don't think he saw it."
"Then what did you do?"
"I had sent you the e-mail, but I didn't feel I could go to Runnerströms Torg. I didn't know what to do. At first I was planning to go to Copenhagen. But I didn't feel up to driving down to Malmö. I'm not a driver. Something could have happened."
"So you simply drove into Ystad. What did you do then?"
"Nothing."
"You stayed in the car until some policemen found you?"
"Yes."
Wallander tried to think about where they should go from here. He wanted Martinsson to be present, as well as Alfredsson. He got up and left the room. Irene was at her desk. She shook her head when she saw him.
"How is the food coming on?" he asked sternly.
"Sometimes I think all of you are nuts."

"That's probably true, but I have a boy back there who doesn't eat hamburgers. I guess there are people like that. And he needs food."

"I called Ebba," Irene said. "She said she would take care of it."

That put him in a better mood. If she had talked to Ebba then everything would be taken care of.

"I'd like to speak to Martinsson and Alfredsson as soon as possible," he said. "Please get hold of them."

At that moment Holgersson hurried in through the front doors.

"More shooting?" she said. "That's what I heard. What happened?"

Briefing Holgersson right now was the last thing he needed, but Wallander knew he had no choice. He rapidly filled her in on the day's events.

"Have you sent out an alert to the neighbouring districts?"

"It's been taken care of."

"When can we have a meeting about this?"

"As soon as everyone comes back in."

"It feels to me as if this investigation is getting out of hand."

"We're not quite at that point," Wallander said, and didn't bother to hide his annoyance. "But feel free to relieve me of my responsibilities if you like. Hansson is the one who's been in charge of the search operation."

She had a few more questions, but Wallander had already turned his back and started walking away.

Martinsson and Alfredsson came in at 5 p.m. Wallander and Modin sat down with them in one of the smaller conference rooms. Hansson had called to say there was still no sign of the man who had vanished into the fog.

No-one knew where Höglund had got to. Wallander barricaded the door. Modin's computers were up and running.

"We're going to go through everything from the beginning," Wallander said.

"I'm not sure we can do that yet," Alfredsson said. "There are too many things we can't see clearly yet."

Wallander turned to Modin. "You said you had thought of something new," he said.

"It's hard to explain," Modin said. "And I'm very hungry."

Wallander felt irritated with him for the first time. Modin might be a computer whizz, but he was far from satisfactory in other respects.

"The food is on its way," Wallander said. "If you need something right now we have good old Swedish rusks, and some leftover pizza. Take your pick."

Modin got up and sat down in front of his computers. The others gathered behind him.

"It took me a while to work this all out," he began. "At first I was convinced that the number 20 which kept turning up had something to do with the year 2000. We already know that Y2K will cause a number of problems in many computer systems. But I never found the missing zeroes, and I also noticed that the countdown looked as if it was set to go off much sooner than the end of the year. Whatever it involves. But I concluded that it had to do with October 20 instead."

Alfredsson shook his head and seemed to want to protest, but Wallander held him back.

"Go on."

"I started looking for the other pieces of the puzzle. We know something here proceeds from the left to the right. There is an end point and that's how we deduce that something is going to happen. But we don't know what. I decided to surf the Web for information about the financial institutions we had already identified. The National Bank of Indonesia, the World Bank, the stockbroker in Seoul. I tried to see if they had anything in common, the point one is always searching for."

"What point would that be?"

"The point of weakness. The one spot where someone could enter the system without anyone noticing."

"But there's a lot of awareness about hackers these days," Martinsson said. "And the business world is getting faster at responding to computer viruses when they emerge."

"The United States already has the capacity to conduct computer wars," Alfredsson said. "Earlier the talk has been about computer-programmed missiles, or 'smart' bombs. But soon that will be as antiquated as cavalry. Now the objective is to dismantle the enemy's networks and knock out their missiles. Or better yet, to direct the enemy's missiles against himself."

"Is this really true?" Wallander said, sceptically.

"It is definitely in the works," Alfredsson said. "But we should also be honest about the fact that there are many things we just don't know. Weapons systems are complicated."

"Let's get back to Falk's computer," Wallander said. "Did you find those weak points?"

"I'm not sure," Modin said hesitantly. "But I think there is a way to see a connection between all of these institutions. They do have one thing in common."

"And what is that?"

"They make up the cornerstones of the global financial network. If you compromised them enough you would be able to set in motion a crisis that could derail all of the world's financial systems. The stock markets would crash.

There would be panic. Everyone would rush to take out their money. Currency exchanges would fluctuate wildly until no-one could be sure what the rates should be."

"And who would be interested in causing anything of this nature?"

Martinsson and Alfredsson spoke at the same time.

"Many people," Alfredsson said. "It sounds like the highest form of terrorism imaginable. And there are many people out there eager to cause chaos and destruction."

"Taking out the global financial network would be the ultimate act of sabotage." Martinsson said.

"Does everyone in this room think that that's what we're looking at here? And that something like this is housed in a computer in Ystad?" Wallander said.

"It's definitely something like this," Martinsson said. "I've never come across anything like it before."

"Is it harder to break into than the Pentagon?" Alfredsson said.

Modin narrowed his eyes. "It's certainly not less complicated."

"I'm not sure how best to proceed in this kind of a situation," Wallander said.

"I'll talk to my people in Stockholm," Alfredsson said. "I'll send in a report that will later get sent on all over the world. We have to alert the institutions involved so that they can take precautions."

"If it isn't already too late," Modin mumbled.

Everyone heard him, but no-one made any comment. Alfredsson left the room in a hurry.

"I still find it hard to credit," Wallander said.

"Well, whatever it is in Falk's computer, there are people ready to kill to keep the system and countdown going," Martinsson said.

Wallander gestured at Modin so that Martinsson would understand that he should choose his words with more care.

"The question is: what we can do?" Wallander said. "Is there anything we *can* do?"

"There's often a button to push," Modin said abruptly. "If you infect a computer system with a virus you often hide it in an innocent and common command. But in order to set off the virus several things have to come together at once. The commands need to be carried out at a precise time, for example."

"The best thing we can do now is carry on with what we've been doing," Martinsson said. "We need to warn the institutions that they're in danger of an attack so that they can double up on their security procedures. Alfredsson will handle the rest."

Martinsson scribbled a few words on a piece of paper. He looked up at Wallander who bent over to read them: *The threat against Modin is serious.*

Wallander nodded. Whoever had been spying on Modin from the road between the fields had known how important he was. He was in the same situation that Hökberg had been in.

Wallander's phone rang. Hansson was calling to let him know that the search for his attacker had not yet yielded any results, but they would continue unabated.

"How is Nyberg doing?"

"He is comparing fingerprints."

Hansson was still out near Backåkra, where he would stay for now. He didn't know where Höglund was.

They ended the conversation. Wallander tried to phone Höglund, but her phone had no signal.

There was a knock on the door and Wallander went to unblock the door. Irene came in with a box.

"Here's the food," she said. "Who's supposed to take care of the bill? I had to pay the delivery man out of my own pocket."

"I'll take care of it," Wallander said and stretched out his hand for the receipt.

Modin ate. Wallander and Martinsson watched him in silence. Then Wallander's phone rang again. It was Elvira Lindfeldt. He went out into the hall and closed the door behind him.

"I heard on the radio that shots were fired in an incident near Ystad," she said. "And there were policemen involved. I hope that wasn't you."

"Not directly," Wallander said vaguely. "But we have a lot going on right now."

"It made me worried, that's all. I had to ask. Now of course I'm getting curious, but I won't ask any more questions."

"There isn't much I can tell you," Wallander said.

"I understand that you don't have a lot of free time at the moment."

"It's too early to say. But I'll be in touch."

When the conversation was over Wallander thought about the fact that it had been a long time since anyone had worried about him. Let alone cared about him.

He went back into the room. It was 5.40 p.m. Modin was still eating. Wallander and Martinsson left to get some coffee.

"I forgot to tell you that I cross-checked the list of names I got from Sydkraft. But I didn't find anything."

"We didn't expect to," Wallander said.

The coffee machine was on the blink again. Martinsson pulled out the plug and then put it in again. Now it was working.

"Is there a computer program inside the coffee machine?" Wallander said.

"Hardly," Martinsson said. "Though I guess you can imagine more sophisticated machines that would be controlled with tiny computer chips."

"What if someone went in and changed the program? Could they change it so that tea came out instead of coffee? And milk when someone wanted latte?"

"Of course."

"But how would it get triggered? How could you get it to start?"

"Well, you could imagine that a certain date has been entered in. A date and a time, perhaps an interval of an hour. Then the eleventh time that someone presses the button for coffee, the virus is triggered."

"Why the eleventh?"

"That was just an example. It could have been any number that you had chosen."

"Is there anything you can do once that change occurs?"

"You could pull out the plug and restart it," Martinsson said. "You can hang out a sign saying the machine is broken. But the program that runs the machine would have to be replaced."

"Is this what Modin is talking about?"

"Yes, but on a larger scale."

"And we have no idea where Falk's coffee machine is."

"It could be anywhere in the world."

"And that would mean that whoever sets off the chain reaction wouldn't need to be aware of it."

"It would be an advantage if whoever it was were nowhere near where the virus first arises."

"So we are looking for the symbolic equivalent of a coffee machine," Wallander said. He walked to the window and stared out. It was already dark. "I want you to do something," he said. "I'd like you to write a memo about what we just talked about. The threat of a global financial collapse. Get Alfredsson to help you. Then send it on to Stockholm and all of the international police agencies you can think of."

"If we're wrong we'll be the laughing stock of the world."

"We'll have to take that chance. Give me the papers and I'll sign them."

Martinsson left. Wallander stayed in the canteen, deep in thought. He didn't notice when Höglund came in. He jumped when she appeared at his side.

"You know the poster of that film," she said, "the one you saw in Hökberg's wardrobe?"

"*The Devil's Advocate*. I have the video at home, I just haven't had time to watch it."

"I don't think the film is so important, actually," she said. "But I've been thinking about Al Pacino. He resembles someone."

Wallander looked at her.

"Who does he resemble?"

"He looks like the man in her sketch. Carl-Einar Lundberg. He actually looks a little like Al Pacino."

She was right. Wallander had seen a picture of Lundberg in a file she had put on his desk. He just hadn't thought about the resemblance until now. Another detail fell into place.

They sat at a table. Höglund was tired.

"I went to talk to Persson," she said. "I thought I would be able to get something more out of her. Silly me."

"How was she?"

"She is still impregnably nonchalant. That's the worst thing. I wish she looked as though she slept badly and cried at night. But she doesn't. She just sits there chewing her gum and seems mildly irritated at having to answer my questions."

"She's hiding her feelings," Wallander said. "We just can't see it."

"I do hope you're right."

Wallander briefed her on Modin's hypothesis of an impending financial collapse.

"We've never even been close to something like this," she said when he finished. "If it's true."

"We'll find out on Monday, I guess. Unless we think of some way to intervene."

"Do you think we will?"

"Maybe. Martinsson is contacting police from all over the world, and Alfredsson is getting in touch with all of the institutions on Falk's list."

"There isn't much time. If it really is set for Monday. It's the weekend already."

"There is never enough time," Wallander answered.

By 9 p.m. Modin was exhausted. It was agreed that he should not spend the next few nights at home, but when Martinsson suggested that he sleep at the station he refused point-blank. Wallander thought of calling Sten Widén to see if he had space for an extra person, but decided against it; and for security reasons he could not stay with anyone on the investigative team, since they could also be considered a target.

Finally Wallander thought of someone to ask. Elvira Lindfeldt. She was completely unconnected, and it would also give him a chance to see her if only for a short while. He did not mention her name, but said he would take Modin to a safe place for the night.

He called her at 9.30 p.m. "I have a question that may seem a little strange," he said.

"I'm used to strange questions."

"Could you put someone up for the night?"

"Who would that be?"

"Do you remember the young man who came to the restaurant that night?"

"His name was Kolin?"

"Modin."

"Has he nowhere to sleep?"

"I'm only going to say that he needs a place to stay for a few nights."

"Of course he can stay here. How is he going to get here?"

"I'll give him a lift. We'll be there shortly."

"Would you like anything to eat when you arrive?"

"Some coffee would be good. That's all."

They left the station at 9.50 p.m. By the time they passed Skurup, Wallander was satisfied that no-one was following them.

Elvira put the receiver down slowly. She was happy, in fact more than happy. She was overjoyed. This was an amazing stroke of luck. She thought about Carter who was about to take off from the Luanda airport. He would be happy too. After all, this was exactly what he had wanted.

CHAPTER THIRTY-SEVEN

The night of Saturday, October 18, Wallander would remember as one of the worst in his life. Afterwards he would think back to a near accident that night as a sign. As they passed the turning to Svedala, someone had suddenly decided to overtake him just at the moment that a huge truck was bearing down on them from the other direction. Wallander turned as sharply as he could without driving off the road, and managed to avoid the car, but it had been close. Modin was asleep in the seat and didn't notice anything, but Wallander's heart was pounding inside his chest.

He kept driving and his mind reverted uneasily to what Höglund had told him about Martinsson and his games. He had an unpleasant sense of being on trial and not being sure of his own innocence. The anxiety and worry was nagging at him from all sides.

When he followed the sign off the main road for Jägersro, Modin woke up.

"We'll soon be there," Wallander said.

"I was dreaming," Modin said. "Someone tried to attack me."

Wallander found the house easily enough. It was in the far corner of a housing development that looked to have been built between the wars. He drew up.

"Who lives here?" Modin said.

"A friend of mine," Wallander said. "Her name is Elvira.

You'll be safe here. I'll send someone to pick you up in the morning."

"I don't even have a toothbrush," Modin said.

"We'll take care of it somehow."

It was pretty late, but Wallander had imagined that he would have a cup of coffee, look at her lovely legs and stay until about midnight.

But they had only just gone inside when Wallander's phone rang. It was Hansson. He could tell that something was up by the tension in his voice. They had found traces of the man they thought had shot at Wallander. Once again it was a person out walking their dog who had helped them. He had spotted a man who seemed to be hiding in the bushes and generally behaving oddly. Since he had been seeing police cars driving to and fro all day, the dog owner thought it best to call in with his information. The dog owner had told Hansson that the man looked as though he was wearing a black raincoat.

Wallander quickly introduced Elvira to Modin, thanked her for her hospitality, and left. He thought about the curious fact that dog owners had been such a help during the investigation. Perhaps these civilians were a resource that the police should make more use of in future. He drove much too fast and soon arrived at the place north of Sandhammaren that Hansson had described. He had stopped at the station on the way to pick up his gun.

It was raining again. Martinsson had arrived a few minutes before Wallander. There were officers there in full protective gear, as well as several dog units. The man they were closing in on was in a small pocket of forest bordered on one side by the road to Skillinge and by open fields on the other. Although Hansson had been effective in mobilising police into the area, Wallander could see at once that the man had a good chance of escape. While they were discussing their plan of advance, a message came in on Hansson's radio. A police patrol to the north thought they had seen the suspect. The radio contact broke off. In the distance came the sound of a shot followed closely by a second, and from Hansson's radio came very clearly: "The fucker's shooting at us." Then silence.

Wallander feared the worst. Martinsson seemed to have disappeared. It took him and Hansson six minutes to get to where the radio transmission had come from. When they saw the patrol car with its lights on they readied their weapons and got out of their own vehicle. The silence was deafening. Wallander shouted out to the others, and to his and Hansson's great relief there was an answer. They ran, bent double, to the patrol car and found two policemen there, scared out of their wits. One of them was El Sayed, the other Elofsson. The man who had shot at them appeared to be in a clump of trees on the other side of the road. They had been standing next to the car when they heard the sound of breaking twigs. Elofsson had directed his flashlight towards the trees while El Sayed had established radio contact with Hansson. Then came the shots.

"What's on the other side of those trees?" Wallander said.

"There's a path down to the sea," Elofsson said.

"Are there any houses there?" No-one knew. "We'll try to surround him," Wallander said. "Now that we have a pretty good idea where he is."

Hansson managed to locate Martinsson and told him their position. Meanwhile, Wallander dispatched Elofsson and El Sayed deeper into cover. All the time he expected the gunman to turn up alongside the car with his gun cocked.

"What about a helicopter?" Martinsson said, when he had joined them.

"Good idea. Make sure it has strong spotlights. But don't let it get here until all of us are in place."

Martinsson turned to his radio and Wallander studied the terrain. Since it was dark he couldn't really see anything, and since the wind had picked up it was impossible for him to determine if the sounds he heard were real or imagined.

Martinsson crept over to him. "A helicopter is on its way."

Wallander had no time to answer. At that moment another shot went off. They steeled themselves.

The shot had come somewhere from the left. Wallander had no idea who the intended target was. He called out to Elofsson and El Sayed called back. Then he also heard Elfosson's voice. Wallander knew he had to do something. He called out into the darkness.

"Police! Put down your weapon!"

Then he repeated the phrase in English.

There was no answer, only the wind.

"I don't like this," Martinsson whispered. "Why is he still there shooting at us? Why doesn't he leave? He must assume that there are reinforcements on the way."

Wallander was thinking the same thing. Then they heard police sirens in the distance.

"Why didn't you tell them to be quiet?" Wallander didn't try to hide his irritation. "Hansson should have known."

At the same moment El Sayed cried out. Wallander thought he glimpsed a shadow run across the road and out into the field that lay to the left of the car. Then it was gone.

"He's getting away," Wallander said.

"Where?"

Wallander pointed to where the shadow had been, but Martinsson couldn't see anything. Wallander had to act fast. If the suspect made it across the field he would reach a larger stretch of forest and then it would be harder to corner him. He told Martinsson to move, then he jumped into the car, turned it on and pulled it violently around. He hit something, but he didn't stop to look what it was. The headlights were shining straight out into the field.

When the light hit him the man stopped and turned. The raincoat flapped in the wind. Wallander saw the man raise one arm. He dropped under the dashboard. The bullet shattered the windscreen. Wallander rolled out of the car, yelling to the others to get down. Another shot. It took out a headlight. Wallander wondered if the man was just a lucky shot or if he had meant to hit it. It was much harder to see now.

The sirens were closing in. Suddenly Wallander was afraid that the approaching cars were going to be a target. He shouted to Martinsson to radio the cars and tell them not to approach until they received an all-clear.

"I've dropped the radio," Martinsson said. "I can't find it in this shit."

The man in the field was running. Wallander saw how he tripped and almost fell. Wallander got to his feet.

"What the hell are you doing?"

"We have to take him," Wallander said.

"We have to surround him first."

"If we wait to do that he'll get away."

Wallander looked at Martinsson who shook his head. Then he started running. The mud immediately started caking up under his shoes. The man was beyond the reach of the light now. Wallander stopped and made sure his safety catch was off. Behind him he heard Martinsson shouting to El Sayed and Elofsson. Wallander stayed outside the light from the remaining headlight and speeded up. Then one of his shoes sank into the mud and came off. Wallander angrily ripped off the other one. His feet were at once soaking wet and cold, but it was easier to walk over the mud. And then he caught sight of the man, who was also having trouble walking over the ploughed mud.

The distance between them was still such that Wallander did not fancy his chances of hitting his legs. He heard a helicopter in the distance, but it did not come closer. It seemed to be awaiting further orders. They were out in the middle of the field now and the light from the car was very faint. He wasn't that good a shot. The man he was pursuing had twice in a row missed his mark but had hit the headlight from very far away. Wallander frantically tried to think of something that would work. He couldn't understand why neither Hansson nor Martinsson ordered the helicopter to advance.

Suddenly the man stumbled again and fell. Wallander saw that he was looking for something. It took him a split second to understand that he had dropped his weapon and was looking for it. They were about 35 metres apart. I don't have enough time, he thought, but he was already running and jumping across the stiff furrows. Three times he almost lost his balance. Then the man saw him. Even in this light Wallander could tell he looked Asian.

Wallander's left foot slipped out from under him, as if he had been on an ice floe. He couldn't recover his balance and fell head first into the mud. At that moment his opponent found his gun. Wallander was now up on one knee and saw that the gun was aimed straight at him. Wallander squeezed his trigger. The gun didn't work. He squeezed again with the same result. In a last desperate attempt to survive Wallander threw himself into the mud and tried to slide down into it. That was when the shot was fired. Wallander flinched, but had not been hit. He lay motionless and waited for his opponent to fire again. But nothing happened. Wallander had no sense of how long he lay there. He felt as if he were watching himself, observing the situation from a distance. So this is how it would end: a pointless death in a muddy field. This is where he had brought his dreams and ambitions. Nothing would come of them now. He would vanish into the final darkness with his face pressed into the cold, wet clay, and he was not even wearing shoes.

Only when he heard the sound of the fast-approaching helicopter did he dare to think he might survive. He carefully looked up.

The man lay on his back with his arms spread. Wallander got up and slowly approached. He could see the floodlights from the helicopter starting to search the far end of the field. Dogs were barking and somewhere far away he heard Martinsson's voice.

The man was dead. That shot he had heard had not been meant for Wallander after all. The man lying in the mud had shot himself in the temple. Wallander was overcome by a sudden onset of nausea and dizziness and had to sit down. His clothes were cold and wet and now he started shaking.

Wallander looked down at the body. He didn't know who this man was or why he had come to Ystad, but his death was a relief. This was the man who had entered Falk's flat when Wallander was there waiting for Marianne Falk. He had twice tried to kill Wallander. Probably he was also the one who had dragged Hökberg to the power substation, and thrown Landahl into the propeller shaft on the Polish ferry. There were many question marks, but as Wallander sat there on the muddy field he felt that something at least had come to an end.

He no longer had to fear for his colleagues' or Modin's safety.

There was no way for him to know that he was wrong about this assumption. It was something he would only come to understand in time.

Martinsson was the first to reach Wallander. The latter stood up. Elofsson was also nearby. Wallander asked him to try to find his shoes.

"Did you shoot him?" Martinsson said, in disbelief.

Wallander shook his head. "He shot himself. If he hadn't, I wouldn't be here now."

Holgersson appeared, as if from thin air. Wallander let Martinsson do the explaining. Elofsson reappeared with both of Wallander's shoes, wiping the thick clay from them. Wallander wanted to get away. Not only to be able to change his clothes, but to escape from the memory of what it was like to lie there in the mud expecting the end. The depressingly pathetic end.

Somewhere deep inside there was probably a flicker of happiness, but for the moment a feeling of emptiness dominated.

The helicopter was gone. Hansson had dismissed it and the whole operation was being dismantled. The only ones left were the team who would do the investigation surrounding the gunman's death.

Hansson made his way through the mud. He was wearing bright orange boots.

"You should go home," he told Wallander.

Wallander nodded and started walking the same way he had come. All around him he saw the flickering of flashlights. Several times he nearly lost his footing.

As he reached the road, Holgersson caught up with him.

"I think I have a fairly complete picture of what happened," she said. "But tomorrow we'll have to have a thorough debriefing. It's lucky things turned out as well as they did."

"The main thing is to determine if this is the individual responsible for Hökberg's and Landahl's deaths."

"But why? Why did all this happen?"

"We don't know why yet, but Falk is at the heart of it. Or rather, whatever it is that's in his computer."

"This hypothesis still seems unfounded to me," Holgersson said.

"I can see no alternative." Wallander had no more energy for this discussion. "I have to get into some dry clothes," he said. "If you'll excuse me, I'm going home now."

"One last thing," she said. "And I have to say this. It was completely irresponsible to have gone after this man alone. You should have taken Martinsson along as back-up."

"Things happened pretty fast."

"But you should not have ordered him to stay behind."

Wallander had been wiping lumps of clay from his clothes. Now he looked up.

"Ordered him?"

"Yes, ordered him to stand back while you went in. I shouldn't have to remind you, of all people, that one of the basic rules of police work is never to act alone."

Wallander had forgotten all about the mud now.

"Where did you get the idea that I told him to stay behind?"

"From various reports."

Wallander knew there was only one possible source for this version of events. Martinsson. Elofsson and El Sayed had been too far back to have heard anything.

"Perhaps we should talk about this tomorrow," he said.

"I had to bring this up with you right away," she said. "It's my duty as your commanding officer. You're in a delicate enough situation as it is."

She left him and continued towards her car.

Wallander realised he was trembling with fury. Martinsson had lied. He had told Holgersson that Wallander had ordered him not to follow him out into the field where Wallander had subsequently been trapped and thought he was going to die.

He looked up and saw Martinsson and Hansson coming towards him. The light from their flashlights bobbed up and down. From the other direction he heard Holgersson start up her car and drive away.

Martinsson and Hansson stopped when they reached him.

"Could you hold Martinsson's flashlight for a moment?" Wallander said to Hansson.

"Why?"

"Just do it, please."

Martinsson handed Hansson his flashlight. Wallander took a step forward and hit Martinsson in the face. However, since it was hard to judge the distance between them in the shifting beams of the flashlights, the blow didn't land squarely on his jaw as intended. It was more of a gentle nudge.

"What the hell are you doing?"

"What the hell are *you* doing?" Wallander yelled back.

Then he threw himself on Martinsson and they fell into the mud. Hansson tried to grab them as they fell, but he slipped. One of the flashlights went out, the other landed some distance away.

"You told Holgersson I ordered you to stay behind! You have been spreading lies about me this whole time!"

Wallander pushed Martinsson away and stood up. Hansson was also standing. A dog barked in the background.

"You have been going behind my back," Wallander said, and he heard that his voice had become absolutely steady.

"I don't know what you're talking about," Martinsson protested.

"Behind my back, saying that I'm bad at my job. You sneak away into Holgersson's office when you think noone is looking."

Hansson broke in. "What is going on between you two?"

"We're discussing the issue of good teamwork," Wallander said. "Whether it's better to say what you think to someone's face, or whether you should rather go behind someone's back and complain about them to their superior officer."

"I still don't get it," Hansson said.

Wallander sighed. He saw no point in dragging this out.

"That was all I wanted to say," he said and threw a flashlight at Martinsson's feet.

Then he walked over to a patrol car and told the officer behind the wheel to take him home.

He took a bath and then went and sat in the kitchen. It was close to 3 a.m. He tried to think, but his head still felt empty. He went to bed, but he couldn't sleep. He thought over and over of the field and the terror he had experienced as he lay with his face pressed into the wet clay. The memory of feeling so humiliated at dying without his shoes on. And then his confrontation with Martinsson.

I've reached my limit, he thought. Not only in relation to Martinsson, but perhaps in relation to everything I do.

He wondered what the consequences of his fight with Martinsson would be. He had struck him in the face. It would come down to word against word, just like the case with Persson and her mother. Holgersson had already demonstrated that she put greater trust in Martinsson's accounts than in his own. And now Wallander had shown himself guilty of inappropriate force for the second time in only two weeks. There was no way to get past it.

As he lay in the dark he wondered if he regretted his behaviour. He couldn't honestly feel that he did. It was motivated by a sense of personal dignity. The assault had been a necessary reaction to Martinsson's betrayal. All of the rage that he had been feeling since Höglund had told him about Martinsson had finally bubbled up to the surface.

It was shortly after 4 a.m. when he finally fell asleep.

It was Sunday, October 19.

Carter landed in Lisbon on TAP flight 553 at 6 a.m. The connecting flight to Copenhagen was leaving at 8.15 a.m. As usual, his entry into Europe disturbed him. He felt protected in Africa. Here he was in foreign territory.

At home he had looked carefully at his selection of passports and finally settled on the identity of Lukas Habermann, German citizen, born in Kassel in 1939. After going through customs in Portugal, he went into the nearest toilet and tore the passport into small pieces which he then flushed down the bowl. From now on he was the Englishman Richard Stanton, born in Oxford in 1940. He took an overcoat out of his luggage and slicked his hair down with water. He checked his luggage on to the flight for Copenhagen and went through passport control again, careful to avoid the line to the customs officer who dealt with him on arrival. He encountered no problems. He walked through the terminal until he reached an area that was under construction. Since it was Sunday, there were no workers around. He took out his mobile phone only after making sure that he was alone.

She answered immediately. He did not like talking on the telephone so he only asked brisk questions and received equally succinct answers.

She could tell him nothing about Cheng's whereabouts. He was supposed to have contacted her in the early evening, but he had not called. Carter listened to her extraordinary news with some scepticism. He was not used to being lucky. Finally, he was convinced. Robert Modin had been delivered straight into their hands.

When the conversation was over, Carter thought about Cheng. Something must have happened to him. But on the other hand they had access now to Modin, and he was their biggest threat. Carter put away his phone and went to the executive lounge where he had an apple and a cup of tea.

The plane to Copenhagen took off 5 minutes later than scheduled. Carter sat in seat 3D, on the aisle. The window seat made him feel too trapped. He told the flight attendant he did not want breakfast. Then he shut his eyes and fell asleep.

CHAPTER THIRTY-EIGHT

Wallander and Martinsson met in the corridor outside the canteen at the station at exactly 8 a.m. on Sunday. It was as if they had decided on the time and place in advance. Since they walked towards the canteen from opposite ends of the corridor, Wallander felt as if they were participating in a duel. But instead of drawing pistols, they nodded curtly at each other and went in to get coffee. The coffee machine had broken down again. They read the handwritten sign that had been affixed to the front. Martinsson had a black eye and his lower lip was swollen.

"I'm going to get you for what you did," Martinsson said. "But first we have to finish this case."

"It was wrong of me to hit you," Wallander said. "But that's all I'll take back."

They said nothing more. Hansson came in and watched them, uneasily.

Wallander suggested they may as well have their meeting in the canteen rather than move to a conference room. Hansson put on a pot of water and offered to make them coffee from his private stash. Just as they were pouring it out, Höglund arrived. Wallander assumed it was Hansson who would have told her of the death of the man called Cheng, but it turned out to have been Martinsson. Wallander gathered that he had said nothing about the fight, but noticed that Martinsson looked at her with a new coldness. Probably he had spent the brief night working out who could have given him away to Wallander.

Once Alfredsson joined them they were ready to begin the meeting. Wallander asked Hansson to brief Viktorsson on the night's events. In the present situation it was more than ever important that the prosecutor's office were kept abreast. There would probably be a press conference later in the day, but Chief Holgersson would have to take care of it. Wallander asked Höglund to assist her if she had time. She looked surprised.

"But I wasn't even there."

"You don't need to say anything. I just want you there so you can hear what Holgersson says. Particularly if she happens to say something stupid."

A stunned silence greeted his last comment. No-one had heard him openly criticise Holgersson before. It was not premeditated on his part, it just slipped out. He felt another wave of exhaustion, of being burned out, maybe even old. Of course, his age excused his speaking plainly.

He moved on to the most pressing matter.

"We have to concentrate our efforts on Falk's computer. Whatever is programmed into it is going to take effect on October 20. We therefore have less than 16 hours to figure out what that is."

"Where is Modin?" Hansson said.

Wallander drained the last of his coffee and got up.

"I'm going to pick him up. Let's get going, everybody."

As they filed out of the canteen, Höglund grabbed his arm. He tried to shake her off.

"Not now. I have to get Modin."

"Where is he?"

"With a friend of mine."

"Can't anyone else get him?"

"Of course they could, but I need the time to collect my thoughts. How to use the short amount of time we have most effectively. What does it mean that Cheng is dead?"

"That's what I wanted to talk to you about."

Wallander stopped. "All right," he said, "you have five minutes."

"It seems as if we haven't posed the most important question."

"And what might that be?"

"Why he shot himself and not you."

Wallander was getting irritated. He was irritated at everything and everyone and made no attempt to hide it.

"And what's your opinion on that?"

"I wasn't there. I don't know how things looked out there or what precisely happened. But I do know that it takes an awful lot, even for a person like that, to pull the trigger on himself."

"And how do you know this?"

"You have to admit I have some experience after all these years."

Wallander knew he was lecturing her as he answered, but he couldn't help it. "The question is what your experience is really worth in this case. This person killed at least two people before he died and he would not have hesitated a moment to kill me. We don't know what was driving him, but he must have been a totally ruthless person. What happened was, he heard and saw the helicopter coming and he knew he was not going to get away in time. We know the people involved in this case are fanatical in some way. In this instance the fanaticism was turned on himself."

Höglund wanted to say something more, but Wallander was already on his way to the front door.

"I have to get Modin," he said. "We can talk more later. If our world still exists, that is."

Wallander left the station. It was 8.45 a.m. and he was in a hurry. He drove at a very high speed. At one point he swerved to miss a hare, but one of his back wheels hit the animal. He could see its legs jerking when he looked in the rear-view mirror, but he didn't stop.

He reached the house in Jägersro at 9.40 a.m. Elvira opened the door almost as soon as he rang the bell. She was dressed to go out, but Wallander could tell that she was very tired. In some way she seemed different from when he had seen her last. But her smile was the same. She asked if he wanted a cup of coffee. Wallander looked past her and saw Robert Modin drinking a cup of tea in the kitchen. Wallander wanted nothing more than to drink a cup of coffee with her, but he declined her offer. They had so little time. She insisted, took his arm and almost pulled him into the kitchen. Wallander saw her cast a quick glance at her watch. That made him suspicious. She wants me to stay, he thought. But not too long. She's expecting someone else. He said no thank you again and told Modin to get ready.

"People who are always in a hurry make me nervous," she complained after Modin had left the kitchen.

"Then you've found my first flaw," Wallander said. "I'm sorry about this, but it can't be helped. We need Modin in Ystad right away."

"What is it that is so urgent?"

"I haven't time to explain," Wallander said. "Let me just say that we're a bit worried about October 20. And that's tomorrow."

Tired as Wallander was, he noticed a hint of worry in her face. Then she smiled again. Wallander wondered if perhaps she was afraid, but he dismissed the thought.

Modin came down the stairs. He carried a laptop in each hand.

"And when will I be seeing you again?" Elvira said.

"I'll call you," Wallander said. "I don't know yet."

They drove back to Ystad, at a slightly slower speed.

"I woke up early," Modin said. "I had some new ideas that I would like to try out."

Wallander considered telling him what had happened during the night, but he decided to wait. Right now it was important for Modin to stay focused. They kept driving in silence. It was pointless for Wallander to ask Modin what his ideas were since he would not understand the answers.

They came to the place where Wallander had run over the hare. A murder of crows took off as they appeared. The hare was already dismembered beyond recognition. Wallander told Modin that he was the one who had run him over.

"You see hundreds of dead hares along this road," Wallander said. "But it's only when you kill one yourself that you actually see it."

Modin turned and stared at him. "Could you say that last part again? About the hare?"

Wallander repeated what he had said.

"Exactly," Modin said. "That's it. Of course."

Wallander looked at him, questioningly.

"I'm thinking about what we're looking for in Falk's computer," Modin said. "The way to think about it may be to look for something we've seen a hundred times without really noticing."

Then Modin sank back into thought. Wallander was not sure he had understood this insight.

At 11 a.m. he stopped the car in Runnerströms Torg. From here on in he was dependent on what Alfredsson and Modin would be able to accomplish, with the assistance of Martinsson. The most useful thing he could do would be to try to maintain the large perspective, and not think he would be able to dive into the electronic sphere with the others. He hoped Martinsson and Alfredsson would have the sense not to tell Modin what had happened last night. He should really have taken Martinsson aside and told him that Modin knew nothing about the events, but he couldn't stand to talk to him more than was absolutely necessary.

"It's 11 a.m.," he said, as they had gathered around the desk. "That means we have 13 hours left until it is officially October 20. Time is of the essence, in other words."

"Nyberg called," Martinsson said, interrupting him.

"What did he have to say for himself?"

"Not much. The weapon was a Makarov, 9mm. He thought it would turn out to be the weapon used in the flat on Apelbergsgatan."

"Did the man have any identification?"

"He had three different passports. Korean, Thai and – strangely enough – Romanian."

"Not one from Angola?"

"No."

"I'm going to talk to Nyberg," Wallander said, but first he resumed his general remarks. Modin sat impatiently in front of the computer.

"We have only 13 hours left until October 20," he repeated. "And right now we have three main points of interest. Everything else can wait."

Wallander looked around. Martinsson's face was devoid of expression. The swelling at his lower lip had a hint of blue.

"The first question is if October 20 is the real date," Wallander said. "If it is, what will happen? The third question that follows from this is: if something is about to happen, how can we go about preventing it? Nothing else matters except these three things."

"There haven't been any responses from abroad," Alfredsson said.

Wallander suddenly remembered the paper he should have signed and authorised before it was sent out to police organisations across the world.

Martinsson must have read his mind. "I signed it. To save time."

Wallander nodded. "And no-one has written back or sent other inquiries?"

"Nothing yet. But it hasn't been long, and it is still a Sunday."

"That means that we're on our own for now." Wallander looked at Modin. "Robert told me on the way over that he had some new ideas. Hopefully, they will lead us to new information."

"I'm convinced it's October 20," Modin said.

"Your job is to convince the rest of us."

"I need an hour," Modin said.

"We have 13," Wallander said. "And let us all assume for now that we have no more than that."

Wallander walked away. Best to leave them alone. He drove to the station.

What is it that I've overlooked? he asked himself. Is there a clue in all of this that could bring everything together in a single stroke? The thoughts in his head tumbled around without connecting. Then he thought back to when he had seen Elvira in Malmö. She had seemed different today. He couldn't say exactly what it was, but he knew it was something and it worried him. The last thing he wanted was for her to start finding fault with him at this stage. Perhaps taking Robert to her had been a mistake. Perhaps he had involved her too abruptly into the harsh realities of his life.

He tried to shake off these thoughts. When he got to the station he looked for Hansson. He was in his office researching companies from a list that Martinsson had compiled. Wallander asked him how it was going and Hansson shook his head despondently.

"Nothing hangs together," he said. "The only common denominator seems to be that they are financial institutions. Most of them, but there's also a telecommunications company and a satellite company."

Wallander frowned. "What was the last one?"

"A satellite company in Atlanta, Telsat Communications. As far as I can tell, they rent broadcasting space on a number of communications satellites."

"Which fits with the telecommunications company."

"I suppose you can even get it to fit with the financial companies from the standpoint that they're also involved in the electronic transfer of large sums of money."

Wallander thought of something. "Can you see if any of the company's satellites cover Angola?"

Hansson typed something into the computer. Wallander noticed that he had to wait longer than he usually did with Martinsson.

"Their satellite coverage covers the globe," he said finally. "Even to the poles."

Wallander nodded. "It may mean something," he said. "Call Martinsson and tell him."

Hansson took the opportunity to ask something else. "What was all that about last night?"

"Martinsson is full of shit," Wallander said. "But we won't go into that right now."

Chief Holgersson organised a press conference for 2 p.m. She had tried to reach Wallander beforehand, but he instructed Höglund to say he was out of the office. He stood at his window for a long time and stared at the water tower. The clouds were gone. It was a cold and clear October day.

At 3 p.m. he couldn't stand it any longer and drove to Runnerströms Torg, walking in on an intense debate about how best to interpret a new combination of numbers. Modin tried to involve Wallander, but he shook his head.

At 5 p.m. he went out and bought himself a hamburger. When he came back to the station he called Elvira, but there was no answer, not even an answerphone. He was immediately jealous, but too tired and distracted to dwell on it.

At 6.30 p.m. Ebba turned up unexpectedly. She had brought some food for Modin. Wallander asked Hansson to drive her to Runnerströms Torg. Afterwards he realised that he hadn't thanked her enough.

At 7 p.m. he called the team at Runnerströms Torg and Martinsson answered. Their conversation was brief. They were not yet able to answer a single one of Wallander's questions. He put down the phone and went to find Hansson who was sitting in front of the computer with bloodshot eyes. Wallander asked if there had been any response from overseas. Hansson had only one word in reply: nothing.

At that moment Wallander was overcome by rage. He

grabbed one of the chairs in Hansson's office and threw it against the wall. Then he left the room.

At 8 p.m. he was back in Hansson's office.

"Let's go to Runnerströms Torg," he said. "We can't go on like this. We have to get some idea of where we stand."

They stopped at Höglund's office on the way. She was half asleep at her desk. They drove in silence. When they reached the flat they saw Modin sitting on the floor against the wall, Martinsson on his folding chair and Alfredsson lying flat on the floor. Wallander wondered if he had ever led a more exhausted and dispirited team. He knew that the physical tiredness was due more to their lack of progress than to the events of the night before. If only they had come a few steps closer to the truth, if only they could break down the wall, they could each summon sufficient energy to see it through. But for now the dominant mood was one of hopelessness.

Wallander sat in front of the computer. The others gathered round him, except Martinsson who positioned himself in the background.

"Let's have a résumé of where we are," he said. "What is the situation right now?"

"There are several indications that the date in question is October 20," Alfredsson said. "But we have no indications of a precise time for the event, so we cannot know if it will begin on the stroke of midnight or at any point after that. Quite possibly, the intended event is a form of computer virus that targets all of these financial institutions we have identified. Since they are mostly large and powerful financial institutions we imagine the event has something to do with money, but whether we are talking about a form of electronic bank robbery or not we don't know."

"What would be the worst thing that could happen?" Wallander said.

"The collapse of the world financial markets."

"But is that even possible?"

"We've been through this point before. If there were a significant enough disruption of the markets or a severe fluctuation in the dollar, for example, it might incite a panic in the public which would be hard to control."

"That's what is going to happen," Modin said.

Everyone stared at him. He was sitting with his legs crossed next to Wallander.

"Why do you say that? Do you know it for a fact?"

"No, not for a fact. But I think this is going to be so big we can't even imagine it. We're not going to be able to deduce what is going to happen before it's too late."

"How does the whole thing start? Isn't there a starting point, some kind of button that needs to be pressed?"

"I imagine it will be started by some action so ordinary we would have trouble recognising it as a threat."

"The hypothetical coffee machine," Hansson said.

"The only thing we can do right now is keep going," Wallander said. "We don't have a choice."

"I left some diskettes in Malmö," Modin said. "I need them to keep working."

"I'll send out a car to get them for you."

"I'll go too," Modin said. "I need to get out. And I know of a store in Malmö that stays open late and has the kind of food I like."

Wallander nodded and got up. Hansson called for a patrol car that would take Modin to Malmö. Wallander called Elvira. The line was busy. He tried again. Now she answered. He told her what had happened, that Modin needed to come and pick up the diskettes he had left behind.

She said it was no problem. Her voice sounded normal now.

"Can I expect to see you as well?" she said.

"Unfortunately, I don't have the time right now."

"I won't ask you why."

"Thank you. It would take too long to explain."

Alfredsson and Martinsson were leaning over Falk's computer again. Wallander, Hansson and Höglund returned to the station. When Wallander reached his office the phone rang. It was the reception desk, telling him he had a visitor.

"Who is it and what is it about?" Wallander asked. "I'm extremely busy."

"It's someone who says she's your neighbour. A Mrs Hartman."

Wallander worried that something had happened in his flat. A few years ago there had been a bad leak. Mrs Hartman was a widow who lived in the flat beneath his. That time, too, she had called him at the station.

"I'll come straight away," Wallander said.

When he reached the waiting area, Mrs Hartman was able to assuage his fears. There was no leak, just a letter for him that had been put through her letter box.

"It must be the post," she complained. "It probably came on Friday, but I've been away and only came back today. I thought it might be important, that's all."

"You shouldn't have gone to the trouble, coming down here," Wallander said. "I rarely get post that is so important it can't wait."

After Mrs Hartman had left, Wallander went back to his room and opened the letter. There was no return address on the envelope. To his surprise, it was a notice from the dating agency, thanking him for his subscription and saying that they would forward responses as they arrived.

Wallander crumpled the letter and threw it into the waste-paper basket. The next couple of seconds his mind was a total blank. He frowned, retrieved the letter, smoothed it out and read it again. Then he looked for the envelope, still without knowing exactly why. He stared at the postmark for a long time. The letter had been posted on Thursday.

His mind was still empty.

Thursday. It was the dating agency telling him that his information was now entered in their records. But by then he had already received a reply from Elvira Lindfeldt. Her letter had arrived in an envelope that had been brought directly to his door. A letter with no postmark.

His thoughts were swirling in his head.

He turned and looked at his computer. Was he going crazy? He forced himself to think logically. As he kept staring at his computer a picture was starting to emerge. A plausible sequence of events. It was horrifying.

He ran out into the corridor and into Hansson's office.

"Call the patrol car!" he shouted.

Hansson jerked back and stared at him. "Which patrol car?"

"The one that took Modin to Malmö."

"Why?"

"Just do it."

Hansson grabbed the phone. He got through to them in less than two minutes.

"They're on their way back," he said, putting the phone down.

Wallander breathed a sigh of relief.

"But they left Modin at the house."

Wallander felt as if he had been punched in the stomach. "Why did they do that?"

"Apparently he told them that he was going to keep working from there."

Wallander didn't move. His heart was beating very hard. He had trouble believing that it was true, but he himself had suggested the risk of someone breaking into their computers. These break-ins weren't necessarily limited to the investigation material. Someone could just as easily access other files – such as a letter that someone sent to a dating agency.

"Bring your gun with you," he said. "We're leaving."

"Where to?"

"Malmö." Wallander checked his own gun and ammunition. It had been cleaned and tested for him only this morning.

Wallander tried to explain the situation along the way, but Hansson seemed to have trouble understanding the story. Wallander kept asking him to try Elvira's number, but there was no answer. Wallander put the police siren on the roof and drove faster. He prayed silently to all the gods he could think of to spare Modin's life. But already he feared the worst.

They drew up outside the house shortly after 10 p.m. There were no lights. The house was dark. They got out. Wallander asked Hansson to wait in the shadows by the gate. Then he turned off his safety catch and walked up the path. When he reached the front door he stopped and listened. Then he rang the bell. There was no answer. He rang again. Then he felt the doorknob. It was unlocked. He gestured for Hansson to join him.

"We should send for reinforcements," Hansson said in a whisper.

"There's no time."

Wallander slowly opened the door. He listened. He didn't

know what was waiting for them in the dark. He remembered that the light switch was on the wall to the left of the door and, after fumbling for a while, he found it. Before he switched on the light he took a step to one side and crouched down.

The hall was empty.

Some light fell into the living room. He could see Elvira on the sofa. She was looking at him. Wallander took a deep breath. She didn't move. He knew she was dead. He called out to Hansson. Step by careful step they went into the living room. She had been shot in the neck. The pale yellow sofa was stained with her blood.

Then they searched the house, but didn't find anything. Modin was gone. Wallander knew that could only mean one thing. Someone had been waiting for him in the house. The man in the field had not been working alone.

CHAPTER THIRTY-NINE

He had no idea what kept him going that night. He supposed it was half rage and half self-reproach. But the overriding emotion was his fear for what might have happened to Modin. His first terrified thought when he realised that Elvira was dead was that Modin had also been killed. But they had searched the house and established that it was empty, and Wallander realised that Modin might still be alive. Everything up to this point in the case seemed to have been about concealment and secrets and that must be the reason for Modin's abduction. Wallander did not have to remind himself of Hökberg's and Landahl's fate. But this was not the same situation. Then the police had not known what was going to happen. Now that they knew more, they had a better starting point, even though they did not yet know what had happened to Modin.

Wallander also had to acknowledge that part of what was fuelling him that night was his sense of having been betrayed, and his bitterness that life had once more cheated him of the prospect of companionship. He could not claim to miss Elvira herself. Her death had mainly frightened him. She had accessed his letter to the dating agency and had got on to him solely with the intention of tricking and manipulating him. And he had been thoroughly taken in. It had been a masterful performance. The shame was excruciating. The rage that coursed through him came from many different sources at once. Nevertheless, Hansson would later tell him how collected and calm he had seemed. His evaluation of the situation and his suggested course of action had been impressively swift.

Wallander needed to get back to Ystad just as soon as possible. That was where the heart of the case still was. Hansson would stay in the house, alert the Malmö police and fill them in as necessary. Hansson was also to do something else. Wallander had been very firm on this point. Even though it was the middle of the night, he wanted Hansson to find out more about Elvira Lindfeldt's background. Was there anything that linked her to Angola? Who did she know in Malmö?

"Who was she anyway?" Hansson said. "Why was Modin here? How did you know her?"

Wallander didn't answer and Hansson never asked him the question again. Afterwards he would sometimes ask people about it when Wallander was not present. The fact was that Wallander must have known her since he placed Modin in her care. But no-one knew anything about this mysterious woman. Despite the investigations that they conducted there was always the sense that her relationship to Wallander was not a matter to be delved into. No-one ever found out exactly what had happened between them.

Wallander left Hansson and returned to Ystad. He concentrated on a single question: what had happened to Modin? As he drove through the night he had a feeling that the impending catastrophe was very close. How he was going to prevent it or what it was exactly that needed to be prevented or stopped, he could not say. The important thing was saving Modin's life. Wallander drove at a ridiculous speed. He had asked Hansson to let the others know he was on his way. Hansson had asked if he should call and wake up Chief Holgersson and Wallander had lost his temper and shouted at him. He did *not* want him to call her.

At 1.30 a.m. Wallander slowed down and turned into the station car park. He shivered from the cold as he ran to the front doors.

The others were waiting for him in the conference room. Martinsson, Höglund and Alfredsson were already there, with Nyberg on his way. Höglund handed him a cup of coffee that he almost immediately managed to spill down the front of his trousers.

Then he got down to business. Modin had disappeared and the woman he had been staying with had been found murdered.

"The first conclusion we can draw," Wallander said, "is that the man in the field was not working alone. It was a fatal mistake to assume that that was the case. I should have realised it earlier."

Höglund was the one who asked the inevitable question. "Who was she?"

"Her name was Elvira Lindfeldt," Wallander said. "She was an acquaintance of mine."

"How did she know Modin would be coming to her house tonight?"

"We'll have to tackle that question later."

Did they believe him? Wallander thought he had lied convincingly, but he couldn't tell. He knew he should have told them the truth about the ad to the dating agency and that someone must have broken into his computer and read the letter. But he didn't say any of these things. In his defence, at least what he tried to tell himself, the most important thing was finding Modin.

At this point the door opened and Nyberg came in. His pyjama top peeked out from under his anorak.

"What the hell happened?" he said. "Hansson called from Malmö and seemed to be out of his mind. Impossible to understand a single word he was saying."

"Sit down," Wallander said. "It's going to be a long night."

Then he nodded to Höglund, who summarised the situation for Nyberg.

"Don't the Malmö police have their own forensic team?" Nyberg said.

"I want you to go there," Wallander said. "Not only in case anything else turns up, but also because I need to hear what you think."

Nyberg nodded without saying anything. Then he took out a comb and started pulling it through his unruly, thinning hair.

Wallander continued. "There is one more conclusion we can draw from all this and it is quite simple: something else is going to happen. And this something is somehow rooted here in Ystad." He looked at Martinsson.

"I take it someone is still stationed outside Runnerströms Torg?"

"No, the surveillance has been called off."

"On whose instructions?"

"Viktorsson thought it was a waste of our resources."

"Well, I want a car put back there immediately. I cancelled the surveillance of Apelbergsgatan, which was maybe a mistake. I think I want a car there too from now on."

Martinsson left the room and Wallander knew that he would see that the patrol cars were dispatched immediately. They waited in silence for his return. Höglund offered Nyberg, who was still combing his hair, her make-up mirror so that he could see what he was doing, but he simply growled at her.

Martinsson came back. "Done," he said.

"What we're looking for is the catalyst," Wallander said. "It could be something as simple as Falk's death. At least, that's how I see it. As long as he was alive everything was in control. But then he died, and everything threatened to unravel."

Höglund raised her hand. "Do we know for sure that Falk died from natural causes?"

"I think it must have been natural causes. I believe that because Falk's death was unexpected. He was in excellent health. But he died, and that's what started the chain reaction. If Falk had lived, Hökberg would be tried and convicted of Lundberg's death. Neither she nor Landahl would have been killed. Landahl would have gone on running errands for Falk. And we would have had no idea of whatever it is that Falk and his associates were planning."

"So it's only on account of his dying that we know something is going to happen, something that might affect the whole world?" Höglund said.

"That's how I see it, yes. If someone else has a better hypothesis I would like to hear it."

No-one had.

Alfredsson opened his briefcase and tipped out a number of loose papers, some torn, some folded in half. "These are Modin's notes," he said. "They were lying in a corner. Do you think it's worth our while going through them?"

"That's up to you and Martinsson," Wallander said. "You are the only two who would understand what he's talking about."

The phone rang. Höglund answered it and handed the receiver to Wallander, saying it was Hansson.

"A neighbour claims she heard a car drive away with

squealing tyres at about 9.30 p.m.," he said. "But that's all we have been able to establish. No-one seems to have seen or heard anything else. Not even the shots."

"There was more than one?"

"The doctor says she was shot in the head twice. There are two entry wounds."

Wallander felt sick to his stomach. He forced himself to swallow hard.

"Are you still there?" Hansson said.

"I'm here. No-one heard the shots?"

"Not the immediate neighbours anyway, and they're the only ones we've had time to wake up so far."

"Who is in charge down there?"

"An officer called Forsman. I've never met him before."

Wallander couldn't recall hearing the name either. "What does he say?"

"He says he has trouble getting a coherent picture from what I tell him, there's no motive."

"Placate him as best you can. We don't have time to brief him right now."

"There was one more thing," Hansson said. "Didn't Modin say he was on his way here to collect some diskettes?"

"That was what he said."

"I think I know what room he was staying in, but there are no diskettes there."

"He must have taken them with him. Have you found anything else that belongs to him?"

"Nothing."

"Any sign that anyone else was in the house?"

"One neighbour said that a taxi stopped at the house earlier in the day. A man got out."

"Try to find that taxi. It could be important. Make sure Forsman makes that a priority."

"You know I have no control over what police from another district choose to do or not to do."

"Then you'll have to do this yourself. Did the witness give a description?"

"All he said was that the man looked lightly dressed for the time of year."

It's the man from Luanda, Wallander thought. The one whose name starts with C.

"This is very important," Wallander repeated. "The taxi probably came from one of the ferry terminals, or from Sturup."

"I'll do what I can."

Wallander told the others. "I think the reinforcements have arrived," he said. "Probably from as far away as Angola."

"I haven't been able to get one single answer to any of my inquiries," Martinsson said. "I've been researching sabotage and terrorist groups that go for financial targets. No-one seems to have any data on them."

"You think people like that would be here in Ystad?" Nyberg put his comb down and stared disapprovingly at Wallander, who thought that Nyberg suddenly looked very old. Do the others see me in this way too?

"A man originating somewhere from the Far East turns up dead in a field outside Sandhammaren," Wallander said. "He was claiming to be from Hong Kong, but we know this identity was forged. This is not the kind of thing that ought to be happening around here, but it does. There really are no longer any remote regions left. If I understand anything about the new technology, it is that it enables you to be at the centre of things from anywhere in the world."

The phone rang. It was Hansson. "Forsman is actually

pretty good," he said. "Things are moving right along. He's found the taxi."

"Where did it come from?"

"Sturup. You were right."

"Has anyone spoken to the driver?"

"He's right here. His shifts seem to be very long. Forsman says hello by the way. Apparently you met at a conference last spring."

"Then give him my regards as well," Wallander said. "Let me talk to this driver."

"His name is Stig Lunne. Here he is."

Wallander signalled to the others to pass him a piece of paper and a pen. He told him who he was and what he wanted to know. The driver spoke with such a thick Skåne dialect that it was almost impossible, even with Wallander's experience, to understand him. But his answers were impressively concise. He picked his passenger up at 12.02 p.m. from Sturup. The job had not been booked in advance.

"Can you describe your passenger?"

"Tall."

"Anything else?"

"Thin."

"Is that all? Is there anything else you might have noticed?"

"Tan."

"So this man was tall, thin and suntanned?"

"Yes."

"Did he speak Swedish?"

"No."

"What language did he speak?"

"I don't know. He showed me a piece of paper with the address."

Wallander sighed. He persevered and gathered that the

man had been wearing a summer suit. He thanked the driver and asked him to be in touch if he thought of anything else.

It was 3 a.m. Wallander passed on to the others Lunne's description. Martinsson and Alfredsson had some time ago left to go and read Modin's notes. Now they returned.

"It's hard to get anything from Modin's notes," Alfredsson said. "He writes things like 'What we need to find is a coffee machine that's right under our noses'."

"He's referring to the process that triggers the planned event," Wallander said. "We have talked about it, and it's probably something most of us do every day without thinking twice about it. When the right button is pushed at the right time and place, then something is set in motion."

"What sort of button?" Höglund said.

"That's what we were trying to work out."

They kept talking. At 4.30 a.m. Hansson called again. Wallander made some notes. From time to time he asked a short question. The conversation lasted 15 minutes.

"Hansson has managed to dig up a friend of Elvira Lindfeldt," Wallander said. "She had some interesting information for us. Apparently Lindfeldt worked in Pakistan for a couple of years during the seventies."

"I thought we were still focused on Angola," Martinsson said.

"The important thing is, what was she doing in Pakistan?" Wallander said, and looked closer at the back of the envelope on which he had made his notes. "According to this friend she was working for the World Bank. That gives us a connection. But there's more. The friend also said she expressed strange opinions from time to time. She was convinced that the whole financial order had to be restructured and that this could only be accomplished if the existing scheme of things was essentially torn down first."

"There must be a number of people involved in this," Martinsson said. "Even if we still don't know where or who they are."

"So we're looking for a button." Nyberg said. "Is that it? Or a lever? Or a light switch? But one that could be anywhere."

"Correct."

"So, in other words, we know nothing."

The room was tense. Wallander looked at his colleagues with something that was nearing desperation. We're not going to make it, he thought. We're not going to find Modin in time.

The phone rang again. Wallander had lost count of the times Hansson had called them.

"Lindfeldt's car," he said. "We should have thought of it earlier."

"Yes," Wallander said, "you're right."

"It was normally parked on the street outside her house, but it's gone now. We've alerted the district. It's a dark blue VW Golf with the registration FHC 803."

All the cars in this case seem to be dark blue, Wallander thought.

It was 4.50 a.m. The feeling in the room was tired and heavy. Wallander thought they all looked defeated. No-one seemed to know what to do.

Martinsson got up. "I have to have something to eat," he said. "I'm going down to the burger bar on Österleden. Does anyone want anything?"

Wallander shook his head. Martinsson made a note of what the others wanted, then he left. A few seconds later he was back.

"I don't have any money," he said. "Can anyone lend me some?"

Wallander had 20 kronor. Strangely enough, no-one else had any cash.

"I'll go by the cashpoint," Martinsson said and was gone again.

Wallander stared blankly at the wall. His head was starting to hurt.

But somewhere behind the growing headache an idea formed. He didn't know where it had come from, but suddenly he jumped up. The others stared at him.

"What did Martinsson say?"

"He was going to get some food."

"Not that. Afterwards."

"He said he had to stop at a cashpoint."

"How about that?" Wallander asked. "Something right in front of our eyes. Is it our coffee machine?"

"I don't think I follow," Höglund said.

"It's something we do without thinking twice."

"Buying some food?"

"Sticking a card into a cash machine. Getting cash and a printed receipt."

Wallander turned to Alfredsson. "Was there anything in Modin's notes about a cash machine?"

Alfredsson bit his lip. He looked up at Wallander. "You know, I actually think there was."

"What was it?"

"I can't remember exactly. It didn't strike either me or Martinsson as important."

Wallander slammed his fist into the table. "Where are his notes?"

"Martinsson took them."

Wallander was already on his feet and on his way out

of the door. Alfredsson followed him to Martinsson's office. Modin's crumpled notes lay on the desk beside Martinsson's phone. Alfredsson started leafing through them while Wallander waited impatiently.

"Here it is," Alfredsson said and handed him a piece of paper.

Wallander put on his glasses and looked it over. The paper was covered with drawings of hens and cats. At the bottom, among some complicated and, to him, indecipherable calculations, there was a sentence that Modin had underlined so many times that he had torn the paper. Workable trigger. Could it be a cash machine?

"Is that the kind of thing you were looking for?" Alfredsson asked.

But he didn't get an answer. Wallander was already on his way back to the conference room. He was convinced. What better place? People were using cash dispensers every day, at all times of the day. Somewhere, at some point in time, on the given day, someone would make a transaction and thereby trigger an event that Wallander did not yet understand but had come to fear. He had no way of knowing that this hadn't in fact already taken place.

"How many cashpoints are there in Ystad?" he asked the others after explaining his new idea. No-one knew.

"We can find out from the phone book," Höglund said.

"If not, you'll have to dig out someone senior from a bank and find out."

Nyberg raised his hand. "How can we be so sure that you are right?"

"You can't," Wallander said. "But it beats sitting here twiddling our thumbs."

"What can we do about it anyway?"

"Even supposing I'm right," Wallander said, "we don't

know which cash machine is the trigger. There may be more than one involved. We don't know when or how something is going to happen. But what we can make sure of is that nothing happens."

"You're thinking of having all cashpoint transactions suspended?"

"For now, yes."

"Do you realise what that means?"

"That people will have even more reason to dislike the police. That we'll get abused for a long time. Yes, of course I do."

"You can't do this without the prosecutor's blessing. And after consultation with the bank directors."

Wallander got up and sat in the chair across from Nyberg. "Right now I don't give a shit about any of that. Not even if it becomes the last thing I do as a police officer in Ystad. Or as a police officer, full stop."

Höglund had been going through the phone book. "There are four cash machines in Ystad," she said. "Three in the town centre and one in the shopping precinct. Where we found Falk."

Wallander thought about it.

"Martinsson must have gone to one of the machines closer to Österleden. Call him. You and Alfredsson will have to guard the other two. I'm going up to the one by the department store." He turned to Nyberg. "I'm going to ask you to call Chief Holgersson. Wake her up. Tell her exactly what's going on. Then she'll have to take it from there."

Nyberg shook his head. "She'll put a stop to the whole thing."

"Call her," Wallander said. "But if you like you could wait until 6 a.m."

Nyberg looked at him and smiled.

"One more thing. We can't forget about Robert and this tall, thin suntanned man. We don't know what language he speaks. But we have to assume that he or someone else associated with him is keeping an eye on the cash machine in question. If you have the slightest suspicion about anyone who approaches one of these machines, call the others immediately."

"I have been on many stake-outs in my day," Alfredsson said. "I don't think I've ever staked out a cash machine before."

"Some time has to be the first. Do you have a gun?" Alfredsson shook his head. "Get him one," Wallander said to Höglund. "And now let's get going."

It was 5.09 a.m. when Wallander left the station. He drove up to the shopping precinct with mixed feelings. In all likelihood he was wrong about this, but they had gone as far as they could go in the conference room. Wallander parked outside the Inland Revenue building. He zipped up his jacket and looked around. There was no-one to be seen. Dawn was still some time off. Then he walked over to the cash machine. There was no reason to remain concealed. The radio he had brought with him made a noise. Höglund was broadcasting that they were all in place. Alfredsson had run into problems. Some young drunks had insisted they be allowed to make a withdrawal. He had called for a patrol car to help him out.

"Keep the car circulating between us," Wallander said. "It will only get worse in an hour or so when people get on the move."

"Martinsson withdrew some cash," she said. "And nothing happened."

"We don't know that," Wallander said. "Whatever happens, we're not going to see it."

The radio fell silent. Wallander looked at a shopping trolley knocked over in the car park. Apart from a pick-up truck the car park was empty. It was 5.27 a.m. On the main road a large truck rattled past on its way to Malmö. Wallander started thinking about Elvira, but decided that he didn't have the energy. He would have to come back to it, to puzzle out how he could have let himself be taken in like that. How he could have been such a fool. Wallander turned his back to the wind and stamped his feet. He heard a car approaching. It was a saloon painted with the sign of an Ystad electrical firm. The man who jumped out was tall and thin. Wallander flinched and took hold of his gun, but then he relaxed. He recognised the man as an electrician who had done some work for his father in Löderup. The man greeted him.

"Is it out of order?" he said.

"We're not letting anyone make withdrawals for the time being."

"I'll have to go across town then."

"Unfortunately it won't work there either."

"What's wrong?"

"It's only a temporary malfunction."

"And they called in the police for that?"

Wallander didn't answer. The man got back into his car and drove away. Wallander knew that he would not be able to keep people at bay indefinitely with the explanation of a malfunction, and he was already dreading the moment when word got out to the wider public. How had he supposed it would work? Holgersson would put a stop to it the second she found out. Their reasoning was mere speculation. He would not have a leg to stand on and Martinsson would have more grist for his mill.

Then he caught sight of a man crossing the car park. He was a young man. He had come out from behind the pick-up truck, and he came walking towards Wallander. It took him several seconds to realise who it was. Modin. Wallander was frozen to the spot. He held his breath. He did not understand. Modin stopped, turning his back to Wallander, who knew instinctively what was going to happen. He threw himself to one side and turned. The man behind him had come from the direction of the supermarket. He was tall and suntanned and he was carrying a gun. He was 10 metres away and there was nowhere for Wallander to run. Wallander closed his eyes. The feeling from the field returned. The bitter end. Here but no longer. He waited for the shot that didn't come. He opened his eyes. The man had the gun pointed at his chest, but he was looking at his watch. The time, Wallander thought. It's time. I was right. I still don't know what is going to happen, but I was right.

The man made signs to Wallander to come closer and to put his arms up. He pulled out Wallander's gun and threw it into a rubbish bin next to the cash machine. Then he held out a credit card with his left hand and recited some numbers in heavily accented Swedish: "One, five, five, one."

He dropped the card onto the pavement and pointed his gun at it. Wallander picked it up. The man took a few steps to one side and looked again at his watch. Then he pointed to the cash machine. His movements were more brittle now. For the first time the man looked nervous. Wallander walked to the machine. When he turned slightly he could see Modin still where he had stopped. Right now Wallander didn't care what would happen when he put the card in and entered the numbers. Modin was alive. That was all that was important. But how could he continue to protect him? Wallander was searching for a way out. If he tried to attack the man behind him he would be shot at once. Probably Modin would not have time to escape. Wallander fed the card into the machine, and as he did so a shot rang out. The bullet hit the ground behind him and ricocheted. The tall man turned away. Wallander saw Martinsson on the other side of the street, some 25 metres away. He flung himself at the rubbish bin and pulled out his gun. The man aimed and fired at Martinsson but missed. Wallander raised his gun, sighted and squeezed the trigger. He hit the man in the chest and he collapsed.

"What's happening?" Martinsson shouted.

"It's safe to come over," Wallander shouted back.

The man on the pavement was dead.

"What made you come here?" Wallander said.

"If your theory was correct, then it had to be here," Martinsson said. "It makes sense that Falk would have chosen the cash machine closest to his house and the one he always passed on his evening walks. I asked Nyberg to watch the cashpoint where I was."

Martinsson pointed at the dead man. "Who is he?"

"I don't know. But I think his name starts with a C."

"Is it all finished now?"

"I believe so, but I don't know what it is that's finished."

Wallander felt that he should be thanking Martinsson, but he said nothing. Instead he walked over to Modin. Time enough to talk to Martinsson later.

Modin's eyes were filled with tears.

"He told me to walk towards you. He said that otherwise he would kill my mother and father."

"We'll deal with all that in due course," Wallander said. "How are you feeling?"

"He told me to say I had to stay and finish my work in Malmö. Then he shot her. And we left. I was shut in the boot and could hardly breathe. But we were right."

"Yes," Wallander said. "We were right."

"Did you find my notes?"

"Yes."

"I didn't start taking it seriously soon enough. A cash machine. A place where people come to take out their money."

"You should have said something," Wallander said. "But maybe I should have thought of it myself. We knew it had something to do with money, after all. It should have been an obvious hiding place for something like that."

"A cash machine as the launching pad for a virus bomb," Modin said. "It has a certain finesse, don't you think?"

Wallander looked at the boy beside him. How much longer could he handle the strain? He was struck by the sense of having stood like this sometime before, with a boy at his side, and he realised that he was thinking of Stefan Fredman. The boy who was now dead and buried.

"What was it that happened?" Wallander said. "Do you think you can tell me?"

Modin nodded. "He was there when she let me in. He threatened me. They locked me in the bathroom. Then I heard him start screaming at her. I could understand him since he was speaking English. At least the parts I could hear."

"What did he say?"

"That she hadn't done her job. That she had shown weakness."

"Did you hear anything else?"

"Only the shots. When he came to unlock the door I thought he was going to kill me too. He had the gun in his hand. But he said I was his hostage and that I had to do what he told me. Otherwise he would kill my parents." Modin's voice had begun to wobble.

"No hurry for the rest," Wallander said. "That's enough. That's plenty, in fact."

"He said they were going to knock out the global financial system. It was going to start here, at this cash machine."

"I know," Wallander said. "But now you need to sleep. You have to go home to your parents now."

They heard sirens close by. Now Wallander could see a dark blue VW Golf parked behind the pick-up. Impossible to see from where he had been standing.

Wallander felt how exhausted he was. And how relieved.

Martinsson came over. "We need to talk," he said.

"I know," Wallander said. "But not now."

It was 5.51 a.m. on Monday, October 20. Wallander wondered vaguely what the rest of the winter was going to be like.

CHAPTER FORTY

On Tuesday, November 11, all the charges against Wallander in the Eva Persson assault case were dismissed. Höglund was the one who gave him the news. She had also played a key role in the direction the investigation had taken, but he only found that out later.

A few days before, Höglund had paid a visit to Eva Persson and her mother. No-one knew what had been said during that visit; there had been no record of the conversation, no third party present, although these had been ordered by the court. Höglund did tell Wallander that she applied a "mild form of emotional blackmail". What that had entailed, she never told him, but Wallander was in time able to put together a reasonably clear picture. He assumed that she had told Persson to turn her thoughts to the future. She was cleared of the murder of Lundberg, but bringing false charges against a policeman could have unpleasant consequences.

The following day Persson and her mother had withdrawn the charges against Wallander. They acknowledged that his version of the events had been correct and that Persson had tried to hit her mother. Wallander could still have been held accountable for his actions in the situation, but the whole matter was swiftly dropped, much to everyone's relief. Höglund had also seen to it that a number of journalists were advised of the charges being dropped, but that item of news never made it into the papers.

This Tuesday was an unusually cold autumn day in Skåne, with gusting northerly winds that were occasionally close to storm strength. Wallander had woken early after an unsettled night. He could not recall his dreams in detail, but they involved being hunted and almost choked to death by shadowy figures and by objects bearing down on him.

When he arrived at the station around 8 a.m., he only stayed for a short while. He had decided finally to get to the bottom of a question that had been troubling him for a long time. After casting his eye over a few forms and after making sure that the photo album Marianne Falk had lent to the police had been returned to her, he left the station and drove to the Hökbergs' house. He had spoken to Erik Hökberg the day before and arranged the meeting. Sonja's brother Emil was at school and her mother was on one of her frequent visits to her sister in Höör. Erik looked pale, and perhaps he had lost weight. According to a rumour that had reached Wallander, Sonja Hökberg's funeral had been an intensely emotional affair. Wallander stepped into the house and assured Erik that his business would not take long.

"You said you wanted to see Sonja's room," Erik said. "But you didn't say why."

"I'll explain it to you. Why don't you come with me?"

"Nothing has been changed. We don't have the energy. Not yet."

They walked upstairs and into the pink room, where Wallander had once sensed that something was out of place.

"I don't think this room has always looked as it does now," he said. "At some point Sonja redecorated it, didn't she?"

Hökberg looked baffled. "How do you know that?"

"I don't know. I'm asking you."

Erik swallowed. Wallander waited patiently.

"It was after that time," Erik said. "The rape. She suddenly took everything down from the walls and got out all her things from when she was a little girl. Things that had been stored in boxes in the attic for years. We never understood why, and she never said anything about it."

Something was taken from her, Wallander thought. And she tried to run away from it in two ways: by reverting to a childhood where everything was still all right and by planning a revenge by proxy.

"That was all I wanted to know," Wallander said.

"Why is it so important to you now? Nothing matters any more. It won't bring Sonja back. Ruth and Emil and I are living half a life, if that."

"Sometimes one feels a need to get to the bottom of things," Wallander said apologetically. "Unanswered questions can hang on and on. But you're right, of course. Sadly, it cannot change anything."

They left the room and went back downstairs. Hökberg asked if he would like a cup of coffee, but Wallander declined. He wanted to leave this depressing place as soon as possible.

He drove back, parked on Hamngatan and walked to the bookshop that had just opened for the day. He was finally collecting the book he had ordered for Linda. He was shocked at the price. He had it gift-wrapped. Linda was coming the following day.

He was back in his office by 9 a.m. At 9.30 he gathered up his files and went to one of the conference rooms. Today they were having a final meeting to discuss the Tynnes Falk case before handing the documents over to the prosecutor. Since the investigation of the murder of

Elvira Lindfeldt had involved the Malmö police, Inspector Forsman was to be at the meeting.

Wallander had not yet heard about the dropped charges against him, but this was not anything that weighed heavily on his mind. The important thing was that Modin had survived. This gave him comfort when he was overwhelmed by thoughts that he might have been able to prevent Jonas Landahl's death if he had been able to think just a little further ahead. Part of him knew that this didn't make sense, but these thoughts came and went regardless.

For once Wallander was the last to enter the conference room. He said hello to Forsman and did in fact remember his face from the conference they had both attended. Only two people were missing. Hans Alfredsson had returned to Stockholm and Nyberg was in bed with the flu. Wallander sat down and they started reviewing the case material. They had so much to cover that the meeting ran on until 1 p.m., but at that point they could finally close the books on it.

Wallander's memories of the case had started losing clarity and definition in the three weeks that had gone by since the shooting incident at the cashpoint. But the facts they had uncovered since then strongly supported their initial conclusions.

The dead man's name was Carter and he came from Luanda. They had now pieced together an identity and history for him, and Wallander thought he had at last been able to answer the question he had asked himself so many times during the investigation: what had happened in Angola? Now he knew at least the bare bones of the answer. Falk and Carter had met in Luanda during the 1970s, probably by accident. How that first meeting had gone and what had been said was impossible to reconstruct, but the two clearly had had a great deal in common. They shared many traits in which pride, a taste for revenge and a confused sense of being among the chosen few had predominated. At some point they had begun to lay the plans for an attack on the global financial system. They would fire their electronic missile when the time was right. Carter's extensive familiarity with the structures of financial organisations, coupled with Falk's innovative technological knowledge of the electronic world that connected those institutions, had been a potentially lethal combination.

Together they had built up a secretive and tightly controlled organisation that came to include such disparate individuals as Fu Cheng, Elvira Lindfeldt and Jonas Landahl. These three had been pulled in, brainwashed and forever ensnared. The picture that had emerged was of a highly hierarchical organisation in which Carter and Falk made all of the decisions. Even if the evidence was as yet insubstantial, there were indications that Carter had himself executed more than one unsatisfactory member of the group.

To Wallander, Carter seemed like the archetypal crazed and ruthless sectarian leader, driven by cold calculation. His impression of Falk remained more complicated since he had never been convinced that Falk was possessed of the same ruthlessness. However, Falk did appear to have had a carefully guarded but deep-seated need for affirmation. During the 1960s he had swung from the extreme right to the politically radical left. Finally, he had entirely broken with conventional politics and embarked on his demonic plottings against the human race.

The police in Hong Kong had established the true identity of Fu Cheng. His real name had been Hua Gang.

Interpol had his fingerprints at the scene of several crimes, including two bank robberies in Frankfurt and Marseilles. Though he could not prove it, Wallander suspected that this money had been used to finance parts of Falk and Carter's operations. Hua Gang had been in organised crime for a long time and had been a suspect in murder cases both in Europe and Asia without ever having been convicted. There was no doubt that he had been the killer of both Sonja Hökberg and Jonas Landahl. Fingerprints and reports from witnesses confirmed this. But Hua Gang had been working under the direction of Carter, and perhaps Falk. There was still work to be done in mapping the reach and entire workings of the organisation, but the information they had suggested that there was no longer a reason to fear the group. With Carter and Falk out of the picture the organisation essentially had ceased to exist.

Wallander was never able, satisfactorily, to determine why Carter had shot Elvira Lindfeldt. Modin had reported as much as he could about the angry accusations Carter had flung at her before she died. Wallander assumed that she had known too much and become a liability. Carter must have been in a state of near desperation when he reached Sweden.

Still, he had come uncomfortably close to succeeding. If either Modin or Wallander had put the credit card into the machine at exactly 5.31 a.m. that Monday, October 20, they would have unleashed an electronic avalanche. The experts who had been tracing the infiltrations Falk had made into the bank networks had been amazed. Falk and Carter had exposed the major financial institutions of the world as shockingly vulnerable to attack. Security specialists around the world were working non-stop to rectify these deficiencies, while yet more groups were trying to construct an accurate picture of what would have happened had the plan actually been set in motion.

Luckily, of course, Wallander had not put Carter's Visa card into the machine. And nothing had happened, other than that a selection of cash machines in Skåne had gone haywire for the day. Many of them had been shut down, but as yet no problem had been located. Just as mysteriously, they had, in due course, resumed normal working order.

They never did find a satisfactory answer to why Sonja Hökberg was thrown against the high-voltage wires at the power substation, nor why Falk had been in possession of the blueprints. They had, however, found out how the burglars had gained entrance to the station. That had been thanks to Hansson's doggedness. It turned out that Moberg, one of the technicians, had come home from leave to find that his house had been broken into. The keys to the station had not been stolen, but Hansson maintained that whoever committed the burglary must have copied them and then had them duplicated by the American manufacturer, probably in return for a considerable sum of money. A simple check had revealed an entry visa in Landahl's passport, proving that he had been in the United States in the month following the break-in at Moberg's house. The money may have come from Hua Gang's bank robberies in Frankfurt and Marseilles.

Some loose ends were painstakingly tied up, others remained unsolved. They found out that Tynnes Falk had kept a post-office box in Malmö. But they could never work out why he had told Siv Eriksson that he had his mail sent to her address. His journal was never recovered, nor were the fingers that had been severed from his hand. The coroner's office did, however, determine that he had died from natural causes. Enander had been right about one thing: it was not a heart attack. Falk's death was the result of a burst blood vessel in his brain.

Other information trickled in. One day Wallander found a long report on his desk from Nyberg in which he described how they had determined that the empty case in Landahl's cabin on the ferry had, indeed, belonged to Falk. Nyberg had not been able to find the contents, but he assumed that Hua Gang had thrown them overboard in an effort to delay the identification of the body. They only ever recovered his passport. Wallander put the report aside with a sigh.

The crucial task had been the mapping of Carter and Falk's strange world. Wallander knew now that their ambitions had known no bounds. After their intended crippling of the world markets they had plans to strangle important utilities worldwide. They had been motivated in no small part by their vanity and an intoxication with their sense of power. Wallander thought that it was this weakness which had tempted Carter to have the electrical relay brought to the morgue and to have Falk's fingers cut off. There had been religious overtones in the macabre world where Carter and Falk had figured as not only overseers but also as deities.

Although Carter and Falk had lived in the idiosyncratic realm of their own deranged fantasies, Wallander had started to sense that at least their plan had cast attention on an important insight: the bewildering vulnerability of modern society.

Sometimes he thought about it for a long time late at night. During the past three decades a society had been emerging which he did not fully recognise. In his work he was forever confronted with the consequences of brutal forces that hurled people to the outer margins. The walls surrounding these outcasts were dauntingly high: drugs, unemployment, social indifference.

These changes were accompanied by a parallel development in which members of society were being connected ever more tightly by new technological innovations. But this highly efficient electronic network came at the cost of increased vulnerability to sabotage and terror.

At the heart of his thinking on these changes was his heightened sense of personal vulnerability. He knew he was in danger of being mown down by Martinsson. He also felt harassed by the constantly changing conditions of the workplace and the new demands being made on them all. In the future, society would need a new kind of policeman. Not that his kind of experience and knowledge were no longer valuable, but now there were whole domains of knowledge he simply didn't have. He was forced to accept that he had, quite simply, become old. An old dog who could no longer be taught new tricks.

During those long nights in his flat he often thought he no longer had the energy for police work. But he also knew that he had no choice but to go on, for at least another ten years. There were really no alternatives. He was an investigative police officer, a homicide detective. Travelling around to schools and lecturing on the dangers of drugs or drunken driving was not an option for him. That would never be his world.

The meeting finally ended and the dossier was handed over to the prosecutor's office. No-one could be charged since all the suspects were dead. But the prosecutor had a report on his desk that could well lead to an indictment of Carl-Einar Lundberg.

It was after the meeting was over that Höglund came to his office to tell him that Persson and her mother had recanted. Naturally Wallander was relieved, but he was not particularly surprised. Although he had his doubts about the ability of Swedish justice to prevail, he had always expected the truth in this particular case to come out in the end.

They sat and talked for a while about the possibility that he could now counter the accusations. Höglund urged him to take up the issue of his mistreatment for the sake of the whole force, but Wallander was reluctant. He thought the best thing would be for the affair to be buried in silence.

Once Höglund had left, Wallander sat staring into space for a long time. His head was empty. Finally, he got up to get a cup of coffee.

At the door to the canteen he bumped into Martinsson. In the past few weeks Wallander had felt a strange and for him unfamiliar ambivalence. Normally he did not shy away from conflicts, but what had happened between him and Martinsson was more difficult and went deeper. There were elements of lost friendship, betrayal, camaraderie. When he bumped into Martinsson in the canteen he knew the moment had come. He could put it off no longer.

"We should talk," he said. "Do you have a minute?"

"I've been waiting for you."

They went back to the conference room where they had spent the whole morning. Wallander got straight to the point.

"I know you've been going behind my back. I know you've been spreading lies about me. You have questioned my ability to lead this investigation. Why you have done all this covertly instead of coming to me directly only you know. The only excuse I can think of for your behaviour is that you are laying the groundwork for your future career, and that you are willing to do anything to get where you want to go."

Martinsson was calm. Wallander thought that his words seemed well rehearsed. "I can only tell you how it is. You have lost your grip and the only thing I'm guilty of is that I didn't say this earlier."

"Why didn't you tell me to my face?"

"I tried to, but you don't listen."

"I do listen."

"You think you do, but that's not the same thing as really listening."

"Why did you tell Holgersson that I had ordered you not to follow me into the field that time?"

"She must have misunderstood what I said."

Wallander looked at Martinsson. The urge to punch him in the face was still there, but he knew he wouldn't do anything of the sort. He didn't have the energy. He was not going to be able to shake Martinsson. The man seemed to believe his own lies. At the very least he would not be able to get him to change his official line.

"Was there anything else you wanted to talk about?"

"No," Wallander said. "I have nothing else to say."

Martinsson got up and left. Wallander felt as if the walls had come tumbling down around him. Martinsson had made his choice and their friendship was gone, broken off. Wallander wondered with growing despondency if it had ever really been there in the first place. Or had Martinsson always been waiting for his opportunity to strike?

Waves of grief washed over him. And then there came a wave of rage. He was not going to give up. For the next few years at least he would remain in charge of the most complicated investigations in Ystad. But the feeling of having lost something was stronger than his rage. He asked himself again how he would have the energy to carry on.

Wallander left the station directly after his conversation with Martinsson. He left his mobile in his office and didn't tell Irene anything about where he was going or when he would be back. He got into his car and took the road to Malmö. As he was approaching the exit for Stjärnsund he decided to take it. He didn't know why. Perhaps the thought of two broken friendships was too much to bear.

Wallander's thoughts often returned to Elvira. She had entered his life under false pretences and in the final analysis he suspected she would even have been prepared to kill him. But he could not stop himself from thinking about her the way he himself had actually experienced her. A woman at a dinner table who had listened to what he had to say. A woman with beautiful legs who had dispelled his loneliness for a brief time.

When he turned into Sten Widén's ranch it looked abandoned. Widén had put up a "For Sale" sign some time ago, but now there was on top of it a "Sold" sign. The house was empty. Wallander walked to the stables. The horses had gone. A lone cat sat in a pile of hay and looked at him suspiciously.

Wallander found it upsetting. Sten Widén had left already and he had not even bothered to say goodbye.

Wallander drove away from the stables as fast as he could.

The following day, he did not go into the office. He drove in circles on the small roads around Ystad all afternoon. From time to time he got out and stared over the barren fields. At dusk he started driving back. He stopped at the grocer's on the way back and paid his bill. That evening he listened to the whole score of Verdi's *La Traviata* twice in a row. He also spoke to Gertrud over the phone and they arranged that he would stop by in the morning.

The phone rang shortly before midnight. Wallander jumped. Oh God, not again, he thought. Don't let anything have happened. Not now, not yet. None of us can handle it.

It was Baiba calling from Riga. It had been about a year since they had spoken last. "I just wanted to see how you were doing," she said.

"I'm fine. How about you?"

"Fine."

The silence bounced from Ystad to Riga and back again.

"Do you ever think about me?" he asked.

"Of course. Why would I have called otherwise?"

"I was just wondering."

"And you?"

"I think about you all the time."

Wallander knew she would see through him. He was lying, or at least exaggerating. He didn't know why exactly. Baiba was something that was over, that was fading. But he could not altogether let go of the thought of her, or of the memories of their time together.

They talked for a while on other topics, then the conversation ended. Wallander put the phone down slowly. Did he miss her? He didn't know. It was as if firewalls were not a phenomenon relegated to the world of computers. He had a firewall himself, and he didn't always know how to get past it.

The next day, Thursday, November 13, the gusty winds had died down. Wallander woke early even though he had the day off. He couldn't remember the last time he had had a day off in the middle of the week. He had decided to use some of his flexitime since Linda was coming to visit. He was to meet her plane at 1 p.m. at Sturup. He was going to use the morning to trade in his car and to visit Gertrud.

At 8 a.m. he got up, made his coffee and read the paper. He cleaned the flat, changed the sheets in Linda's old room and put the vacuum cleaner away. The sun was shining and that cheered him up. He drove to the car showroom on Industrigatan. He settled for another Peugeot, a 306 this time, 1996 registration. It had few miles on it and Tyrén, the dealer, gave him a good price on his old car. He was finished by 10.30 a.m. It gave him a good feeling to get a new car, as if he had scrubbed himself clean.

He drove to the house in Svarte where Gertrud lived with her sister. He had a cup of coffee and listened somewhat absent-mindedly to their chatter.

He left their house at 11.45 a.m. When he got to Sturup there was still half an hour to wait. As usual, he felt nervous about seeing Linda. Was it always the case that parents eventually became afraid of their own children? He had no answer. He had another cup of coffee in the airport café. He noticed Höglund's ex-husband sitting a few tables away. Wallander assumed he was leaving on another business trip. A woman that Wallander hadn't seen before was with him. Wallander felt hurt for Ann-Britt. Wallander moved to another table and sat with his back to the man so as not to be recognised. He wondered why he was reacting so strongly.

The plane landed on time. Linda was one of the last to get off. When they saw each other, Wallander's nervousness disappeared. She was just as open and cheerful as before.

Her easygoing nature was the opposite of his own. She was also not as outrageously dressed as she had been on some previous occasions. They collected her case from the baggage claim and Wallander walked her to the new car. He wasn't sure that she would have noticed the difference if he hadn't said anything.

They drove towards Ystad.

"How are things?" he said. "What are you doing these days? You've been a bit secretive this past while."

"It's such a nice day," she said. "Can we drive down to the beach?"

"I asked you a question."

"You'll get an answer."

"When?"

"Not just yet."

Wallander took the next exit and drove down to Mossbystrand. The car park was empty, the burger bar closed for the year. She opened her case and took out a thick sweater, then they walked to the shoreline.

"I remember coming here when I was little," she said. "It's one of my earliest memories."

"Often it was just you and me. When Mona needed time to herself."

There was a ship on the horizon. The sea was very calm.

"What about that picture in the paper?" she said, suddenly.

Wallander felt his stomach tighten. "It's over now," he said. "The girl and her mother recanted. It's over."

"I saw another picture," she said. "In a magazine. Something happened outside a church in Malmö. It said you threatened a photographer."

Wallander thought back to Stefan Fredman's funeral and the film he had taken from the man's camera. The photographer must have had an extra roll. He told her what had happened.

"I hope I would have done the same thing," she said.

"Luckily you're not going to find yourself in these situations," Wallander said. "You're not a police officer."

"Not yet."

Wallander stopped short and looked at her. "What did you say?"

She kept walking and didn't answer immediately. Some seagulls flew overhead, screeching.

"You think I've been secretive," she said. "And you want to know what I've been up to. I didn't want to tell you about it until I had made up my mind."

"Do you mean what you just said?"

"Yes, I want to be a police officer. I've already applied to Police Training College, and I think I'm going to get in."

Wallander still couldn't believe it. "Is this true?"

"Yes."

"But you've never talked about it before."

"I've been thinking about it for a long time."

"Why didn't you say something?"

"I didn't want to."

"But I thought you were going to go into the antique business and restore old furniture?"

"For a while I thought so too, but now I know what I really want to do. And that's why I came down here, to tell you. Ask you what you think. Get your blessing."

They started walking again.

"This comes right out of the blue," Wallander said.

"You told me about what it was like when you told Grandad that you were going to be a policeman. If I remember correctly his answer came pretty quickly."

"He said no before I had finished talking."

"And what do you say?"

"Give me a minute and I'll let you know."

She went and sat down on a tree trunk half buried in the sand. Wallander walked down to the water. He had never imagined that Linda would want to follow in his footsteps, and it was hard for him to come to terms with what he had heard.

He looked at the sunlight reflected in the water.

She shouted to him that his minute was up. He walked back.

"I think it's a good thing," he said. "I think you'll be just the kind of police officer we're going to need in the future."

"Do you mean that?"

"Every word of it."

"I was worried about how you would react."

"You didn't have to worry."

She got up from the log. "We have a lot to talk about," she said. "And I'm hungry."

They went back to the car and on to Ystad. Wallander tried to digest the news as he drove. He didn't doubt that Linda would make a good policewoman. But did she realise what she was in for? The fatigue and the burn-out?

But he also felt something else. Her decision somehow justified the one he had made so long ago in life. This feeling was buried underneath the others. But it was there and it was strong.

They sat up talking for a long time that evening. Wallander told her about the extremely challenging case that had started and ended by the same run-of-the-mill cash machine.

"Everyone talks about power," she said when Wallander

had finished. "But no-one really questions institutions like the World Bank, or the enormous influence they wield. How much human suffering have they caused?"

"Are you sympathetic to Carter and Falk and their cause?"

"No," she said. "At least not to the means they chose to fight back."

Wallander became steadily convinced that her decision was a long time in the making, not an impulse that she would come to regret.

"I'm sure I'm going to need to ask you for advice," she said, before going to bed.

"Don't be too sure I have any advice to give."

Wallander stayed up for a while after she had gone to bed. It was 2.30 a.m. He had a glass of wine in his hand and had put on one of Puccini's operas. The volume was low. Wallander shut his eyes. In his mind he saw in front of him a burning wall. He readied himself. Then he ran straight through the wall. He only singed his hair and his skin. He opened his eyes and smiled. Something was behind him. Something else was only just beginning.

The following day, Friday, November 14, the stock markets in Asia unexpectedly began to fall. Many explanations were offered, not a few of them contradictory. But no-one managed to answer the most important question: what was it that had set the process in motion?